"Might I ask what you have done with Lady Chester?"

"Done with her?" She laughed, a natural, rich sound, as if laughter came easily to her. He liked that. "Why, I have tied her up and stuffed her in an armoire."

"Have you indeed? I daresay she'd rather enjoy that. Although I doubt she is tied up and locked away. What has happened to her?"

"Nothing dire, I assure you. She was simply persuaded to allow me to meet you here in her place."

She drew a deep breath and met his gaze directly. "Because I have a proposal for you. It's rather more difficult to say aloud than I had thought it would be."

He sipped his wine and studied her. "Is it a business proposal?"

"I certainly wouldn't term it business, although I daresay some people might think so."

"Personal, then?"

"Exceptionally so."

"A proposal of an exceptionally personal nature?" He laughed. "That sounds like a proposal of marriage."

"Exactly." She heaved a sigh of relief. "I do thank you, my lord. It's so much easier to hear you say it than to say it myself."

By Victoria Alexander

VICTORIA ALEXANDER

LET IT BE LOVE

AVON BOOKS
An Imprint of HarperCollins*Publishers*

This is a work of fiction. Names, characters, places, and incidents are products of the author's imagination or are used fictitiously and are not to be construed as real. Any resemblance to actual events, locales, organizations, or persons, living or dead, is entirely coincidental.

AVON BOOKS
An Imprint of HarperCollins*Publishers*
10 East 53rd Street
New York, New York 10022-5299

Printed in the U.S.A.

This book is dedicated with
great affection to my dear friend
Bob Gillum,
who has at last found the heroine of his story.
May you live happily ever after.
You deserve it.

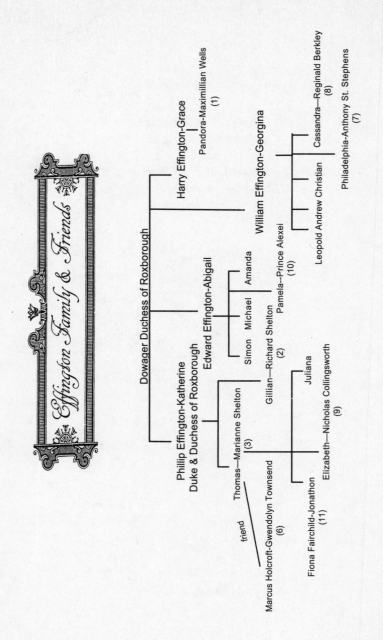

Effington Family & Friends

Dowager Duchess of Roxborough

Harry Effington-Grace
Pandora-Maximillian Wells
(1)

William Effington-Georgina

Cassandra—Reginald Berkley
(8)

Leopold Andrew Christian

Philadelphia-Anthony St. Stephens
(7)

Pamela--Prince Alexei
(10)

Edward Effington-Abigail

Amanda

Simon   Michael

Gillian—Richard Shelton
(2)

Phillip Effington-Katherine
Duke & Duchess of Roxborough

Thomas—Marianne Shelton
(3)

Juliana

Elizabeth—Nicholas Collingsworth
(9)

friend

Marcus Holcroft-Gwendolyn Townsend
(6)

Fiona Fairchild-Jonathon
(11)

Royal House of Pruzinsky

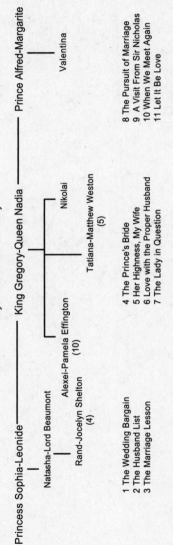

Princess Sophia–Leonide ———— King Gregory–Queen Nadia ———— Prince Alfred–Margarite

Natasha–Lord Beaumont

Alexei–Pamela Effington
(10)

Rand–Jocelyn Shelton
(4)

Nikolai

Tatiana–Matthew Weston
(5)

Valentina

1 The Wedding Bargain
2 The Husband List
3 The Marriage Lesson

4 The Prince's Bride
5 Her Highness, My Wife
6 Love with the Proper Husband
7 The Lady in Question

8 The Pursuit of Marriage
9 A Visit From Sir Nicholas
10 When We Meet Again
11 Let It Be Love

Prologue

December 1853

"$\mathcal{W}$e are a rather grim group today," Oliver Leighton, the Earl of Norcroft, noted to no one in particular and gazed idly at the usual gathering of his closest friends in the lounge of their favorite club.

"What's not to be grim about?" Nigel Cavendish, son of Viscount Cavendish, stared at the brandy in his glass. "Life is moving at a remarkably fast clip. Yet another year is drawing to an end. We are all another year older and another step closer to the inevitable doom that lies in wait for us all."

"I hate arriving in the middle of a conversation." Jonathon Effington, the Marquess of Helmsley and heir to the Duke of Roxborough, sank down in the lone unoccupied chair and grinned at his friends. Today, as always, Helmsley exuded jovial good spirits and an unrelentingly cheerful nature that charmed men and women alike. It could be most annoying. "Yet the expressions on all your faces are as easy to read as the *Morning Times.* I gather *doom* is in reference to the prospect of marriage?"

"What else would make grown men cower in such a fashion?" Gideon Pearsall, Viscount Warton, drawled in the cynical manner he had honed to a fine art.

"What else indeed," Cavendish muttered.

Helmsley raised an amused brow.

"Certainly, we have all accepted that it is our duty to marry and provide an heir to our titles, estates, fortunes, to carry on the family name and so forth, but acceptance and eagerness are two entirely different matters. Marriage is a daunting prospect relished by no sane member of the masculine gender." Warton signaled to an ever-vigilant waiter for another round of refreshment. "And a prospect none of us will be able to avoid much longer."

Warton alone among them had not avoided it entirely, but that was a subject that by unspoken agreement was not— was never—to be discussed.

"I don't know that I still wish to avoid marriage," Helmsley said mildly.

"Of course not." Oliver snorted. "Precisely why we have noted you loping down the aisle at breakneck speed."

Helmsley accepted a glass from the waiter. "I simply haven't found the right woman yet."

"The right woman?" Warton rolled his gaze toward the ceiling. "You mean the woman who will set your heart aflame?"

"Not to mention your loins," Cavendish said.

"A woman who will challenge your mind," Oliver added with an overly dramatic flourish. "As well as the rest of you."

Helmsley's amused gaze slid around the circle. "Have I mentioned this before, then?"

"Each and every time the topic turns to potential brides." Warton sighed. "Let us see if we can remember all the requirements for the future Lady Helmsley. There are a fair number, if I recall."

"As well there should be," Helmsley said, his voice firm. "My wife shall one day be the Duchess of Roxborough. Such a position is not easy to fill."

"Nor is the position of perfect wife," Oliver said.

"Perfect is relative," Warton said, "the perception of

which is highly individual. I, for one, do not find his qualifications culminate in perfection at all."

Helmsley raised his glass in a toast. "To whatever passes
for perfect, then."

"Perfect?" Oliver snorted. "Your idea of perfect is more in
tune with what rational men would call difficult."

Warton heaved a long-suffering sigh. "All that spirited-
nature nonsense."

"Sounds like a lot of trouble to me," Cavendish said
darkly.

"It does, doesn't it?" Helmsley frowned in a good-
natured manner. "Was I drinking excessively at the time?"

"Probably." Warton shrugged. "Such discussions on the
relations between men and women and what we do and do
not desire generally come toward the end of a long evening
of excess. Usually after we have thoroughly dissected the
sorry state of contemporary politics and preceding the inevitable pondering of the true meaning of existence in the
world."

"That does seem to require excessive drinking," Cavendish murmured.

"Although we must note, Helmsley's requirements do
not vary considerably whether he is inebriated or cold
sober. There is something to be said for consistency, I suppose, or perhaps it's simply obstinacy." Oliver studied his
friend.

One wouldn't note his stubborn nature simply to look at
him. Jonathon Effington was an attractive sort, his good
looks accentuated by his confident friendly air. Add to that
his title, his prospects and his family wealth, and one could
only wonder why he hadn't yet found the bride who would
perfectly fill his expectations. Certainly there was no lack of
eager candidates vying for the position of the future
Duchess of Roxborough. But Helmsley had long ago made
it clear he did not wish for the type of submissive, well-
behaved, proper bride English society was so adept at pro-
ducing. He claimed such a wife would bore him to tears,
and Oliver wasn't sure he wasn't right. Still, Cavendish was
right as well: Such a wife would be a great deal of trouble.

"As foolish as it sounds to the rest of us, Helmsley has declared he does not wish for a wife who is overly docile or blindly obedient." Oliver raised his glass to his friend. "God have mercy on him."

"God had better," Warton said. "A woman of that nature certainly wouldn't."

"I wouldn't mind blind obedience, myself." Cavendish paused for a moment as if debating the merits of obedience, blind or otherwise. "A woman who would do precisely as I wished, when I wished, without asking annoying questions. I should think that would be an excellent quality in a wife. Yes, I quite like that." A frown creased his brow. "Still, I would be willing to sacrifice a certain amount of obedience for the sake of appearance. She should definitely be pretty. I would not like an ugly wife. And she should be of good family, of course, with a respectable dowry."

"None of which is of true importance when one is deciding upon a woman to spend the rest of one's life with," Helmsley noted in an annoyingly lofty manner, then grinned. "Admittedly pretty and the rest of it is preferable."

"One does have to bed her, after all." Warton sipped his brandy in a thoughtful manner. "Although an enormous fortune would certainly make a less-than-attractive face and figure more palatable."

Helmsley raised a brow. "I would not have thought it possible, but you are more cynical than unusual tonight."

" 'Tis the undue influence of the season. All this good will toward men, urchins singing in the streets, high spirits run amok." Warton shuddered. "It quite goes against my nature."

It was a lie and every man present, including Warton himself, knew it, but he did so love playing the role of jaded cynic. And who would tell him otherwise? It was part of an unspoken agreement among the longtime friends not to shatter anyone's illusions about himself unless it was of the utmost necessity to do so.

To all appearances, they were an odd group to have

formed such a bond. While they shared a similarity of position and age, they were as disparate as if they were from different civilizations. Warton, with his dark handsome features and brooding nature, was given to cynicism in direct contrast to Cavendish's boyish good looks and penchant for getting into scrapes. Helmsley was the true optimist among them and liked little better than a good joke or a good wager or a good investment. As for Oliver himself, well, he wasn't entirely sure how he described himself, save that he thought in some odd way he shared some of the characteristics of each of the others, for good and ill.

The men had attended school together, but had not truly become friends until recent years when they found themselves frequenting the same clubs and same social events. Oliver's friendship with Helmsley had begun when he had enthusiastically, and futilely, pursued the hand of Helmsley's youngest sister. How all four of them had drifted into friendship as fast and firm as this had become was still a matter of some debate.

And there were moments when nothing but honesty between them would serve. Certainly there had been any number of occasions through the years when the group had been forced to make one of its members—usually Cavendish—face unpleasant facts about himself for his own good. Generally in situations that had involved the fairer sex, the potential for extreme embarrassment and an excess of alcohol.

Oliver wondered if, in the spirit of the season, which did seem to call for a fair amount of honesty, this wasn't one of those moments.

"You, Jonathon Effington, Lord Helmsley, heir to the Duke of Roxborough"—Oliver aimed an accusing finger—"are a nice man."

"Women like you," Cavendish added.

"Yes, I know. It works out rather well, to my way of thinking." Helmsley grinned. "What's wrong with being nice?"

"For one thing, it makes every other man look bad in comparison. Beyond that"—Warton's eyes narrowed—"it drives the rest of us mad."

Helmsley laughed. "Don't be absurd."

Oliver leaned closer. "Do you realize when you end a liaison with a woman or a flirtation with a young lady they never seem to hate you?"

"Well, of course not. Why would . . ." Jonathon paused. "What exactly do you mean?"

Oliver lowered his voice in a meaningful manner. "Have you ever infuriated a woman to the point where she flung a vase at your head?"

"Or slapped you across the face?" Warton asked. "Hard?"

"Or thrown your clothes into the fire so that you were forced to make your way to your discreetly waiting carriage clad in nothing more than a flimsy woman's dressing gown?" Cavendish said.

At once all eyes and a corresponding number of raised brows turned toward him.

"Perhaps that's only happened to me," Cavendish said under his breath. "Nonetheless, Helmsley, you do see the point, do you not?"

"I don't know that I do. I consider myself a gentleman," Helmsley said staunchly. "And yes, I suppose I am nice. I see nothing wrong in that."

"Except what one has sacrificed for nice." Warton sipped his liquor in a sage manner.

"Sacrificed?" Helmsley's brow furrowed in suspicion. "What have I sacrificed?"

"Passion." Warton's voice was smug.

Helmsley snorted. "Nonsense, I—"

"There's never been passion in any of your relationships, old man," Oliver said, "beyond the obvious sort of passion, that is."

"That's ridiculous." Indignation rang in Helmsley's voice. "I've experienced no end of passion. Why, I reek with passion. Passion practically follows me down the street. I've certainly never had any complaints about a lack of passion." He threw back the rest of his drink. "Lack of passion, hah!"

"Not that kind of passion," Oliver said. "We're talking about passion of the spirit. Of the heart."

Warton nodded. "Love, if you will."

Cavendish raised his glass. "Love."

"Love, Jonathon." Oliver eyed him. "Or passion. Whatever you wish to call it. You are never carried away. Never overwhelmed. Which is precisely why you and whatever lady has caught your eye for a time can go your separate ways without recrimination on either side."

"Or promises of undying affection on her part." Warton waved blithely. "Even threats—"

"Or family members vowing to track you to the ends of the earth to carve you like a goose if you so much as . . ." Cavendish paused, then winced. "Only me again?"

Warton eyed the other man with equal parts awe and disbelief. "One does wonder where you find the time."

Cavendish grinned wickedly. "One makes the time."

"This is not the least bit amusing." Helmsley's tone was mild. "I am as passionate as any of you, probably more. I simply pour most of my passion into my prose."

Oliver bit back a grin. Helmsley fancied himself the next Charles Dickens, but he had yet to publish so much as a single verse. His failure to do so was in many ways a credit to his integrity. Helmsley's godfather was a well-respected publisher and his mother wrote novels of adventure and romance. He certainly could have had his work published, but he preferred to submit his offerings under an assumed name, wishing his writing to succeed on its own merit rather than his family connections. Thus far, his integrity remained intact, although his pride was sorely tested.

"Perhaps"—Helmsley considered his friends thoughtfully— "it is not my lack of passion that has prompted this charge against me but my skill and, I might add, success in dealing with the fairer sex."

Oliver and Warton traded glances.

Cavendish snorted in disdain. "Just because you have never been involved in a scan—"

"Nor shall I. I"—Helmsley got to his feet and bowed to the others with a dramatic flourish—"am a true gentleman.

That coupled with my charm and an innate understanding of the nature of women is why, when a lady and I decide to part company, it is without recrimination, frenzied promises and"—he glanced ruefully at Cavendish—"threats of dismemberment. As for the question of a perfect bride, I make no apologies for knowing precisely what I want and knowing as well that when I find it I shall waste no time in making the lady in question my wife. And furthermore I admit that knowledge brings me a great deal of satisfaction, as does knowing"—he flashed a triumphant grin—"that it drives the rest of you mad."

"One day, old man, that confident nature of yours will be your downfall." Warton's manner was ominous.

It wasn't that Helmsley was especially better behaved than the rest of them, it was just that he had never actually been embroiled in a situation he could not talk his way out of. That, coupled with the annoying tendency of women to immediately forgive him for whatever transgression had occurred because he was so blasted nice, and a fair amount of luck, had kept his public reputation, if not completely spotless, at least eminently respectable.

"Take, for example, that rendezvous you have every year at your family's Christmas Ball." Warton studied Helmsley curiously. "Have you no concern as to the consequences should someone uninvited stumble upon that little assignation?"

Helmsley thought for a moment, then shrugged and grinned. "No."

It was common knowledge among the men that Helmsley had a Christmas tradition of sorts—a private meeting with whatever woman had captured his fancy at that particular Christmas in the library at Effington House at some point during the annual Effington Christmas Ball. Helmsley claimed the encounters were relatively innocent, consisting merely of conversation, champagne and perhaps an embrace and a kiss or two. Nothing, he insisted, that would provoke a true scandal, no ruination of virgins or writhing about on the library rug. Still, such claims were made with a distinctly wicked twinkle in his eye, and as much as

Helmsley prided himself on his honorable nature and his position as a *true gentleman*, no one—save the ladies involved—was especially certain exactly what did transpire in the Effington House library during the Christmas Ball each and every Christmas Eve.

Jonathon Effington, the Marquess of Helmsley, heir to the Duke of Roxborough, had never been caught.

That too drove his friends mad.

"I say, just out of idle curiosity, mind you," Cavendish started in a casual manner, "who is the lady this year?"

"Yes, Helmsley, do tell," Warton drawled. "Who is this year's lucky miss?"

"I cannot believe you would ask such a thing. A gentleman never reveals the name of a lady under such circumstances." Helmsley shook his head in a mock mournful manner. "Besides"—an altogether ungentlemanly grin flashed across his face—"there's more than a week until the ball."

Oliver chuckled. "So there is no lady as of yet."

"Ah, but there will be, old friend." Helmsley paused. "Would you care to make a small wager on it?"

Oliver shook his head. "No."

"We might as well throw our money into the streets," Warton added wryly. "If nothing else, you do have our confidence."

Helmsley laughed. "And on that note I shall bid you all a good day. Christmas is but a week away and I have a great deal to accomplish between then and now."

"Go, then." Warton waved him off. "And take that nauseating good cheer with you."

Helmsley laughed again, the friends made their farewells and a moment later he was off, the faint whistle of a Christmas carol lingering in his wake.

"I do wonder, though"—Warton studied Helmsley's retreating figure thoughtfully—"exactly what would happen if Helmsley did find a woman who met all his qualifications."

"A woman with spirit to challenge his mind." Oliver

chuckled. "I daresay such a woman would have no end of other qualities Helmsley might not find as enchanting."

"In my experience, spirited women tend to be stubborn and single-minded. And not overly concerned with propriety. Not at all the type of woman who could be a duchess. Of course, he might well enjoy that." Cavendish thought for a moment. "Or"—He grinned—"she would drive him mad."

It was a delightful thought.

For a long moment, the trio was silent.

"It's really rather a pity . . ." Warton began.

"Precisely what I was thinking," Oliver said slowly.

Warton's brow furrowed. "Of course, no one in particular comes to mind."

"No one he hasn't met." Oliver shook his head. "Therefore it would have to be someone entirely unknown."

"It would be the least we could do—"

"In the name of friendship and in the spirit of the season—"

"What?" Confusion rang in Cavendish's voice. "What is the least we can do in the name of friendship and the spirit of the season?"

"Why, give Helmsley precisely what he wants, of course." Oliver grinned. "The woman of his dreams."

"It's a brilliant idea." Warton heaved a resigned sigh. "It's a shame we can't do something about it."

"I do have a cousin who should be arriving from Italy any day now," Oliver said slowly.

"A cousin?" Warton brightened. "Is she the type of woman to appeal to Helmsley?"

"I have no idea." Oliver thought for a moment. "My mother corresponds with her regularly, but we haven't seen her for years. My recollection of her is of a somewhat plump, freckled, red-haired, quiet creature. Not an especially attractive child, but pleasant enough in nature, as I remember."

"Perhaps she's changed?" Cavendish said.

"Perhaps. She's five-and-twenty now—"

"And not yet married?" Cavendish asked.

"No. Indeed, her father's displeasure at her failure to wed is the one item Mother has repeatedly mentioned in regards to my cousin's letters."

"Not wed at five-and-twenty?" Cavendish winced. "That's a bad sign."

"I doubt she would serve our purposes." Oliver shrugged. Fiona's letter announcing her imminent arrival was brief and contained no sense of the young lady's character. Or why she had decided to return to England after nearly a decade. Of course, her father had died several months ago and perhaps she simply wanted to at last return home. "Besides, I would hesitate to offer up a family member in this cause."

"Pity. I should love, just once, to see Helmsley head over heels for a woman who is precisely what he claims he wants. It would be the quintessential Christmas gift." A slow grin grew on Warton's face. "And it would indeed drive him mad."

One

Six days later . . .

"What am I to do, Oliver?" Miss Fiona Fairchild paced the width of her cousin's parlor and ignored the amused, or perhaps bemused, expression on his face.

Fiona and her sisters had arrived at Oliver's home a scant hour ago accompanied by the Contessa Orsetti, who had graciously agreed to chaperone them on their journey from Italy. She was traveling to England anyway and said it was certainly no bother. Aunt Edwina had greeted the party with an enthusiasm that quite warmed Fiona's heart and provided a significant measure of relief as well. For one thing, Aunt Edwina was thankfully nothing like the contessa, who could be both overbearing and presumptuous. For another, her aunt and cousin had had very little warning as to their arrival and it had been more than a dozen years since they'd last seen one another. After sending the contessa on her way, Aunt Edwina had spirited the younger girls off to settle them in their accommodations. Fiona had preferred to wait in the parlor for Cousin Oliver to return home.

His greeting had been just as warm as his mother's, but Fiona had had no time for idle pleasantries. In truth, she had no time to waste at all. She had a crisis of immense proportions confronting her and Oliver might well be her only salvation.

"I refuse to marry a man I've never seen, let alone met, and an American at that. He would probably wish to live in his own country and I have spent far too many years away from England already. This is my home and I have missed it more than I can say."

Oliver leaned casually against the fireplace mantel and studied her. "But you are not averse to marriage in and of itself?"

"Of course not. I wish to marry. Whatever would I do if I did not marry? I am rather a good match, you know." She turned to him and ticked the points off on her fingers. "I am of good family. I can run a household. I am an excellent hostess. I speak three languages fluently and several others adequately. And the mirror tells me, as have any number of suitors, that I am pretty as well."

"You are not as . . . *round* and speckled as you were as a child," Oliver murmured. "You have turned out nicely. Quite nicely."

"Surprisingly so." She grinned with the satisfaction of a woman who was indeed pleased with the way she'd turned out. "Thank you, cousin." Her smile vanished. "What am I to do?"

Oliver's brows drew together. "I cannot believe Uncle Alfred would leave you in such a position."

"He was, unfortunately, doing what he thought was best for me. He had encouraged me to marry for years before he fell ill."

"I assume there were offers?" Oliver's gaze traveled over her in an appreciative manner.

She was well aware of precisely what he saw: a figure no longer plump but curved and appealingly lush, hair that had deepened from a bright, almost orange color to a rich mahogany, intelligent green eyes that tilted upward slightly at the corners and a porcelain complexion marred only by an annoying smattering of pale freckles across the bridge of her nose that men oddly enough seemed to find enchanting. Fiona Fairchild had become a true beauty and she well knew it. Why, hadn't men compared her to a Renaissance painting?

Still, she could be as ugly as sin, for all it mattered.

"Yes, of course." She waved away his comment. "Aside from the aforementioned attributes, I am heir to a significant fortune. At least I was. When Father realized he would not recover . . ." A wave of sadness passed through her and she ignored it. She had mourned for her father upon his death nearly four months ago, and would mourn and miss him for the rest of her days, but at the moment she had the pressing matter of how to resolve the circumstances he had left her in to consider. "He took matters into his own hands.

"In spite of his urgings, Father felt my failure to wed was in part his fault. It wasn't, of course. I simply never met a man with whom I should wish to spend the rest of my days." She shrugged. "You must understand that after my stepmother died, I took over her duties in regards to running the household, acting as Father's hostess and helping with my stepsisters."

"There are three, aren't there? And two are twins?"

Fiona nodded. "And I could not care for them more than if they were my own flesh and blood, which in itself compounds my dilemma. Father knew if I had only myself to consider I would never marry a man I had not met."

"What would you do with your life, then?" Oliver asked mildly. "I cannot see you becoming a governess."

"Nor can I." She wrinkled her nose. "Or a lady's companion or anything else of that nature. I would probably do exactly what I have done."

"Throw yourself on the mercy of your closest living relative?" He grinned.

"Most certainly." She flashed him a blinding smile. "You and dear Aunt Edwina would never abandon me and throw me into the streets. Still, I—or rather we—cannot impose on your hospitality forever."

"You are certainly welcome to do so. I daresay my mother is beside herself at the idea of having four young women under her wing. She has long bemoaned the fact that she had no daughters and only one son who has not yet done his duty and provided her with a daughter-in-law."

Fiona laughed. "That does seem to be a constant theme in her letters." She sobered and shook her head. "Regardless, we cannot live here for the rest of our days as . . . as poor relations."

"You most definitely can," Oliver said staunchly. "You are the closest thing I have to a sister."

"Oliver—"

He held up a hand to stop her. "However, I can understand how you would not wish to be"—he rolled his gaze toward the ceiling—"*poor relations*, although Mother and I would certainly never think of you as such. Now . . ." Oliver's brow furrowed. "Let me see if I understand this correctly. Uncle Alfred left the bulk of his fortune to you, primarily in the form of a dowry, with substantial amounts also set aside for each of your stepsisters to provide for their dowries."

Fiona nodded.

Oliver studied her. "He left nothing for you to live on? To maintain a household, that sort of thing?"

"A minimal amount for household expenditures, mostly in the hands of his solicitor, only enough to provide for expenses until such time as my"—it was hard not to choke on the word—"*intended* arrived from America. Father knew if he left too great an amount at my disposal I would find a way to elude this marriage he has arranged. He was right, of course." She resumed her pacing. "Once I learned of the terms of his estate, I used everything I could get my hands on plus what little I had saved to pay for our passage here. I can assure you, from now until the day I die I shall have a tidy surplus of cash hidden in my mattress for unforeseen circumstances."

"In the event you once again have to flee a foreign country to avoid an unwanted marriage?" Oliver's voice was serious but there was an amused twinkle in his eye.

She ignored it. "Exactly. Which reminds me." She paused, clasped her hands behind her back and adopted a casual tone. "I should mention, as most of that money was intended for household expenses, there might perhaps be an unpaid account, a creditor or two who might take it upon themselves to follow us—"

Oliver raised a brow. "All the way from Florence?"

She waved dismissively. "Expenses might have been a bit more than father anticipated. Honestly, Oliver, you needn't look at me that way. Death is not an inexpensive proposition, you know. Mourning clothes for four young women do not come cheaply—"

He frowned. "Your clothing does not appear suitable for mourning."

"That too was Father's doing. He stipulated mourning clothes for no more than three months, as he did not feel black was attractive on young women. I suspect he did not wish for me to meet my future"—she wrinkled her nose—"*husband* looking like an overblown, red-haired crow. It was most thoughtful of him." She cast Oliver a rueful glance. "I look dreadful in black."

"I doubt that," he murmured.

"At any rate, about expenses," she continued, "you have no idea the number of people who felt compelled to call on us for weeks and months afterward and offer their sympathy, all of whom expected refreshment. Burying Father and all that entailed was quite costly."

"I had no idea."

"No, I'm sure you wouldn't." Fiona sighed.

Oliver's father had died when he was a boy and the very idea of someone else controlling his finances, whether from this world or beyond the grave, was foreign to him. And why shouldn't it be? He was a man and in control of his own destiny. Fiona liked being female and considered herself quite accomplished in feminine skills and wiles. Still, at moments like this, it was most frustrating not to have the power accorded a man in this world. Especially when one's own monarch was a woman.

"It's all right here." She moved to the valise she had placed on a side table, opened it, and pulled out a copy of her father's will. "All the unpleasant details." She handed it to Oliver. "Father's solicitor in Florence says there is nothing I can do about it. And two others I consulted agree. While there is no particular deadline involved, I think it would be best if, at the very least, I was betrothed to someone else before my intended—I forget his name—arrives from America—"

"America? He's not *in* Italy, then?"

"No." She pushed her hair away from her face. She hadn't taken the time since her arrival to tidy up and no doubt she was a bit disheveled in appearance. Not at all her usual manner, but it was of scarce concern at the moment. "Perhaps I am not telling this properly. It is somewhat complicated."

"Perhaps," Oliver said wryly.

"Very well, then." She paused for a moment to get her thoughts in order. "When Father realized he would not recover, he changed his will, dividing his fortune among the four of us in the form of dowries, with a larger portion allocated to me so that I might provide for the others, and a minimal amount set aside to provide for expenses until such time as I wed. None of us get anything beyond that until I marry. Even if Genevieve, Arabella and Sophia wished to marry, all of whom are of an eligible age to do so, although Belle and Sophie are only seventeen, which I think is entirely too young, and they are a bit flighty—"

"The point?"

"The point is . . ." She paused. This part was especially upsetting and still difficult to believe. "That even if my sisters wed, they will not receive their dowries unless, or until, I am married. Their futures are entirely dependent upon my actions."

"Can your father do that?" Oliver glanced at the papers in his hand then back to her. "Is it legal, I mean? To compel you to marry?"

"My father was a clever man with a heretofore unknown diabolical streak." She narrowed her gaze. "He's not forcing me to do anything. It is entirely my choice. If I want my inheritance, and the means to a good marriage for my sisters, I shall marry. Until I do, be that a month or ten years from now, the money remains firmly in an account of trust administered by his London solicitors."

"So if you don't wed, your sisters don't get their dowries either?" Oliver said slowly.

"Exactly."

His gaze met hers. "Your father was really quite determined, wasn't he?"

"Indeed he was."

"And where does this American fit in?" He moved to a writing desk, spread the will before him and stared at the papers.

Fiona followed him. "Perhaps you've forgotten, but we spent nearly four years residing in Paris before we moved to Florence. In addition to his diplomatic duties for the queen, Father had a fair number of investments and business associates from various parts of the world. Whatshisname's father—whose name also escapes my memory—was among them. He was in Italy last year and he and Father renewed their acquaintance." She peered over his shoulder at the will and suspicion hardened her voice. "I wouldn't be at all surprised if this wasn't when the two of them hatched this scheme to merge their families with a marriage between their offspring."

Oliver scanned the papers. "Hold on a moment. I see where you are required to marry 'a suitable gentleman of good character and financial means' but nothing that specifically requires you to marry this whatever-his-name-is."

"I've already noted that and it may well be my means of escape." She paused and sent a silent request for forgiveness toward the heavens and her father, although, given his final acts, she wasn't entirely certain her prayer was aimed in the right direction. "Apparently Father was too ill to realize that was a rather large flaw in his grand scheme. It is also where you come in."

Oliver raised a brow. "Me?"

"Yes, well." She searched for the right words. As much as this had seemed like an excellent plan when it first came to mind, at the moment it seemed nothing less than stupid. She drew a deep breath. "I need you to find me a husband."

Oliver's head jerked up and he stared at her as if she had suddenly grown two heads. "What do you mean, a husband?"

"You know, a husband. You know what a husband is, you've obviously avoided becoming one long enough to know what it is." She waved impatiently. "Someone suitable, of good character and so forth and so on. Preferably someone not on his last legs, and I would prefer that he was handsome with a pleasant nature—a sense of humor would be nice as well—but the quality I need most is *willing*, because I need him as quickly as possible. The moment Whatshisname arrives in Florence, his beast of a father will tell him I've fled and he'll be right on my heels."

Oliver continued to stare as if one of her heads had actively started drooling. "Have you considered the possibility that Whatshisname might not want to marry you?"

"Not want to marry me?" She scoffed. "Don't be absurd." She stepped to the closest chair and sank into it in a most unladylike manner, but she didn't feel especially ladylike at the moment. "Honestly, Oliver, men have desired me for my looks alone. This American creature has the additional incentive of an impressive fortune plus the posthumous approval of my father. I can't imagine him not wanting to marry me. Especially if he is anything like his father. Short, rotund, with very little hair and a calculating disposition, he eyed me as if I were a brood mare he was considering purchasing. I cannot imagine the son is any better." She glanced at him. "And do stop staring at me, it is most disconcerting."

"You're just not at all as I remember." Oliver shook his head. "I always thought you were shy and reserved."

"When I was a child, I was, for the most part. One changes with the years, cousin. You have, haven't you?"

"Indeed. I scarcely ever climb trees anymore and I can't remember the last time I played with tin soldiers." He smiled, then sobered. "If this American does follow you here, what then? He certainly can't force you to marry him."

"Of course he can, in that I will have no choice." She leapt to her feet and paced the room. "I am very realistic about myself, Oliver."

He chuckled. "So I've noticed."

"My flaws as well as my attributes. And do not be fooled by appearances, I am not nearly as perfect as I look. I have any number of nasty flaws." She shook her head. "I am a weak person, cousin. I do not relish the idea of poverty and I quite enjoy spending money. We have already agreed that aside from marriage, I have no useful way to make my way in the world. If I have not come up with a way to escape, I shall be compelled to marry Whatshisname, as much to save my sisters as myself, of course." She glanced at him. "Although they would not do well impoverished either."

He snorted. "No doubt."

Fiona moved closer to him, took his hands and looked into his eyes. "Will you help me."

"Find a husband?" He shook his head. "I thought you didn't want to marry a man you've never met."

"I don't, but if I have to marry, and it appears I do, I would prefer him to be English. I am not averse to selecting a match that would be to my liking. Come, now, cousin." She widened her eyes and adopted a persuasive tone that had been known to work effectively on any number of gentlemen. "Surely you have friends who are looking for a wife?"

"Most of my friends are actively avoiding marriage at the moment."

"But you could come up with, oh, say, a selection, an assortment, I can choose from?"

"An assortment?" He laughed. "Like sweets?"

"With any luck at all, yes. A choice of suitable matches. An array of acceptable candidates." She forced a slight catch to her throat. "Please, Oliver."

"I don't—"

"I warn you, I do not intend to give up. Either you help me find an appropriate husband or"—she dropped his hands, stepped back and squared her shoulders—"I shall have to find one myself. And with your father and my father both deceased, you, as the Earl of Norcroft, are the head of the family. Therefore . . ."

"Therefore?" he said slowly, with a distinct flash of apprehension in his eye.

"Therefore, as head of the family, I should think you'd wish to avoid public scandal. I cannot guarantee that my pursuit of an appropriate match will be the least bit discreet." She folded her arms over her chest. "In fact, I think the best way to begin my quest would be directly and honestly. An advertisement in the *Times* would serve. Something along the lines of, 'Attractive heiress seeks suitable match. Candidates must be of good quality and willing to wed immediately.' "

"You wouldn't." He stared in horrified disbelief.

"Oh, but I would." She shrugged. "I am a desperate woman, Oliver. Desperate women must resort to desperate means."

"I said you and your sisters are welcome here."

"I said I don't want to be a poor relation." She pressed her lips into a firm line. "Well?"

"Good Lord, you are stubborn. I cannot believe . . ." He paused and his eyes narrowed. "And single-minded as well.

"I do know what I want."

"And spirit." A slow smile spread across his face. "You have a great deal of spirit."

She huffed impatiently. "I don't know what that has to do with anything."

"You, my dear cousin, would be a challenge for any man." His smile broadened into a grin.

"I do like to think so."

He studied her silently for a long moment. Fiona held her breath. She hadn't really intended to threaten to advertise for a husband and wasn't entirely sure she could do such a thing. Still, she was indeed desperate.

"Helmsley," Oliver said abruptly.

"Who?"

"The Marquess of Helmsley. Jonathon Effington."

"Jonathon Effington?" Her heart skipped a beat. "He is not yet married, then?"

Oliver laughed. "No, he is definitely not married. But he wishes to be."

"Does he?" She forced a light note to her voice. "How . . . perfect."

"Perfect? I daresay Helmsley would be anything but . . ." He paused and considered her. "Why?"

She widened her eyes innocently. "Why, what?"

"Why do you think Helmsley of all people would be perfect? Have you met him?"

"No, of course not. I've never spoken two words to the man," she said with an offhand wave. "I did see him once, however, before my family left London, oh, what, nine years ago now?" It would be nine years exactly this coming Christmas Eve and the Effington Christmas Ball. "I liked the look of him, that's all. Unless he's changed dramatically, he was quite dashing. And if I am to marry anyone with the speed my situation requires, I should just as soon like the looks of the man."

Oliver studied her suspiciously. "I'm not certain I believe you."

"Oh, but I do like the looks of him."

And was there anything about the man that a woman wouldn't like? Unless her memory had completely failed her, Jonathon Effington was tall with nicely broad shoulders, hair a rich sable in color and he danced as if he was born on a ballroom floor. He had a delicious dimple that appeared when he laughed and eyes that sparkled with mischief. Oh, certainly she had never danced with him or heard his laugh at anything but a distance or gazed into his eyes.

"That's not what I meant, and you well know it."

"Regardless, you must admit he is a catch even Father would have approved of. He would be a more than suitable match."

"And you are not the only lady in London to think so. Helmsley is one of the most eligible bachelors in the country. He will one day be the Duke of Roxborough and he is obscenely wealthy."

"I told you he was perfect." She beamed. "Now all we have to do is convince him that I am perfect for him."

"And do you have an idea for that as well?"

"None whatsoever." She sighed. "I have had gentlemen attempt to convince me to marry them, but I have never been in the position of trying to entice one to marry me. There is always the possibility of embroiling him in a scandalous situation which would then compel him to marry me, to save my honor and all that."

Oliver raised a brow. "You would do that?"

"Unfortunately, I'm afraid I wouldn't. Oh, I am certainly desperate enough to do so, but even I have certain standards of behavior. Besides, I should have to live with him for the rest of my days and I would prefer to avoid the resentment that a forced marriage would surely provoke."

"Good."

"I'm glad you approve, although it would be much easier if I were the type of woman who would force a man into an unwanted marriage. Oliver." She leaned toward him. "Aren't you and he friends? Can't you think of something?"

"Something that will make an old friend marry a woman he has never met? That's a rather formidable challenge." Oliver grinned. "However, challenge might well be the key."

"What do you mean?"

"Helmsley comes from a family of very strong-willed women." He chuckled wryly. "You may trust me on this point. There was a time when I fancied myself in love with his younger sister. At any rate, he was once vehement about what he wished for in a wife. Quiet, reserved, well-behaved, that sort of thing."

"Oh, dear," she murmured.

"However, in recent years he has come to realize that that particular type of woman would bore him to tears. He wants a woman with intelligence, who knows her own mind. He wishes for a bride who would be more of a"— Oliver grinned—"challenge."

"I don't know that I've ever attempted to be a challenge before, but I can certainly try," she said quickly. "And I definitely know my own mind."

"Indeed, a woman who would flee across half of Europe rather than wed the man her father has selected for her would be just the type of woman to pique Helmsley's interest."

"Excellent."

Jonathon Effington was precisely the kind of man she'd always dreamed of marrying. Indeed, although she had never said it aloud to anyone, had in truth pushed the thought from her mind years ago, Jonathon Effington was the very man she'd always wished to wed, even if he had no idea she existed.

With Oliver's help, that was about to change.

"What do we do now? Will you arrange introductions or . . ." She drew her brows together. "I do plan to be honest with him, you know. Marriage is permanent and I should not wish to begin such an endeavor with deceit."

"Honesty is indeed the best way to proceed." Oliver nodded. "Everything aboveboard, and all that."

"Well, perhaps not everything," she murmured. The memory of a number of incidents that skated perilously close to scandal came to mind.

"Not everything?" Oliver's brow raised.

"One cannot be a challenge and completely honest," she said in a lofty manner. "I shouldn't wish for him to know all my . . . secrets, as it were. Not that I have any particular secrets," she added quickly, "although I suppose one could consider—"

"That's quite enough." Oliver shuddered. "I have no desire to know anything more than is absolutely necessary. Simply give me your assurance that your *secrets* do not include anything that would preclude your being seen as a respectable match—"

"Oliver!" She cast him an indignant glare. "How could you think such a thing?"

"My apologies, cousin." He had the good grace to look chagrined. "We haven't seen each other for a very long time and, in truth, we do not really know one another at all. You have the manner and appearance of a woman who, well . . ." He shook his head in a wry manner. "I sincerely doubt that there are many men who would not risk scandal for you."

"I shall take that as a compliment." She grinned, then sobered. "Including Jonathon Effington?"

"Especially Jonathon Effington. You are precisely what he claims he wants in a wife. I shall be doing him a favor." He chuckled. "Oh, this should be a great deal of fun."

"Fun is the last thing I need, Oliver." Fiona sighed. "I need a husband."

And Jonathon Effington was not merely what she needed, he was exactly what she wanted.

Four days later, at the Effington Christmas Ball . . .

"Efficient as always, Henry."

Jonathon Effington slanted a glance at the butler, who, as he had done every year at this particular point during the Effington Christmas Ball, had stationed himself beside the Venetian mirror and console table that stood in a discreet alcove in the corridor that led to the Effington House library. And, just as he had every year, he bore a bottle of the house cellar's finest champagne and two glasses.

"Thank you, my lord," Henry said coolly.

Jonathon bit back a grin. Henry Mansfield was no more than a decade older than Jonathon himself and Jonathon was the lone member of the family to call him by his given name. Aside from that one deviation, long permitted and accepted by both men, Henry's demeanor was polished and never anything less than perfect. Probably ran in his blood. He was at least the third Mansfield to serve as the Effington House butler, and thereby serve the Duke of Roxborough and family, succeeding to his position several years ago when his uncle, the previous butler and a Mansfield as well, had retired to a cottage in the country.

Jonathon turned his attention back to his image. He had had an earlier meeting tonight in the library with the man he hoped would soon become his brother-in-law, but the assignation he was on his way to now was entirely different and much more pleasurable. He made a minor adjustment in the fold of his cravat. "What do you say, Henry, will I do?"

"You are perfection itself, my lord," Henry drawled.

Jonathon laughed. Henry was never overtly sarcastic, yet Jonathon knew exactly what the butler's tone now implied. The two men had known one another most of their lives. Indeed, in their younger years Henry had both assisted Jonathon in his various exploits and, on occasion, provided much-needed rescue.

"Scarcely perfection, but acceptable, I should think." Jonathon studied his reflection critically.

He was not the handsomest among his friends, but he was not unattractive. In truth, he was quite pleased with his appearance. And women certainly didn't seem to find him at all lacking. Why, they even liked the annoying way his thick brown hair insisted on flopping over his forehead instead of obediently staying put. He flashed a wicked grin at his image. And they did seem to adore his smile and the twinkle in his eye and the lone dimple in his cheek. Gad, he was undeniably a good-looking devil.

"Passionless, my ass," he said under his breath.

Henry's brow quivered slightly. "I beg your pardon, my lord?"

"Nothing, Henry, just thinking aloud." Jonathon's smile faded and he stared at the face in the mirror.

He would not have admitted it to his friends, but their charge last week as to the lack of passion in his relationships had dwelled in the back of his mind. He'd tried to ignore it, brush it off as the absurd notion that it was, yet it had lingered still like a melody that repeats over and over and can easily drive one mad.

He did concede, if only to himself, that perhaps they were not entirely wrong, although certainly he *had* been in love on occasion. Any number of times. It was simply not the kind of love, the kind of grand passion, as it were, that would lead one to behave in a ridiculous manner or to make promises one had no intention of keeping. Upon reflection, he had never led a woman to believe he offered more than he had. If his relations with women were somewhat superficial, well, it had served him and whatever lady was the object of his attentions at the moment nicely. And partings had always been amicable.

It was not a bad way to live one's life. Jonathon had no doubt that when the right woman made her appearance the passion his friends claimed he had never experienced would follow.

Not tonight, however. This evening his annual liaison in the library was with the exquisite Lady Chester. Judith was a petite blond-haired, blue-eyed widow with a delightful and well-earned reputation for savoring the amusements life offered and absolutely no desire for remarriage. He chuckled to himself. It would not be the first time he and Judith had shared a private evening, nor, he suspected, would it be the last. Still, one never knew what to expect with Judith, and it was Christmas Eve.

Jonathon accepted the glasses Henry offered in one hand, took the bottle in the other, then started toward the library. He took two steps, then glanced back at the butler and raised a brow. "Well?"

"Well, what, my lord?" Henry's impassive expression did not flicker.

"Advice, Henry, words of wisdom. Your traditional Christmas Eve soliloquy."

"I would not term it a soliloquy." Henry's voice did not waver, but a distinct gleam of amusement shone in his eye.

"Yet it is as much a tradition as the Effington Christmas Ball itself or the way my mother will find ever larger trees to decorate every year or . . ." Jonathon's grin widened and he glanced pointedly down the corridor toward the library.

"That is indeed a tradition," Henry said mildly. And who would know better than he?

When Jonathon had had his first tryst in the library during the Christmas Ball, he had been all of seventeen and

Henry was merely a footman. Still, he had managed to procure the necessary wine and glasses and had offered as well a few words of advice on dealings with the fairer sex from the vantage point of an older man's experience.

"Very well." The butler's clear gaze met Jonathon's. "Do take care, my lord. Remember that women are fickle creatures and prone to read more into a gentleman's words and actions than he might intend." Henry delivered precisely the same words and in precisely the same tone as he did every year. "Do not lose your head. Do resist overly compromising positions, lest an uninvited guest stumble upon"— he cleared his throat—"your assignation."

"Thank you, Henry. I am now fully prepared." Jonathon grinned, again started for the library, then paused. "Henry, have you ever been in love?"

"In love?" Henry shook his head. "Not yet, my lord, but I have not ruled out the possibility in the future."

"Nor have I."

For a moment, Henry's customary aplomb faltered. "Sir, am I to understand Lady Chester—"

"Good God, no," Jonathon said quickly. "Not that she's not a charming woman and I am exceedingly fond of her, but she is no more interested in me beyond this evening than I am in her."

"Yet, I cannot recall you ever meeting a lady in the library for a second time."

"Yes, well . . ."

It was difficult to explain the relationship he had with Judith. Even he wasn't sure he completely understood it. Through the years they had developed into something more than friends and something less than lovers, although they had certainly shared a bed on more than one occasion. He wasn't entirely sure why he had invited Judith to join him tonight although they did always have an excellent time together. Perhaps it was simply easier and safer to be in the company of a lady one knew well than play the games one did with a heretofore unknown female.

Henry studied him calmly. It was most disconcerting. Henry always saw far more than Jonathon would like.

"No. Lady Chester and I will have an amusing, momentary respite from the ball, a pleasant interlude, but nothing more than that." Jonathon's voice was firm.

"As always, my lord."

"Indeed." Jonathon raised the glasses in a toast of sorts. "As always."

He nodded, turned and strode down the corridor, his pensive mood swept away by the thought of the delectable widow awaiting him.

Judith was the perfect choice for this evening. There was no better way to mark the season than with a bottle of good champagne and a beautiful woman in one's arms. And if the lady in question expected no more than one was willing to give, so much the better. Besides, she would probably be the first to agree that he was no more what she wished, if she were in the market for a husband, than she was what he wanted.

No, he knew precisely what he wanted and, as much as his friends thought it was most amusing, when at last he found such a woman he would not hesitate to pursue, and win, her hand as well as her heart. And he'd do so with unbridled, imagined, never-before-seen passion.

But not tonight.

He grinned, nudged open the library door with his foot and stepped into the room. The library was a long, large room with book-laden shelves reaching upward to a distant ceiling, an oversized desk opposite the door and a fireplace at the far end of the room with a sofa strategically positioned in front of it for whatever purposes may be deemed necessary. The gaslights in the room were dimmed and even the fire did not dispel the shadows at that end of the chamber. Still, there was the distinct silhouette of a woman lingering in the darkened corner.

"Ah, Judith, forgive my tardiness." Jonathon moved to the desk, set down the glasses and expertly opened the champagne. "I had planned on arriving before you."

"Had you?" she said, her voice a shade huskier than usual. Quite exciting, really. This evening might be far better than he had expected.

"Indeed I had." He filled two glasses. "I wanted to greet you with champagne already poured." He picked up the glasses and turned. "I do so hate . . ." The words died in his throat.

A vision, definitely not Judith, but a vision all the same, stepped out of the shadows. "You do so hate what?"

"Surprises," he murmured, and handed her a glass. "You're not Lady Chester."

"I'm not?" She sipped the champagne and gazed at him in an innocent and most effective manner. "Are you sure?"

"I haven't a doubt in my mind." His gaze slipped over her and he very much liked what he saw. But then, who wouldn't?

She was much taller than Judith, but not overly tall, with hair a deep, warm red. He had always liked red hair. Her eyes were lovely, green in color and almost almond in shape. The low cut of her gown emphasized her lush figure. She was indeed a vision—no, a goddess, vibrant and fiery and straight from any healthy man's dreams. Jonathon had always been extremely healthy.

"Might I ask what you have done with Lady Chester?"

"Done with her?" She laughed, a natural rich sound as if laughter came easily to her. He liked that too. "Why, I have tied her up and stuffed her in an armoire."

"Have you indeed? I daresay she'd rather enjoy that." She laughed again.

"Although I doubt she is tied up and locked away." He studied the goddess curiously. "What has happened to her?"

"Nothing dire, I assure you. She was simply persuaded to allow me to meet you here in her place."

"Persuaded? By you?"

"No." She shook her head. "I've never met the lady. Lord Norcroft spoke to her."

"Did he?" Jonathon raised a brow. "Lord Norcroft, you say? How very interesting."

She smiled in a noncommittal manner.

He chose his words with care. What was Oliver up to?

"Why would Norcroft persuade Lady Chester to allow you to take her place?"

"Well." She frowned and thought for a moment, then drew a deep breath and met his gaze directly. "Because I have a proposal for you."

"A proposal?" He kept a pleasant smile on his face, but suspicion coursed through him. "What kind of proposal?"

"It's rather more difficult to say aloud than I had thought it would be." She wrinkled her lovely nose and appeared ill at ease. Jonathon wasn't entirely sure he believed her.

He sipped his wine and studied her. "Is it a business proposal?"

It would be just like Oliver to send him an interesting investment proposition in the guise of a beautiful woman. Particularly if the investment was more *interesting* than sound.

"I certainly wouldn't term it business, although I daresay some people might think so," she added under her breath.

"Personal, then?"

"Exceptionally so."

"A proposal of an exceptionally personal nature?" He laughed. "That sounds like a proposal of marriage."

"Exactly." She heaved a sigh of relief. "I do thank you, my lord, it's so much easier to hear you say it than to say it myself."

"Hear me say what?" He stared in confusion. "My dear lady, I have no idea what you are talking about."

"It's really quite simple. You said it yourself. I'm talking about a proposal of marriage." She leaned toward him and spoke clearly, as if his intelligence were in question. "Between you and me."

"You and me?" he repeated slowly. *Marriage?*

"I can see you still don't quite understand do you?" She gazed at him in a most sympathetic manner. "That's my fault, I'm afraid. I am not very good at explanations, especially complicated ones."

"You're not?" *Marriage?* "Perhaps you could give it a try?"

"Oh, absolutely." She downed the rest of her champagne,

placed the empty glass on the desk, clasped her hands together and drew a deep breath. "My Lord Helmsley . . ." She paused and a slight frown creased her forehead. "Might I call you Jonathon? I know it's terribly presumptuous of me and not at all proper, but it does seem that a discussion of this kind requires a sort of, well, intimacy that might otherwise be considered"—she thought for a moment—"naughty."

"Naughty?"

She nodded. "Naughty."

"One would hate to be thought naughty," he murmured. "Jonathon it is, then. And you are?"

"Oh, dear, imagine that, I have quite forgotten to introduce myself." She laughed lightly. "I shall attribute it entirely to nerves. I have never proposed marriage before."

"To my everlasting relief. I should hate to think you made a practice of this, Miss . . . ?

"Miss Fairchild. Fiona Fairchild." She held out her hand to him. "But you must call me Fiona."

"I would be delighted." He took her gloved hand and brushed his lips across it. Fairchild? It was vaguely familiar, but he couldn't quite place it. His gaze never left hers. "Fiona."

"I like the way that sounds." She tilted her head and studied him thoughtfully. "Jonathon and Fiona. It sounds . . . right. As if it were meant to be."

"Meant to be?" He didn't like the sound of that one bit. Particularly as the subject was marriage. He wasn't entirely sure he should continue whatever game this woman and Oliver played. Still, he did hate to surrender before knowing if it was a game he might win. "Fated, perhaps?"

"Exactly." She cast him a radiant smile that did something odd to the pit of his stomach. For a moment her words were obscured by the roar in his ears and the blood pounding in his veins and nothing in the world mattered save her smile and her eyes. ". . . destiny of a sort, I should think."

He shook his head. "What?"

"I was saying that as you are not yet married, it does indeed seem like destiny or providence or something of that nature."

He narrowed his gaze. "Why?"

"Because I am perfect for you." She beamed that amazing smile again, but he firmly ignored it. He obviously needed all his wits about him.

"Perfect for me?" he said slowly.

"Do you respond to everything with a question?"

"Forgive me, Miss Fairchild—Fiona. I have never been the object of a proposal before."

"No, of course not." She waved away the comment. "How silly of me not to realize you might well be every bit as discomforted by this as I am." She paused. "Now, then, where was I?"

"You are perfect for me," he said wryly.

"Ah, yes. Well." She squared her shoulders and met his gaze in an unflinching manner. "Your future wife will be the Marchioness of Helmsley and one day the Duchess of Roxborough. In very many ways, I have spent my entire life preparing for such a position.

"My mother was the sister of an earl, my father the younger son of a marquess. I have traveled extensively and am fluent in several languages. I can run a household with both efficiency and elegance and I am an excellent hostess." She spread her hands in a modest gesture that didn't seem the least bit modest and smiled. "As I said, I am perfect."

"Perfect perhaps if I were simply filling the position of marchioness or duchess, but are you indeed perfect for me? As a wife, I mean." Jonathon chose his words with care. There was something afoot here and he was determined to discover precisely what it was.

"Oliver thinks so."

"He does, does he?" So she called Oliver by his given name. This was most interesting and implied a relationship of a close nature. Whatever game his friend was playing, Jonathon would play along for the moment. Besides, whoever this woman was, she was undeniably lovely, and rather amusing as well.

He sipped his champagne and cast his gaze over her. "Why?"

"He says I'm stubborn and single-minded. He says as well that I have an inordinate amount of spirit and I am far too intelligent for my own good. In truth, it makes no sense to me." She shook her head, a puzzled look on her face. "I have always considered those qualities more a problem than an asset, at least in the eyes of men, but Oliver says they make me a challenge. And he further says you wish for a challenge in a wife."

"I am an unusual man. I do enjoy a challenge. . . ." And hadn't he admitted it to his friends just last week? "I will further confess that a lovely woman"—And hadn't they found it most amusing?—"who is as well a challenge is . . ."

Surely it was no coincidence that this green-eyed goddess now appeared in Judith's place assisted by Oliver?

At once the answer struck him and he was hard-pressed not to laugh. He should have known. He should have realized the truth the very moment this woman had said she was perfect for him. This was obviously some sort of joke. An elaborate scheme concocted by his friends to make him look like a fool.

"Is . . . what?" Fiona—if that was indeed her name—prompted.

"Is"—he cast her his most charming smile—"perfect." He turned to refill his glass and hers. Just how far would this woman go at the direction of Oliver and the others?

He handed her a glass and she accepted it with a grateful smile. She was obviously an actress. And a good one at that. That innocent widening of her eyes. The slightly unsure expression that would cross her face, the slight hesitation, the touch of discomfort. And Fairchild probably had a familiar ring because he had heard her name in connection with some play or other. He might even have watched her onstage, although surely he would have remembered if he had seen her before tonight. In truth, he couldn't imagine ever forgetting her. This was a woman who would linger in a man's mind.

"So tell me, Miss Fairchild—Fiona—why a woman as

lovely, as accomplished and as much of a"—he chuckled—
"*challenge* as you are should have to resort to proposing
marriage to a man you have never met."

"It's complicated."

"You've mentioned that."

"It bears repeating." She sipped her champagne and
thought for a moment. "My father wished me to marry—"

"As fathers tend to do."

She nodded. "And as I hadn't wed before he died, he
arranged for me to marry the son of an acquaintance of
his." She glanced at him. "Yet another man I have never
met.

"Go on."

"Until I marry, I receive no inheritance or dowry. Nor do
my three sisters receive their dowries unless or until I wed."

He choked back a laugh. "That's the most ridiculous
thing I've ever heard."

She heaved a dramatic sigh. "I know."

"So your future and the futures of your sisters are dependent upon your actions?" It was remarkably difficult to
restrain from laughing aloud at the dramatic nature of her
story. "You alone can save them from a life of poverty or
servitude?"

"Exactly." Her green eyes misted with tears at the very
thought. It was a nice touch.

"I see."

What a fabrication. What a far-fetched tale. And surely he
had heard that plot performed onstage before. He would
not be the least bit surprised if an entire cast tripped into
the room at any moment. Or at the very least the play-
wrights, the authors of the farce:

Norcroft, Warton and Cavendish.

Oh, they were fiendish fellows, these friends of his. No
doubt they had plotted this scheme after he had left them
last week. There were likely significant wagers among
themselves as to what he would do. Perfect wife indeed.
They probably thought he would run like a frightened rabbit when confronted with such a woman and the imminent

prospect of marriage. This Fiona Fairchild certainly filled all his qualifications, but then she would, wouldn't she?

She had obviously been rehearsed.

"Oliver says you have declared that when you find the woman who meets all of your qualifications you shall marry her at once." She stared at him with an uncertain smile on her face.

Well rehearsed.

Still, no one liked a good joke better than Jonathon himself, and this was no exception.

"So at this point I am supposed to take you in my arms and agree to marry you?"

"It sounds rather silly when you say it that way." She frowned. "That would be most convenient but is probably too much to expect."

"What do you expect?"

"To be perfectly honest, Jonathon"—she glanced at him—"and I do wish to be perfectly honest—"

"As do we all."

"I didn't know what to expect. Nor do I know precisely what to do. I only know that if I do not marry, my sisters and I shall lose everything. And the longer I wait to wed, the greater the chances are that I shall be forced to marry someone I have no desire to wed."

"And you do desire to marry me?"

A charming blush colored her cheeks. It was most impressive. "I think we would suit nicely. And"—she flashed him a slightly wicked grin—"you do come highly recommended."

"By Norcroft?"

"Certainly but you are one of the most eligible bachelors in England. Why, I should be interested in you even if my situation were not of a desperate nature."

"I'm flattered as well as curious." He considered her for a moment. "You are a beautiful woman and I cannot imagine any man not wishing to marry you. Why, then, have you reached the advanced age you have without being wed?"

"Advanced age?" She raised a brow. "I would scarce call five-and-twenty advanced."

He shrugged. "Many people would."

Annoyance flashed in her eyes. "Would you?"

"I would expect the kind of woman I want to be"—he thought for a moment—"*independent* enough to have resisted the urge to marry simply for the sake of marriage."

"Good." She paused. "I have, however, had offers of marriage, you know."

"I would expect nothing less."

She wrinkled her nose. "This is most awkward."

"Awkward? Not at all."

"Well, I certainly find it so." She held out her glass and he obediently refilled it. She did indeed seem discomforted, but then Jonathon had no doubt she was skilled at deception. He would expect no less of Oliver. "I never imagined, at the moment I did at last pursue marriage, I would be the one issuing the proposal." She tossed back her champagne. "So, then, we should end this, don't you think?"

"End this?"

"End this discussion." She waved impatiently. "By the way, that is most annoying."

"What is?"

"The way you answer everything with a question."

He chuckled. "I should hate to annoy you. It would make me less than perfect for you."

She stared in surprise. "My dear Jonathon. I never said you were perfect for me. Why, I really know nothing about you, save for your family position, your title, your prospects—which admittedly do make you a relatively perfect match for any woman—and Oliver's assurances that you are a nice man."

His brow raised. "A nice man?"

"A very nice man," she amended.

It was obviously time to be something less than nice and past time to take control of this scheme. His friends expected him to run from this allegedly perfect creature. It would certainly turn the tables on Oliver and the others if instead he accepted her proposal with—he grinned to himself—*open arms*. Indeed, once the truth was revealed and this plot of theirs laid to rest and they were all appropriately chastised, why, he would not be at all averse to getting to know the lovely actress better. And with something far less permanent than marriage in mind.

Regardless of what wagers may have been laid, Jonathon had no doubt he would be the ultimate winner.

"Very well, then, Fiona." He took another swallow of his champagne and set the glass aside. "I accept."

She stared. "You accept?"

"I do indeed." He stepped toward her and was most gratified when she stepped back.

"Just like that?"

Oh, this was good. The slight glimmer of panic in her eyes, the faint tremor in her voice. Very effective and almost believable.

"You are obviously the type of woman I have always wanted." He shrugged. "Therefore I see no reason to postpone the inevitable."

"The inevitable?" she said slowly.

"Now who is answering with a question?"

"I simply didn't expect this to be so . . . so easy."

"What did you expect?" He moved closer and again she stepped back. This was fun, although he would have thought she would be a bit bolder. Still, a charming virginal hesitance was called for if her story was to be believed. Oliver had taught her well.

"I'm not sure, really." She wrung her hands together and feigned dismay creased her lovely forehead.

"You're not changing your mind are you?"

"Oh, no, of course not." She sighed. "In truth, if you are indeed willing to marry me, I have no choice."

"But you find me entirely too easy?"

"Yes, I do. I never imagined you would agree to marry so quickly. I thought you would need much more convincing and some time to consider my proposal. Certainly I have little time to spare, but I have grown accustomed to the idea of marrying someone I don't know, whereas this is new to you."

"I don't believe in wasting time when an opportunity

presents itself." He flashed her a wicked grin. "You, my dear Fiona, are definitely an opportunity."

Her eyes widened. "Be that as it may, I thought as well you would wish to speak to Oliver about my, um, about me."

"And I fully intend to speak to him as soon as possible." His voice was firm. "All about you."

"You only have my word as to my background and family and everything else I have told you." Unease edged her voice. "I also assumed you would want to determine for yourself whether or not we will truly suit one another before a commitment of this nature."

"But our meeting was arranged by Norcroft and he is one of my dearest friends. Who better to know if you are indeed perfect for me than a man who has known me for years and, as my friend, has only my best interests at heart?"

She didn't so much as flinch at his declaration.

"My dear Fiona, I have long said that when I find the woman who is precisely what I want, I should not hesitate to make her my own."

"Still . . . don't you wish to—"

"What I wish is to take you in my arms." He suited his actions to his words and pulled her into his embrace, noting a slight reluctance on her part. Obviously part of the act. "And kiss you thoroughly to seal our bargain."

"Do you?" She stared up at him, her green eyes wide with a skillful mix of trepidation and anticipation.

"I can think of nothing I would rather do more."

"Then, I suppose . . ." Her voice had a charmingly breathless quality no doubt honed to perfection on the stage. She raised her chin and her gaze met his in a determined manner. "You should do precisely that."

"Indeed I should." Regardless of who she really was or the jest she was a part of, he fully intended to enjoy this. "And I shall."

He pressed his lips to hers and for a moment she stilled, as if uncertain, then her lips opened beneath his. She tasted delightfully of champagne and Christmas spices, secrets and desire. His and possibly hers as well. Excellent. He slanted his mouth harder over hers and his kiss deepened in a greedy manner that was less polished than usual, but he wanted her more than he had expected. In his arms and eventually in his bed.

She had obviously been kissed and kissed well before now. Still, there was something in the way her hands rested lightly on his shoulders or the slight restraint in the feel of her body pressed against his or a reluctant eagerness in her response that struck him as odd. Perhaps she wasn't as experienced as most actresses of his acquaintance. Or perhaps she was very skilled at her profession.

He scarcely cared at the moment. His mouth plundered hers and desire rose within him. He pulled her tighter against him. The feel of her body next to his, the intimacy of his mouth on hers, caught at something deep inside him, perilously close to his heart, although that was absurd. She was an expert at this and well used to eliciting such reactions from a man. Even so, Jonathon was not at all used to being affected in any manner that was not entirely physical. No doubt it was all that talk of perfection and fate.

He gently ended the kiss and raised his head. Her eyes were closed, her lips slightly open and she seemed unable to move.

Whether that was part of her charade or not, he quite liked it. And liked as well the faint dusting of freckles across the bridge of her nose. He chuckled and her eyes fluttered open.

"Oh, my." Her words came in the manner of a woman who has just been well and truly kissed and enjoyed it. Jonathon was confident this particular moment was no act. "That was quite . . ." Her eyes were wide and a bit glazed. "Quite wonderful."

He smiled down at her. "I thought so. But then it would be, wouldn't it?"

"Why would it?" She fairly sighed the words.

"Because we are perfect for one another." He grinned with satisfaction. "Fated for each other and all that."

"All that." She smiled up at him with that brilliant smile that reached inside him and twisted him in knots.

He swallowed hard. No matter what else happened, he would never forget that smile.

She stepped out of his arms with a reluctant sigh, moved back as if to put distance between them and absently smoothed the skirt of her gown.

"In spite of the challenge I apparently present, I do plan on making you a good wife." Fiona glanced at him with a determined look in her eye. "You will not be sorry, Jonathon."

He shook his head to clear it. Regardless of her act, she was still a remarkable woman, and when this was all said and done he had every intention of pursuing a closer acquaintance. "I cannot imagine I will be the least bit sorry."

"I should take my leave now." She glanced around the library. "This would be most improper if we were found here alone. I should hate to begin our marriage with any kind of scandal or gossip of an untoward nature."

"No, we wouldn't want that."

"Now that this is decided, we should probably proceed quickly." She leaned toward him in a confidential manner. "I am fairly certain the man my father wished me to marry will no doubt make an appearance at some point soon and it would be best if I was wed before then."

"By all means. Speed is definitely called for." Not that there was any spurned suitor or dead father or anything beyond an elaborate hoax. He could hardly wait to see the faces of his friends when he informed them that he knew of their joke all along.

She pulled a calling card from her glove and handed it to him. "I have written the address where I am staying on the back of my card. Since our return from Italy, my sisters and I have been residing with my cousin and aunt and shall do so indefinitely. Or at least"—she glanced at him in a manner that was almost shy; excellent acting—"until we wed."

"I shall call on you within the next few days so that we might begin making arrangements."

"Dear Lord, I hadn't thought about an actual wedding ceremony." She paused as if she were really considering the details of such an event. "Something small, I should think, and as soon as arrangements can be made."

"Absolutely. I wish to spend as much time with you as possible as well. Now that I have found the perfect woman, I cannot wait to get better acquainted with her." He flashed her a knowing grin. "Far better acquainted."

Her eyes widened in apparent surprise. Oh, she was very good indeed. Then a slight smile curved her lips. "I shall look forward to it, Jonathon." She stepped closer and, before he could say a word, framed his face in her hands and pressed her lips to his. Her body molded against his and he could feel the shape of her through petticoats and corset and all those annoying layers women were compelled to wear. Before he could respond, she pulled away. "Very much so."

She cast him a wicked smile of her own, not at all the kind of smile an innocent lady of good breeding sacrificing herself in marriage to save her sisters would wear. Nor did she kiss like an innocent. It was at once shocking and most exciting. It was almost a pity this Fiona Fairchild was a fraud.

She turned and swept from the room.

"Excellent performance, my dear," he said softly, then chuckled.

He couldn't wait to find Oliver and the others, including Judith. She was obviously in on the joke. Well, he had seen through their little charade and had nicely turned the tables on them. Any minute now they would hear Fiona's report about what had transpired in the library. He hated to miss the expressions on their faces when she told them he had agreed to marry her. Perhaps he would wait for them to come to him to confess their failed plot and beg his forgiveness. Just the thought of them simmering in their own ill-conceived juices brought a grin to his face. No, Jonathon could not resist a good joke any more than they could. He propped a hip on the desk and picked up his glass. He would give them a few minutes to consider what their hoax had wrought and how to now correct it. He chuckled with anticipation. He could hardly wait.

He took a long sip of champagne and idly glanced at the engraved card in his hand: Miss Fiona Fairchild. Perhaps that was indeed her real name. No matter. He turned the card over and read the address written in a fine, firm hand. It was a house on Bedford Square. She certainly had picked a prestigious address. Didn't Oliver live on Bedford Square? Indeed, this was his address. Of course, as he had arranged this scheme it only made sense. . . .

The faintest sense of unease washed through him.

My sisters and I have been residing with my cousin and aunt.

Surely that was part of the act? Although presenting a card with Oliver's address written on it was going a bit far. After all, Jonathon would recognize the location immediately and the joke would be at an end.

If it was a joke.

Of course it was a joke. It was just the kind of thing Norcroft and Warton and Cavendish would delight in. Why, Oliver didn't even have a cousin. Did he? Jonathon racked his brain. Fiona had said her mother was the sister of an earl. If he remembered correctly, Oliver's aunt was long dead and had been married to a diplomat of some sort. What was his name? Fargate? Fairfax? His breath caught. *Fairchild?*

Surely he was mistaken. It couldn't possibly be. . . . Oliver would go to great lengths for a good joke, but he would never involve a member of his own family in something of this nature. Jonathon groaned aloud.

Fiona Fairchild was the Earl of Norcroft's cousin.

And Jonathon had just agreed to marry her.

Panic, pure and simple and overwhelming, gripped him. It was a mistake. A dreadful, dreadful mistake. Surely Fiona—Miss Fairchild—would understand that? And certainly Oliver would understand it as well?

Of course, if that ridiculous story she had spun was true, and right now he very much feared it was, the woman would not be inclined toward releasing him from his agreement. She was desperate to avoid an unwanted marriage. And while she had said he was not her perfect choice, she did seem to like him. At least if her kiss was any indication.

In spite of his declarations to his friends, he had no desire to wed anyone—perfect for him or not—at the moment. Why, he was still a young man. There were any number of things he wished to do before tying himself down with a wife and the accompanying responsibilities a wife and— God help him—children would entail. Oliver and the others were right. The very idea of imminent marriage—no matter how perfect the woman might be—was terrifying and chilled him to his very bones. Marriage was something one should approach slowly and with a fair amount of caution and reserve.

Not something one should agree to when alone with a beautiful stranger and a bottle of champagne and a fervent belief that he was the victim of an elaborate hoax!

He started toward the door. He would certainly be the butt of the joke now and for the rest of his days if he did not find Fiona at once and stop her before she told anyone of their betrothal. Especially before she told Oliver or Oliver's mother or—he groaned aloud—his own mother. Worse, he might be forced to actually marry her.

A heartbeat before he reached the door, it jerked open and he came face to face with his sister Lizzie, Lady Langley.

"Did you, by any chance, see anyone . . . someone . . ." He craned his neck to see around her.

"Someone?" Lizzie stepped past him into the library. "You mean a woman? Very pretty? Rather upset?"

"Yes," he said eagerly. Although he wasn't at all sure why Fiona would be described as upset. Indeed, she had had a charming smile on her face when she had left the library.

Unless she had had second thoughts? His spirits lifted. Perhaps she had come to her senses about wedding any man she didn't know, especially him. Or perhaps, as she had apparently avoided wedded bliss nearly as long as he had, the thought of marriage itself was as daunting to her as it was to him even if she had no other choice. But if Lizzie had seen Fiona in the corridor, he had an excellent chance of catching up with her.

"No." Lizzie's voice was cool, although there was the distinct possibility she would not tell him even if she'd seen

Fiona. His sister was not at all tolerant of his Christmas Eve trysts.

"I see." If Lizzie hadn't seen her, Fiona had probably already returned to the ballroom.

"Have you seen Nicholas?" Lizzie said.

"Nicholas?" Jonathon murmured, still staring down the passageway as if to will Fiona's return to the library by sheer desire alone. He might yet be able to find her among the crowd at the ball, although as he knew from past experience finding one lone female amid the revelers in the ballroom at the height of the evening was nearly impossible. Still, he could try.

"Yes," she snapped. "Nicholas Collingsworth? Sir Nicholas? Your dear old friend?"

"Yes, of course." Jonathon cast one last, longing look down the corridor, then slipped Fiona's card into his waistcoat pocket.

Lizzie had problems of her own, and regardless of the circumstances Jonathon now found himself in, he owed his sister whatever assistance he could provide. While he was confident she would soon be happily wed, the least he could do was help her along that path. It was a debt long past due.

He heaved a sigh and turned toward his sister.

"Well?" Lizzie said impatiently. "Have you seen him?"

"Briefly. . . ."

By the time he finished with Lizzie and Nicholas, it might well be too late to find Fiona and clear up this *misunderstanding* tonight. He would have to call on her, and Oliver, as soon as possible. But between family festivities and obligations on Christmas Day tomorrow and Boxing Day after that, it would be at least two days before he could see her again.

Surely nothing irrevocable would happen in the span of a mere two days?

Three

One, two or three days later, depending on one's point of view and level of desperation . . .

"Do you think he's changed his mind?" Genevieve Fairchild's offhand question hung idly in the air of the parlor Aunt Edwina—Lady Norcroft—had assigned to the sisters. Gen reclined on a chaise, her gaze remained fixed on the magazine she held in front of her, although she, and everyone else in the room, was acutely aware of the significance of the question, though no one had dared voice it aloud before now. "It's been two full days, three if you count today as well."

"I don't count today," Fiona said, and continued to pace the floor just as she had done yesterday and the day before in those few, yet endless moments when holiday festivities had not compelled her attention. Aunt Edwina had taken advantage of having a full house to arrange all sorts of festive activities. It would have been a great deal of fun if Fiona hadn't had the pressing matter of her impending marriage on her mind.

Sophia Fairchild looked up from her embroidery and

traded knowing glances with her twin sister Arabella who sat writing at a ladies' desk.

"I would count today, if I were you," Belle said under her breath.

"Three days is a very long time," Sophie murmured.

"Two days," Fiona snapped. "It's only been two days. And as one was Christmas and the other Boxing Day, they scarcely count at all. Why, a very good argument could be made that Lord Helmsley and I came to our agreement less than a full day ago."

"If you want to delude yourself and live in a world peopled with fairies and elves and other creatures that don't exist," Gen said as if she were speaking more to herself than the others.

Fiona stopped and glared at the younger woman. "I am not deluding myself. Lord Helmsley is a man of honor. He agreed to marry me—rather more quickly than I thought he would, but he agreed nonetheless. And I have every confidence that he will live up to his word."

"Do you?" Gen tossed the magazine aside and sat up. "Then why haven't you told Cousin Oliver of his lordship's agreement?"

"I haven't had the chance," Fiona said staunchly.

"You've avoided him, is what you've done," Belle said. "We've all noticed it."

"I have not," Fiona lied.

Sophie snorted. "You most certainly have. And in increasingly creative ways."

Belle jumped to her feet, hooked her thumbs in imaginary lapels and addressed her twin in a deep voice. "Come, now, Cousin Fiona, do tell me what transpired between you and Lord Helmsley, as he is one of my dearest friends and you are a member of my family."

"Oh, dear, Cousin Oliver"—Sophie's voice was unnaturally high—"I would, but . . ." She rose, stretched out one hand toward her twin in a pleading manner and rested the back of the other on her forehead. "As much as I should like to tell you everything, I fear I must swoon now."

Gen shifted out of her way and Sophie collapsed theatrically beside her onto the chaise.

"Poor, poor Fiona." Gen patted her sister's head and heaved a dramatic sigh. "She is such a fragile thing and bears such awesome responsibilities now that the girls are all alone in the world."

"That is not the least bit amusing." Fiona tried and failed to stifle a laugh. "I understand Sophie is supposed to be me and Belle is Oliver, but who, pray tell, are you?"

"Aunt Edwina, of course." Gen clasped her hands under her chin and gazed heavenward. "Dear, courageous Fiona. Taking care of her orphaned sisters when she should be raising a family of her own." Gen grinned. "She thinks you're wonderful."

"She thinks I am one step away from permanent spinsterhood," Fiona said wryly. It had not escaped Aunt Edwina's notice that Fiona was five-and-twenty and unwed.

"Not for long, with any luck at all." Sophie studied the older girl. "You've told Oliver about Father's will. Why haven't you told Aunt Edwina?"

"Aunt Edwina would have you married in less than a day." Belle smiled smugly. "And to an excellent catch too, I would wager. I daresay she has any number of friends with eligible sons who would marry you without so much as a by-your-leave."

"It shouldn't be that difficult, really." Belle surveyed Fiona with a critical eye. "Your age scarcely shows at all."

"Thank you." Fiona resisted the urge to snap and drew a deep breath. "I haven't told Aunt Edwina because this situation is embarrassing and humiliating and I'd prefer that as few people know as necessary. Besides, I thought having Oliver's assistance was preferable to his mother's."

"I can see that. Oliver is quite dashing." Gen grinned in a wicked manner. "Rather a shame he's a cousin."

"Only by marriage." An eager note sounded in Belle's voice. "His aunt, Fiona's mother, was Father's first wife. And as Father adopted us when he married Mother, why, there's no true blood connection at all."

"I am very much aware of that," Gen said thoughtfully.

"Well, put it out of your head right this moment." Fiona cast a firm glance at each sister in turn. "Oliver is not a potential match for any of you. We need family here in London more than anything else. And he and his mother are all we have."

"Pity," Sophie murmured.

"Besides, Aunt Edwina is already talking about bringing you all out into society this spring." Fiona adopted a casual manner. "Should any of you find a match before then, well, I should hate for you to miss a London season and all it entails."

Gen glanced at her discarded magazine. "The gowns."

"The parties," Sophie added.

"The gentlemen." Belle grinned.

Fiona sighed reluctantly. "It would be a pity to settle on Oliver before any of you have had the opportunity to see who else might be—"

"I would hate to disappoint Aunt Edwina." Sophie struggled to sit up on the chaise. "She sees us all as the daughters she's always wanted, and I for one quite like having a mother around, even if she's not my own."

"I think Mother would have liked Aunt Edwina's plans for us, for a season and whatever else she has in mind." Gen nodded. "Mother would have especially liked how much Aunt Edwina likes, well, us."

The girls' mother, Fiona's stepmother, had died shortly after Fiona's eighteenth birthday when Gen was ten and the twins barely nine years of age. The younger girls had spent much of their lives without a mother and even in the scant week they'd been in London, Aunt Edwina had proven to be a delightful substitute. She was thoughtful and wise and thus far had spoiled them all in a manner only a woman who had long wanted daughters could do.

"And it's not as if we were all Fiona's age. Gen, Sophie and I have plenty of time to find suitable husbands." Belle cast a pointed glance at Fiona. "Of course, just how suitable depends on whether or not we have a dowry."

"I am well aware of that." Fiona's voice was grim.

"Perhaps you should pay a call on Lord Helmsley rather than waiting for him to call on you?" Gen said.

Fiona shook her head. "It wouldn't be all proper."

"Proper?" Belle scoffed. "And it was proper to ask him to marry you in the first place?"

"You could bring Oliver with you and no one could complain about that." Sophie leaned forward. "Of course, you would have to tell Oliver everything first."

"It can't be avoided, I suppose." Fiona wasn't sure why she was reluctant to tell Oliver what had transpired in the Effington House library.

It was entirely possible that she didn't want Oliver, or anyone, to know that Jonathon Effington was more than likely the one man in all the world that she wouldn't mind marrying under these circumstances, or any circumstance, for that matter. It sounded absurd, even to her, but there you had it. It was even more ridiculous when she considered that, in the nine years since she'd last seen him, she hadn't given him more than an occasional passing thought—at least for the past eight years or so. Why, she had very nearly forgotten him altogether. And she had never considered him as a potential husband until Oliver had brought up his name.

It had seemed so easy when she and Oliver had come up with the idea of marriage to Jonathon. A simple *Here I am, my lord, the very woman you have always wanted, and oh, by the way, did I mention I have to marry as soon as possible?* But once alone with Jonathon, it had been difficult to get the words out. In truth, it all felt unseemly and more than a little pathetic. Not to mention desperate. Certainly she was desperate, but still . . .

Now he was the only one she wanted and their meeting in the library only made her want him more. She had long wondered what it would be like to be the lady in the library with Jonathon Effington on Christmas Eve. Had wondered from the moment she had seen him in that very room nine years ago.

She and her family were to embark for France a few days after Christmas Day, 1845. Her parents had been invited to the Effington Christmas Ball and even though Fiona had barely turned seventeen, she'd been allowed to attend because, as her stepmother had said, who knew how long it would be before Fiona had the chance to attend her next London ball?

The Christmas Eve event was everything Fiona had ever dreamed a grand ball would be. Decorations wrought from greens and ribbons festooned every nook and cranny. Music and laughter filled the air. Skilled dancers whirled about on the ballroom floor in an endlessly changing kaleidoscope of bright colors and flashing jewels. Lovely ladies in the latest French fashions flirted with dashing men in fine formal attire. But none was more dashing than the young Jonathon Effington.

Fiona had seen Jonathon from across the room and he had quite taken her breath away. Upon later reflection she had realized that he wasn't perhaps the handsomest gentleman there or the most charming, but there was something in his manner that was irresistible, as if he were surrounded by light. At least in her uncritical eyes. The man simply exuded life, and when he laughed, delightful shivers ran up her arm.

It had taken her nearly an hour to work up the courage to approach him, if only to wish him a happy Christmas. In the year that followed, Fiona would grow nearly two inches in height and her plump figure would evolve into a much more attractive form. But on that Christmas Eve, Fiona was the first to admit she resembled nothing so much as an overripe Christmas plum. Still, with the desperate drama inherent in a girl of that age who has just seen the man who may well be the one true love of her life, the man she might never see again, she had to at least make his acquaintance. Or she would surely perish.

She had just managed to nonchalantly edge away from her parents' side when she saw Jonathon slip out of the ballroom. What could she do but follow him? After all, it was probably fate that she had been allowed to attend the ball in the first place and, even at seventeen, she knew one didn't laugh in the face of fate. She watched him turn down a corridor, scurried after him, then peeked around a corner in time to see him accept a bottle and glasses from a servant and continue down the hallway. She'd ducked behind a potted palm just in time to avoid detection by the servant passing by her on his return to his duties.

Fiona had then carefully made her way down the hall until she heard the unmistakable sound of feminine laughter coming from a half-opened door. She had flattened herself against the wall and cautiously peeked into the room.

Jonathon had been locked in a scandalous embrace with a lady. A woman of questionable morals, given the way she was embracing him back.

Fiona had stifled a gasp and jerked away from the door as if singed. Even today, the shock of that moment was as sharp as if it had happened yesterday. And even today, she had the good grace to blush at the memory of how she had peeked again, just to make certain, of course, that she had seen what she'd thought she'd seen, and then had returned to the ball in a most dejected state.

She'd pined over Jonathon Effington for a time, but the excitement of travel and their new life in Paris eased her dismay. In truth, as the years passed, and her chubby figure had slimmed and her orange hair darkened and young men had actively sought her favors, why, she'd forgotten about Jonathon Effington altogether.

Until now.

"Yes, of course. That's the thing to do." Fiona squared her shoulders. "I shall tell Oliver of Lord Helmsley's willingness to wed and we shall call on him together."

"Good." Gen nodded, then met her older sister's gaze. "We are grateful that you are willing to do this for us, but—"

"But it doesn't seem at all . . . right." Belle sighed. "You shouldn't have to sacrifice your life in a marriage not of your choosing because Father was mad."

Fiona gasped. "Arabella Fairchild!"

"Well, not mad, I suppose"—Belle shrugged—"but definitely not in his right mind. How could he have been to be willing to condemn his own child to a loveless marriage?"

"We haven't talked about love, you know." Sophie stepped closer and searched Fiona's face. "Don't you think about that? Don't you want to marry a man you love? A man who will love you?"

"Of course I do, but . . ." Fiona paused to gather her thoughts. "I've had twenty-five years to fall in love and it hasn't happened. If I had fallen in love and married, and indeed Father gave me every opportunity to do so, we would not be in this mess to begin with. At this point, I have no choice. And everything might well be for the best. Lord Helmsley is an excellent match. Besides . . ." She cast her sisters a weak smile. "If I have not had the occasion to fall in love by now, I daresay I never will."

"Could you love Lord Helmsley?"

"In time, perhaps." She had certainly fancied herself in love with him once long ago when she was very young and hadn't known any better and hadn't known him. Not that she knew him now, but at least they had spoken. And kissed. Which was really very nice, as he was exceptionally good at it. "I certainly do not find him objectionable in any way. He is quite dashing and charming and handsome enough—"

"Not that we would know," Gen muttered. The sisters were still annoyed that they had not been allowed to attend the ball, but Aunt Edwina had insisted it would not do, as she had great plans for their debuts in the spring.

"You'll meet him soon enough," Fiona said firmly. "It's decided, then. I shall find Oliver, tell him everything and together we shall pay a call on Lord Helmsley."

She started toward the door, but Sophie caught her arm. "Are you certain you wish to do this?"

Gen stepped toward her. "Surely there's another way. We just haven't found it yet."

"We could all find positions." Belle closed her eyes as if praying for strength. "As maids."

"You couldn't," Sophie murmured.

Fiona stared at her sisters. "Why this sudden concern? We have known for weeks that this day was coming."

"Yes, but now that it has come, we feel dreadful about it."
Sincerity rang in Gen's voice.

"Simply dreadful," Belle echoed, her tone perhaps a
shade less sincere than her sister's. Skeptical eyes turned
toward her and she huffed. "Well, we do, although admittedly I would not do well as a maid. And none of the rest of
you would either."

"We would make terrible maids." Sophie sighed. "Still, it
might be better than living with guilt for the rest of our
lives."

Fiona raised a brow. "I suspect you shall all manage to
bravely carry on." Once more she turned to leave. "As shall
I."

"Dear Lord, Oliver, tell me this is a joke," Jonathon said the
moment Oliver stepped into the parlor.

Oliver stopped in midstride. "Very well. It's a joke."

"Thank God." Relief washed through Jonathon and he
collapsed in the nearest chair. "I thought surely it had to be
some sort of hoax perpetrated by you and Warton and
Cavendish, with an assisting hand from Judith as well. But
then she gave me her card and it had your—"

"What's a joke?" Oliver asked.

Jonathon's stomach clenched. "Do you have a cousin by
the name of Fiona Fairchild?"

Oliver stared for a moment, then a slow smile spread
across his face. "Indeed I do."

Jonathon groaned. "Then I am doomed."

"Doomed?" Oliver raised an amused brow. "I gather this
is in reference to your meeting with Fiona during the
Christmas Ball?"

"How could you do that to me?" Jonathon glared. "I'm
your friend. One of your oldest friends." He narrowed his
gaze. "And it seems to me you do not have that many that
you can afford to squander one."

Oliver laughed. "It went well, then?"

"You are not taking this at all seriously."

Oliver stepped to the cabinet where he kept his liquor
and withdrew glasses and a decanter of something—

hopefully something potent. Jonathon needed potent at the moment.

"How can I, when I have no idea what transpired between you and my cousin. For all I know, it was your usual Christmas Eve romp." Oliver glanced at him over his shoulder. "Although I would hope not. I have come to regard her more as a sister than a cousin and I find I have become somewhat protective."

"They are not romps," Jonathon muttered, although, in truth, on more than one occasion they could certainly have been called romps. Not that it mattered at the moment. He studied his friend. "She has not told you, then?"

"She's not said a word." Oliver filled the glasses. "In fact, every time I attempt to speak to her about it she changes the subject or makes an excuse to leave my presence or distracts me in some way." Oliver crossed the room and handed Jonathon a glass. "She's very good at distraction."

At once the memory of a brilliant smile flashed through Jonathon's mind. "I can see where she would be." He took a sip, pleased to discover excellent Scottish whiskey of an appropriate quality and strength, and thought for a moment. "Then she's made no claims? No irrevocable announcements?"

"Not a one." Oliver settled in a chair that matched Jonathon's and narrowed his eyes. "What kind of irrevocable announcement?"

Jonathon leaned closer to his friend. "I swear on the graves of every Effington that has come before me, I thought she was part of a hoax." He jumped to his feet and paced the room, glass in hand. "I thought you and Warton and Cavendish had hired some woman—"

Oliver raised a brow.

"A beautiful woman," Jonathon said quickly, as if the compliment to Oliver's cousin would improve the situation. "An actress, probably."

"You thought my cousin was an actress?"

"An *accomplished* actress. I thought she was very good." Jonathon stared at his friend. "Is that ridiculous story true? About her father's will?"

Oliver nodded.

"Are you certain? This isn't some absurd plot on her part to trap me into marriage? I mean, I am considered quite a catch."

"Immodestly so." Oliver snorted. "But you're not the only marriageable man in London with a good title and tidy fortune. Without any effort at all, I can name several. Why, Freddy Hartshorne's prospects are every bit as good as yours and he would no doubt jump at the opportunity to wed a lady with Fiona's lineage, not to mention her looks."

"Come, now. Hartshorne is short, stubby and has hair redder than hers. They would have children who looked like carrots." Jonathon waved away the comment. "Besides, he's an idiot."

"As, apparently, are you." Oliver paused. "And it was not Fiona who thought of you. You were my idea."

Jonathon groaned. "Why? Why would you do such a thing to me?"

"I was doing you a favor. My cousin is everything you claim to have ever wanted in a prospective wife."

"She does seem to be," Jonathon admitted in a grudging manner. Indeed, in the two days since their meeting he'd realized it had taken a lot of courage as well as determination for Fiona to approach him. The woman obviously had spirit. He took another sip of his whiskey. "But I don't wish to be married."

"You've said over and over again—"

"I lied." Jonathon shrugged helplessly. "I didn't realize myself that I'd lied until I came face to face with the truth of it. Face to face with marriage." He resumed pacing. "I'm not ready for marriage, Oliver. Oh, I know it's my duty and all that, but I'm still a young man—"

"You're two-and-thirty."

"Yes, but men can get married at any age. We're not like women, we age better. I am certainly not the callow youth I was ten years ago."

"Older but no wiser?"

"I thought I was wiser until now."

"What exactly passed between you and my cousin?"

Oliver said slowly. "Fiona's silence led me to believe she might well have lost her nerve. Or that you rejected her out of hand."

"Not exactly," Jonathon murmured.

Oliver stared.

Jonathon blew a long breath. "I agreed to marry her."

Oliver grinned and raised his glass to his friend. "Well done, old man. I must say, you had me worried for a few minutes there."

"I wasn't serious. I thought she, the whole thing, was a joke."

"Well, it wasn't."

"I know that now. But I didn't know that at the time." A hopeful note sounded in Jonathon's voice. "Therefore, I would think, since I agreed to wed under false pretenses as it were, my agreement would be invalid."

Oliver stared in disbelief. "Do you forget you're dealing with a woman who is trying to save her sisters from poverty?"

"You're the head of the family, can't you provide for them? Can't they live with you?"

"As poor relations?" Oliver shook his head. "That is precisely what Fiona is trying to avoid. She has a fair amount of pride."

"Not so much that she wouldn't ask a total stranger to marry her," he said sharply.

Oliver's eyes narrowed. "I daresay it was not easy for her."

"Probably not." Of course it hadn't been easy for her. "My apologies." If Jonathon hadn't been such a fool and attributed every moment of hesitance or flash of unease in her eyes to acting—good acting, he amended—he would have seen that and realized the truth before it had been too late. "But it was all a misunderstanding. A dreadful, dreadful misunderstanding. Surely she will understand that?"

"I'm not sure I understand," Oliver said slowly. "You're saying you asked my cousin to marry you—"

"I *agreed* to marry her," Jonathon amended. "She did all the asking."

"Nonetheless, promises were made, were they not?"

"Well, yes, but only—"

"Then I would think you are obligated. Honor-bound."

"Trapped is more like it." Jonathon downed the rest of his whiskey. "Like a rat. No." He smacked the glass down on a table and aimed an accusing finger at the other man. "It's your fault I'm in this mess and it's up to you to get me out."

"I think not. Besides, I rather like the idea of you marrying my cousin. And the fault here, old friend, lies entirely with you. Jonathon." Oliver studied him for a moment. "Did she lie to you? Or misrepresent herself in any way? Did she entice you or threaten you or do anything other than be perfectly honest with you?"

"She was damned enticing," Jonathon snapped, then sighed. "But no, it was nothing like that. I suppose she was completely honest, but I didn't know that."

"And now you do." Oliver grinned. "Welcome to the family."

"No, Oliver." Jonathon stared at his friend for a long time. "Regardless of how *perfect* she might be for me, I will not marry because of a mistake. I shall simply have to make her understand that I—"

"Make who understand what?" a feminine voice sounded from the entry.

Oliver got to his feet. Jonathon braced himself and turned toward the doorway. His breath caught. Fiona Fairchild was every bit as lovely in the light of day as she was by gaslight.

Fated for each other and all that.

Fate? Hah. Not if he had anything to say about it.

"Good day, Miss Fairchild." Jonathon adopted his most formal manner.

"Jonathon." She smiled and the room—the world— brightened around her. She sailed toward him with an ethereal grace as if her feet did not quite touch the floor. "I have looked forward to seeing you again."

She extended her hand, but he seemed frozen in place, unable to do anything but stare. In the back of his mind he realized he was indeed an idiot who wanted nothing more at the moment than to melt at the feet of this goddess in a small stupid puddle of adoration and, yes, desire.

Oliver nudged him with a sharp jab of the elbow.

"As have I," Jonathon murmured, and took her hand. He raised it to his lips, his gaze fastened on hers, and it took every ounce of self-control he possessed not to lose himself in the green of her eyes. It struck him that regardless of the awkward circumstances, he had indeed looked forward to seeing her again. Still, if he did not gather his wits about him, he would be wed before he knew it. He released her hand abruptly and stepped back. "I hope you are well, Miss Fairchild."

She narrowed her eyes slightly at the overly polite note in his voice. "Quite well, thank you for asking. And you?"

"I'm well. As well. Thank you." Jonathon winced to himself. He sounded like a blithering idiot. Of course, he felt like a blithering idiot. But how on earth did one tell a lovely young woman—or any woman, for that matter—that he had no intention of marrying her? Especially when he had already agreed to do so. And agreed with a fair amount of enthusiasm.

"The weather is exceptionally fine as well." Oliver's voice was thoughtful, but there was a definite spark of laughter in his eye. "Although I daresay it might snow. What say you, Helmsley, might it snow?"

"It might. It might indeed." Jonathon nodded with relief. The weather was at least a safe topic. "The feel of snow is definitely in the air."

Fiona looked from Jonathon to Oliver and back. "Make who understand what?"

"I must say, I find myself in rather a quandary at the moment." Oliver shook his head. "Here one of my closest friends has asked for my assistance and, as he so gallantly put it, I do not have so many friends that I can afford to squander one. Although"—he fixed Jonathon with a wry glance—"I would dispute him on that point." He wagged his eyebrows at Fiona. "People quite like me, you know."

She laughed. "I have no doubt."

"On the other hand, there is my cousin, one of the few

blood relations I have in the world—excepting, of course, my mother, who scarcely ever needs anyone's help in any-thing—who needs my assistance as well. I find my loyalties are quite divided. Therefore"—he started toward the door—"I shall do what any intelligent man in my position would do and leave the two of you alone to sort out whatever it is you need to sort out without me." Oliver glanced back. "I shall, however, be within calling distance should either of you feel the need for rescue of any kind." With that, Oliver took his leave.

Fiona studied Jonathon carefully and he resisted the urge to shift from one foot to the other in the manner of a small child.

He cleared his throat. "Miss Fairchild—"

"Make who understand what?" she said for the third time in a tone considerably cooler than before.

"I believe we have something of a problem."

"What kind of problem?"

"I'm not entirely sure how to say this," he said under his breath. "It's really quite awkward."

"It was awkward for me when last we spoke." She crossed her arms over her chest. "Apparently it's your turn."

"Apparently," he muttered, then met her gaze directly. "I feel I should be perfectly honest with you."

"As I have been with you."

"Aha, but that's precisely the problem," Jonathon said quickly. "I didn't know you were being honest."

She raised a brow. "You didn't? What did you think?"

"I thought . . . well . . . that is to say . . ." He drew a deep breath. "I thought you were an actress."

"An actress?" She stared at him for a moment, then burst into laughter. "An actress?"

"A very good actress," he said quickly. It wouldn't hurt to flatter her as much as possible.

"As good as, oh, say, Sarah Woolgar or Mary Ann Kee-ley?"

"Every bit as good." He paused. "Perhaps even better."

"What a relief." She grinned. "I should hate for you to think I wasn't very good at my chosen profession."

"Oh, no, I thought you were excellent." Relief washed through him. She was definitely amused and did not seem the least bit upset. This would be easier than he'd expected.

"I am a bit confused, though. Why did you think I was an actress?"

"Oh, any number of things led me to that conclusion. Erroneously, I might add."

"You needn't add that," she said pleasantly. "But please go on."

"First of all, you had taken Lady Chester's place in the library." He leaned toward her in a conspiratorial manner. "This is just the sort of prank that she would find most amusing."

Her eyes widened slightly in a most fetching manner. "Prank?"

"Yes, of course." He chuckled. "And then you mentioned Oliver's name and his assertion that you were my perfect match. You see, it was no more than a fortnight ago that he and the others—"

"The others?" Her words were measured.

"Warton and Cavendish. Decent enough chaps most of the time, although they do like a good joke on occasion."

"Do they?"

"Indeed they do. Why, I can tell you things . . ." He caught himself. "No, that would be most inappropriate."

"And we would hate to be inappropriate," she murmured.

"At any rate, the last time we found ourselves talking about the inevitability of marriage—no more than a fortnight ago, I might add—I mentioned that I was not at all reluctant to wed. And when I found the woman who met all of my qualifications, I would marry her at once. The woman who was"—he cast her a pointed glance—"perfect for me. So you can see how when you presented yourself as the perfect potential bride, in Lady Chester's place, bandying Oliver's name about, well, you can certainly understand how I thought it was a hoax."

"A hoax?" she said slowly.

"And a good one too, I might add." He chuckled. "That nonsense about your inheritance and your sisters' dowries being withheld until you marry. And your father arranging a marriage for you."

"You thought that was nonsense?"

"I did at the time, and you have my apologies for that," he said quickly. "Now I see I was mistaken."

"Not entirely." She blew a frustrated breath. "It is *nonsense*. Nonetheless, as absurd as it is, it is my life." She paused and her brow furrowed in thought. "Let me make certain I fully understand what you are trying to say."

"Excellent." He nodded eagerly.

"When we met in the library during the ball—when I took Lady Chester's place—you thought I was an actress sent there by my cousin and your other friends." She glanced at him. "Is that correct so far?"

He nodded. "Absolutely."

"And you thought this because I appeared to be exactly what you had told them you wanted in a prospective bride?"

"Correct again." She certainly seemed to have a grasp of the situation thus far. His hopes rose.

"Adding to this assumption was the admittedly absurd—but true nonetheless—circumstances I find myself in."

"Yes, yes, go on." She was clearly as clever as she was lovely. Precisely what he had indeed claimed he wanted in a future wife. He pushed the inconvenient thought aside.

"And all these erroneous assumptions on your part led you to the inescapable conclusion that I was part of a hoax perpetrated by your friends?"

"Exactly." He heaved a sigh of relief. "So you see, when I agreed to marry you I was simply turning the tables on them. Going along with the joke, as it were."

"So when you agreed to marry me, you were not"—she thought for a moment—"sincere?"

That didn't sound at all good. "Although I wasn't actually *insincere*. Not in the truest sense of the word. As I said, I was going along with—"

"Did you or did you not mean it when you accepted my proposal?"

"Of course I didn't mean it. It was a misunderstanding. Completely on my part," he added quickly. "And I accept full responsibility. I am entirely to blame."

"Then you concede I did not lie to you or mislead you or coerce you in any way?"

"Absolutely not," he said staunchly.

"I was honest and entirely candid?"

"Without question."

"Well, then, my Lord Helmsley—Jonathon—I believe in one respect you were right all along." She cast him that brilliant smile, and for the briefest flicker of a moment he regretted that it was all a mistake. "The joke is indeed on you."

Four

"On me?" Jonathon's smile faltered. "What do you mean, the joke is on me?"

Fiona struggled to keep a pleasant expression on her face. For one brief, shining moment when she had entered the parlor and Jonathon had gazed at her with the most wonderful look in his eyes—almost like a man in love—she had believed her troubles were at an end. Damn the man anyway. She should have known when it took him three days—counting today—to call on her. Now the world crashed down about her head. No. Her resolve hardened, she would not permit it to do so. Or rather, she would not permit *him* to do so.

She drew a deep breath. "You said I did not mislead you, indeed I was completely honest?"

"Well, yes, but—"

"Therefore my proposal was issued in good faith?"

"I suppose, but . . ." He frowned. "Women are not supposed to issue proposals in the first place."

"No, my lord, women are supposed to know their place in this world. They are supposed to do exactly as they are instructed by fathers or husbands or brothers in all matters up to and including when they should marry and to whom," she said, a shade more sharply than she'd intended. "But I daresay a woman who was a *challenge* would not hesitate to take matters into her own hands, especially when it involved issues as important as proposals of marriage."

He stared at her. "Perhaps, but—"

"And did you not want a challenge in this imaginary perfect bride of yours?"

"I might have said that, but—"

"Then consider yourself challenged, my lord!" Her restraint snapped and she whirled away from him. She spotted a decanter of sherry on a cabinet. Excellent. Spirits were certainly called for at the moment, at least to steady her nerves. Why, even her hands were shaking with anger. She stalked to the decanter, sloshed some of the sherry into a glass, drew a deep swallow, realized at that moment it wasn't sherry, and promptly choked.

"I say, Miss Fairchild." Jonathon stepped toward her. "Are you all right?"

"Quite," she sputtered, and thrust out her hand to keep him away, although she wasn't the least bit all right.

"Whiskey should really not be drunk that quickly if one is unused to it."

"I thought it was sherry." She choked the words. "It looks like sherry."

"Appearances can be deceiving." He paused in a significant manner. "Exactly as I have been trying to—"

"You thought I was an actress!" She glared at him.

"I've explained that," he said warily.

"My mistaken conclusion was influenced by anger. Yours was the result of, I don't know, *lust* perhaps?" A horrible thought struck her. "Did you think I was a whore as well?"

"Of course not." Even as he said the words, she could see in his eyes that the idea that she was at least of questionable virtue had indeed passed through his mind.

She gasped.

"See here, Miss Fairchild, I can tell you I have known any number of actresses who were not, well—"

"Whores?"

"Yes, although admittedly they do tend to be of looser

morals . . ." His voice trailed off helplessly as if he had no idea what to say now that would not make the situation worse. It would have been rather endearing if she wasn't so furious.

She narrowed her eyes and resisted the urge to wrap her hands around his neck. "Is that why you took the liberty of kissing me?"

"Not at all," he said staunchly. "Your morals had nothing to do with it. I kissed you because I very much wanted to kiss you."

"And to seal our bargain?"

"No! I was not making a bargain. I was making a mistake."

"In that you thought I was an actress with loose morals?"

"Yes! That was definitely a mistake. Although you did nothing to correct that impression. Indeed"—a smug smile lifted his lips—"you kissed me back. And I must say, Miss Fairchild, it was not the kiss of a woman who has never been kissed before."

She scoffed. "Of course I've been kissed before. You yourself pointed out that I am far from my schoolgirl days."

"You've been thoroughly kissed," he said pointedly.

"And you have obviously kissed thoroughly," she snapped. "You are very skilled at it. I assume you have had a great deal of practice!"

He shrugged in a modest manner.

"I do hope you enjoyed it, as your days of practicing are quite at an end."

"What?" His brow furrowed.

"No husband of mine is—"

"I am not going to be your husband." His voice rose.

She stepped to him and poked a finger at his chest. "You agreed!"

"I told you it was a mistake."

"Nonetheless"—she emphasized every word with a jab of her finger—"you gave your word and I am holding you to it."

He caught her hand and glared down at her. "I am not going to be trapped into marriage."

She gritted her teeth. "I did not trap you."

"I feel trapped!"

"You feel trapped? You haven't the vaguest idea of what trapped truly feels like." She stared up at him. "To know that the one man that for your entire life you trusted and loved above all others has left you in an untenable situation where your only recourse is to marry one stranger or throw yourself on the mercy of another! That, my lord, is trapped!"

His expression softened. "I am sorry."

She gazed up into his blue eyes and for a moment wanted nothing more than to stay like this, with her hand in his, caught between the two of them forever. And wished as well they had met under different circumstances when she could indeed be the type of woman he'd always wanted and he would be the man her dreams were made of. "Save me, Jonathon," she said softly, and raised her lips to his. "Rescue me."

"I would like nothing better than to rescue you, Fiona." His head bent to hers, his voice low and inviting. "You might well be everything I have ever claimed to want."

"Then marry me," her lips murmured against his.

"No," he whispered, and pressed his lips to hers.

For the length of a heartbeat she reveled in the warmth of his lips on hers and the longing that rushed through her at his touch, exactly as it had on Christmas Eve. Not that it mattered. Her anger rekindled and she shoved him away.

"You are a cad, Jonathon Effington! The very worst kind of beast, and don't you dare try to kiss me ever again!"

He chuckled. "I didn't just try, I did kiss you."

She sniffed. "Hardly."

He stepped closer. "Perhaps I should try again, then?"

"You're refusing to marry me, yet you want to kiss me?" She glared in disbelief. "Have you no shame?"

He thought for a moment, then grinned. "No."

"If you come one step closer to me I shall scream, thus attracting the attention of the entire household, including Aunt Edwina. It should be a most compromising position to be found in. No doubt she will insist on marriage at once." She studied him for a moment. "Upon further consideration . . ." She opened her mouth to scream.

Before she could get so much as a squeak out, he had moved to her, pulled her into his arms and clapped his hand over her mouth.

"Now, now, Miss Fairchild. We shall have none of that." There was a distinct twinkle of amusement in his eyes and her anger rose. She struggled against him. "If you promise to behave like a reasonable person, I shall release you."

She glared at him, wishing that just this once looks really could be lethal.

"Well? Do you promise?"

What choice did she have? His hand wasn't even in a good position to bite. Pity. She nodded.

"I'm not entirely sure I believe you." He grinned, and she vowed to hurt him at the earliest opportunity. "I suppose I shall just have to trust you." He released her and stepped out of range.

She cast him her most scathing look, then moved to the door and flung it open. "Oliver!"

"You needn't yell." Oliver lounged beside the door. "I've been right here all along."

She raised a brow. "Then you have heard everything?"

"I missed something between how trapped you are and what a beast he is, but other than that, I pretty much caught it all."

"Good." She turned and stalked back to the center of the room. "Then I won't have to repeat it." Abruptly she turned on her heel and glared at her cousin. "This is almost as much your fault as it is his, you know."

"That's what I was thinking," Jonathon said under his breath.

"My fault?" Oliver's brows pulled together. "How is this my fault?"

"You told me I was exactly what he wanted in a wife. You said he would jump at the opportunity to marry me—"

"I don't think I ever said jump," Oliver murmured.

"You said he was nice!"

Oliver shrugged. "I was wrong."

"I say, I am nice." Indignation sounded in Jonathon's voice. "Ask anyone."

"Hah!" Fiona crossed her arms over her chest and studied each of the two men in turn.

She'd thought, and still did think for the most part, that Oliver had been sincere in his suggestion of Jonathon as a husband. Now, however, it was apparent that his motives might not have been entirely pure. Of course, he couldn't possibly have imagined that Jonathon would think she was part of a hoax.

As for Jonathon, as much as she needed a husband she couldn't marry a man who had no desire whatsoever to marry her. Indeed, a man who had strenuous objections. What kind of life would that be? He would resent her for the rest of his days. Why, regardless of how *nice* he was, he'd no doubt have an *actress* in his bed before her vows were out of her mouth.

Still, Jonathon offered her only hope for salvation at the moment.

"Oliver"—she met her cousin's gaze—"I will assume that you were sincere when you suggested Lord Helmsley as a prospective husband and had no intention of tricking him in any way."

"On my word, Fiona, I had no idea he would think your situation . . ."—he cast a pointed look at Jonathon—"your *dire* situation was a ruse. And I never would have put you in such a position. Although I do have to admit"—Oliver tried and failed to hold back a grin—"if it had been a joke it would have been a damn fine one. Brilliant, really."

"Not that I would have fallen for it," Jonathon said under his breath.

"No, you would have been too clever for that," Fiona snapped, then closed her eyes and prayed for calm. She drew a deep breath and leveled Jonathon a firm look. "As for you, I am willing to concede that your agreement to marry was"—she grimaced—"a misstatement—"

"A mistake," Jonathon corrected.

"*Said in error.*" She clenched her teeth. "That you did indeed believe I was part of a hoax—"

Jonathon heaved a sigh of relief. "Thank God."

"However"—she smiled in a pleasant manner—"I do intend to hold you to it."

Oliver choked back a laugh.

Jonathon's eyes widened. "What?"

"Unless you can come up with a better solution to the absurd dilemma that is my life. And when I say you"—she shifted her gaze from Jonathon to Oliver—"I mean both of you."

"I am completely at your service." Oliver nodded a bow.

"I don't really have a choice," Jonathon said under his breath to Oliver. "Do I?"

"I don't see one, aside from marriage." Oliver thought for a moment. "You should keep in mind as well there is always the possibility of legal action on Fiona's part. Breach of promise, that sort of thing."

"Nonsense." Jonathon scoffed. "I have excellent solicitors."

"As do I," Oliver said firmly. "And as Fiona is a member of my family, they would be at her disposal to use as she sees fit."

Jonathon glanced at his friend. "Would she do that?"

"She is a desperate woman." Oliver shook his head. "I might if I were her."

"It would create a huge scandal."

"Indeed it would." Oliver grinned. "Might be worth it to at last see you in the midst of something truly tasty."

"I am still in the room, you know." Fiona glared at the men. They were both most annoying. "And I would much prefer that you not discuss me and what I might or might not do, as if I were not here."

"Yes, of course," Oliver said.

"My apologies," Jonathon murmured.

She studied the two of them for a moment, then squared her soulders. "Since I first learned of the provisions of my father's will, I have, needless to say, considered all aspects of my situation. I have come to the conclusion that I essentially have three options.

"First, I can resign myself to my fate. Surrender to my father—my dead father—complete control over my future and marry Whatshisname—"

"Who is Whatshisname?" Jonathon asked Oliver.

"The American her father has arranged for her to marry."

"An American?" Jonathon shuddered. "I can see why she objects."

She ignored them. "There's a possibility I could convince him to agree to a marriage of a temporary nature."

Oliver frowned. "Divorce?"

"As distasteful as that is, and as difficult as it is to arrange, yes, or possibly annulment. The solicitors I consulted believe either would satisfy the conditions of the will. However, this would depend entirely upon the type of man Whatshisname is. My inheritance and dowry represent a considerable fortune, you know."

Jonathon glanced at Oliver. "How considerable?"

"Quite considerable," Oliver murmured.

"It would take a man of impressive character to let it, and me, go. It would also take brilliant legal maneuvering as well. I am not willing to risk everything based on either character or brilliance. Furthermore, when I marry I would much prefer it be for the rest of my life.

"Secondly"—she directed her gaze toward Jonathon—"I can force Lord Helmsley to live up to his agreement and marry me."

Jonathon opened his mouth, probably to object, then closed it again and smiled weakly. He obviously had more intelligence than he had displayed thus far.

"Unfortunately"—given her circumstances she could not believe she was about to say this—"I cannot imagine a more dreadful way to begin a life together than with a marriage that does not appeal to both parties."

"I say, Miss Fairchild"—sheer relief rang in Jonathon's voice—"that is damnably decent of you. I cannot tell you—"

"My decision"—she thrust out her hand to quiet him—

"regarding my second option is contingent upon the success of my third."

Oliver chuckled. "I suspected there would be a condition."

Jonathon swallowed hard. "And that third option?"

"I fully plan on marrying someday, Lord Helmsley, and therefore someday my inheritance and my sisters' dowries will be released. However, the chances seem excellent that Whatshisname will appear to claim his"—she winced—"*bride* before someday arrives. I fear I shall have no other choice but to marry him, if only to resolve this mess." She pinned Jonathon with a firm glance. "My character is considerably weaker than you may think, my lord."

Jonathon stared in obvious disbelief.

Oliver snorted.

"Therefore, I—or rather we—need to find some way for me to get, to put it bluntly"—she fairly spit the word—"*money*. I need to make my fortune."

Jonathon scoffed. "Women don't make their fortunes. They marry fortunes."

"I tried that," she snapped, then forced a measure of calm. "Aunt Edwina plans on introducing the girls to society in the spring. Even though I did not have a London season, I suspect it's quite costly."

"I am more than happy to foot the bill for whatever is required," Oliver said quickly. "I can certainly afford it and it will keep my mother occupied. If she's busy shepherding three young women through the straights and narrows of the season with an eye toward suitable husbands for them all, she'll be far too busy to concern herself with my marital state."

"That's very generous of you, Oliver." She cast him a grateful smile. "And while I am willing to accept your hospitality for as long as is necessary, I cannot expect you to take on the financial burden of all four of us for the rest of our days. Beyond that, Gen is eighteen, Sophie and Belle are seventeen—"

"The sisters," Oliver said in an aside to Jonathon.

Jonathon nodded.

"—and there is every possibility their somedays shall occur before mine—"

Jonathon raised a curious brow. "Do they all look like her?"

"Not in the least," Oliver said. "They all have dark hair, dark eyes and they're shorter than she is. But all three are lovely. They should have no problem finding husbands. I daresay they'll be snatched up in their first season."

"Not if they don't have acceptable dowries!" Fiona glared at the men. Were they really this dim? Did they not understand the prospects of a good marriage for a penniless girl were bleak? "I need to find a means to come up with the money for—"

"There is another option. Why didn't I think of it before?" Jonathon smacked the palm of his hand against his forehead. *"We* could find you a husband." He turned to Oliver. "You said it yourself. Freddy Hartshorne would marry her in a minute."

Oliver cast Fiona a wary glance. "I'm not sure that—"

"Oh, it's a splendid idea. Brilliant, really." Excitement rang in Jonathon's voice. "And Hartshorne's not the only possibility. Let me think. There's Kensington and McWilliams and"—he grinned—"maybe even Warton and Cavendish. That would serve them right."

Oliver shook his head. "I don't think—"

"God knows if she wants an Effington, I have a dozen cousins I'd be willing to name who would—"

"Absolutely not." Fiona clenched her fists by her side. "I will not be peddled like yesterday's fish!"

"But you're not yesterday's fish, Fiona." Jonathon paused. "May I still call you Fiona? We were, after all, more or less engaged."

"And you might be again if you're not very careful," Oliver warned quietly.

She gritted her teeth. "By all means. *Jonathon.*"

"You're a wonderful catch, Fiona, not at all like fish, yesterday's or otherwise. You listed your qualities for me the other night." He counted them off on his fingers. "You can run a household in seven different languages and you travel efficiently." He frowned. "Or something along those lines. At any rate, you might well be perfect."

She stared at him. "What about stubborn? Opinionated? Challenging?"

"That's what makes you perfect for him," Oliver murmured.

Jonathon waved off her comment. "We needn't mention those."

"Needn't mention those? Where? In the sales brochure? In the advertisement?" Surely he wasn't serious? Perhaps he was simply mad? What he looked at the moment was disgustingly eager. As if this were indeed a brilliant idea. Without warning the absurdity of it all struck and she burst into laughter.

Jonathon grinned and nudged Oliver. "See, she likes the idea."

"Or her mind has snapped under the strain." Oliver studied her. "Are you—"

"Daft? I don't know." She sniffed and tried to catch her breath. "It's just all so ridiculous."

Jonathon pulled a handkerchief from his waistcoat pocket and handed it to her. "Much of life is ridiculous, really. It simply depends how one looks at it. I have a sister who is about to marry the man who once broke her heart because he thought he was doing the right thing. Quite silly when you think about it."

"Why?" She dabbed at her eyes with the handkerchief. "If he was doing what he thought was right?"

He shrugged. "It just seems to me that when you stumble upon the person who is truly the love of your life you should let nothing stand in your way."

Her gaze locked with his and for a long moment they stared at one another.

"He does have a point," Oliver said, and the moment was shattered. "At least this way you would have an opportunity to select your own husband, which you did say you wished to do—"

"I am not going to ask another man I have just met to marry me." She shook her head firmly. "It was difficult enough, as well as humiliating, to do so once. It did seem like a good idea originally, but now . . ."

"Then we are back to choice number three," Oliver said. "Making your fortune. It won't be easy, especially given as we have no idea how much time we have to do so." Absently he paced the length of the room.

"Which eliminates any kind of investment possibility." Jonathon's brows furrowed in thought and he too began to pace. "Anything that would generate the kind of funding she needs would take a considerable amount of time." He stopped and glanced at her. "Do you have any skills?"

"I have been mistaken for an actress on occasion." She cast him a pointed glance. "Perhaps I could go on the stage?"

"Don't be absurd." Jonathon scoffed. "You weren't actually acting. Surely there is something you are good at?"

"There are many things I am good at," she snapped. "I can efficiently run a full staff of servants. I can organize a dinner party for a hundred people on less than two days' notice. I can select the appropriate fashion, furnishings or flowers for any occasion."

"All of which makes you well trained to be a wife but little else." Oliver sighed. "This may indeed be hopeless."

"Nonsense," Jonathon said staunchly. "It's far too early to give up on option three."

"Especially as that would require acceptance of option two," Oliver pointed out.

"Come, now, Fiona, surely you have some sort of marketable talents?" Jonathon looked at her hopefully.

"Only when it comes to marketing me for marriage." She heaved a frustrated sigh. "It's hopeless. I might as well resign myself to marrying Whatshisname and pray he turns out to be a decent sort."

"Not yet." Jonathon shook his head. "Surely the three of us can come up with something."

"I must say, you surprise me." She studied him curiously. "I would think you of all people would encourage me to comply with my father's wishes. It would certainly do away with any obligation you feel toward me."

"Ah, yes, but the guilt." Jonathon clasped his hand over his heart in mock remorse. "The guilt would be more than I could bear."

She resisted the temptation to smile. "Guilt?"

"Absolutely. If I had gone through with my agreement to marry you, you would not have to marry Whatshisname. In addition, you requested my assistance, you asked for rescue and I failed you. I shall have to live with that guilt for the rest of my days, especially as I now know how it feels to be faced with a marriage one does not want. No." Resolve shone in Jonathon's eyes and he resumed pacing. "There is a solution. We simply have to find it."

Oliver paced in one direction, Jonathon in the other. In a part of her mind not occupied by the desperation of her dilemma Fiona wondered how they managed to avoid knocking into one another.

"Helmsley here writes stories," Oliver said, "although he has never sold anything or seen anything in print."

"Yet." Jonathon's voice was firm. "I have not had anything published yet. You don't by any chance—"

"Only letters." Fiona blew a long breath. "In truth I have no skills beyond what any woman of my station has. I embroider, admittedly not very well. I play the piano adequately and sing better than I play, but my voice is not exceptional. I do draw rather well, but—"

Oliver raised a brow. "How well?"

"Very well." In truth she was quite proud of her artistic abilities. "I have studied for years. My portfolio is in my room."

"May we see it?" An eager note sounded in Oliver's voice.

She stared at her cousin. "It's nothing more than a pastime. I seriously doubt—"

"I have an idea, and it might well be brilliant." Oliver grabbed her arm and steered her toward the door. "But it would help if we could see your work first."

"I really haven't shown many people my work."

"Then we shall be doubly honored," Jonathon said in a gallant manner.

She glanced from one man to the other. Certainly, at this point if she couldn't trust them she couldn't trust anyone at all. Besides, she was probably just being silly. "Very well."

"Excellent." Oliver beamed. He opened the door and practically pushed her into the hall, closing the door behind her. Apparently she wasn't the only one a bit undone by her situation.

Fiona found a passing maid and sent her to fetch the portfolio. She turned to go back into the parlor, then decided instead to wait by the stairs. Besides, she could use a moment to herself. Whatever Oliver had in mind, she hoped it was a good idea. No, a lucrative idea. She certainly needed one.

It was all Jonathon's fault. If he was a man of his word . . .

No. She sank down on a bench by the stairway. As much as she wanted to, she really couldn't blame him for this. It was entirely her own fault. She should have married long ago. She'd had more than a few proposals through the years. And several of them quite acceptable. Men who were handsome and charming and wealthy. She would have done well to have wed any of them, but she'd just never felt the kind of affection that she'd wanted to feel for the man she would spend the rest of her days with. She'd liked them, most of them, but she'd never found anyone who made her heart leap and her toes tingle and all those things that she'd heard came along with love.

The closest she'd ever come to anything approaching those sorts of feelings was the brief infatuation she'd had at the tender age of seventeen with Jonathon Effington, a man she'd never even spoken to at the time. Now that she had, now that she'd been in his arms, it was rather shocking to realize he might well be the one man for her. Certainly there was something wonderful in the pit of her stomach and even perhaps in her heart when he'd kissed her. Not that it mattered. As much as she thought she could easily fall in love with him and thought as well, given the look in his eye, he could fall in love with her, there was simply not enough time.

And indeed, wasn't time at the very heart of her problem? Hadn't she always thought there would be enough time to meet the right man? To fall in love? To marry? But there was always another grand ball, another spring outing, another flirtation, another day or week or month planned, and she'd been having entirely too much fun to worry about the distant future.

Without warning it had seemed nineteen had turned to two-and-twenty, and two-and-twenty had turned to five-and-twenty. And her father had died and had left in his wake a means to force her to do what he'd never forced her to do when he'd been alive. Because he too had believed in love. And love, for his daughter, was precisely why he had made the arrangements that he had.

Not that she didn't intend to do everything possible to thwart those arrangements.

Regardless of whatever scheme Oliver had in mind, her only real options were to marry a man she had no desire to wed or to force marriage to a man who had no wish to marry her. As dreadful as it sounded, it would be better to take her chances with Whatshisname. At least he was probably willing to marry.

Of course, she had no intention of letting Jonathon know that yet. Aside from her anger, she'd been surprisingly disappointed. Perhaps even hurt. She shouldn't have been, of course, it made no sense at all. But nothing about her life at the moment made a great deal of sense. And the very least Jonathon deserved for reneging on his agreement was uncertainty about his own fate for as long as possible.

The maid appeared with her drawings and Fiona returned to the parlor.

Oliver and Jonathon were engaged in an earnest discussion, probably about her, each with glass in hand. She would wager it wasn't sherry. They cast her similar guilty looks.

"Let's see these, then, shall we?" Oliver said in an all-too-jovial manner.

"I am looking forward to it." Jonathon's eagerness matched his friend's. They were definitely plotting something. She sent a quick prayer toward the heavens to save her from the plots and plans of well-meaning men.

She started to hand over the portfolios, then abruptly realized what a poor idea it was and groaned to herself. If she hadn't been so preoccupied, she never would have forgotten the need to take certain precautions. She held the collection close against her chest. "I really don't think this is a good idea. I'm not at all used to letting anyone see my work."

"This is not the time for modesty, Fiona," Oliver said firmly. "Your drawings could provide your salvation."

"I doubt that," she muttered, then drew a deep breath. "Very well, but you should know, my work might not be precisely what you are expecting."

Jonathon and Oliver traded glances.

"I'm sure it's wonderful." Jonathon moved to her and practically snatched the portfolio from her hands. "We're quite looking forward to seeing it."

"Indeed we are." Oliver briskly led Jonathon to a large game table in the far corner of the room, leaving Fiona to trail behind them.

The men opened the portfolio and started paging through it.

"Very nice," Jonathon murmured.

"Not bad at all," Oliver said thoughtfully. "Rather good, really."

"Thank you," Fiona said, more to herself than to them. They were paying her no heed at the moment anyway. This would be an excellent time to make her escape. She casually inched toward the door. Still, taking her leave now would be the height of cowardice. She blew a resigned breath and stayed where she was—halfway between the men and the door—and noted for future reference that she could easily be out the door before anyone could stop her.

"I like this one. . . ."

She could tell exactly where they were in her drawings by their comments; innocuous and complimentary right now, they were probably still paging through the landscapes in the first section of the portfolio. Next in order would be a series of still lifes, followed by studies of faces and hands, mostly those of her sisters. At this point, anyone who happened upon her portfolio uninvited would probably grow bored. If not, the next group of drawings, details of various works of Renaissance masters, might well dissuade the casual viewer from further perusal. However, if one was made of sterner stuff and continued, one would find her drawings of ancient sculptures. She did so like the way light played on the intricately carved folds and creases of the marble and enjoyed capturing it with pen and pencil. After that . . .

A noticeable silence fell over the far end of the room.

She braced herself.

A long, low whistle came from one of the men. Jonathon, she thought.

Oliver turned away from the table and cleared his throat. "Fiona?"

She adopted an innocent tone. "Yes?"

"Are these drawings from . . ." Oliver paused as if he couldn't find the right word or it was simply too painful to say aloud.

"Life?" Jonathon tossed the word over his shoulder and continued to lean over the table to study her drawings. She really preferred that he didn't.

"When you say life," she said slowly, "what precisely do you mean?"

"You know exactly what I mean." Oliver crossed his arms over his chest. "I mean are these drawings of real people?"

"Models, I should think," Jonathon murmured.

"Real nonetheless." Oliver studied her. "Well?"

"Of course they are," she said in a lofty manner. "One cannot create art if one cannot work from life. Art imitates or enhances life."

"These scarcely need enhancement," Jonathon said under his breath. "Clothing, perhaps, but—"

"That's quite enough, thank you." Fiona crossed the room, stepped between the two men and began collecting the drawings that were now scattered across the table. "I knew I should never have shown you my work."

"Did your father know about these?" Oliver asked in a tone every bit as condemning as any father's could ever be.

"Father knew full well of my studies." She snatched a drawing from Jonathon's hands. He cast her a wicked grin. She ignored it.

"Surely Uncle Alfred did not condone the drawing of naked people by his oldest daughter?"

"I daresay Father would not have condoned the drawing of naked people, or indeed acknowledge that beneath their clothing people in general are naked," she said in a matter-of-fact manner. "Father was not of an artistic nature."

Jonathon chuckled. "I'd wager he didn't know."

"He didn't know?" Oliver stared. "He never asked to see your work? Never wished to check on your progress? Never wanted to see if you were cavorting with naked women and men?"

"Don't be absurd, Oliver, there was no cavorting." She rolled her eyes toward the ceiling. "I can't believe you would say such a thing. They posed. I drew them. That's all."

"Good God, old man, you sound like my father." Jonathon turned back to the stack of drawings and pulled several out to array across the table. "Besides, I don't think they look like they're cavorting."

"Oh, just look at them." Oliver huffed. "They're . . . they're . . . they're smiling!"

"Not all of them. A few are quite pensive." Fiona paused. "I suppose some do look happy enough."

"Of course they look happy." Jonathon studied the nudes. "They're naked." He glanced at her in a most considering manner. "I know I tend to be extremely happy when I'm naked."

She didn't intend to, but without thinking she cast him one of her most flirtatious smiles. "Do you?"

"Indeed I do." Jonathon's gaze met hers in a look that could only be described as intimate, and a delightful shiver passed through her.

"Stop that at once! There will be no happiness here!"

Oliver glared. "And you have not answered my question, cousin. About your father's knowledge of your activities?"

"Father considered art of little importance and therefore considered my studies to be of little importance as well. They were an indulgence on his part. I neither disagreed with him nor did I mind." Her gaze roamed over the drawings. In spite of their admittedly embarrassing nature, she was proud of them. "His attitude allowed me a relative amount of freedom."

Jonathon choked back a laugh.

Oliver groaned. "But Fiona, to have drawn naked people you have to have seen naked people."

"It does generally prove necessary to do so." Again she gathered together the drawings.

"Have you no shame, Fiona?" Jonathon's voice was serious, but it was obvious he found throwing her words back at her along with Oliver's shock and her own discomfort most amusing.

She glanced up at him. "I see nothing to be ashamed of. All modesty aside, I think my work is very good."

He smiled down at her. "I quite agree. It's most impressive."

"But they're naked!" Shock colored Oliver's face. "I demand an explanation."

"Do you?" She stared at him in surprise. Admittedly she did not know her cousin all that well, but in their acquaintance thus far he certainly hadn't struck her as the kind of man who would be prudish about things like this. She'd thought he might be surprised by her drawings, but not to this extent. "Why?"

"Why? Because . . . because . . . they're naked!" Oliver's eyes narrowed. "And because as head of the family, it is my duty to make certain you avoid activities that would compromise you in any way."

She studied him for a moment and realized there were some things about her life before now that might be best to keep from him. Pity she hadn't managed to cull the more surprising drawings from the portfolio before she'd handed it over, but she did have a great deal on her mind.

Fiona sighed in surrender. "Very well, Oliver. For years I have studied art with an Englishwoman, a Mrs. Kincaid, a very talented artist now living in Italy. A free thinker as well, I believe you would call her. During the course of my studies, it was only logical to progress from pears in a bowl to people."

Oliver groaned. "Naked people."

"Probably naked pears as well." Jonathon leaned toward Fiona and lowered his voice. "He doesn't seem to mind fruit without clothes."

"This is not the least bit funny." Oliver glared at his friend.

"No, of course not." Jonathon struggled to look appropriately somber.

"You really needn't be concerned about this, Oliver," Fiona said quickly. "There were several of us who took lessons from Mrs. Kincaid and we all agreed it would be best if the subject of our work remained—"

"Unexposed?" Jonathon offered helpfully.

She raised a brow. "Not precisely as I would have phrased it, but yes. We agreed it might be something of a problem if the subject of our work became public knowledge. Besides"—she shrugged—"we were all the daughters of prominent foreign fathers, none of us Italian, and none of us planned ever to have to earn our keep. It was indeed simply a pastime." She looked at Oliver. "Surely you're not suggesting this is how I make my fortune?"

"Certainly not now!" Outrage colored Oliver's voice.

"Why not now?" Jonathon said.

"Because it's not what we were . . . well, the idea was . . ." Oliver waved at the drawings. "Perhaps some of these, but—"

"What idea?" Fiona asked.

"Look at these, Oliver." Jonathon quickly organized the drawings into stacks.

Fiona frowned. "Whatever are you doing?"

"Patience, my dear." He flashed her a quick smile. "As I was saying, in this pile are her landscapes. Fair enough in terms of technique, but not especially inspired. Here are her still lifes." He rested his hand on the second stack. "Once again, she draws a fine apple and very nice bowl, but there's nothing particularly special about them. Now"— he shuffled the papers—"in this stack are her drawings of details of well-known works. Copied, I would suspect, at the Academia galleries?" He looked at her. "Uffizi or Pitti?"

She nodded.

"I thought as much." He turned back to her drawings. "In these you see, well, something special, the beginnings of life, as it were. Of course, it could be that she is simply an excellent copyist."

Oliver eyed him suspiciously. "How do you know so much about art?"

"My dear Norcroft, I have no exhaustive knowledge on any one subject in particular. However, I do know a little about a great number of things." Jonathon sighed in an overly dramatic manner. "It's a curse." He turned his attention back to the drawings. "Now pay attention. Here, when she draws the statues, you can practically feel the smooth texture of the marble."

"Do you really think so?" Fiona looked up at him. She was not used to extensive flattery. Mrs. Kincaid had always said she had a talent granted to her by God and wasn't it a pity she would never use it for anything worthwhile. Her sisters had seen some of her drawings through the years and, while complimentary, had never been overly interested. Indeed, with the exception of other students, no one had seen Fiona's work.

"I do." Jonathon nodded firmly, then directed his attention back to her drawings. "Up to this point her work is good but not extraordinarily so. However, look at her studies of hands and faces." He glanced at her. "Your sisters, I presume?"

She nodded.

"I thought so." He looked at Oliver. "Are you following me thus far?"

"I am managing to struggle along," Oliver snapped.

"Good." Jonathon nodded. "It's when she begins drawing from life that her work starts to have a life of its own. You can see it in the faces of her sisters and the drawings of their hands, but when she draws entire figures . . ." He shuffled through the sheets and pulled out a study of a reclining man. "The very lines on the page seem alive. There's a depth here that is lacking in her renderings of inanimate objects. You can almost feel the warmth of their bodies. They look as if they might move at any moment. Indeed, you wonder if you stare at them long enough you might not see them breathe."

"You see all that?" Fiona stared. She was flattered, of course, but wasn't entirely sure she believed him.

"Yes, I do." Jonathon met her gaze directly. "I think they're quite remarkable."

"Thank you." The loveliest feeling of warmth washed through her, and for a moment she wasn't sure if it was due to his appreciation of her work or appreciation of an entirely different sort that shone in his blue eyes.

"They might well be the best naked people ever drawn in the history of the world, but they are still naked people." Oliver glared. "And the drawing of them, why, even the discussion of them, is scandalous."

"Oliver, it's art." Fiona sighed. "Not obscenity."

"No, they're not the least bit obscene." Jonathon's gaze met Oliver's. "Fiona's drawings are some of the finest I've ever seen in or out of galleries and museums. And I think we should capitalize on what she does best."

Oliver's eyes widened. "Naked people?"

Jonathon shrugged. "Why not?"

"What do you mean, capitalize?" Fiona asked.

They ignored her.

Oliver shook his head. "Think of the scandal."

"There would be no scandal if no one knows the name of the artist." A persuasive note sounded in Jonathon's voice.

"Even so . . ." Oliver shook his head.

"Come now, Oliver," Jonathon said. "It was a good idea a few minutes ago and I think it's even better now."

"A few minutes ago we were talking about innocent

artistic dabbling, not . . . not"—Oliver waved at the table—"*these.*"

"What idea?" Fiona glanced from one man to the next. "Do you honestly believe people will pay for my drawings?"

"Not just for your drawings." Oliver threw up his hands in surrender. "But for your drawings coupled with a story."

She shook her head. "I am no writer."

"Then this is indeed your lucky day." Jonathon grinned. "Because I am."

Five

Fiona studied him for a long moment. A note of caution edged her voice. "Are you a good writer?"

Oliver choked.

Jonathon ignored him. "I like to think so."

"And do others think so as well?" she said slowly.

"Not yet, but I'm confident that someday they will." In truth, while no one had yet seen fit to publish his work, he had had some very encouraging letters of rejection.

Fiona looked at her cousin. "So is this what the two of you were talking about when I left the room? Is this the idea you mentioned?"

"More or less," Oliver muttered. "Not that we had any idea that your drawings would be—"

"Quite as wonderful as they are," Jonathon said quickly. Fiona certainly did not need to hear another tirade from Oliver on the propriety of her work.

"I'm not sure I understand." She narrowed her eyes suspiciously. "You propose to write a story to go along with my drawings?"

"Exactly. An illustrated book. Folio-sized, I think. Nicely bound, perhaps in leather. Designed to appeal to a . . ."

He thought for a moment. "*Select* clientele. There's quite a market for this sort of thing. A discreet market, but a market nonetheless. Naturally, it would be sold by subscription only and not made available to the general public."

Oliver groaned. "Good God."

Fiona's eyes widened. "Are you suggesting something of an obscene nature?"

"Most decidedly not!" Indignation rang in Jonathon's voice. "I am not talking about obscenity. I am talking about"—he picked up one of her sketches and waved it—"art."

"Art?" Suspicion sounded in her voice.

"Art." Jonathon nodded. "Magnificent, evocative and, yes, frankly, erotic."

"You think my drawings are . . ." She drew a deep breath. "Erotic?"

Jonathon shrugged. "Well, they are smiling."

Oliver muttered something unintelligible.

"Yes, but . . ." She pulled the sketch from his hand and scanned it as if looking for something he saw that she did not. "I don't understand. They don't look the least bit erotic to me. Most of these drawings are of individuals simply posed. I see nothing especially provocative about them."

"They're naaakkkeddd." Oliver drew the word out as if he could force understanding with emphasis.

Jonathon paid him no mind and concentrated his attention on Fiona. "It's not merely that they're not clothed, although that certainly is significant. Nor is it that they're well drawn, although that too is important. But these drawings are not those of Michelangelo or da Vinci—"

She raised an indignant brow. "I never for a moment claimed my work was comparable—"

"No, no, I didn't mean . . . that is to say . . ." He ran his hand through his hair and searched for the right words. "What I meant was that your drawings are exciting in an erotic sort of way precisely because they were not drawn hundreds of years ago." That was it, of course. "These are not renderings of long-dead Renaissance matrons or Italian nobles now moldering in their graves, but living breathing people you can conceivably pass on the street—"

Oliver snorted. "Not on my street."

"—people you might converse with. People who are"— Jonathon thought for a moment—"accessible or attainable, I think."

"Real?" she asked.

He nodded. "Exactly."

"I see." She considered the drawing thoughtfully. "And real makes them—"

"Absolutely." Jonathon's voice was firm.

Fiona's gaze shifted from the drawing in her hand to Jonathon. "This might be the most ridiculous thing I've ever heard."

"Or the most brilliant." Jonathon grinned.

Fiona looked at her cousin. "Oliver?"

"Yes, yes, I suppose it could be brilliant," Oliver admitted in a grudging manner. "And even lucrative."

Fiona considered the matter. "I assume this would be done anonymously?"

"Most definitely," Jonathon said. "Both the artist and the writer would remain nameless."

Fiona studied him. "And would I have any say in the story?"

"In *my* story?" Jonathon shook his head. "Oh, I don't know if that would—"

"Without question," Oliver said, and slanted Jonathon a pointed glance. "They are your drawings and it is your future. In fact, I think you should peruse every line, every word as it is written."

Jonathon pushed aside a twinge of irritation. No one had ever had a say in one of his stories. On the other hand, none of them had ever sold either. And in truth it scarcely mattered what he wrote, the end result would be the same.

She met Jonathon's gaze and smiled slowly. "Then will this . . . endeavor of ours require that we spend a great deal of time together?"

He stared down into her green eyes. "Every minute, I

should think, if we wish to accomplish this as quickly as possible."

"When should we begin?" Her voice was soft and full of promises that went well beyond art and literature.

The oddest mix of desire and guilt stabbed him. "Tomorrow?"

Her smile widened. "I shall look forward to it."

She gathered her drawings up into the portfolio, tied it, started toward the door, then turned back to him and offered her hand. "Until tomorrow, then?"

He brushed his lips across her hand and gazed into her eyes. "Until tomorrow."

Fiona favored him with a final flash of her brilliant smile and left the room.

Jonathon stared after her and wondered that he remembered to breathe. Spending every minute possible with Miss Fiona Fairchild had far more appeal than he had ever imagined.

"If you do not take care, old friend, you'll be wed before you know it," Oliver said in a low voice directly behind him. "Whether you wish to be or not."

Jonathon scarcely heard him. Was Fiona indeed the perfect woman for him? The perfect wife? There was certainly something about her that held him spellbound. She was beautiful, of course, but he was not unused to beautiful women. But she was, as well, clever and determined and talented. And quite admirable. And to a man wishing to avoid marriage, probably very, very dangerous.

Jonathon shook his head to clear it and turned to his friend. "Did you say something?"

Oliver refilled their glasses. "I am head of the family, and as such she is my responsibility. Do keep that in mind. And keep in mind as well that I will not hesitate to demand marriage should there be anything whatsoever of a questionable nature."

Jonathon gasped in feigned dismay. "Are you saying you don't trust me with your cousin?"

"I wouldn't trust you with a three-hundred-year-old great-aunt, let alone a beauty like Fiona." Oliver handed him a glass. "Trust aside, this scheme of ours will never work."

"Of course it will work. It's working so far." Jonathon took a sip of the whiskey. "She doesn't suspect a thing."

"She's not stupid."

"No, she's not. It's one of the things I rather like about her."

Oliver narrowed his eyes. "Then you could simply marry her and we could end this farce."

Jonathon grinned. "Where would be the fun in that?"

Oliver settled down in a chair and stared at his friend. "It's a complicated plan. I don't know if we can pull this off without her suspecting."

"Why would she suspect? You and I will handle all the details. And you've said it yourself: Fiona is desperate." Jonathon aimed his glass at his friend. "Mark my words, she'll be so grateful she'll not question the success of it. In fact, I daresay success is the easiest part of it all."

Oliver grimaced. "The trick is in the details."

"And they will make or break this scheme." Jonathon paced the room, drink in hand, trying to sort out said details. "Given the nature of her drawings, we should go with something simple. Classic. A retelling or reworking of a timeless story. A myth or legend, something of that nature. Greek or Roman, perhaps. No, better yet, an entirely new myth—"

"Can you have an entirely new myth?"

"Literary license." Jonathon waved off the comment. "It should not take long to write the story. All we need is a few lines per page written so that her drawings become illustrations. Although she may need to draw a few more—"

"From memory only," Oliver said with a grim firmness.

"Yes, yes, whatever." Jonathon thought for a moment. "Once we have the story and the illustrations together, I shall ask Sir Ephraim to produce a handful of copies—"

"Will he do that?"

Sir Ephraim Cadwallender had been a close friend of Jonathon's parents, the Duke and Duchess of Roxborough, for as long as he could remember. Aside from their friendship, Sir Ephraim and the duke had been involved in various successful business ventures through the years and Sir Ephraim often credited Jonathon's father with his own success.

"Certainly." Jonathon paused to sip his drink. "It might be costly, but it will be well worth it.

"At any rate, we show Fiona the books. We tell her subscriptions have been quite impressive. Within a week or so we present her with a bank draft, from my accounts of course, as we want to keep her participation in this endeavor anonymous, that will be a start toward the money she needs for her sisters. Which means when this American appears she won't have to marry, because she will be well on her way toward earning her own fortune."

"And as these books are to be sold privately," Oliver said slowly, "Fiona will never know none were printed beyond those we show her and none were actually sold. Which also eliminates any possibility of scandal."

"Exactly." Jonathon grinned. "It's brilliant."

"It is clever." Oliver studied him. "Are you prepared to support her for the rest of her days, then?"

"Don't be absurd." He scoffed. "This is a temporary measure. We are simply providing Fiona with time. She is beautiful and charming and is indeed what any number of men would wish for in a wife. Now that she is back in London, and more amenable to marriage than she might have been in the past, I daresay she'll be properly wed within a year. And her inheritance and that of her sisters will be released."

"Until then, you are willing to fund this endeavor?"

"I am," Jonathon said staunchly.

"I had no idea you were so noble."

"I'm not. I'm practical. A breach-of-promise suit will cost me far more than this deception of ours. Besides"—he blew a long breath—"I feel very much responsible for her now. Regardless of whether I thought it was a joke or not, I did agree to marry her. She proposed to me in good faith and it was obviously a difficult thing for her to do." He sank into the chair beside the other man's. "No, Oliver, I owe her this."

"You do realize she'll be furious if she learns the truth," Oliver said mildly. "With both of us, but I suspect the full brunt of her wrath will be directed toward you."

Jonathon shuddered. "That's a frightening prospect."

Still, it wasn't the prospect of Fiona's ire that scared him the most. The woman simply did things to him. In truth, she took his breath away in a manner that had nothing to do with her looks. As no woman had ever done before. And when he gazed into her green eyes or took her in his arms, the oddest feelings swept through him. It had bothered him since the moment they met on Christmas Eve. Desire he recognized, but there was something more, something intense that reached inside him and tied his stomach in knots and stuck in his throat. Something he'd never felt before. Something that perhaps caught at his heart.

It was a silly idea. Accepting it meant he believed in all sorts of nonsense like love at first sight and fate. It was surely nothing more than the circumstances they found themselves in and that business of her being what he'd always wanted. Why, he barely knew the woman and he certainly wouldn't consider marriage to anyone he'd had no more than a few conversations with. Even if she was what he'd always wanted, not that he knew what that was at this point. No, if she was the right woman for him, surely he would not be plagued with doubts and indecision and terror at the very mention of marriage.

He'd never had doubts or indecision or terror about anything in his life. That he did so now was significant, but why it was significant eluded him, therefore it was best not to consider it at all. Even so, the question nagged at the back of his mind.

"All things considered, I don't think we should completely abandon the idea of finding Fiona a husband, without her knowledge, preferably." Oliver's voice was thoughtful. "Lady Chester's Twelfth Night Ball is next week. We should take the opportunity to introduce her to as many eligible gentlemen as possible." He chuckled. "We could have her wed by Easter."

"We cannot count on that," Jonathon said quickly, and shook his head. "No, I think our original plan is best."

"But if she were to marry, there would be no need . . ." Oliver studied his friend curiously. "Are you having second thoughts?"

"Not at all. I think our plan is sound and almost flawless."

"That's not what I meant."

"I know what you meant." Jonathon adopted a firm tone. "I assure you I am not having second thoughts about anything."

And for the moment, at least, Jonathon could almost believe it himself.

". . . and so"—Fiona drew a deep breath—"we're going to write a book together."

"I knew Lord Helmsley would change his mind," Belle said under her breath.

"Doesn't it take a long time to write a book?" Gen asked.

"Why would he change his mind?" Sophie frowned. "Rather beastly of him, I would say."

Gen shook her head. "And you really don't have all that much time if you're going to avoid marriage to that American. What was his name?"

"I have no idea." Fiona shrugged. "Nor do I care."

Sophie brightened. "Shouldn't Cousin Oliver challenge his lordship to a duel or something? For dishonoring you?"

Fiona groaned. "I have not been dishonored."

"Daniel Sinclair," Belle said.

All eyes turned toward Belle.

"The American. His name is Daniel Sinclair. I'm very good with names," Belle said smugly. "Now, about this book?"

Fiona stared at her sister for a moment longer. Gen was the most practical of the younger girls, Sophie the sweetest, but Belle was an ongoing enigma. Sometimes selfish, sometimes selfless, one never knew what she would come up with next. She was a constant source of surprise.

"Yes, the book." Fiona gathered her thoughts. "It's not going to be a very long book, so I daresay it won't take long to write. Lord Helmsley proposes to write a story to go along with my drawings. The book itself will consist mostly of my work."

Gen grimaced. "Oh, not those dreadfully boring pictures you do of hills and trees and streams and whatever else you stumble upon when out-of-doors?"

"No—"

"Or those dull, tedious drawings of grapes and candles and bowls and the occasional trussed chicken." Belle shuddered. "I cannot imagine any kind of story worth the effort of reading that has anything whatsoever to do with trussed chickens."

"I rather like my still lifes." Fiona huffed. "But no, those won't be included either."

"Oh." Sophie's eyes widened. "Then this will involve the naughty pictures?"

Fiona held her breath. "What naughty pictures?"

Her sisters traded knowing glances and matching smiles.

Gen crossed her arms over her chest. "The ones with the naked people."

Fiona groaned to herself but kept her expression impassive. "Those are simply drawings of statues and—"

Belle snorted. "Hah! We've seen your drawings of statues and they are decidedly different from your drawings of naked people."

Sophie cast Fiona a pitying look. "We can certainly tell the difference, you know." She paused, then added, "Even if we've never seen naked people cavorting—"

"No one was cavorting!" Fiona gritted her teeth. By God, did everyone who looked at those pictures immediately think of cavorting and frolicking and possibly even drunken orgies with laughing dark-haired men with lone dimples and invitation in their eyes? At once she pushed the shocking thought from her mind.

She drew a deep breath and faced her sisters. "You've been looking at my drawings."

"Indeed we have." Gen grinned. "For several years now."

"But you've never shown any interest in my work."

"There's nothing at all interesting about fruit." Belle rolled her eyes toward the ceiling. "Or trees."

"We do rather like the ones of us, though. We think they're very good." Sophie cast her older sister a chastising look. "But you stopped showing any of your pictures to us long ago."

"I didn't think you particularly cared."

"We didn't, really, for the most part," Belle said under her breath. "It was mostly fruit, after all."

"We were shocked, Fiona, at first." Gen paused. "Then we decided, as it was part of your art studies, that it was probably acceptable."

"As long as no one knew," Sophie added quickly. "Besides, we all agreed there was every possibility none of us would ever see naked people—"

"Naked men in particular," Belle pointed out.

"—until we were married." Sophie wrinkled her nose. "If then."

Gen considered Fiona thoughtfully. "Can one really make one's fortune writing a book?"

Belle scoffed. "I daresay you can if it has naughty pictures in it."

"They're not naughty, they're art." Sophie sniffed.

"They're naked," Belle smirked. "Naked people drawn by artists who are famous and more often than not dead, hanging on the walls of a museum, are art. Pictures of naked people in a book are naughty."

"Although," Gen said slowly, "I suspect they might sell well."

"Let's hope so," Fiona said sharply. "Our futures depend on it."

"In respect to our future . . ." Gen studied her older sister. "Regardless of whether you call it art or naughty, won't this book of yours and Lord Helmsley's be cause for scandal?"

"Not if no one knows of our involvement. It will be published anonymously. Our names will never be connected to it." Fiona narrowed her gaze. "And I want your solemn promises right now that you will never, never reveal this to a solitary soul."

The girls exchanged glances.

"I realize none of you have ever been especially good at keeping secrets, but secrecy now is of the utmost importance." Fiona met the gaze of each sister in turn. "Should I be embroiled in the level of scandal this could produce, each of you will be disgraced as well." She shook her head in a mournful manner. "I daresay Aunt Edwina would not look kindly upon sponsoring girls in society whose sister has—"

"We won't say a word," Gen said quickly.

"Never." Sophie nodded. "Even if we were tortured by American savages."

Belle sniffed. "And we're offended that you think for so much as a moment that we would."

"Good." Fiona breathed a sigh of relief. The last thing she needed to worry about was word of this absurd venture becoming public. Why, she'd be ruined before she could so much as mutter a word of explanation. And any chance of ever finding a suitable husband would vanish. Whether you called it art or something else altogether, no gentleman would consider taking a wife who drew pictures of naked people, particularly naked men. Whether they cavorted or not.

Except perhaps one.

Jonathon didn't seem the least bit shocked by her drawings. Instead he was amused and complimentary. Indeed, he was enthusiastic about her work. It was most heartening. Jonathon was an unusual man, not at all what she'd expected of the son of a duke. But then she suspected she was not entirely what he'd expected either.

That too was most heartening.

The one thing that did not lift her spirits after Jonathon's admission that he'd thought she was part of a hoax and he had no desire to marry her was this book scheme of Jonathon's and Oliver's. Even with a *select clientele* she couldn't imagine she could earn the kind of money she needed and in a timely manner. It was possible, she supposed, if indeed there was an eager, if discreet, market for books of this nature. She simply had to trust Jonathon and Oliver in the matter. At the moment, what choice did she have?

"Are you sure he doesn't want to marry you?" Gen asked.

Belle considered her sister. "Perhaps he just doesn't want to marry you right now?"

"Isn't it possible he might change his mind?" Sophie's voice was thoughtful. "After all, he did kiss you."

"Yes, he did." Fiona smiled with the memory. "And quite nicely too."

Belle raised a brow. "How nicely?"

Fiona grinned. "Very nicely. The man has kissed before."

"Well . . ." Belle drew the word out slowly.

"I know what you're thinking, and you can put it out of your mind right now," Fiona said in her best no-nonsense voice. "Regardless of our circumstances, I have no desire to marry someone who does not want to marry me."

"There are ways—"

"I will not trap him into marriage." Fiona shook her head.

"Pity," Belle murmured.

Fiona stifled the urge to agree with her sister, but she'd meant what she'd said about not forcing a man into marriage. Still, she had no intention of giving up the idea of marriage to Jonathon either. As far-fetched as she thought this book nonsense was, it would serve the lovely purpose of allowing her to spend a great deal of time with his lordship. And who knew what might happen then?

There was the promise of something quite wonderful in his eyes when he looked at her. And the hint of something equally wonderful deep inside her when she looked at him. It wasn't at all like the feelings she'd had for him when she was a girl. This was hesitant, tentative, as if the emotion was entirely too powerful to acknowledge all at once. Deeper, richer and much more important. Like a stew that has simmered almost unnoticed for a very long time. Or a drawing that has been worked and reworked until it was something special and unique and perfect.

Whatever it was that lingered between the two of them, it was well worth exploring. After all, she had nothing to lose and perhaps a great deal to gain.

$\mathcal{Six}$

The very next day . . .

$\mathcal{J}$onathon paced the length of Oliver's library, his brow furrowed, an occasional unintelligible muttering coming from his lips. It would have been amusing if it wasn't so, well, dull.

"Anything yet?" Fiona said hopefully, and not for the first time.

Fiona sat at one end of a long table that had been brought in precisely for the purpose of working on *The Book*, as she now thought of it, poised to write down his every word, although to this point she had done nothing but tap her pen, fight her growing impatience and watch Jonathon pace, which he claimed helped him to think.

"Soon," Jonathon murmured.

Thus far—Fiona glanced at the empty page before her—he had done a great deal of pacing and possibly a great deal of thinking, but it had yet to yield any results. Every now and then Jonathon would break stride, step to the table and study one or more of her drawings.

With the exception of the space directly in front of her, the table was covered with the drawings of nudes she had produced over the last few years. There were thirty-seven separate drawings in all. The majority were of women posed either individually or in groupings of twos and threes. All the studies of nude men were individual and comprised barely a third of the total. In truth, while it may appear otherwise, there were only two different men who had ever posed for Fiona and the other students, both of whom, at various times, had been intimate friends of Mrs. Kincaid.

Fiona stifled a yawn and casually glanced at the clock on the mantel at the opposite end of the room. It was too far away and too small to make out the time, but surely they had been in here forever. Oliver had left them alone to work on *The Book* with a promise to keep Aunt Edwina away. All three agreed she would never understand and probably did not have a good sense of *art*. Regardless, Oliver had pointedly left the door open and a footman was stationed in the hallway to avoid any hint of impropriety.

Admittedly, watching Jonathon pace was not entirely unpleasant. He did cut a dashing figure, after all, but surely there was something she could be doing to help other than sitting here waiting to capture whatever literary gems dropped from his lips.

An image of Jonathon opening his mouth and an emerald popping out flashed into her head and she choked back a laugh.

He glanced at her. "Did you say something?"

"No. Nothing." She smiled pleasantly, then paused. "However, I do have something to say." She got to her feet, braced her hands on the table and leaned toward him. "Jonathon, we've been at this for hours and you've yet to dictate a single word."

"Surely it hasn't been that long." He pulled a gold watch from his pocket and checked the time. "Why, I've scarcely been here a full hour yet."

"It seems much longer."

"It takes time, you know, to come up with an idea for a story. One just doesn't pull it out of the air."

"What a shame," she murmured.

"It's exceptionally difficult. Not at all like"—he scoffed—"drawing."

"Drawing?"

"Yes. You have to admit, art is much easier than literature."

She straightened and crossed her arms over her chest. "I needn't admit anything of the sort, but do tell me why."

"With art you start with something already created. Scenery or a vase of flowers or"—he paused for emphasis—"a nude figure, and you simply draw what you see. Literature starts with nothing but an idea, and usually a vague one at that." He tapped his head with his forefinger. "It comes entirely from right here."

She snorted. "It certainly hasn't come so far."

"It's not easy." His tone was lofty. "It takes time."

"How much time?"

"One cannot write on command. Conjure up a story at a moment's notice."

She studied him thoughtfully. "I can."

He scoffed. "You cannot."

"Would you care to wager on it?"

"No!" He paused. "What would we wager?"

She thought for a moment. "A hundred pounds."

He gasped. "A hundred pounds?"

"There's no time like the present to begin making my fortune. And you can certainly afford to lose a hundred pounds."

"Nonetheless, you don't have a hundred pounds to wager. What do I get if you lose?"

"I won't lose." She smiled.

"Then it would be exceedingly foolish of me to wager."

She shrugged. "As you wish."

He studied her carefully. "If I take your wager, I do want something on the table on the slim chance that you do lose."

"I really have little to wager." She waved at the drawings laid out on the table. "My work, of course. An admittedly very nice wardrobe." She smiled. "I do rather like pretty gowns, especially if they're French."

"I have all the French gowns I need, thank you."

"I have some jewelry."

"Nor do I want your jewelry."

"What then do you want, Jonathon, should I lose? Which I won't."

"I don't know. Given your limited finances, something simple, I should think." He smiled in a slow and somewhat wicked manner. "A kiss would suffice."

"A kiss?" Surprise sounded in her voice, although she should have expected as much. "From a woman you do not wish to marry?"

"A kiss is not cause for marriage." He grinned. "If it was, I would be married a dozen times over."

"As would I." She raised a shoulder in an offhand shrug. "However, we have already kissed. Twice, I believe."

"But it was under false pretenses."

"Ah, yes. I thought you were going to marry me and you thought I was a who—"

"An actress," he said quickly. "A very good actress. And as those kisses were part of a mistake, I daresay they don't count. When you consider it that way, we have never really kissed at all."

She narrowed her gaze. "We haven't?"

"No. And a first kiss, with you, might well be worth a hundred pounds."

"A mere kiss, worth a hundred pounds?" She laughed lightly. "I am flattered."

"It's not a mere kiss, it's a first kiss, and as such very important." His voice was somber, but his eyes twinkled. "Why, who knows what might happen after a first kiss."

"You are a charming devil, Jonathon." And a dangerous one at that. Still, there was no real harm in enjoying a bit of flirtation with him. "So we have a wager, then?"

"Indeed we do." He waved a grand gesture at her drawings. "Do your best, Fiona, compose a story."

"Very well." She circled the table. "Before you began your pacing and thinking, I believe you mentioned writing something along the lines of a Greek myth. Something of a classical nature."

"It seems to go nicely with the"—he cleared his throat—"dress or lack thereof, as well as the settings."

"Possibly." She positioned herself before the table and studied the drawings in an effort to look at them with a fresh eye. As if she were seeing them for the first time.

For the most part, each figure was drawn, or at least started, during a different lesson and generally completed during the next few lessons or so, usually without the model's presence. Some of the more complicated drawings, those with more than one figure, had taken several sessions with posed models. Aside from the lack of clothing and perhaps setting, there was no particular theme that connected the works. For the first time, Fiona tried to look at them as a whole rather than as separately produced pieces. As if they were indeed trying to tell a story.

"Well?" Jonathon said with a smug note in his voice. "It's not so easy, is it?"

"I've barely begun to consider this," she muttered.

He was right, though, about some sort of story based on myth. The figures, as well as their surroundings, sketched in with as few lines as possible so as to be vague and no more than hinted at, seemed to call for exactly that. The nudes were positioned on stone benches or leaned against marble columns or reclined beside fountains. If one looked at the pictures as illustration, a story of sorts did indeed begin to take shape.

"You said you could do it at a moment's notice." He paused significantly. "I think that was the wager. If you now find you cannot—"

"Of course I can." She did have a glimmer of an idea, but nothing more. Still, the only way to win this wager might be to start talking and hope something brilliant came out. Even something that made no sense at all would be better than nothing. The wager didn't stipulate that it had to be a good story. "The ancients used myth as a way of explaining what they had no explanation for. Primarily the natural world. The rise of the sun. The arrangement of the stars—"

"The phases of the moon." He nodded. "Go on."

"Well . . ." *Well, what?* She stared at the drawings for a

long moment and abruptly noted a pattern of sorts. "Here we have twelve drawings of individual women." She rearranged the display, placing the selected dozen drawings aside. "They represent the . . ." The what? A dozen eggs? A dozen tea cakes? "The . . . the months of the year." She flashed him a triumphant smile.

"Continue."

"Very well." She put the drawings with two female figures on one corner of the table, those with three figures in another and those that consisted of male nudes in yet a third. "The males represent two primary yet opposite forces."

"But there are more than two drawings."

"Different poses but the same men." She waved off his objection.

"The faces look different to me," he murmured.

"I daresay no one will note their faces, nor notice any difference in appearance," she said dryly. "Besides, for purposes of our myth, two will serve. Now, then, as I was saying, they represent forces of nature. Opposing forces. Light and dark, perhaps. Or day and night—"

"Good and evil?"

"Possibly," she said slowly. "But that doesn't seem quite right either. If the twelve ladies are the months of the year, then the two men are—"

"Winter and Summer." He rested his hands on the edge of the table and leaned forward, his gaze roving over the drawings. "By Jove, that's good. That's very good."

"Yes, it is." She cast him a smug smile, then turned back to her works. "Winter and Summer each want the months of the year. They want the . . . the *favors* of the ladies. . . . No. They want to possess them. That's it. They are locked in an endless battle over possession. They want them, the months, the ladies, because . . ." She gestured aimlessly. The answer seemed to be just out of reach. "Because . . ."

"Because the months, that is the ladies, are lovely and passionate and exciting, and"—he furrowed his brow—"the men—"

"Gods," she said. "They have to be gods."

"Absolutely. The gods then want the months because . . ." He thought for a moment, then grinned. "Because they are selfish beasts, as ancient gods were prone to be. Always thinking of themselves and what fun they could be having. Frolicking and eating grapes with lovely women at their beck and call. Ancient gods could never have too many cavorting *months* around them, you know."

"They're not cavorting," she said absently, and tried to focus her thoughts. "The more months each god possesses . . . Of course." She straightened and smacked her palm against her forehead. "The more months a god possesses, *the greater his power*! Over the earth, the sky—"

"The very universe itself!"

"Exactly." Excitement rang in her voice. "Winter and Summer are locked in battle, in endless combat, for all eternity over possession of the months!" She stopped and wrinkled her nose. "Although we should call them something other than months. *Months* just doesn't have the right sound to it."

"Goddesses?"

"Something less than goddesses, I should think."

"Less than goddesses but definitely more than mere mortals." Jonathon moved to a bookshelf and perused the leather-bound volumes. "Surely there's something here that might help."

Fiona joined him. "Homer perhaps?"

He nodded. "There are all sorts of deities flitting around the *Iliad* and the *Odyssey*." He thought for a moment. "What about graces?"

"I think there were only three." She continued to scan the shelves.

"It's our story and our myth. I daresay we can do precisely as we please." He pulled a book out and flipped open the cover. "If we want a dozen graces, we can have a dozen graces."

"But we do want it to make a certain amount of sense."

"I doubt if that's necessary." He paged through the book. "Given the nature of what we are trying to do, and the fact that myths are fictional in the first place, making sense might not be required."

"Probably not," she murmured, and glanced at the book in his hand. "Have you found something?"

"Not really." He snapped the book shut and replaced it on the shelf. "What about muses?"

She shook her head. "Too fanciful, I think. Our story is about forces of nature, not the arts."

"I've got it." Jonathon smiled with satisfaction. "Nymphs. If I remember my classical studies right, they were minor goddesses."

"Excellent. Nymphs it is, then." Fiona returned to the table, grabbed a sheet of paper, scribbled *Winter* on it and then wrote *Summer* on a second sheet. Quickly she divided the stack of male drawings into two piles, placed the page with Winter on one and Summer on the other. "Now." She took six of the female drawings and put three on each god's stack. "Winter and Summer have each won the hearts and loyalty of three nymphs."

"Summer has June, July and August and Winter has January, February and"—he frowned—"December?"

"I definitely think of December as winter," she said firmly. "The days are the shortest of the year and it's invariably cold. Much more so than March."

"Very well, then, Winter and Summer each have the uncontested possession of three months apiece." Jonathon moved to her side and studied the piles of drawings. "Should we have a god of Spring and Autumn as well?"

"I don't think so." She drew her brows together. "The remaining months, or rather nymphs, the ones who would belong to Spring or Autumn if we had two additional gods—"

"Perhaps they were vanquished by Winter and Summer because they were weak?"

"Excellent. So those nymphs are now free and the object of constant struggle between Winter and Summer. It's the loyalties, even the affection of those nymphs that is always in question." She thought for a moment. "So it's not really a face to face battle between Winter and Summer. It's a competition, but it's subtler than that. Each of the gods is always trying to convince one of the spring or autumn nymphs to join him."

"Through whatever means necessary. Trickery or bribery or . . ." He raised a brow. "Seduction?"

"Definitely seduction, I should think." She met his gaze firmly. "Don't you?"

"Seduction seems like the right way to proceed." He stared down at her. "With gods and nymphs, that is."

At once she was aware of how very close they stood to one another. Side by side, their shoulders nearly touched, and she wondered why she hadn't noticed his proximity before. Or was it the word *seduction* that made her so aware of him?

"And nymphs, being what they are, can be very susceptible to"—she swallowed hard—"seduction."

"They are fickle creatures." His gaze dropped from her eyes to her lips and back. "You can never count on a nymph to be truly faithful."

"One would be a fool to ever depend on a nymph." How much more foolish to depend on a man? Especially one with broad shoulders and an infectious laugh and a wicked dimple in his cheek?

"Is that it, then?" His voice was low and . . . *seductive.*

"Is what what, then?" She stared into his blue eyes. Endless and oh, so inviting. He could say whatever he wished about their previous kisses not counting, but she could well recall the warmth of his lips on hers. The hard feel of his body pressed against hers.

"All you have of the story?" He lowered his head closer to hers as if he were about to claim his kiss.

It might be worth a hundred pounds to kiss him again. To feel the way his kiss weakened her limbs and made her blood pound and her head spin. Surely that was only because he was so very skilled at it.

"No." She fairly sighed the word.

He stilled, his lips a bare breath from hers. "No?"

"No." She couldn't quite hide the regret in her voice.

He paused. "Are you sure?"

"I am." She shook her head slowly. "That's not all to the story."

"The story?" Confusion crossed his face, then he winced and straightened. "Ah, yes, the story."

"The story." She drew a deep breath and clasped her slightly unsteady hands together. The last thing she wished him to notice was that she wanted him to kiss her. More than she'd expected. "Well, it's a myth."

"And?" His tone was abrupt and he crossed his arms over his chest. "Go on."

She studied him for a moment. Obviously, given his newly grumpy manner, he'd wanted to kiss her just as much as she'd wanted to kiss him. Possibility even more than he'd expected. She stifled a satisfied smile.

"And myths, as we agreed earlier, are for the express purpose of explaining a facet of nature that had no understanding, at least to the ancients." She gestured at the drawings spread across the table. "Our story explains precisely why those months between winter and summer, the seasons of spring and fall, are sometimes colder than expected and sometimes warmer."

His eyes narrowed in confusion. "What?"

"Come, now, Jonathon, you're deliberately being obtuse. You understand exactly what I'm saying." She rolled her gaze toward the ceiling. "When Winter is doing his best to seduce March, to keep her by his side, March is cold. But when Summer has flattered and cajoled and March is ready to fall into his waiting arms, March is much warmer than usual. When March is uncertain, torn between the two gods, we have storms. How severe depends on March's emotions and the efforts of the gods to win her. The same applies to April, May, September, October and November."

He stared at her for a long silent moment.

"Well? Say something."

He blew a long breath. "I owe you a hundred pounds."

The most delightful sense of accomplishment bubbled through her and she grinned. "I know."

"It's really rather brilliant, Fiona."

"It is, isn't it?" She glanced at the drawings. "I think this is going to turn out far better than I ever expected. However . . ." She met his gaze. "I believe the development of this story was more a joint effort than mine alone, therefore I cannot take your money."

"No." He shook his head firmly. "I always pay off my debts."

"It was an outrageous wager in the first place. A hundred pounds against a kiss."

"Outrageous or not, I gave my word."

"You gave your word to marry me as well, yet you had little problem not living up to that promise."

"Because I thought it was all a—"

"Yes, yes, I know, and I would much prefer not to hear it again." She waved away his comment. "Very well, then. I will accept fifty pounds, but no more."

He raised a brow. "Half of the wager, then?"

She nodded.

He smiled slowly. "And do I get half a kiss?"

"I'm not entirely sure I know what half a kiss is."

"Nor am I, but I'm certain together we can find out."

She stared at him. "Are you bent on flirtation with me, Jonathon?"

"Why, I don't know that I'm bent on it. It just seems rather natural to flirt—"

"You have refused to marry me, yet you obviously wish to kiss me." She leaned toward him. "Do you wish more than that?"

His eyes widened. "More?"

"More." Without warning, something inside her snapped and anger gripped her. "Won't one kiss lead to another? A second to a third and so on? Where do you wish it to end?"

"I don't—"

"You don't wish it to end? Yet you don't want it to lead to marriage."

"I didn't really—"

"I have seen your type of man before. You are handsome and charming and make no promises save those in your eyes."

"In my eyes?" Caution edged his voice. "My eyes aren't saying a word."

"Hah! Even you don't believe that!"

He stared at her. "What exactly are you trying to say?"

"I'm saying that you, Lord Helmsley, are an outrageous flirt. And the question that I have is, to what purpose?" She stepped back and folded her arms over her chest. "You have no desire to marry me."

"I say, that's not fair. That really has nothing to do with you. I have only recently learned I have no desire to marry anyone at the moment. You simply made me realize that."

Fiona stared in disbelief. She wasn't sure if she wanted to scream or crack her hand across his face. Either would be most satisfying.

Jonathon winced. "I didn't mean that exactly the way it sounded."

"How did you mean it?"

"Fiona, you are intelligent and beautiful, and just from the brief time we have spent together I can certainly see you would not be meek and mild as a wife." He ran his hand through his hair. "And I doubt that I have ever met any woman more suited to be a duchess than you."

"Is it love you're looking for, then?"

"Quite frankly, I have never given love any serious consideration." He blew a long breath. "My friends claim I have never been in love."

"Are they right?"

"I didn't think they were, but"—he shrugged in a helpless manner—"in truth, I don't know."

"I see." She drew a deep breath. "You need to understand I have no such hesitation about marriage. Regardless of whether this scheme of yours and Oliver's is successful or not, I fully intend to marry one day. I hope to do so for . . . affection, possibly love, but even if I ultimately marry simply to settle my finances I shall do so with my honor intact."

His eyes widened. "Fiona, I never—"

"Didn't you?" She shook her head. "You look at me as if I am a morsel you wish to devour."

"I don't mean to offend you."

"The problem is not that I'm offended! I am flattered and intrigued. Far too intrigued. And that, my lord, is the problem."

His mouth dropped open and he stared.

She stepped very close to him and stared up into his eyes. "When you stand near me and gaze into my eyes with a look that says there is nothing you want so much in the world than to take me in your arms and kiss me, I want to kiss you back. I want everything those eyes of yours promise. And that is very, very dangerous to my life and my future." She stepped back. "Therefore, there will be no more kisses waged. We shall work to put together this book with a cordiality tempered with formality. I am willing to be pleasant, but I prefer to be impersonal. This"—she gestured at the table—"will be difficult enough to do without panting over one another as if we were animals."

"May I say something?"

"No. There is nothing more to say." She brushed past him and collected her drawings and packed them into the portfolio. "We have done quite enough for today. I think we should start again tomorrow. We have the basis for our myth. Now we, or I should say you, as you are the writer, need to simply come up with the appropriate words."

She nodded sharply and started toward the door.

"Fiona."

She braced herself and turned. "Miss Fairchild, please."

"As you wish." He stared at her for a long moment. "You have my apologies for anything I have done that you feel is inappropriate."

"Do you believe in honesty, my lord?"

He nodded. "Under most circumstances."

"Then know this." For a moment she debated the merits of what she was about to say. Although, in truth, it scarcely mattered. "Like you, I do not think I have ever truly been in love before, and I very much fear I could easily fall in love with you. As you have no interest in marriage, that would only lead to the breaking of my heart and my ultimate ruin. I will not allow that. Now, then, I shall bid you good day." She nodded, turned and swept from the room.

"Fiona," he called. "Miss Fairchild."

She ignored him, not pausing for so much as a single moment until she reached the relative safety of her own rooms.

Fiona tossed aside the portfolio, then sank down on her bed and buried her face in her hands. What on earth had come over her? How could she have been so . . . so honest? She certainly hadn't planned on confessing anything at all, let alone how enticing she found him. Her plan, if indeed she'd had anything that approached an actual plan, was to spend time with him and charm him into . . . what? Marriage? Love?

She had no idea. He confused her, as did the feelings he provoked in a way no man had ever confused her before. Lord knows she'd been involved in any number of flirtations and with men probably even better at it than him. Yet she'd never before been so tempted by a man. Never before even suspected surrender was a possibility. Never before so much as considered tossing away her future for the magic to be found in his arms or even, God help her, in his bed. Yet with Jonathon she wanted nothing more than to surrender to his charms. And had, in truth, wanted that, wanted him, from the moment she'd taken Lady Chester's place in the library. Or perhaps from the moment she'd first seen him all those years ago.

Nonetheless, she had her sisters to consider, and they would not be well served if Fiona indulged her desires. No, she needed a husband, not a lover.

And if Jonathon was not interested in the first position, she was not about to grant him the second.

Jonathon stared at the now-empty doorway.

What exactly had he done to provoke that? Nothing the least bit out of the ordinary. Yes, he had flirted with her, but he flirted with every woman who was lovely and amusing. It was only natural that he would . . .

He groaned to himself. He should have known better. Fiona wasn't simply any woman. She was in a desperate position and had already asked him to marry her. He winced at the thought. And she had been rejected. His flirtation would only encourage any romantic inclinations she might have toward him. Why, she'd said she could easily fall in love with him.

And couldn't he fall in love with her just as easily? The unbidden thought flashed through his mind. It was absurd, of course. Ridiculous. Admittedly she provoked all sorts of unfamiliar emotions within him, but those were surely due to the odd situation they found themselves embroiled in and nothing more than that. Still, if his friends were right and he had never experienced a true passion of the heart, would he even know love when he found it?

He needed advice and he needed it at once. Certainly he had two sisters he could turn to, but lust and desire and confusion were not exactly topics one discussed with one's sisters. Nor did he wish to talk about such things with either of his parents, although he suspected both would understand. Oliver wasn't a possibility either. He was Fiona's cousin, after all, and had her best interests at heart. And neither Cavendish nor Wharton had ever been overly successful with women. Why, Jonathon would trust his own instincts before he would rely on advice from either of them. Besides, they'd probably find all this the height of amusement.

No, he needed someone who could help him unravel the workings of the female mind, and for that, perhaps, only a female would do.

Seven

The next morning, far earlier than anyone with any sense would pay a call . . .

"You woke me up at this ungodly hour to ask about love?" Judith, Lady Chester, lounged on the chaise in her bedchamber ensconced, more than attired, in some frilly pink confection of a dressing gown. She stared at Jonathon as though he had taken leave of his senses. The small, fluffy white beast that she claimed was a dog lay curled by her side and stared with nearly the very same expression. It was most disconcerting.

Jonathon perched on the edge of a French armchair that was far too delicate for comfort. But then, nearly everything in Judith's boudoir was far too delicate for anyone whose tastes were not distinctly feminine, with the possible exception of the fresh flowers, always unusual and interesting. Judith had a passion for flowers, and the more exotic and costly they were, the more she liked them. She fancied herself a bit of a gardener, although she had a complete staff to handle the more distasteful chores of actually planting and tending to plants.

"It's half past nine, which most people do not consider ungodly. Besides, I sent you a note last night advising you of my intention to call this morning." Jonathon narrowed his eyes. "And I said nothing about love."

Judith yawned in a most indelicate manner. "It's all about love, dear heart. All this man and woman nonsense. On occasion, it can also be about passion or lust or money, but for the most part it's always about love. Or rather it's always best when it's about love."

He raised a brow. "I never imagined you to be such a romantic."

"I don't know a woman who isn't a romantic in one way or another." She studied him for a moment. "Including your Miss Fairchild."

"She's not my Miss Fairchild," he said sharply.

The fluffy creature picked up his head and growled. His mistress smirked. "But you want her to be."

Frustration brought him to his feet and he paced the pastel-hued Aubusson carpet. "I don't know what I want."

"Of course you don't, you poor, poor stupid man." Judith settled back on the chaise and watched him with far too much amusement in her eyes. "I should apologize to you, I suppose, for my part in this. But when Norcroft said his cousin very much wished to meet with you privately, I saw no real harm in it. And indeed, as I had had a much more interesting invitation for the evening—"

He stopped and stared. "You weren't at the ball, then?"

"For a few moments." She shrugged. "Long enough to establish . . . my wherabouts."

"What are you up to, Judith?"

She laughed. "Nothing of any significance, I assure you. Or perhaps something of great importance. I have not yet decided. And it's none of your concern."

"Nonetheless, I—"

"Jonathon, the topic for discussion today is your life, not mine," she said firmly. "Now, then, of all the men I have ever known, I would have chosen you least resistant to marriage. So why don't you simply marry the girl?"

"Don't be absurd. I scarcely know her."

"My dear man, you can't possibly ever know anyone, not

truly, until you marry them. Until you share a life and a sense of permanence. Until you have the opportunity to complain about her spending and she has the chance to berate you about your bad habits and your equally bad companions."

"I would call neither my companions nor my habits bad," he said loftily.

She laughed. "You are scarcely perfect, my lord."

"I never claimed to be perfect." He paused. "Although I am a good catch."

"And modest as well."

"Do stop it, Judith, and tell me what I am to do."

"You could have married me years ago."

He shot her a skeptical glance. "You have never been particularly interested in marriage."

"Once was quite enough." She patted the dog in an absent manner and the creature rested his head on her lap, although his gaze never left Jonathon. "Besides, I rather cherish the unique understanding you and I have cultivated through the years."

He smiled. "Friends who have shared a bed on occasion?"

"You do realize that will come to an end when you marry?" Her gaze met his. "Not our friendship, we will always be friends, but the rest of it."

"Of course." Judith may well be a bit freer with her favors than other women of his acquaintance, but she did not involve herself with married men and to his knowledge never had. "I should hate to lose your friendship." Jonathon smiled even as he realized there were few women alive who would tolerate the kind of friendship he and Judith had shared.

She studied him for a long moment. "Don't you think it rather significant that you are asking for advice in the first place?"

"No." He drew his brows together and tried to think of the last time he had asked for advice about a woman and failed. "Do you?"

"Absolutely. You have never lacked in confidence and

you have certainly never asked for my assistance regarding whatever lady had captured your attention at the moment."

"This is different," he said staunchly.

"Oh?"

"*She* is different." He wasn't entirely sure how to explain.

"She scarcely seems different to me. Oh, her circumstances are certainly unique enough, but"—Judith waved aimlessly—"I daresay she's no different than any young woman seeking a husband. A bit more desperate, perhaps, but really no different. Women marry all the time to improve their financial circumstances." She sat up abruptly, the dog scrambling to keep from sliding onto the floor. "I should meet her as soon as possible. Especially if she really is different. I certainly can't give you proper advice without meeting your Miss Fairchild."

Nonetheless, Jonathon wasn't at all sure a meeting between Judith and Fiona was advisable, regardless of how he might or might not feel about Fiona. Or Judith either, for that matter. "Judith, I'm not sure—"

"I shall send Norcroft a note at once." She scooped the dog up in her arms, got to her feet and swept across the room. Jonathon could have sworn the animal cast him a threatening look as they passed.

"Judith . . ." He trailed after her.

"I shall make certain he brings Miss Fairchild to the Twelfth Night Ball." Judith placed the dog in a basket festooned with lace and ribbons and seated herself before a small desk. "I shall send her an invitation as well." She glanced at Jonathon. "You don't think she'll be offended, do you? To be invited so late, that is. The other invitations went out weeks ago."

"Not at all," Jonathon said weakly. Certainly he and Oliver had every intention of bringing Fiona to Judith's ball, but Jonathon had never imagined the two of them actually *meeting*.

"You know, this is the first ball I've had in town in years." Judith pulled out a sheet of paper from a writing box on the desk, then dipped a pen into an ornate inkwell. "I do usually prefer *intimate* parties at my house in the country, but sometimes one just feels the need for a large, extravagant event even if for no real reason."

"Of course," he murmured.

"It's been ten years since my husband died. A full decade that I have been a widow." She paused in an almost wistful manner. "I have had a great deal of fun."

Jonathon stared. As much as they were friends and had been for a number of years, he wasn't sure he had ever heard her mention her late husband before. Or sound the least bit wistful.

"I should take my leave." He edged toward the door. "Miss Fairchild and I are to continue our work this morning."

"Jonathon." Judith set down her pen and swiveled in the chair to face him. "You've come for my advice, so here it is. Take the opportunity this book scheme affords you to become better acquainted with this woman."

"Better acquainted?" He shook his head. "She will not allow—"

"I am talking about friendship." She blew an exasperated breath. "Offer her the hand of friendship. Surely you can do so without flirtation of any kind?"

At once the image of a brilliant smile and irresistible green eyes flashed through his mind.

"Well, for heaven's sakes, do at least try to suppress that natural inclination of yours to be charming." She rolled her gaze toward the ceiling. "She has said she could fall in love with you. You cannot allow that if you cannot return her affection."

"No, of course not."

"However, I should point out some of the very best relationships between men and women that I've ever witnessed result from a shared friendship as well as love. Make friends with her and along the way explore your own feelings."

He blew a long breath. "I don't know what my feelings are."

"Therein lies the need for exploration as well as the problem. Jonathon." Her tone sobered and she met his gaze directly. "If she is indeed what you have always wanted, you can ill afford to let her go. That might be the greatest mistake of your life."

"And if she isn't?"

"Then you have lost nothing."

"I suppose." He cast her a firm look. "I assume you will keep everything we have discussed entirely confidential."

Her eyes widened. "My dear Jonathon, I have kept better secrets than this for you." She paused. "As you have kept for me."

He grinned. "You do have some interesting secrets."

"As do you. Well, perhaps not quite as interesting," she said wryly, then shook her head. "You do realize if she finds out that you are providing the money that she believes is being earned by the sale of your book, she may never forgive you. From what you have told me, it sounds as if she has a great deal of pride. Women with pride do not take well to what they might perceive as charity."

"She won't find out," he said firmly. "I will make certain of that. Only Norcroft and I will ever be privy to this scheme."

"And myself, of course."

"Yes, but you know how to keep a secret."

"I do indeed, when necessary. Oh, and Jonathon." She tapped the end of her pen thoughtfully against her bottom lip. "I must confess you have piqued my curiosity. When you have this handful of books printed"—she smiled in an altogether wicked way—"reserve a copy for me."

"... her body was lush and ripe and the first rays of his brother Sun turned her flesh to gold. Winter wanted her ..."

Jonathon paused to find the right words. "With a need that ached in his loins."

"Ached in his loins," Fiona murmured, her head bent over the page she scribbled his words on. "That's very good, my lord."

"Thank you, Miss Fairchild," he said in the polite yet

pleasant tone he had adopted from the moment they had begun their work here in Oliver's library an hour or so ago.

He had given Judith's advice a great deal of thought on the carriage ride here and had decided to follow it. Why not? She was right about his not doing anything to encourage Fiona's feelings. And right as well about his need to determine exactly how he felt about her. As for making friends, that too made a certain amount of sense.

Still, it would be easier to consider friendship if words like *loins* and *flesh* and *ache* could be avoided, since, in his mind, they naturally led to words including *lust* and *desire* and . . . *Fiona.*

She glanced up at him. "And?"

"And?"

Fiona didn't seem to be the least bit bothered by any of it. He could have been dictating children's stories, for all the effect it seemed to have on her.

"And what is the next line?"

"The next line?" Good God, he could barely remember his own name, let alone come up with a next line. And wasn't it exceptionally warm in here? He drew a steadying breath. "The next line."

"Yes, the next line. The following sentence. What comes after *ached in his loins.*" Her tone was cool and unruffled. "Do you have a next line?"

If she was not affected by all this talk of *need* and *aching,* he was certainly not going to let her know he was. "Of course." He thought for a moment. "She paid him no heed. As if she had no knowledge of his presence."

"Good, good," she said under her breath, writing down every word, her gaze on her work. "Go on."

The late morning sun slanted in through the window and her hair glowed a dark copper color in the light. As if she were indeed touched by the sun itself. "No knowledge of his gaze upon her porcelain skin." She looked like an ancient enchantress recording spells of magic and potions of love to be used to enthrall a knight or a lord or the son of a duke. "Of the desire coursing through his—"

"Can skin be porcelain and golden at the same time?" she said abruptly.

"What?" The question rudely jerked him back to here and now.

"Can skin be porcelain and golden at the same time?" she said again, somewhat slower, as if his intelligence were such that she needed to make a special effort to make certain he understood, and frowned at the paper in front of her. "It seems to me *porcelain* evokes a very cool feeling, while *golden* brings to mind something considerably warmer."

He stared at her in disbelief, all thoughts of irresistible magic wielded by bronze-haired goddesses at once vanquished by irritation.

"Well?" She looked up at him. "Which is it? Porcelain or golden?"

"It's both."

She shook her head. "It can't be both."

"It most certainly can if I say it can. It's . . . it's literary license. It's fiction. I am the author. I can do whatever I want." He crossed his arms over his chest. "And if I wish this particular nymph to have skin that is both porcelain and golden, she shall have skin that is both porcelain and golden. Write it down."

"Very well." She shrugged and turned her attention back to the paper and said under her breath, "But it makes no sense."

He watched her write and suspicion washed through him. "Are you writing what I said?"

She cast him a pleasant smile. "No."

"No?"

"No. I changed it." She looked down at the paper. "It now reads: *no knowledge of his covetous gaze upon the warmth of her skin.*"

"I never said covetous."

"No, but you should have. I like it. Next sentence, please."

"If you are not going to write precisely what I say, then perhaps I should be the one doing the writing."

"Would you?" She rose to her feet. "Then I can be the one to pace the room and mutter under my breath and occasionally groan in the throes of creative despair." She fluttered her lashes and smiled in an overly sweet manner.

He stared at her and without warning annoyance was swept away by absurdity. He struggled to keep a grin from his face. "Creative despair?"

She raised a brow.

He laughed. "Am I being ridiculous, then?"

"You are being . . ." She smiled slowly, a genuine smile this time. "Most amusing."

"Am I?" He chuckled. "I do not intend to be."

"Nonetheless you are." She studied him for a moment. "Is this how you always write?"

"I don't think so. I do on occasion pace when trying to think of the proper phrase or word, but I am fairly certain I do not groan in the throes of creative despair." He shrugged. "Although I might. I have never had a witness to my writing before, nor have I ever attempted to dictate a story."

"Do you think Mr. Dickens groans and mutters and paces?"

"No." He heaved a resigned sigh. "I think Mr. Dickens's genius is such that he simply touches pen to paper and the words flow unimpeded."

She laughed. "Surely not. I would think he struggles every bit as much as you do."

"Possibly, but I would wager his struggles are tempered by the sure and certain knowledge that the world is waiting with breathless anticipation for his next work." Jonathon grimaced. "The world is neither waiting for my words nor does it know I exist."

"Perhaps someday."

"Perhaps." He shook his head. "Although I seem to have a better gift for investment than for writing, at least in terms of success. I have yet to sell a single story, whereas my investment ventures have thus far proven profitable."

"Will this venture prove profitable?" The question echoed in her eyes.

"I shall make certain of it, Miss Fairchild." He met her gaze with a confident smile.

"I am most appreciative, my lord," she said softly.

For a long moment her gaze locked with his. His smile faded. The green of her eyes deepened with something he couldn't quite place. Something wonderful. The moment between them stretched and lengthened. The oddest sensation of tension, electric and compelling and not the least bit what he had ever felt for a friend, crackled in the air between them. He wanted to move toward her, sweep her into his arms, his bed, his life. Kiss her until they were both senseless with—

She cleared her throat. "Shall we continue, then?"

"Good God, yes," he murmured.

A charming blush tinged her cheeks. "With the story?"

"The story." He drew a deep breath. "Yes, of course, the story. Where were we?"

She pulled her gaze from his, sat down in her chair and picked up the pen. "The last line was: *no knowledge of his covetous gaze upon the warmth of her skin.*"

"Covetous." He snorted.

She ignored him. "Then I believe you started to say something about coursing desire?"

"Desire?" Dear Lord, not desire. "*Coursing* desire, you say?"

"Or possibly desire coursing. I did not quite get it down. I was concerned with covetous at the time."

"Very well, then." He clenched his jaw, firmly thrust aside all desirous thoughts of Fiona, covetous or otherwise, and forced himself to concentrate on the desires of Winter as regards whatever nymph he had in his sights. "What nymph is this again?"

She shuffled through the papers on the table. "April, I think."

"April." He thought for a moment. *"No knowledge of his covetous gaze upon the warmth of her skin . . ."* He glanced at Fiona.

She smiled down at the paper in an annoyingly satisfied manner.

He continued. "No knowledge of the desire coursing through his veins. Surging in his blood. Grasping him—

no—gripping him with a fire that demanded quenching. He could . . . take her. Yes, that's good." Very good, in fact. Far better than *covetous*. "Or rather, should take her. Now. As was his due, without—"

"Wait!" Fiona wrote frantically. "You are going entirely too fast."

"Sorry."

"What came after surging through his blood?"

"Gripping him with a fire that demanded quenching."

"Gripping him with a fire," she repeated as she wrote, "that demanded quenching."

"He should take her now as was his due—Good Lord, Miss Fairchild!" He stared at her. "Don't you find this difficult?"

"Not if you slow down," she muttered.

"I didn't mean the dictation." He huffed. "I meant the topic. Don't you find this embarrassing?"

"Not at all, my lord." She glanced up at him. "Do you?"

"Well, yes, somewhat."

"Why?"

"Because I am not used to discussing topics of this nature with properly bred young women." The moment the words were out of his mouth, he regretted them. Why, he sounded as stuffy as his father.

"Really?" She sat back in her chair. "Who do you discuss topics of this nature with?"

"What?"

"You said you were not used to discussing such topics with properly bred young women. Who do you discuss such things with?"

"Why . . ." he sputtered. "I don't!"

"Perhaps you should have thought of that, then, before we began this project," she said primly. "I believe it was your idea."

He glared at her. "This doesn't bother you at all, does it?"

"What, my lord?" She blew an exasperated breath, set her pen down and looked up at him. "The words we are using or the fact that you are wasting a great deal of our time being uncomfortable at their use?"

He gritted his teeth. "The first."

"No, of course not. They are simply words, after all. I am an artist and you are a writer. You tell your stories with words, I tell mine with pen and charcoal." She shrugged. "The words you use have no more effect on me than the subjects of my drawings."

He raised a brow. "Naked men?"

"And women." She studied him for a moment. "You are more shocked than you originally let on about my work, aren't you?"

"Not at all," he said staunchly, then paused. "Admittedly, I might be more surprised the better I get to know you—"

She laughed. "I do not seem like the type of woman who would draw nude figures?"

"In many ways, Miss Fairchild, you seem like the type of woman who would do almost anything that struck her fancy," he said wryly. "But I also think you have certain boundaries of behavior you will not breach."

"Oh?"

"For example, I am fairly certain you will not trick a man into marriage, nor will you force a man to wed who does not wish to."

"I wouldn't wager on that." A warning sounded in her voice.

"I would." He grinned. "Shall we say a hundred pounds?"

"Don't be absurd." She scoffed. "If you lost, you would lose far more than money, you would lose your freedom."

"Very well, then. I'll wager my freedom. And if I won, what would I win?"

She laughed. "But you could never win. You are betting on my behavior. On something that I would or would not do. Something that I have full control over. It is a fool's wager."

"I have been called a fool on more than one occasion." He wagged his brows wickedly. "What do you have to wager that would be comparable to my freedom?"

"My virtue," she said without pause.

"Yes, well . . ." He tried and failed to keep the surprise from his voice. "That is comparable."

She laughed. "Now I have truly shocked you." She leaned toward him. "Is it because of what I am willing to bet in a wager that I cannot lose? Or is it simply because I have said the word *virtue* aloud?"

"You have said *naked* aloud." His tone was dry. "Not to mention *coursing desire* and"— he shook his head in a mournful manner—"*covetous.*"

She heaved an overly dramatic sigh. "Oh, dear, I am shocking."

"Yes, you are, and I find it quite charming." He grinned. "But you're right, such a wager as we've discussed would be nothing short of stupid on my part. And I agree, only a fool would engage in such a gamble knowing he cannot possibly win."

"And you are no fool."

"I try not to be." He studied her for a moment. "Miss Fairchild." Jonathon pulled up a chair and sat down beside her. "Would you like to be friends?"

She narrowed her eyes in obvious suspicion. "What do you mean, *friends*?"

"I mean friends. Comrades. Something more than acquaintances and less than . . . Well, you know what friends are."

"Certainly, but—"

"We are going to be spending a great deal of time together. Given our conversation yesterday regarding any potential feelings you could develop toward me"—Jonathon winced to himself; this was most awkward not only because of the possibility that she might feel something for him, but because of his confusion toward her—"and my own . . . reluctance regarding marriage, it seems that friendship would be the safest course for us both. You have informed me in no uncertain terms that you do not wish for any sort of flirtation on my part, and I must tell you it's damnably hard to avoid."

"Imagine that," she murmured.

"You're quite lovely, Miss Fairchild, and clever and amusing, and I find I enjoy your company, but . . ." He blew a long breath. "I feel things are most unsettled between us. I hope that if we can at least be friends—"

"Agreed."

"—then perhaps our work together would not—"

"I said I agree."

He drew his brows together. "You agree?"

"On friendship between us." She nodded. "I think it's an excellent idea."

"You do?"

"Even I am aware that your efforts to suppress your obviously natural inclination toward flirtation are most difficult for you. Indeed, today you have seemed like a thread stretched to the breaking point."

"I have?"

She lowered her voice in a confidential manner. "And it's apparent the subject matter we are dealing with is not helping."

"You could say that," he said under his breath.

"Therefore, in the interest of friendship and your well-being, I propose we divide our time." She thought for a moment. "We could write a bit, finish a few pages—as much as you can bear—"

"See here, Miss Fairchild." Indignation rang in his voice. "I daresay I can hold up—"

"—then we'll stop," she continued without pause, "and spend some time getting to know one another. Perhaps we could each ask the other a question about something we are curious about." She glanced at him. "Nothing too personal, of course."

"However, some personal questions are allowed. Among friends, that is," he added quickly.

"I suppose. I daresay we can decide on a question-by-question basis."

"Excellent." He sat back and beamed at her. "Would you like to go first? With a question, that is?"

"I think I prefer that you go first," she said slowly. "I cannot think of a question at the moment and I do hate to squander the opportunity."

"Very well." He waved at the drawings strewn across the table. "How did all this come about? You said you went from pears to people. Surely there was more to it than that?"

"It was"—she thought for a moment—"a natural progression, I would say. I began my studies with Mrs. Kincaid years ago. Eleanora Kincaid is a wonderful artist, although I daresay no one has ever heard of her and probably never will. She left England as a young woman and supplements the commissions she receives for portraits and murals and the like with art lessons. At first we drew still lifes and landscapes and that sort of thing. Then we started going to museums and galleries to study works of the great masters. She encouraged us to draw what we saw there including ancient Roman and Greek sculptures." She glanced at him. "You realize most of them are not clothed?"

"I do realize that, although they are also made of stone and cool to the touch."

"Quite, and therefore not much of a challenge, really." She nodded. "We studied anatomy from books as well as statues, but eventually it wasn't enough and we needed to draw from life, from living, breathing people." She leaned toward him. "It's quite a different thing, you know, to copy what you see in a book or render an inanimate figure made of marble to drawing a living being." She grinned. "They have a tendency to move. It's most awkward."

"No doubt."

"At any rate, a few years ago, Mrs. Kincaid decided, for purposes of improvement and challenge, that it was time to move on to something more demanding and she hired models to pose for us."

"Female and male models?" he asked.

She shook her head. "Just women at first. I believe it's rather difficult to find men to pose naked in front of a group of young women."

"I can well imagine," he murmured. "I would certainly find it embarrassing, to say the least."

"Really? But it was simply a task for which they were well

compensated. There was nothing at all personal about it. On their side or on ours."

"Nonetheless, I would never . . ." He shook his head. "I can't even envision . . ."

"Can't you?" She looked at him as if assessing his qualifications to pose nude. "What a shame."

He huffed. "Miss Fairchild, if you think I am the type of man to shed my clothes in the name of art—"

She laughed. "I didn't think that at all. However, as a writer, I would think you would well be able to imagine how a man in that position, surrounded by young women, all staring dispassionately at him as if he were nothing more than an object, might feel. Or how he might respond."

At once the image of her gazing dispassionately at his nude body popped into his head. He wasn't at all sure he liked the idea of her—or any woman, for that matter, but her in particular—gazing at his naked form in a *dispassionate* manner. If Fiona were ever to look upon him when he was unclothed, he did hope that she would have some sort of passionate response. Lord knows he would, if the situation were reversed.

Without warning the image changed to include her in a similar state of undress.

"Well?"

"I do have a rather vivid imagination," he muttered.

"I thought as much." She chuckled. "As I was saying, it is difficult to find male models. However, Mrs. Kincaid was never long without male companionship—"

"Miss Fairchild!"

"Have I shocked you again?" She stared at him in disbelief. "I had no idea you were so easily shocked."

"I'm not." He paused. "Usually."

"Are you shocked at what I know or what I say?"

"Both." He sighed. "Neither. My apologies, do continue."

"There's really not much more to say." She shrugged. "Mrs. Kincaid convinced her . . . *companion* to pose. After they were no longer"—she flashed him a quick teasing look—"*companions,* she persuaded her new companion to do so as well."

"Were you not embarrassed by all these"—he grimaced—
"companions? These *naked* companions."

"No," she said blithely. "After all, they weren't my companions."

He tried and failed to stifle a gasp.

"I am sorry." She laughed. "I couldn't resist that. You are
great fun to shock."

"I am glad you're enjoying it."

"Oh, I am." She grinned, then her expression sobered. "I
do admit it was a bit uncomfortable in the beginning, but
eventually one looks at a naked body very much as one
looks at a vase or a piece of fruit. The work itself becomes
more . . . alive, I think, than the subject." Her brows drew
together thoughtfully. "You should understand, this was a
very small group of students. Seven of us altogether and
not one under the age of twenty. We were all great friends
and the subject of this aspect of our work was our secret.
Some of us were more talented than others, some better
with charcoal, others with paint, but we each took what we
did quite seriously. Although none of us expected ever to
have to earn our own living." She smiled wryly. "My
friends would be as shocked as you to learn of this project."

"They won't. No one will. Ever," he said staunchly ignoring the fact that just today he had told Judith, but Judith
was an expert at the keeping of secrets. "Anonymity is crucial. Besides"—he grinned—"if seven women can keep the
subject of their work secret for years, we can surely do no
less."

She studied him for a long moment. "I do appreciate your
efforts with this, you know."

"It's entirely my pleasure."

"Why are you doing it?"

"Is that an official question?"

She laughed. "Yes, I suppose it is."

"It seems the least I can do to help a friend in your situation."

"Are we friends already, then?"

"Somewhat, I hope. In truth, Miss Fairchild, I have never

had a woman—a woman aside from my sisters, that is—ask me for help in any sort of endeavor of this serious a nature. Which is precisely what you did when you asked me to marry you." He met her gaze directly. "You were completely candid with me and I regret that I was not as forthright with you. Apologies alone do not seem sufficient to rectify my error in judgment. I feel a certain obligation to help you avoid the fate you so very much wish to avoid. You asked for rescue and I did not provide it. I have long thought of myself as an honorable man and I am not proud of my refusal."

"I see." Her gaze searched his. "And if my fate cannot be avoided? If we cannot earn the funding I require? If I see no other choice but to marry the man my father selected?"

"You won't," he said firmly.

"This all seems so very speculative to me." She blew a long breath. "I have any number of doubts as to its success, whereas you are completely confident."

"I am indeed." He nodded. It was easy to be confident, since he knew precisely where her funds would come from. Not that she would ever know. "Rest assured, Miss Fairchild, with this endeavor you will be rescued."

"I am fortunate, then, to have found a friend such as you." She smiled and his stomach twisted.

"I am the fortunate one." At once he realized he did indeed feel fortunate.

"Because you will at last see your work in print, even if anonymously?"

"Yes, of course," he murmured. Surely there was no other reason to feel as if he had just won an impressive wager? An immense lottery? The world itself? "That's it."

"I thought so. Very well." She drew a deep breath. "He should take her, now, as was his due."

"Indeed." His gaze slipped to her lips.

"And then?"

Her words wrapped around him and without thought he leaned closer to her. "And then?"

"What comes next?" Her voice was soft and so enticing.

"Next?" He was close enough to kiss her. Surely a kiss, to seal a friendship, would be permissible?

"The next line, my lord? We should get back to our work." The corners of her lips tilted upward in a slight, vaguely smug smile, as if she knew precisely what he was thinking. She pointedly turned away from him and read from the page. *"He should take her, now, as was his due."*

As well he should. Jonathon pushed the errant thought from his head and got to his feet. "Of course. The next line." He paced a few steps, then paused to study her, and smiled slowly.

"And knew, in the manner in which all gods knew such things, she wished it as much as he."

Eight

The following morning, not nearly as early as the day before, but still earlier than one would have preferred if one had one's choice, but then on occasion, one doesn't . . .

"There is nothing like a new gown to raise a girl's spirits." Aunt Edwina circled the stool Fiona stood on in her aunt's parlor and studied the fabrics draped over the younger woman. She'd been in a tizzy of excitement ever since Lady Chester's invitation for Fiona had arrived yesterday afternoon and had wasted no time in summoning her favorite dressmaker.

Aunt Edwina fingered a length of copper-colored silk and glanced at the seamstress. "This will do beautifully, I think."

"I agree, madame." Madame DuBois, a Frenchwoman and, according to Aunt Edwina, one of the best and costliest dressmakers in the city, scrutinized Fiona with an even more critical eye than her aunt. "It suits her coloring and complements both her hair and her eyes."

Madame DuBois's entourage, consisting of a young man with a somewhat haughty demeanor and two women of indeterminate age, murmured their assent.

"I really don't need a new gown," Fiona said halfheartedly, and stared at her reflection in the mirror. Madame was right. The silk was beautiful in and of itself and it did look well on her. "I was scarcely at the Christmas ball for any time at all. I could certainly wear the gown I wore then, or I have any number of others that will suit."

"Nonsense. One can never have too many gowns." Aunt Edwina's gaze met Fiona's in the mirror and her eyes twinkled. "Besides, it's much more fun to dress you properly than to dress myself."

"Nonsense, my lady," the Frenchwoman said staunchly. "You are a joy to dress. You have kept your figure and you do not look a day older than when we first met."

"Thank you, madame, and never fear you have not lost me as a client." Aunt Edwin laughed. "But even you must admit it has been a number of years since a fabric flattered me, or, I should say, I flattered a fabric in the way my niece does."

All three women stared in the mirror.

"She is indeed lovely, my lady." Madame DuBois nodded. "It will be a privilege to create a gown that will enhance her beauty."

"There will be a great many eligible gentlemen at this ball." Aunt Edwina and Madame DuBois exchanged meaningful glances in the mirror.

"And she is not growing younger," Madame DuBois said under her breath.

"And she is standing right here," Fiona muttered, not that anyone paid her any notice. She could be invisible, for all it mattered.

She was not the least bit used to being ignored by a dressmaker. Indeed, Fiona had been in full control of such matters since her stepmother's death. Still, it was lovely to leave every decision in Aunt Edwina's capable hands. An odd pang of regret mingled with gratitude stabbed her. In truth, it was rather nice to have a mother again.

"We only have a week." Aunt Edwina frowned. "Will that be enough time?"

Madame sniffed. "But of course."

Fiona suspected Madame could do just about anything she set her mind on if the price was right.

"This is just the beginning, you know." An eager light shone in Aunt Edwina's eye. "She has three sisters I plan to sponsor this season."

Madame chuckled in a manner that would have been considered mercenary from anyone else. "I shall look forward to it. As for this one . . ." Madame circled Fiona slowly. "I think something to reveal the curve of the shoulders." She paused and peered up at Fiona. "The freckles, are they everywhere?"

Fiona sighed. "Just my nose."

"The sun, no doubt. She should take care." Madame continued her perusal. "Pity the waist is not smaller, but a snug bodice will make it seem so and push up the bosom as well." Madame glanced at Aunt Edwina. "She has a good bosom. We must show it to advantage. Gentlemen love a generous bosom."

Aunt Edwina beamed as if she were somehow responsible for, and therefore proud of, the generous nature of Fiona's bosom.

Madame stepped back and nodded. "She will be as a princess. Heads will turn, my lady."

Aunt Edwina flashed Fiona a grin. "I do so love it when heads turn."

Madame signaled to her minions and without a sound save the swishing of the fabrics, the two women unwrapped the lengths of material from around Fiona and the young man extended his hand to help her down from the stool.

Aunt Edwina accompanied the Frenchwoman to the door and Fiona heard snatches of conversation about designs and fittings and that sort of thing. She'd never noted before the endless details of arranging for things like the commission of a new gown. She'd simply taken care of it for herself and her sisters. It was delightful not to have to do so now. She already felt more than a little like a princess.

Aunt Edwina swept back into the room. "Madame

DuBois is a genius. You will indeed be exquisite. We shall find you a suitable husband in no time."

Fiona held her breath. If her sisters had told their aunt about her predicament she would have to throttle them all, individually or as a group. "A suitable husband?"

"Yes, of course, my dear." Aunt Edwina shook her head. "Why, even Madame Dubois noted that you are not quite as young as would be preferable for a quest of this nature. You're what?" She cast her gaze over Fiona. "Six-and-twenty?"

"Five-and-twenty."

"Oh, that's much better." Aunt Edwina breathed a sigh of relief. "There is something about five-and-twenty instead of six-and-twenty that does not sound nearly so . . . so . . ."

"Old?" Fiona raised a brow.

Aunt Edwina laughed. "I was going to say distressing. Not that you are distressed of course. I think you are carrying on bravely and I'm very proud." She took Fiona's hand and led her to a settee. "Come, my dear, and sit with me for a bit. We have not had the chance for a good chat since your arrival."

Aunt Edwina settled herself on the settee and patted the place beside her. "I blame myself for all of this, you know."

Fiona sat down and studied her aunt cautiously. "Blame yourself for all of what?"

"For your unwed state, of course." She heaved a remorseful sigh. "When your stepmother died, I should have insisted Alfred send you and your sisters back here to live with me instead of dragging you all off to Italy."

Fiona shook her head. "We never would have left Father."

"Then I should have persuaded him to seek a way for you all to return. If you had been here these last years, you would have had a proper London season and would no doubt be happily wed by now with children of your own. No, I shirked my responsibility to my husband's only sister, your poor dear mother, to see to your well-being, and I shall not shirk it any longer.

"But it's not at all too late. With your looks you shall most certainly be considered a prize, especially given your inheritance. I have not asked, but I assume it is sizable." She drew her brows together in concern. "Although Oliver did mention that he was consulting his solicitor about details of your father's will. There isn't a problem, is there?"

"No," Fiona said weakly. Other than not receiving her inheritance or her sisters' dowries until she wed, and an unknown American no doubt on his way to claim her as his bride this very moment, coupled with writing a book of an erotic nature with the man who had rejected her proposal of marriage, there was no problem at all. "None whatsoever."

"Good. Fiona . . ." A troubled expression crossed her aunt's face. "May I ask you something of a rather personal nature?"

Fiona braced herself. "Certainly, what is it?"

"You're not one of those women who . . . well, I'm not quite sure how to say it." Aunt Edwina's brow furrowed. "Who prefer never to marry, are you? A reformer? A suffragist? Not that I don't feel there is a great deal that needs reforming in this world. And between us, I think it's a travesty that half of the population of this country has no say in its governance. Unfortunately, it is the way of the world in this day and age. But women have always wielded a great deal of power, albeit subtly and admittedly through their influence on men, primarily husbands.

"I can't say that I understand if indeed you are a . . . a free thinker." Aunt Edwina squared her shoulders. "But you shall certainly still have my affection if for, whatever reason, you don't wish to marry—"

"Oh, but I do wish to marry." Fiona laughed with relief. She'd had no idea what her aunt was going to ask, but Fiona's beliefs as to the rights of women and any desire she might have to solve the ills of the world were not high on the list of possibilities.

"Thank goodness." Aunt Edwina studied her niece. "Then you are waiting for the right man? For love, perhaps?"

Fiona wrinkled her nose. "Is that silly?"

"No, darling, not at all." Aunt Edwina leaned toward her in a confidential manner. "I have noticed Lord Helmsley here a number of times of late."

"His lordship is Oliver's friend. He and I have simply discovered that we share . . ." Fiona struggled for the right word. Lust? Desire? "Common interests. Yes, that's it. Common interests. In art and literature."

"Really?" A speculative light gleamed in Aunt Edwina's eyes. "He is extremely eligible, you know. Is there a possibility—"

"I don't think so," Fiona said firmly. The last thing she needed was her aunt trying to make a match for her with Jonathon. "I suspect Lord Helmsley and I are destined to be nothing more than friends."

"It's not at all uncommon for friendship to turn to something more."

"I doubt that will be the case here. Lord Helmsley is pleasant enough, but . . ." Fiona shrugged.

"What a shame." Disappointment sounded in Aunt Edwina's voice. "Well, I suppose there is something to be said for friendship."

"One can never have too many friends," Fiona said brightly, and groaned to herself.

She hated deceiving her aunt, but it could not be helped. One simply didn't tell a woman like Aunt Edwina that Jonathon had suggested friendship as a way to keep their relationship from becoming more improper than it already was.

Friendship between them was an excellent idea if, of course, Fiona could keep from throwing herself into his arms.

Jonathon was not the only one having a difficult time keeping himself in check while concocting tales of ribald gods trying to seduce provocative nymphs. It was necessary for the proper telling of the story to use words like *ache* and *need* and *want*, and Jonathon used them far better than he gave himself credit for, but she was not unaffected. Indeed, it was most difficult to remain cool and serene and an ongoing struggle for her not to let on that she was every bit as bothered as he.

She had always thought women were made of sterner stuff when it came to controlling their prurient desires than men were. Fiona had certainly never lost control, never been swept off her feet or given in to desire, although admittedly there was the distinct possibility she had never been as sorely tempted before. Certainly she had been involved in flirtations and had been kissed any number of times. On occasion, she'd even kissed back. But nothing in her experience had ever been so intense, so overwhelming as these feelings she had for Jonathon. The man truly did make her ache with a heretofore unknown longing. Jonathon wasn't the only thread stretched to the breaking point.

Still, she had a great deal more to lose than he did. Her virtue as well as her heart.

". . . and I believe Oliver mentioned she is a friend of his as well."

"What?" Fiona shook her head in confusion. "Who is a friend of whom?"

"Do pay attention, dear." Aunt Edwina cast her a chastising look. "I was saying that Lord Helmsley is apparently a friend of Lady Chester's. But then Lady Chester has a great many friends and a great many gentlemen friends. However, as she is discreet and a widow, one tends to overlook such things. Besides, she is a charming lady and really rather tragic when you think about it." Aunt Edwina shook her head in sympathy. "Poor thing. She was scarcely married a few years when her husband died, oh, at least ten years ago, now, I think.

"I can understand it, really. Her behavior, that is, not his death. She is young and lovely and has a great deal of money. One can do very much as one wishes with a great deal of money and no family encumbrances. In truth, I rather envy her the freedom she has enjoyed." Aunt Edwina grinned in a wicked manner. "I would have done precisely the same had I lost your Uncle Charles at a younger age. But I had Oliver's future to consider and therefore responsibilities that I could not ignore. Still," she mused, "I have not had a bad time of it."

"Aunt Edwina!" Fiona stared in surprise. Perhaps Aunt Edwina was the type of woman who would understand what was happening between Fiona and Jonathon after all.

"Oh, dear, I don't mean to shock you. I have not lived a life of scandal." The older woman smiled in a satisfied manner. "But I have not been entirely without amusements through the years either. However"—her smile took on an air of conspiracy—"I do think it would be best if this was never mentioned to Oliver. I should hate to shatter any illusions the dear boy might have about his mother. Besides, I think he shocks rather easily."

Fiona choked back a laugh. "No doubt."

"But enough about that. Fiona." Aunt Edwina took her niece's hands and met her gaze directly. "I want you to know how delighted I am that you and your sisters are here. This is your home now and I want you to think of it as such, for now and always."

Aunt Edwina's declaration caught at Fiona's heart. She'd meant what she'd said about she and her sisters not being poor relations, dependent on anyone's charity. Still, until she married, they were exactly that. Aunt Edwina had no idea of her situation and at once Fiona realized it wouldn't matter to her if she did. Her aunt had a kind and generous nature and Fiona had no doubt she would never treat them as anything less than members of her family.

"We are not a large family, Fiona. Oliver is the last of his line, and other than you and your sisters there are no more Fairchilds. Aside from my son, all I have is you," Aunt Edwina said simply.

Would it be so wrong to accept the home her aunt offered, if only for the sake of her sisters?

Aunt Edwina heaved an overly dramatic sigh. "I did so always wish for daughters of my own."

Fiona bit back a smile.

"It would be a pity if the only family any of us have—"

Fiona laughed. "Enough, Aunt Edwina. Of course we shall consider this our home, and we are most grateful."

"Good." Her aunt beamed. "Now we simply have to find you a good match and all will be right with the world. We needn't wait for the season for that, you know. Lady Chester's ball is the perfect place to begin and there is not nearly as much competition as there will be later in the year."

"How very . . . fortunate," Fiona said with a forced smile.

"Although the opportunities to make a good match are far more plentiful in the spring," Aunt Edwina continued without pause. "There are so many social events one scarcely has a moment to breathe. If you have not found a husband before then, with my sponsorship and your looks, I daresay we shall still have you wed before the end of the season." She patted her niece's hand in a confident manner. "You needn't worry about a thing."

"I'm not the least bit worried," Fiona lied, although in truth, barring the far-fetched success of *The Book*, she would probably be wed long before spring to Whatshisname and already living among the native savages in America.

"As for your sisters, it's selfish of me, I know, but I rather hope at least the twins don't make a match this year. I should like to think we had another season to look forward to after this one. I don't mind saying I am probably more excited by the thought of it all than they are."

Her aunt's excitement was contagious and Fiona grinned. "I'm sure we will all have a grand time."

"Indeed we will. I haven't looked this forward to spring since my own first season." Aunt Edwina heaved a sigh of pure bliss. "I tell you, Fiona, I dearly love Oliver, but it's not the same with a son during the season. Young women and their mothers are looking for suitable matches, while young men are looking for escape. Which leaves their poor mothers to smile in a weak manner and fabricate excuses about their sons not being ready to settle down or having too many responsibilities to take on that of a wife or on occasion mutter something about"—Aunt Edwina's voice lowered and she refused to meet Fiona's gaze "—the madness afflicting the male members of the family."

"Aunt Edwina!" Fiona choked back a laugh. "You didn't?"

"I might have." Aunt Edwina thought for a moment, then shrugged. "Yes, I believe I did, but in that case it was to the mother of a young woman who was far and away too fast and loose and will probably end her days in scandal. I thought it was best if she set her cap for someone else, and saying Oliver might have an inherited tendency toward insanity seemed like a brilliant idea at the moment."

Fiona laughed. "I assume this is something else I shouldn't mention to him."

"I daresay he'd like this," Aunt Edwina said wryly. "Now, then." She got to her feet. "Oliver suggested I take your sisters to the British Museum this morning and then perhaps we might pay calls on some of my friends and I daresay we will be gone most of the day. Would you care to join us?"

"Thank you, but no." Fiona stood. "I may draw today or possibly write."

"No doubt you have any number of friends in Italy who are anxious for word from you. Correspondence is endless, isn't it?" Aunt Edwina shook her head. "I am dreadful at keeping up with it." She frowned. "I should probably stay home as well, I suppose."

"Oh, but the girls would be very disappointed," Fiona said quickly, and wished she had had the sense to keep her mouth shut.

"As would I." Aunt Edwina nodded and moved toward the door. "Besides, they are Englishwomen and it is past time they learned of their heritage and what it means to be a proper Englishwoman. In addition, we shall have a most enjoyable time." She reached the door and glanced back at her niece. "And the moment we get you married"—Aunt Edwina smiled in a determined manner—"we shall have to find a wife for Oliver as well."

Fiona sat at the table in the library awaiting Jonathon's appearance and reread all they had written yesterday. It was suggestive rather than explicit, with a sort of erotic elegance. At least in her opinion. Even so—a hot blush flushed up her face—it was most definitely arousing. But would it appeal to the elite clientele Jonathon aimed for? In short, would it sell?

Fiona heard voices in the hall and braced herself for another day of pretending that she was not the least bit effected by Jonathon's words. Or the images they conjured in her mind. Or the tremulous feeling they triggered in her stomach. Or, for that matter, the heat in the room that didn't seem the least bit excessive at the start of their day but bordered on oppressive by day's end.

The door flew open and a petite blond lady sailed into the room. "Good morning, my dear."

The woman looked a few years older than Fiona, was quite a bit shorter and extremely pretty. Fiona rose to her feet, and caution edged her voice. "Good morning."

The blonde's assessing gaze swept over the younger woman. It was most discomforting. Fiona resisted the urge to shift from one foot to the other. "My, you are pretty. Why, one would never imagine you are as old as you are."

"Thank you." Fiona forced a pleasant note to her voice. "I daresay you don't look as old as you are either."

The lady's eyes widened and she stared, then abruptly burst into laugher. "Well said, Miss Fairchild." Her brows drew together. "You are the elder Miss Fairchild, aren't you? Miss Fiona Fairchild?"

"If there is a Miss Fairchild even older, she is no doubt in even more dire straits than I," Fiona said wryly. "And you are?"

"How rude of me not to have introduced myself before I began making comments of a personal nature. I tend to forget those sorts of details on occasion. I am Lady Chester." She cast Fiona a genuine smile. "But you must call me Judith."

"Judith," Fiona said slowly. So this was Jonathon's friend? "How nice to meet you."

"Is it?" Judith raised a brow. "Why?"

Because you are Jonathon's friend. "I have heard a great deal about you."

"Most of it scandalous, no doubt." Judith leaned toward her in a confidential manner. "And all of it true."

Fiona stared and in spite of herself returned Judith's smile. There was something engaging and genuine about this woman. And surprisingly candid. "All of it?"

"No, not really." Judith straightened and shrugged. "Probably about half is true and the rest is, well, jam on the toast, as it were. And rather a pity, I think, not to have earned every bit of an interesting reputation. I would have had an even better time of it than I have." She grinned in a wicked manner. "And I have had a very good time."

Fiona laughed.

"Oh, good, a sense of humor. I was afraid you might be one of those women with no appreciation of the amusing nature of the world." Judith glanced around the room and gestured gracefully at Fiona's chair. "Please, do sit down. I really don't plan to stay more than a few minutes, and in truth I am rarely up and about at such an uncivilized time of day.

Fiona grinned. "It's nearly midday."

"I know." Judith shuddered and perched on the edge of a nearby wing chair. "You probably wonder why I am here at all."

"It had crossed my mind." Fiona settled into her chair.

"I wanted to extend a personal invitation to you to attend my ball." Judith smiled brightly.

"I am most appreciative," Fiona said in a cautious manner, "although as your invitation arrived yesterday, hand-delivered by one of your servants, I believe, I'm still somewhat confused as to your appearance here now."

"Very well, then, you've caught me. I confess, I simply wished to meet you in person." Judith studied her curiously. "You have quite set Lord Helmsley on his ear, you know."

"Have I?"

Judith nodded. "The poor man even came to me for advice."

"Is that good?" Fiona held her breath.

"Very good. I have known his lordship for many years, and he is not one to ask advice about anything."

"How interesting," Fiona murmured.

Judith studied her for a long moment. "May I be completely candid, Fiona—oh, may I call you Fiona?"

"Please."

"As I said, I have known Lord Helmsley for a very long time and I consider him a dear friend. He has never failed to"—she thought for a moment—"come to my assistance when I have needed him to do so. That he feels he failed to do so with you weighs rather heavily on his conscience."

"I'm afraid I don't know what you mean," Fiona said slowly.

"You know precisely what I mean. I know about your situation in regards to your father's will." Judith shook her head in exasperation. "Lord save us all from well-intentioned men. And I know as well about Jonathon's scheme to earn the money you need to save you from an unwanted marriage."

"Lord save us all from well-intentioned men," Fiona repeated under her breath.

"My dear girl, it certainly could succeed. From what Jonathon has told me, your work is excellent and, frankly, in an endeavor of this nature, I'm not sure the words are nearly as important as the pictures."

"I fear they're too . . . artistic. I mean, they really don't show anything except for unclothed bodies."

Judith raised a brow. "And is that not enough?"

"I just don't think my drawings are . . . prurient enough. What I mean to say is that they don't show people, well"—she grimaced—"cavorting."

"Do they need to cavort?"

"I don't know." Fiona sighed. "I should trust Oliver and Jonathon—after all, this was their idea, and I daresay they have more of a sense of these things than I do—but I always thought something of this nature would have to be more, well, *more*."

Judith eyed her wryly. "But if your drawings were *more,* as you put it, then you would be rather *less* than what you are. At least in terms of how society judges such things. A properly bred young woman who draws nudes might well be courting scandal, but only the stuffiest among us would not grudgingly forgive that in the name of art. However, even art would not be an acceptable excuse for depictions of naked frolicking."

"It is all supposed to be anonymous," Fiona said quickly.

"And so it shall." She leaned forward and met Fiona's gaze firmly. "I am very good at keeping secrets. At least secrets that are meant to be kept. All of this shall go no further than you and me. Jonathon confided in me and I would not speak of it to anyone save you, as it does seem to me it is more your secret than his. That is, you have the most to lose." Judith settled back in her chair. "Or possibly the most to gain."

Fiona shook her head. "I simply want to provide for my sisters' futures."

Judith's brow rose. "Then you've given up the idea of marriage to Jonathon?"

"It seems rather pointless. He wishes to be nothing more than friends."

Judith snorted. "He wishes to be far more than friends."

"Has he said something—"

"No, nor would he. He's far too confused at the moment." Judith considered Fiona thoughtfully. "But there is a look in his eye when he speaks of you. I have never seen it before. If I were a jealous sort, I would have to rip your throat out."

"I thought you were simply friends."

"I am intensely loyal and quite possessive of my friends," she said loftily, then grinned. "And I very much hope we can be friends."

Fiona returned her smile. "I hope so too."

"One can never have enough friends in London," Judith said firmly. "Even at this time of year, when life moves at a considerably slower pace than it does as spring approaches,

London society is full of any number of pitfalls for the uninitiated."

"Pitfalls? Such as, oh, I don't know . . ." Fiona pulled her brows together. "Working with one of the most eligible bachelors in the country to write an erotic book based on your own illustrations? That kind of pitfall?"

"Actually, I was thinking more in terms of wearing an overly formal gown to a very informal occasion, but yes, I suppose your example works as well." Judith grinned. "You and I are going to be very good friends."

Fiona laughed.

"Now, then, aside from the intricacies of fashion, which I shall leave in your aunt's capable hands, there are any number of faux pas you can avoid if you are armed with the proper information."

Fiona shook her head in confusion. "The proper information?"

"You know the sort of thing," Judith said blithely. "Whose husband might be dallying with whose wife. Which lady's jewels might be fake because she has sold them to pay her gambling debts. Which gentlemen casting about for a wife with a good dowry might not be as wealthy as they appear and, better yet, which gentlemen are."

Fiona frowned. "Gossip?"

"Gossip is the lifeblood of London society. Why, we simply could not function without gossip." Judith paused. "Of course, if you think it's somehow"—she closed her eyes as if praying for strength—"*wrong,* I daresay—"

"Not at all," Fiona said quickly. "I have always thought gossip serves a . . . a useful purpose. As a method of communication."

"Exactly." Judith nodded. "No worse than the newspapers, I say."

"Simply an oral method of passing along pertinent information instead of a written means."

"And more than likely every bit as accurate."

"Or at least as interesting," Fiona added.

"More so, usually," Judith said firmly.

"Why"—Fiona bit back a grin—"one could really think of gossip as a public service."

"And as such it's our duty." Judith sprang to her feet and raised her chin in a noble manner. "Our civic duty."

Fiona followed suit. "To society. To our country."

"To our queen!"

Fiona met the other woman's gaze and they both burst into laughter.

"I daresay the queen would not share our opinion, but then"—Judith's eyes twinkled with amusement—"we shall not tell her. Now, where to begin?"

Judith sat back down and Fiona took her seat.

"Let us start with those eligible gentlemen who are expected at my ball." Judith smiled slowly. "Forewarned is forearmed, especially when it comes to matters of this sort. Jonathon is not the only prospect for a good match and it certainly cannot hurt to know precisely who else is. Besides, I suspect there is the distinct possibility of jealousy on Jonathon's part if he sees other men taking an interest in you and you in them."

"I have no intention of tricking him into marriage."

Judith huffed. "I said nothing about trickery. Simply allow the man's natural instincts to prevail."

"Still." Fiona shook her head. "Deliberately provoking jealousy scarcely seems fair."

"Fair has nothing to do with any of this." Judith raised a brow. "Do you or do you not need a suitable husband?"

"Yes, but—"

"Are you willing, then, to abandon all hope and blindly submit to marriage with the man your father chose? A man you have never so much as seen?"

"No, of course not, but—"

"Do you wish to wager your entire future on the questionable success of your book?"

"No, but—"

"Is Jonathon Effington what you want?"

"Yes," Fiona said without thinking, then sighed. "It's not at all what I had planned, but yes, he is."

"Good." Judith nodded. "Then we shall have to do whatever necessary to make certain you have him and he has you. Now that I have met you, I haven't the slightest doubt that you are indeed perfect for one another. The least I can do as his friend is to ensure his happiness." Judith cast her a satisfied smile. "And yours."

Nine

Later that afternoon, the heat in the library had risen considerably . . .

"A title," Jonathon said abruptly.

"What?" Fiona jerked her head up from her writing and stared. Her eyes were wide and she appeared very much as though she was just as effected by their writing as he was. Good.

Under other circumstances, Jonathon would never stop when a story was going well. But Summer was currently waging a heated battle to possess September and it was all he could do to keep his concentration on the simmering passions on the page and not the continued, if unacknowledged, simmering in the library.

"We need a title," he said, a vague note of relief sounding in his voice. Anything to get away from consideration of Summer's covetous gaze, and indeed *covetous* was most appropriate, upon the long, luscious limbs of September. Which only led Jonathon to speculate on the length of Fiona's limbs, just how luscious they might be and the delight to be found as they wrapped around . . . He blew a long breath. "We have not decided upon a title."

"A title." Fiona leaned back in her chair.

"We need to call it something other than"—he smiled—
"*Fiona's Book.*"

She raised a brow. "You've been calling it *Fiona's Book*?"

"It seemed appropriate. It is your fate in the balance."

A smile curved the corners of her lips. "That's really
rather nice."

"I am a nice man." He shrugged as if the pleasure she
took in his naming the book for her was of little consequence and was surprised to note her delight did indeed
matter. A great deal. "Besides, it's a beautiful name. It
means 'fair,' I believe, and it suits you."

"Does it? Fair as in somewhat average?" She frowned in
a mock-serious manner. "Or fair as in extremely pale?"

"Fair as in . . . *fair*." He huffed in exasperation.

The woman could be most annoying, and she well
knew it. An ordinary woman would be swooning at his
feet at such a compliment. Of course, an ordinary woman
wouldn't make him feel as inept as a schoolboy. And for
whatever reason, Fiona made him feel precisely that. It was
obviously due at least in part to their work. What healthy
man wouldn't be affected by spending his every waking
minute thinking of erotic phrases to accompany drawings
in which the subjects, regardless of what anyone said, could
well be described as *cavorting*, and doing so in the company
of a woman who was beautiful and amusing and intelligent? A woman who was, God help him, willing to be his
friend, even his wife, but nothing somewhere in between.

It was enough to drive a man mad.

He leaned over the table and shuffled through the pages
they'd written, all the while trying not to notice how near
he was to her. Why, with scarcely any effort at all he could
lean closer and brush his lips across hers.

And probably get his face soundly smacked for it. All that
there-shall-be-no-kissing nonsense. He grudgingly admitted it made sense. Who knew where a kiss might lead? And
one kiss with Fiona would not be nearly enough.

He found the page he wanted, pulled it aside and read,

tapping his forefinger on the paper for emphasis. *"The nymph was fair of face and form and figure."*

She stifled a smile. "Oh, that fair."

"Yes, that fair. You are extremely fair of face and form and figure. In truth, you are exceptionally lovely and any man would be lucky to have you." *Even me.* The thought came from nowhere and he pushed it aside.

"Any man?"

"Yes." He clasped his hands behind his back and resumed his pacing in an effort to put a definite end to the discussion. It was best to keep matters between them away from anything of a personal nature that did not fall under the strictest definition of friendship.

Pity, he had never wanted a friend, even Judith, quite the way he wanted Fiona. "Now, then, as for a title."

"I like *Fiona's Book*," she said with a smile.

"As do I, although it defeats the purpose of anonymity," he said in his loftiest manner.

Usually pacing like this helped him to think. Blast it all, the only thing he could think about at the moment was her. At least if he was on his feet and moving there was some distance between them.

"Then I suppose we should come up with something else." She widened her eyes in an innocent manner. "What if we title it *Jonathon's Book*?"

He cast her a vile glance and she choked back a laugh. "No, I didn't think you'd like that."

He ignored her. "As the story is in the nature of a myth or a legend, we could have either word in the title."

"*Jonathon's Myth?*"

He stopped short and glared. "Do be serious, Miss Fairchild, we have a great deal to accomplish today and the question of a title is of the utmost importance."

"Yes, of course." She studied him curiously. "Might I ask what has brought on this foul mood of yours?"

"My mood is not foul," he snapped, then grimaced. "Perhaps it is foul. My apologies." He ran his hand through his hair. "I have not slept well of late."

She tried not to grin and failed. "Of late?"

He gritted his teeth. "Since Christmas Eve."

Her grin widened. "Oh?"

"My life has been rather unsettled since then."

"*Your* life has been unsettled?"

"Indeed it has." He glared at her. "I am not at all used to it and I must say I don't like it. My life has always been rather, well, *settled*."

"Dull, you mean?"

"I most certainly do not." Indignation washed through him. "My life has never been the least bit dull. On the contrary, I have always liked my life. I like my family as well as my friends. I have never lacked for male or female companionship. I enjoy the excitement of a speculative investment as well as the writing of stories that may never be read by anyone other than myself. Moreover, for the most part, I generally know what is going to happen on any given day and I like that as well."

"And you do not consider that dull?"

"In spite of how it might sound, I have always managed to have a great deal of fun, so no, I do not consider it the least bit dull. I consider it"—he thought for a moment—"well in hand. I am in complete control of my life. The master of my own fate, as it were." He narrowed his eyes. "Or at least I was."

"And now?"

"Now I have no idea what tomorrow may bring. It is most disconcerting." He heaved a frustrated sigh. "I do not recall ever having been disconcerted in my life. It is . . ."

"Confusing?"

"Exactly."

"I see." She considered him with a sympathetic eye. "I am truly sorry to have embroiled you in my affairs. However"— she met his gaze firmly—"you did bring it on yourself. All you had to do was say, *Why, no, Miss Fairchild, regardless of your excellent qualifications, I will not marry you.* Instead, in your arrogance and belief that the entire world revolves around you, you jumped to the conclusion that I, my situation, my very life, was nothing more than a ruse perpetrated by your friends to make a fool out of you." She smiled in a pleasant manner.

He stared at her for a long moment. As much as his immediate impulse was to argue with her, he couldn't. Unfortunately, she was right and he had been, well, an ass. Not that he would admit it aloud.

"Was that an apology?" he asked.

She shrugged.

"It didn't sound especially sincere to me."

"Perhaps you weren't listening?" she said sweetly.

"Oh, I was most certainly listening. But I believe a legitimate apology would not include charges of arrogance."

"Even if true?"

He chuckled reluctantly. "Especially if true."

She laughed.

He liked the way she laughed as if for this one single moment she hadn't a care in the world. Damnation, he enjoyed being in her company. If he could just get his mind off the more delectable possibilities her company suggested. All sorts of interesting ideas that the writing of *Fiona's Book* or *Jonathon's Myth* only exacerbated. Things like *desire* and *temptation*, which naturally led to thoughts of *seduction* and *surrender*. Hers or even his, it made no difference.

Desire. Temptation. Seduction. Surrender.

She stared at him. "What?"

Good God, had he said that aloud? He groaned to himself.

"Did you say something?"

"Did I . . . yes. Yes, I believe I did indeed." He drew a deep breath. "I said desire, temptation, seduction."

Her gaze met his. "And surrender."

"And surrender." He nodded. "Yes, I certainly said surrender. Fine word, *surrender*. It means to . . . to . . . submit, you know. To yield, to capitulate."

"I know what surrender means. What I don't know is why you said it. Nor do I know why you also said desire and seduction."

"Don't forget temptation," he said weakly.

"Oh, I would never forget temptation."

"Nor would I," he muttered.

"Well?" There was a definite twinkle of amusement in her eye as if she knew full well precisely what he'd been thinking and exactly what had been, and indeed still was, on his mind. The corners of her mouth quirked upward in the vaguest hint of a smug smile.

And there it was again. That awful feeling that his life was no longer under his control. That forces that had nothing to do with him had taken it—no—had snatched it from his hands. Forces that had swirled around him since the moment Fiona Fairchild had appeared from the shadows and into the forefront of his life.

"Well . . ." It was time to take his life back. Past time. "I've been considering the merits of desire and seduction." His gaze met hers. "As well as temptation."

Caution sounded in her voice. "The merits? What do you mean, the merits?"

"I mean the benefits, the virtues, as it were. As well as the merits of surrender."

She stared up at him. "Surrender?"

"Yes. What do you think?"

She licked her lips as if her mouth were abruptly dry. He resisted the urge to grin. "I'm . . . I'm not sure."

"Although I must say seduction has a great deal of appeal as well, as does desire and temptation. But I think my preference is for surrender." He smiled pleasantly. "What do you say, Miss Fairchild? Will you agree to surrender, then?"

She stared in obvious disbelief, then rose to her feet and raised her chin. "Surrender is not a possibility, my lord, nor will it ever be. I told you once before, I—"

"Miss Fairchild." Jonathon rested his hands on the table and leaned toward her. "I think surrender will suit our purposes rather well."

She gasped. "Your purposes, perhaps, but as I think our individual intentions are completely at odds—"

"Therefore I propose *The Surrender of the Seasons* as a title for"—he straightened—"*Fiona's Book.*"

"A title?" Her eyes widened. "You were talking about a title?"

"Of course." He cast her an innocent look. "What did you think I was talking about?"

"I thought . . . well, you said . . . and . . . a title?"

He nodded and resisted the urge to laugh. "A title."

"A title, of course, yes. Exactly." She nodded with enthusiasm. "I thought you were talking about a title."

"Unless you preferred *The Seduction of the Seasons,* as you seem to have rather strong feelings about surrender."

"No." She shook her head. "Not at all. Surrender"—she winced slightly at the word—"is acceptable."

He shrugged. "Either will work, I suppose. Although, personally, I do still prefer"—he flashed her a wicked grin—"surrender."

"I'm not surprised." Her gaze locked with his and a glimmer of admiration showed in her eyes. Or perhaps it was recognition. At once he realized she played this game every bit as well as he did. "I think surrender sounds"—she lowered her voice—"perfect."

"You do?"

"Oh, absolutely." She paused. "Although desire is appropriate as well. Let me think." She tapped the end of her pen on her lower lip. "What about *Desire of the Gods*?"

"Acceptable, I suppose." His gaze followed the movement of her pen. It was extremely distracting. No doubt deliberately. "As you say, *desire* is an appropriate word. For our purposes."

"Isn't it, though?" She ran the end of the pen along her lip and his stomach twisted. Fiona's skill at flirtation was as polished as Jonathon's. How very interesting. "But perhaps even better would be . . . temptation?"

And most effective. He swallowed hard. "Temptation?"

"For our purposes, that is."

"Yes, yes, our purposes."

"*Temptation* too is an excellent word. Although upon further consideration I must admit that I agree with you." She reached forward across the table and tapped the end of her pen on his chest. "As to the merits of surrender, that is."

Enough, however, was enough. His writing might lack,

but in the fine art of flirtation he was an expert. He caught her hand. "In the title?"

She nodded. "Of course."

"As in *The Surrender of the Seasons*?"

She met his gaze directly. "Or *A Nymph's Surrender*."

"*Surrender to the Gods*."

She nodded. "*A Divine Surrender*."

"Better yet"—he took the pen from her hand and tossed it aside—"*A Fair Surrender*."

"*A Fair Surrender*?"

How far would she allow this game to go? How far would he permit it? He pulled her hand to his lips, his gaze locked on hers. "*A Very Fair Surrender*."

"My lord." She tried to pull her hand away, but he held it fast. "I think—"

"Miss Fairchild, throughout all of this you have been candid and honest with me."

"Yes?" Her voice had a breathless quality.

"I have not been similarly so with you, in regards to your proposal of marriage, that is. I should like to remedy that now." He lightly kissed the palm of her hand and she shivered beneath his touch. "I should like to be completely honest."

"You would?"

"I would indeed, and in all honesty, I must tell you . . ." His gaze drifted to her lips and back to her eyes. "A woman has never caused me to lose sleep before."

"Never?"

"Never." He shook his head. "I have been unable to think of anything except you."

"You haven't?"

"You are in my thoughts day and night."

"Oh, my," she murmured, staring in what might be disbelief or simply surprise.

"You have muddled my mind, Miss Fairchild. You have confused my senses." He kept hold of her hand and moved toward the end of the table, drawing her along with him, Fiona on one side, Jonathon on the other. "I have never been befuddled in my life until now."

"Never?"

They reached the end of the table and he stepped toward her. "Not that I can recall."

"Are you sure?" Her voice didn't so much as waver, but there was a definite touch of confusion in her eyes. Good. It was her turn to be confused. "Perhaps your memory is faulty?"

"My memory is excellent." He smiled down at her in a slow and leisurely manner.

"Well, then . . ." She squared her shoulders, stepped closer to him and looked into his eyes. "Do you intend to do something about it? Your befuddlement, that is?"

"Oh, I do, Miss Fairchild." He pulled her into his arms. "I do indeed."

"Perhaps," she said slowly and with a great deal of reluctance, "this would be the proper moment, in the interest of friendship and getting better acquainted and your well-being—"

"My well-being?"

"Our well-being, then, to ask a question."

"Unless I'm very much mistaken"—he bent and kissed the side of her neck just below her ear—"you already have."

She shuddered. "Have I?"

"You asked what I intended to do about my befuddlement." He ran his lips along the line of her jaw.

She sucked in a hard breath. "And did you answer?"

"Not entirely." His lips murmured over her skin. "But what I intend to do right now is kiss you."

"I suspected as much." Her breath was shallow. "And did you have a question for me?"

"Do you want me to kiss you?"

"I said there would be no more kissing. I don't think—oh, my, that's very nice."

"I thought so." He smiled against her neck.

"Still, it's not the wisest course." Her voice was barely more than a whisper.

"Answer my question," he fairly growled. "Do you want me to kiss y—"

"Yes." Fiona stared up at him, an odd mix of determination and desire in her eyes. "Yes, I do. I think it might well be the only way to ease this—"

"Miss Fairchild." He pulled her firmly against him. "Kissing you will not ease anything." He brushed his lips over hers. "But it will be most delightful."

He pressed his lips harder to hers. For a moment she was still. Then her body relaxed against his, an odd sort of sigh whispered through her and her mouth opened to his.

Abruptly she pulled away. "This is a dreadful mistake, you know."

"Yes, I know," he said solemnly.

She studied him as if to gauge his sincerity, then nodded. "As long as you know."

She grabbed the lapels of his coat and pulled him back to her, kissing him with an eagerness that did indeed speak of desire and temptation and seduction and surrender and . . .

He pulled away and stared at her. "Upon further thought, I might not know. Why is it a mistake? Other than the obvious impropriety."

"Because one kiss with you, Jonathon Effington"—she wrapped her arms around him and smiled—"is not nearly enough." She pulled his head to hers, and pressed her lips hard against his.

Her body molded to his and he gathered her closer against him. Her lips were soft and warm and just the nicest bit demanding. And there was a heady scent about her, that of sun and spring and all sorts of delights. He could easily lose himself in the feel of her mouth on his, the heat between his body and hers, the anticipation surging with the blood in his veins. . . .

One kiss is not nearly enough.

Not for her and definitely not for him. He had known it from the moment they'd met. One kiss was simply the beginning, a prelude, a prologue. . . .

Good Lord, what was he doing? What was he thinking? Or rather, he wasn't thinking, at least not with his head. There could be no more kisses or anything else, regardless of how tempting, unless he was prepared to do the honorable thing and marry her. And he wasn't.

He'd become far and away too involved with this woman. Why, they'd become well acquainted and one would think that alone would be enough to quell any surges of lust. But if anything, their fledgling friendship had only intensified more intimate feelings. However subtly it had happened, this woman had worked her way into his life. She dominated his thoughts, if not other parts of his body.

And it would end badly. He knew it as surely as he knew his own name. How could it end otherwise?

He might well break her heart. He had never broken a heart before and the idea was not appealing.

Or she might break his. That held no appeal either. He had seen his friends in the throes of a broken heart and it was to be avoided.

He pulled away. "Fiona, I think—"

"Did you hear that?" Her brow furrowed. "Voices in the entryway?"

"No, I didn't hear a thing." Save the thudding of his own heart. "Fiona—"

Abruptly she stepped out of his arms, turned toward the table, grabbed the pages they had written along with her drawings and stashed them all in the portfolio. She moved quickly to her seat, put them on the chair and promptly sat on them, the wide skirt of her gown providing an effective hiding place.

She folded her hands on the table and smiled up at him in a polite and formal manner as if they had not just been in each other's arms. "You were saying, my lord?"

He stared in confusion. "I was saying . . . what are you—"

Without warning the barely open door swung wide and a trio of exuberant young ladies swept into the room in a flurry of chatter and cold air from the out-of-doors. All three were much the same in appearance, although one was a few inches taller.

"We're back," the first said brightly, her hat dangling from her hand. She caught sight of Jonathon and pulled up short. "You must be Lord Helmsley."

"*The* Lord Helmsley?" the tallest said with the raise of an arched brow.

The third narrowed her eyes. "The same Lord Helmsley who agreed to marry Fiona and then thought better—"

Fiona stood. "Is Aunt Edwina with you?"

The girl who had just spoken shrugged, pulled off her bonnet and patted her hair. "She is conferring with the cook about supper."

"Good." Fiona breathed a sigh of relief, took the portfolio from the seat behind her and tossed it on the table. "My lord, I don't believe you have met my sisters."

"I have not had the pleasure," he murmured, although *pleasure* might not be the right word. Given the way they stared at him, *ordeal* might be more appropriate.

Fiona's sisters studied him as if he were a specimen under glass. A specimen they found lacking in some manner, like an insect missing a leg or a moth with a mangled wing. An ugly moth.

There was, however, nothing lacking in these three as far as he could see. They were all lovely, with dark hair and dark eyes and, as well as he could tell given they were still clad in cloaks, as fair in figure as their older sister. The two shorter girls were obviously twins, although the taller sister looked as much like the others as to give the appearance of triplets. Oliver's assessment of them was correct: These three would have no problem finding suitable husbands.

Jonathon glanced at Fiona. "Are they armed?"

Fiona laughed. "Only with their wits." She waved a hand at the girls. "My lord, I should like to present my sisters. My oldest sister, Miss Genevieve Fairchild."

The taller girl stepped forward and extended her hand. "My lord."

Jonathon took her gloved hand, raised it to his mouth and lightly brushed his lips across it. "A pleasure to meet you, Miss Fairchild."

"No doubt," she murmured, and met his gaze firmly. At once he realized Genevieve Fairchild would be as obstinate as her older sister one day if she was not already.

"And my youngest sisters, Miss Sophia Fairchild and Miss Arabella Fairchild."

One, he wasn't sure which, offered her hand. He took it and again brushed a quick kiss across it. "Miss Fairchild."

"Arabella." Arabella Fairchild smiled in a slow and surprisingly seductive manner. It was apparent that flirtation was as natural to this young woman as her next breath. Fiona would have her hands full keeping this sister from scandal. "It is indeed a pleasure to meet you at last, my lord."

He released her, turned to the remaining sister and took her hand. "Therefore you must be Sophia."

"Indeed I must, my lord." Sophia studied him curiously. "We have heard a great deal about you."

"Oh?" He slanted a quick glance at Fiona. "Good or bad?"

Sophia grinned. "Both."

"I see." He chuckled. "At least it's not all bad."

"It would be better if you had kept to your word," Genevieve said with a pleasant smile as if she were commenting on nothing more significant than the weather. She removed her hat and began pulling off her gloves. "I'm referring of course to your agreement to marry Fiona."

"Indeed it would be better." Sophia nodded. "Then she would not be forced to marry—" She glanced at her twin.

"Mr. Sinclair," Arabella said.

Jonathon glanced at Fiona. "Who?"

"Whatshisname," Fiona said.

"The American. Yes, of course." He addressed the younger girls. "Surely your sister explained to you that my agreement to marry was a—"

"Yes, yes, we know all that." Genevieve waved off his comment. "You thought she was an actress or something of that nature. A player in a farce."

"Even so, we think you should not have reneged on your promise." Arabella crossed her arms over her chest. "You quite had our hopes up, you know. Now we are all devastated, distraught—"

"And shocked as well." Sophia shook her head. "Yours

were not the actions of an honorable man. We expected much more from a friend of Cousin Oliver's and the son of a duke."

"I say, that's not fair." Indignation sounded in his voice. He glanced at Fiona. She smiled but didn't come to his defense. Obviously he would get no rescue from that quarter. Not that he needed it. He did, after all, have sisters of his own and was therefore not completely unaccustomed to the emotional outbursts of young women. He addressed the younger girls in a firm manner. "It was a misunderstanding and I freely admit, it was completely on my part. I am doing what I can to make amends."

"You mean with this book of Fiona's drawings?" Genevieve cast a skeptical glance at the portfolio on the table.

"The book that will no doubt be the downfall of us all?" Sophia asked. "The cause of a scandal of immense proportions?"

"We shall all be ruined. None of us will ever marry." Arabella shook her head mournfully. "We might as well fling ourselves off a cliff right now."

Fiona smothered a laugh.

"No one will fling anyone off anything," he snapped, and glared at Fiona. "You told them? About the book?"

"Of course I told them." She huffed. "It is their futures at risk as well as mine."

He cast a stern look at each in turn. "I do hope each of you understands the importance of secrecy."

"We understand full well exactly what is at stake." Genevieve fixed him with a cool gaze. "Do you?"

"Indeed I do. Miss Fairchild." He met Genevieve's gaze directly. "I have every confidence this endeavor will be successful and generate the funds your sister needs to provide for all of you without having to resort to a marriage she doesn't want to—" He glanced at Arabella.

"Mr. Sinclair," she murmured.

"To Mr. Sinclair or anyone else." He directed his gaze to Sophia. "Furthermore, there will be no scandal as long as each and every one of us keeps all knowledge of this venture to ourselves. And not just for the present but forever. I am arranging for all aspects of publication to remain anonymous and as long as each of us keeps this secret there will be no need for concern."

He turned to Arabella. "No one will be ruined, therefore there will be no need to fling yourself off a cliff. You shall all find suitable matches and be deliriously happy for the rest of your days." He narrowed his gaze. "And if God is just, you shall all have daughters."

Three sets of dark eyes glared at him with distrust and probably dislike. And why not? In many ways he held their fate in his hand. And this too was his own fault.

"He's not nearly as nice as she said he was," Arabella muttered.

"That's quite enough," Fiona said firmly. "Now that you have made Lord Helmsley's acquaintance, and no doubt his day as well, I'm sure you have any number of things you need to attend to elsewhere."

"Yes, of course." Genevieve nodded.

Sophia drew a deep breath and cast him a polite smile. "It was a pleasure to meet you, my lord."

"A pleasure," Arabella murmured.

The girls started toward the door, then Genevieve paused and looked back at him. "You have a great deal of confidence, my lord." Genevieve considered him thoughtfully. "I hope it is not misplaced."

"I assure you, Miss Fairchild," he said coolly, "it is not."

She cast him a last look and a moment later the sisters took their leave.

A muffled laugh sounded behind him.

He turned and eyed Fiona with annoyance. "You could have come to my defense."

Fiona shook her head. "I could have, but it would not have been nearly as much fun. Nor would it have been what you deserved. Now"—she started toward him—"where were we?"

"Where were we?" Caution edged his voice. He knew precisely where they'd been.

"I believe we were interrupted."

"We do need to get back to it." He stepped to the table in a brisk manner and opened the portfolio. "I believe we had just agreed upon a title."

She laughed. "Indeed we had, but that's not what I was referring to."

"I know what you were referring to, Miss Fairchild." He squared his shoulders and adopted a no-nonsense attitude. "However, I feel it is in your best interest that this sort of thing not happen."

"This sort of thing?" She raised a brow. "In *my* best interest?"

"In *our* best interest, then." He blew a long breath. "Miss Fairchild—Fiona—allowing our . . . our baser instincts free rein can only lead to ruin."

"Ruin?" she said thoughtfully, as if the word were new to her.

"Yes."

"My ruin?"

He scoffed. "Certainly not mine."

"I see." Her brows drew together and she considered him for a moment. "Then, as you are already ruined—"

"I would not use the term *ruined*. After all, I am a man, and therefore subject to different standards. Men cannot be ruined."

"Yes, of course. What was I thinking? As I was saying, if it is my ruin at stake, then whether or not this 'sort of thing,' as you put it, does indeed happen should be my decision and mine alone." She cast him a measuring look. "Would you agree?"

"Definitely." He nodded with relief. And what choice was there, really? The woman wanted marriage and he didn't. It would be difficult to keep his distance as long as they continued to work together, but that would have to change. He would see to it.

"Excellent." She smiled. "Then I have decided to continue where we left off."

He stared. "Where we left off?"

She advanced toward him. "I believe I was in your arms and you were kissing me or I was kissing you. No." Her brows drew together. "If I recall correctly, it was a mutual thing. And quite nicely done on both sides, I think."

"Miss Fairchild!" Shock rang in his voice.

"You don't think it was nicely done on both sides, then?"

"Yes. No!" He huffed. "Admittedly it was nicely done. In truth, *nicely* isn't at all the word I would use. Nonetheless—"

"What word would you use?" She moved closer.

He stepped back. "It scarcely matters, it shall not be repeated."

"It? You mean kissing?"

"Yes."

"Then you didn't like it?"

"Whether I liked it or not is not the point."

"But that's precisely the point. I liked it. I liked it a great deal. In fact, I have never liked it quite so much and I have never been the least bit interested in, well, *more.*" She grinned wickedly. "But I am now."

He stared. "*More?* What do you mean by *more*?"

"You know exactly what I mean by *more.*"

"You're the one who said there should be no kissing. You're the one who brought up the possibility of ruin and the breaking of hearts and that sort of thing." In spite of himself the oddest note of panic sounded in his voice. "I am now simply agreeing with you."

"I find I have changed my mind."

"But—"

"You changed your mind about marrying me and I have now changed my mind about"—she cast him a wicked look—"*more* and the dire nature of the consequences of more."

"But you were right, Miss Fairchild, and I was very, very wrong."

"In a moral sense, perhaps. Even so, I am willing to run the risk of immorality."

His eyes widened. "You don't mean that. You cannot be serious."

"Oh, but I do and I am. You are the one that I"—she thought for a moment—"*want* and I have never wanted a man before. It's not at all as I expected, although I daresay I didn't know what to expect," she said as much to herself as to him, and shook her head. Then her gaze met his. "If I cannot have you as my husband, well . . ." She studied him with a curious smile. "I am willing to have you in whatever way I can."

"Do you know what you're saying? What this would mean for the rest of your life?"

"Yes, I believe I do." She clasped her hands together in a prim manner that quite belied the impropriety of her words.

"Fiona, you have not thought this through."

"Admittedly much of it just occurred to me, but it struck like . . . like . . . inspiration. Yes, that's it. As a writer I should think you would understand inspiration."

"I understand inspiration, but this is . . . this is . . ."

"Brilliant?"

"Immoral!" Outrage sounded in his voice.

"Probably. Still, I'm not sure I care."

"How can you not care?" He was almost afraid to hear the answer.

"It's really very simple, Jonathon." She gazed at him as if he were not especially bright enough to understand basic language. "If this scheme of yours succeeds, I will have the money to provide for my sisters as well as myself. I can live an independent life and do precisely as I wish. Why, I can have *companions* if it so pleases me."

He sucked in a shocked breath. "Miss Fairchild!"

"On the other hand, if this doesn't succeed, regardless of my fallen state, I have no doubt I can find someone to marry me, perhaps even Whatshisname. Probably not whom I would prefer, but someone acceptable nonetheless." She eyed him wryly. "There is a great deal of money at stake, you know, and I am rather attractive. Money and beauty are bound to overcome details like virtue, or rather the lack thereof. Furthermore, if I am destined to a marriage of necessity, I should like to know something other than marital duty first." She beamed at him, and for once her smile didn't make him lose his senses. "Lust, as it were."

Her words struck fear into his very soul. He stared in disbelief and abruptly realized this was serious. She was serious. Up to this point, regardless of the actions he had taken to assist her, he wasn't entirely certain he had been taking her dilemma with the seriousness it had required. In truth, hadn't it been something of a lark, just as any number of other things in his life had been a lark?

Now this bright, beautiful woman, a woman who was everything he'd ever thought he'd wanted, was offering herself to him, indeed had chosen him with no stipulations or conditions attached. It was the stuff men's dreams were made of. A heaven right here on earth. Or hell.

"Well?" She studied him curiously. "You cannot tell me this is not precisely what you have wanted."

Of course he wanted her. Only a man long dead and buried wouldn't want her. He'd wanted her from the first moment they'd met and very nearly every moment since then. He should have been ecstatic at her offer. Why instead he felt something more akin to panic would bear examination at a later date. For now, he would have to protect Fiona from himself and, God help him, from her own intentions.

"I must go. Now, I . . . I . . . I have an appointment. Yes, that's it." Jonathon grabbed the portfolio and started toward the door, refusing to meet her gaze. He wasn't at all sure he could see desire simmering in her green eyes and remain steadfast. "I can finish the rest of the story myself. I have your drawings. Indeed, there's no need for us to . . . Silly, really when you think about it. Just asking for trouble," he muttered. "I have recently arranged the purchase of a town house from the man who is to marry my sister, tomorrow actually, and it will provide a quiet place to write without interruption."

"Jonathon, you're babbling." Amusement sounded in her voice.

"Don't be absurd. I never babble. I have never babbled in my life and I do not intend to start now." He headed for the door knowing full well he was indeed babbling, or something suspiciously like babbling. Nonetheless, he knew he had to leave now, at once, before the temptation presented by the willing and delectable Fiona Fairchild proved too much. Even a saint would be hard-pressed to reject what she offered, and he was no saint.

"When will you return?" she called after him.

"When the story is finished," he said, fumbling with the door handle. "And when I have spoken to the printers and arranged for lithographs to be made of your drawings and that sort of thing." Dear Lord, he had no idea what he was saying.

"Do keep in mind we probably haven't much time."

"I know. I shall do everything possible to expedite matters." He forced a businesslike note to his voice. "With luck, I should have it all well in hand sometime next week."

"I will see you before Lady Chester's ball, then?"

"Yes. Of course. Probably. I don't know." He yanked the door open wide.

"Jonathon?"

"What?" He snapped his head toward her, only then realizing she stood no more than an inch or two from him. And realized as well he was trapped with one hand on the door handle and the other gripping the portfolio.

"Jonathon." She rested her palms on his chest. Without thinking, he flattened himself against the door.

"I simply want you to know." She leaner closer, the breath of her words warm against his lips. It was all he could do not to toss caution aside, abandon restraint, drop the portfolio and ravish her right here in the doorway. "That I very much like and I think is most appropriate . . ."

"What?" He could barely croak out the word.

"*A Fair Surrender*." She brushed her lips lightly across his. He jerked back and smacked his head against the door. She winced in sympathy although he could have sworn he saw at least the hint of a stifled smile, and stepped back.

"Good." He drew a relieved breath and edged along the door. "Excellent. *A Fair Surrender* it is, then. It's perfect. For our purposes, that is. Good day, Miss Fairchild." He straightened, nodded and took his leave using every bit of self-determination he could muster not to look as if he were fleeing. Which, of course, he was.

Jonathon didn't breathe normally again until he was safely on the street and well away from irresistible women with ruin on their lovely minds. It was cold and a chill breeze caught at his coat, but he relished it. The crisp air cleared his head and helped him to think and Lord knows he had a great deal to think about. He signaled to his driver that he wished to walk and started down the street, his carriage following at a discreet distance.

Damn the woman anyway. What on earth had possessed her to make such an offer? And it wasn't even an offer as much as it was a declaration. An announcement. Why, she'd given him no choice in the matter whatsoever. She'd made her decision and that was that. It was a good thing for her that Jonathon was descended from generations of Effingtons who were made of sterner stuff than to allow a woman to sacrifice her virtue no matter how willing or eager she may be.

And what in the name of all that's holy was wrong with him? His step slowed. Fiona Fairchild's virtue was no doubt intact, but she had definitely been kissed before and had definitely kissed back. The woman was no stranger to flirtation. By God, she was five-and-twenty and as skilled at flirtation as Jonathon himself!

Fiona was beautiful and willing and a mature adult by anyone's standards. The question wasn't so much what had possessed Fiona to suggest what she had, but why Jonathon had rejected it.

And more, why the answer to that scared the hell out of him.

Fiona stared at the doorway and smiled with the sort of satisfaction that would surely send her to hell for her sins. One should never feel satisfaction at the distress of others, and Jonathon was most certainly distressed. Still—her smile widened—hell might well be worth it.

It was, she supposed, a test of sorts, although she had not intended it as such. Indeed, her intention had been seduction or even surrender. Hers or his, it scarcely mattered. No man had ever made her feel this sort of stomach-wrenching, breath-holding, sharp, aching need before. It was at once exciting and terrifying. She'd never known lust, but she knew with a certainty that came from somewhere deep inside that this feeling that gripped her was more than simple desire of the flesh. Intense and irresistible and inevitable, she wondered if it had lingered in the back of her mind, or rather her heart, since the first time she'd seen him all those years ago.

But this was decidedly different. Then he was a dashing figure on the far side of a ballroom, a charming rogue with a willing lady in his arms and of no more substance really than a figure in a romantic novel. Now she knew Jonathon Effington as a man who was amusing when he wished to be and even more when he didn't. He was intelligent and gracious, with a good heart. In spite of his refusal to honor his agreement to marry, he was an honorable man. He had indeed become her friend and she suspected she could not now live her life without him.

Surely this was love and not merely passion triggered by the brush of his hand or the warmth of his lips on hers or the dimple in his cheek and the sound of his laughter? Regardless, she did indeed want him and all that wanting him entailed. As for the consequences, well, she might not have considered them at length but she'd meant everything she'd said about the lure of money and beauty. If indeed she did have to marry simply to comply with the terms of her father's will, so be it. At least she would have known the joy of being in the arms of the man she loved first.

The man she loved. No, there really wasn't any doubt. She loved Jonathon Effington now and probably always had.

It was however, more than apparent that the ever-confident Lord Helmsley was fraught with doubt as well as confusion. Why else, then, had he fled like a frightened rabbit? He could have laughed off her offer, turned it into an amusing moment and gently but firmly declined. She was, after all, the cousin of his very good friend, reason enough to reject her advances. And surely he'd declined intimate proposals before without turning into a babbling idiot?

She laughed aloud. Jonathon was not at all the type of man to babble. That alone was an excellent indication that what he felt for her went well beyond anything he'd known before. It could be lust, she supposed, although she suspected he was no stranger to lust and probably handled it with far more skill than he'd shown today.

Whether he yet realized it or not, the feelings that held him in their grasp might well be more profound than lust, or at least not lust alone.

Fiona drew a deep breath and sent a quick prayer heavenward.

Dear Lord, let it be love.

Ten

The next day, upon the occasion of the wedding of Lady Elizabeth Langley and Sir Nicholas Collingsworth, Effington House buzzed with talk of undying love and the inevitability of fate. Discussion either most delightful or decidedly uncomfortable, depending upon one's marital status, gender, and state of confusion . . .

The intention had been that of a small affair with only family and friends present. But there was nothing small when it came to an Effington celebration. Even a hastily called wedding with immediate family in attendance, those already in London and those who would travel here by whatever means possible regardless of the winter weather, grew to rather impressive proportions given the number of aunts, uncles, cousins and their varied and assorted spouses and children. Jonathon estimated the crowd at somewhere between sixty and one hundred, too large for the wedding breakfast to be held anywhere but the ballroom. *Small*, when it came to an Effington gathering, was relative.

There was nothing the family liked better than a reason to celebrate, although most had been at the Christmas Ball just last week. Still, that was a far cry from marking the entry and acceptance of a new member of the family.

Jonathon stood off to the side of the room beside a large potted palm which provided a concealment of sorts, not a true sanctuary but enough to offer a momentary respite from the need to be charming and gracious, as was his duty as the future duke, to each and every relative in attendance, and offered as well the ability to observe the proceedings without being drawn into the fray. It was all blessedly festive even if Jonathon was not in an especially festive mood. Regardless, he was making an effort to set aside his own turmoil about virtually everything regarding men and women: lust, love, marriage, friendship. Still, those thoughts—or rather, thoughts of Fiona—lingered in his mind. It was as if the blasted woman had taken up residence there and refused to leave. It was most disconcerting.

"One would think this was your wedding, and not one in which you'd had a choice in the matter either, given the expression on your face." Thomas Effington, the Duke of Roxborough, handed his oldest child, and only son, a glass of champagne and sipped at his own. "Would you care to share what is on your mind?"

Jonathon took a grateful drink. "I fear my thoughts are not especially conducive to a celebration of this nature." His gaze strayed to his sister Lizzie, and her new husband, Jonathon's old friend, Nicholas. "But they well deserve to celebrate and I wish them every happiness."

The newly wed couple stood amid a cluster of well-wishers, each with a glass of champagne in hand, matching expressions of happiness and the occasional exchange of glances secret and intimate. They had decided upon this course, marriage and the rest of their days together, at the Christmas Ball when they had at long last resolved their differences and admitted their true feelings for one another. The sheer speed of their nuptials would cause no end of gossip, although Jonathon would wager neither Lizzie nor Nicholas nor anyone else in the family would care. In truth, this union was ten years past due and never had the joining of two people seemed so right.

"Do you believe in fate?" Jonathon said, more to himself than to his father. "Destiny? That sort of thing."

"In what context? The fate of nations?" His gaze followed his son's. "Or people?"

"It seems to me that Lizzie and Nicholas were always meant to be together. Destined for one another, as it were." Jonathon glanced at his father. "Do you think that's possible?"

"In this case"—the duke nodded—"yes, I believe it is."

"But they didn't realize it, did they? Ten years ago when Nicholas went off to America and left Lizzie to marry someone else."

"We cannot always see what is right in front of us." The elder Effington chuckled. "Especially when it comes to matters of the heart. It often takes longer than anyone would suspect to see the obvious." He paused for a moment. "Did you know when I first met your mother I was charged with the responsibility of shepherding her and two of her sisters through their first season?"

Jonathon raised a brow. "No, I didn't."

"Your sisters have probably heard the story, although I daresay it's not the kind of romantic nonsense one relates to a son." The duke scanned the room until his gaze settled on his wife. The Duchess of Roxborough wore her years well. Even to Jonathon's eyes she was still a fine figure of a woman. A smile curved his father's lips. "I wanted nothing more than to find her a suitable husband."

"Was a will involved?" Jonathon said under his breath.

"A will?" The duke shook his head. "No, I simply wished to get her off my hands and out of my life."

Jonathon looked at his father in surprise. "It wasn't love from the moment you met, then? I had always assumed, given the obvious affection between the two of you, that you knew from the very first that she was the woman for you."

"Oh, I think I did know, I simply didn't accept it. But I had no desire to marry at that point. Certainly I knew it was my duty, but I was having far too good a time of it to wish to be shackled to a wife." He glanced at his son. "I daresay you understand that."

"Somewhat." Jonathon smiled weakly.

"Marianne Shelton was everything I had ever wanted in a woman, in a wife, but I was too stubborn to acknowledge it. It took nearly losing her to bring me to my senses. And then it required a far-fetched and nearly disastrous scheme or two to bring her to hers." He grinned. "Plus one of my poems."

Jonathon winced. "You wrote her a poem? And she married you anyway?"

"Difficult to believe, I know." The duke cast his son a wry glance. "It's the sentiment that's important, my boy, much more than the execution."

"Thank God," Jonathon murmured.

"Thank God indeed." His father laughed. "So . . ." He studied his son. "Who is she?"

Jonathon started guiltily. "Who is who?"

"The woman who has put that look upon your face."

"I have no look," Jonathon said staunchly. "And there is no woman."

"It is of great joy to a father when he realizes that his son does not lie well," the duke said in a dry manner. "It means he has had little experience in doing so."

"I may be improving," Jonathon muttered, then blew a long breath. "It seems I have embroiled myself in an awkward situation. The future of a young woman is at stake."

His father's eyes narrowed. "Oh?"

"It's not as bad as it sounds," he said quickly. "Well, it is, but it's not—"

"An indiscretion?"

"No, nothing like that." *Yet*, a voice in the back of his head noted. He ignored it. "I have no idea how to describe it, Father. Suffice it to say it is a long, confusing story and it makes me look like something of an idiot, which, in truth, I was. I certainly feel like an idiot."

"I see," the duke murmured.

"Which is why I have no choice, really, but to lend her my assistance now. It's the least I can do."

"Yes, of course."

"I feel a sense of obligation, as it were. While it is not entirely my fault that she's in the position she is in, I did not help matters."

"That is a problem. And is there a solution?"

"There is always a solution," Jonathon said with a confidence he did not quite feel, and sipped his champagne. Thus far the solution was to support Fiona and her sisters financially while letting her believe she was supporting herself. It was not a perfect solution, nor was it permanent. There was, of course, a permanent solution.

His gaze again turned to his sister and her husband. "When did you decide to marry her? Mother, that is?"

"When I realized my life was not worth living without her," the duke said simply. "Marriage was a small enough price to pay to keep her by my side, and indeed, as it turned out, it was not a price at all but rather the greatest gift I have ever had. Still, I suppose doubt is inevitable when one considers a step that will change the course of one's life."

"Nicholas hasn't suffered from such doubts. He's wanted to marry Lizzie from the moment he saw her again."

"Ah, but Nicholas lost her once and obviously learned from that loss. Which means he is probably wiser than the rest of us. Few people have the opportunity for a second chance and even fewer are smart enough to grab it. That these two have found one another again speaks of a bond between them that may well last for the rest of their days." He paused. "Which brings us back to fate. And love."

"How did he know?" Jonathon huffed in frustration. "How did you know?"

"I wish I could answer that, but I can't. I have no idea. I only know one minute I was trying to get rid of her and the next I was doing everything in my power to keep her." The duke considered his son for a long moment. "If you care for this woman—"

"In truth, I don't know how I feel." Jonathon shook his

head. "She's amusing and clever and has a great deal of talent and I enjoy her company. More than I expected. But I find her most confusing. Or at least I am most confused when in her presence. It is as though my life is no longer under my direction when I am with her. And I don't like it one bit."

"How do you feel when you are not with her?"

"Confused as well. She is like a melody I cannot get out of my head." Jonathon thought for a moment. "She's lovely, Father, and I do feel a great deal of desire for her. But . . ." He shook his head. "There's more to it than that. I don't know how to explain it."

"Love, perhaps?"

"No," Jonathon said without thinking. "Or rather, I don't know. I don't believe I've ever been in love, so I'm not sure I would recognize it if I saw it." His gaze met his father's. "I could certainly use some advice."

"From someone older and more experienced and full of sage words of wisdom that will guide you through this dilemma?"

"Yes?"

"That would be your mother," the duke said wryly. "At least on this topic."

Jonathon groaned. "I could never talk to Mother about this. If she even suspected I was confused about my feelings for a woman, she'd declare it love, plan a wedding far grander than this one and have me married before I could so much as take a breath."

His father chuckled. "Indeed she would."

"Father, I am serious. I don't know what to do."

"Very well, for what it's worth my advice is to do nothing at the moment. Continue the course you're on with this woman. Either you will realize, as I did, that you cannot live without her and then your path will be clear, or you will discover whatever it is that you've felt has passed."

Jonathon grimaced. "That's not very sage."

"I told you your mother would be better at this. However, if you insist . . ." The duke paused to pull his thoughts together. "All I really know is that lust will get you into all sorts of trouble in this world. But love, love will kill you. Still . . ." His gaze once again turned to his wife, he smiled in a most satisfied manner and raised his glass in a toast. "It's a magnificent end and a glorious way to go."

Hours later, after a lengthy day in which his presence was required far longer than he'd wished, Jonathon at last took his leave and now wandered through his new home. He had arranged to purchase the overly furnished town house from Nicholas, who had owned it for less than two months. Nicholas had bought it only because it was located next door to Lizzie's house. Its purchase was part of his strategy to work his way back into her affections. Now that they were wed, they saw no need to keep both establishments. They planned to sell Lizzie's and acquire an entirely different house that did not carry the ghosts of the past along with it. Jonathon was toying with the idea of buying Lizzie's house as well, simply for the purposes of investment. The properties were in an excellent location.

Of course, it wasn't as if Jonathon did not already have a house of his own, even if he had been residing of late at Effington House. But his residence was still under repair and had been for months, thanks to an untimely accident this past summer, a fire, the origin of which was still unclear.

The house had been in the possession of Cavendish while Jonathon was at the Effington estate in the country. Jonathon still did not know the exact details, only that it involved Cavendish and an actress. The mention of a parrot was made as well, although at that point in his friend's explanation Jonathon had decided he preferred not to hear anything more. It was enough that Cavendish was funding the repairs, as slow as they were, and Jonathon had learned a valuable lesson about loaning his home to anyone whose own house was under repair because of an incident of flooding, the details of which were, again, not clear. Things seemed to happen around Cavendish, usually including a combination of women and spirits and culminating in the occasional life-threatening disaster.

Regardless of the events leading up to his purchase, Jonathon was not at all displeased. He had rather liked the place from the moment he'd stepped in the door, although *liked* might not be as appropriate a word as *fascinated*. And tonight, lit by gaslight with strange looming shadows and the odd occasional creak caused by the footstep of a servant or the settling of ancient timbers, it was even more intriguing.

Jonathon paused in the doorway of the parlor and glanced around. This room and nearly every other one in the house was quite simply stuffed with furniture and curiosities. The previous owner was a bit of an eccentric and had apparently never encountered an oddity he did not feel the need to purchase. He had sold the house and all its contents to Nicholas at an exorbitant price, which Nicholas then passed on to Jonathon without profit, given that they were to be related.

In the parlor alone there were at least two sofas and three times that many chairs, plus tables, clocks, statues and any number of items whose actual purpose was in question, with scarcely a free inch of space to be found anywhere. It was perhaps the most bizarre place Jonathon had ever seen. In spite of that or, more probably, because of it, he . . . well, he liked it.

The only empty spaces in the room were where pieces of Nicholas's antique Chinese porcelain had been placed. The extensive collection was now packed in crates and stacked in the front entry. Jonathon had told Nicholas he needn't worry about his pottery and there was no need for haste in removing it from the premises, but Nicholas had insisted on having it safely crated nonetheless. Perhaps in fear that that Cavendish might arrive for an unexpected and possibly ill-fated stay.

Jonathon chuckled at the thought and crossed the foyer, skirting around the crates, to the library, although to call it a library in the sense of a place to house books was an insult to a true library. The libraries at the Effington residences were spacious and well ordered and lined with books elegantly positioned on floor-to-ceiling shelves. This library was a den of happy chaos with stuffed heads of large animals staring from the walls. Suits of armor ready for battle were propped in the corners. Here were bronze statues, unidentified antiquities and ancient pieces of painted pottery haphazardly crammed into any available space, nearly obscuring shelves of disordered books that formed a vague background to the pandemonium that was, in this house, the library.

He stepped into the room under the crossed spears of two larger-than-life Nubian statues. He liked them as well.

A throat cleared behind him.

"Yes, Edwards?" Jonathon glanced over his shoulder at his—or rather, Nicholas's—butler.

Edwards, as well as the rest of the staff, was on loan to Jonathon until such time as they could be incorporated into Nicholas and Lizzie's new household. Jonathon was most grateful, as much of his previous staff had been hired—pirated, really—by Cavendish's mother, a most determined lady. God knows what had happened to her own servants. In his darker moments, Jonathon questioned the accidental nature of the fire.

"Do you require anything else this evening, my lord?" Edwards said.

"No, Edwards." Jonathon nodded. "You may retire if you wish."

"Thank you, my lord." A faint note of gratitude sounded in the butler's voice. It had probably been an exceptionally long day for him as well.

"Before you go, I must confess I am curious as to, well"— Jonathon gestured at the room—"all this. What do you think of it?"

"It's . . . unusual, sir."

Jonathon nodded at a hat stand fabricated from antlers. "Unusual is something of an understatement. Come, now, Edwards, what do you really think?"

"Very well, my lord." Edwards thought for a moment. "I have visited museums that did not house collections as extensive."

"As have I." Jonathon grinned. "I gather you were not employed by the previous owner of the house, then?"

"No, sir. I was hired by Sir Nicholas," Edwards said coolly. "There was no staff when he purchased the residence. The house had been maintained but unused for a number of years, as the previous owner preferred to reside in the country."

"Do you know anything about him, Edwards? The previous owner, that is. Was he a world traveler? An explorer of some sort?"

"I believe he was simply very wealthy with questionable taste, sir."

Jonathon laughed. "I like it, though. It's interesting. One could explore within the confines of this room, let alone this house, for a very long time and never see everything. It's an adventurous sort of place."

"Lady Langley's children, or rather I should say Lady Collingsworth's children, did seem to enjoy it." The tiniest hint of a smile tugged at the corners of Edwards's lips and Jonathon realized the man was not your usual sort of butler. And wondered as well if, in the best spirit of Lady Cavendish, Jonathon might not be above a bit of servant piracy himself.

"I can see why my nephews would like it. I daresay any boy worth his salt would love it here." Jonathon glanced around with satisfaction, feeling not unlike a small boy himself. "It's a place where boys can be boys."

"Boys of any age, my lord?" Edwards said mildly.

"Probably." Jonathon laughed. "You must admit, the surroundings are decidedly male in nature and appeal."

"It is my understanding that the previous owner, a Lord Halstrom, I believe, was advanced in age and widowed for many years."

"There is certainly a lack of female influence. There's not a hint of anything remotely feminine anywhere in sight." Jonathon chuckled. "This may well be the natural habitat of a man with no obligations to the sensibilities of a woman."

"Indeed," Edwards murmured. "If that is all for this evening, then, my lord?"

"Yes, of course. Good evening, Edwards."

The butler nodded and took his leave. Jonathon made his way through what was little more than a cleared pathway leading farther into the room and ending at a large desk inlaid with mother-of-pearl and intricately carved with dragons and other fanciful beasts in a Chinese style. The top of the desk was bare, in stark contrast to every other surface in the room, only because Nicholas had used this desk from which to run his considerable business interests.

Jonathon settled in the chair behind the desk. Everything here suited him in an odd sort of way, appealed to a sense of exotic adventure, perhaps, that he wasn't aware he had. This was where he would finish the writing for *Fiona's Book*—or rather *A Fair Surrender*. It shouldn't take him more than a day or two, really. He simply needed to concentrate on the task at hand without the distraction of a lingering scent of spring or brilliant green eyes or a smile that twisted his soul. Certainly here he could focus on what he needed to do without interruption. Here there would be no tempting, fiery-haired goddesses with immoral offers on their lovely lips and something he was almost afraid to name in their eyes.

No, this would be the perfect place to work, alone and with his own muse, who, in his mind, had never looked the least bit like Fiona Fairchild. Although at the moment he couldn't remember what his muse did look like, because whenever he attempted to conjure her up the only face that appeared was Fiona's. Damn the woman anyway. Best not to think of muses or goddesses or anything other than the task at hand: an erotic literary accompaniment to drawings of a suggestive, if artistic, nature. He groaned to himself. Certainly that would keep his thoughts from dwelling on Fiona only if he were long dead and buried.

He flattened his hands on the desk and drew a deep breath. Surely he could keep his baser instincts at bay. He was a man of accomplishment, after all. His success in investment ventures had not come easy, but had been achieved nonetheless. He'd been well trained in the responsibilities of his position as his father's heir and no one questioned his abilities to assume the dukedom when that time came. His writing might not have been published as of yet, but he had no intention of abandoning the effort. Determination and perseverance were part of his very nature. He could certainly finish the story once he set his mind to it.

He would begin first thing in the morning and continue to write until *A Fair Surrender* was completed. The quicker he finished, the sooner he could get a sample of the book produced to show to Fiona. Then it was simply a matter of leading her to believe subscriptions were pouring in and the book would be a great success. Within a week or two he could present her with a bank draft, an amount substantial but not so large as to trigger any suspicion on her part. That would alleviate her need to wed anyone in a hasty manner, especially Whatshisname, should he ever appear. She could take her time and eventually find a husband to her liking. It really shouldn't be difficult, given her looks and family and inheritance. The oddest twinge struck him at just how easy it might well be for Fiona to find a suitable husband and he disregarded it. In no time at all any obligation Jonathon might have to Fiona would be alleviated and she, and her sisters, would be off his hands entirely and he could go on with his life unimpeded.

I simply wished to get her off my hands and out of my life.

His father's words echoed in his head and he pushed them aside. This was entirely different. His parents had been destined for one another, fated to be together.

Jonathon and Fiona. It sounds . . . right. As if it were meant to be.

Complete and utter nonsense.

As you are not yet married, it does indeed seem like destiny or providence or something of that nature.

The height of absurdity.

Because I am perfect for you.

And what if she was? He scoffed. It scarcely mattered at the moment. He would not be forced into marriage with Fiona or anyone else because of an agreement made while under the mistaken belief that he was the victim of a hoax. Perhaps someday when he was ready to marry . . .

What if she was taken by then?

He ignored the question and ignored as well the heavy weight that settled in his stomach at the thought. He might well lose her forever, not that he truly had her to lose. The problem was he didn't know what he wanted when it came to Fiona. And until he could answer that, it was best to carry on with his plan. If nothing else, it would provide time for him to understand his own feelings. And wasn't that what both his father and Judith had advised him to do?

This house was the ideal setting in which to get on with it without the distractions that arose whenever females of any type were about. As he and Edwards had agreed, this was a distinctly masculine domicile. The place spoke of collections, of acquisitions, chosen only for their value or their curious natures or their unique appearance rather than frivolous reasons. There was nothing of an emotional nature here. It could well indeed have been a museum.

The oddest thought struck him: Was this what became of men who lived too long alone? Who did precisely what they wanted to do, when they wished to do it? Who had nothing and no one to consider save themselves and their own desires?

Men who waited until it was too late to pursue the one thing, the one person, who would make their lives complete? Men who were, in truth, too stupid or too stubborn or simply too blind to recognize the truth when they saw it? When it stepped out of the shadows and into their lives?

Would this, then, be his fate? Would he grow old sitting at this desk writing stories that no one cared to read? Would he find passion only in the collection of objects? Would his greatest enthusiasm be for accumulation of curiosities?

At once the library that a moment ago had held a promise of secret adventure seemed now cold and bereft. A promise still, perhaps, but of adventure alone, without accompaniment, companionship . . . love.

A chill tripped up his spine and he rose to his feet. Here,

in the dimly lit library in the overstuffed house, he could easily believe in fate and destiny. He could believe as well that the actions taken in the upcoming days would set the course for the rest of his days.

And he could wonder if those days would be spent alone.

Eleven

Five days later, practically an eternity if one were concerned that the object of one's affection did not return said affection, but no time at all if one were convinced, or at the very least hopeful, that the aforementioned object needed time to acknowledge his own feelings. Especially if one subscribed to the old adage about absence making the heart grow fonder and firmly refused to so much as consider the considerably older maxim that decreed out of sight, out of mind . . .

"It's rather startling, isn't it?" Fiona said, as much to herself as to Jonathon. "In a lovely sort of way, that is."

She sat at the table in the library where they had done much of their work together, paging through the preliminary version of *A Fair Surrender* that Jonathon had just presented with a flourish and a satisfied smile. "My drawings and your words."

"To see your work upon a printed page is quite unlike anything I've ever experienced." Jonathon shook his head. "It's most remarkable."

"It's quite wonderful. The book, that is."

"Not yet, but it will be. Remember, this is just a sample so that we may begin taking subscriptions. Even so, all of the twenty-eight drawings we decided—"

"Twenty-eight?" She raised a brow. "When did *we* decide to use twenty-eight drawings instead of all thirty-seven?"

"Admittedly, I decided." He shrugged apologetically. "I am sorry, but the story, as well as the production of the book itself in terms of cost and artistic arrangement, worked best with just twenty-eight of your drawings. Do understand, I selected them with an eye toward the quality of the work as well as the story and believe I made the best choices possible. Not that they were not all exceptional, of course," he added quickly.

"I see."

"I probably should have sent a note to you explaining what I was about, but, given the time constraints, and I furthermore did feel certain you would concur—"

"As indeed I do." She smiled up at him.

He frowned suspiciously. "You do?"

"I most certainly do." She nodded. "I trust your judgment implicitly in this particular endeavor. First of all, Oliver says you have a talent for making investments that prove profitable."

"Never of this nature," he said under his breath.

"Nonetheless, you still possess experience and knowledge that I do not. Besides, you are investing a great deal of your own money." She ran her fingers lightly over the book in front of her. "This is most impressive."

The book itself was larger than a normal volume, folio-sized, with a red leather cover and *A Fair Surrender* emblazoned in gilt encircled by embossed leaves and flowers and fruits, reminiscent of the various seasons of the year.

The frontispiece was a printed version of the cover, precisely the same with the exception of the title. Here, under *A Fair Surrender*, was written *A Mythical Tale of Seduction* and *by Anonymous*. The rest of the volume was arranged so that a section of prose, no more than a few lines per page, preceded a lithographic copy of a drawing.

"It must have cost a small fortune to have this produced so quickly," she murmured.

"But well worth it nonetheless," Jonathon said firmly.

She turned to the first page and read aloud. "*In those days long ago, when the world was young and man had not yet stepped a foot upon it, there lived two brothers who between them ruled the skies and the winds and the very earth itself. And still, it was not enough.*" She glanced up at him and smiled. "Oh, Jonathon, I like it. A great deal."

"Do you? Good." He chuckled in a wry manner. "I rather like it a great deal myself."

"This is your book as much as mine, you know. Which is yet another reason to trust your decisions." She rose to her feet and moved around the table. She stopped before him, a shade too close for the sake of propriety but well within reach should someone decide to kiss someone else. Fiona beamed up at him. "Beyond that, I am certain that you would never do anything that was not in my best interest."

"No," he said staunchly, "of course not. Never."

Her gaze met his and they stared at one another and she wanted nothing more than to fling herself into his embrace. Or for him to take her into his arms. What was the man waiting for?

It had been six very long days since she'd last seen him, and as much as she was confident he had a certain amount of affection for her, if not at least the beginnings of love, it had been decidedly difficult to wait for him to make an appearance and, hopefully, come to his senses. She'd never been a patient person and now that she'd realized he was the only man in the world for her it had been a daily struggle not to hire a carriage and go after him bodily. Indeed she had gone so far as to find his new address and precise directions from Oliver's house to his. That she'd managed to restrain herself was due entirely to the residue of good breeding that decreed proper ladies did not appear on a single gentleman's doorstep unaccompanied. Of course, properly bred ladies did not propose seduction, or surrender, or even marriage.

Regardless, if he had not appeared today, she had

planned to go to him. The news she'd just received demanded it.

Her gaze searched his, her voice soft and inviting. "You will rescue me after all, won't you, Jonathon?"

"I shall certainly do my best." His tone was firm, businesslike, almost impersonal, definitely reserved. Precisely as it had been from the moment he'd walked in the door. He didn't step away, but his manner put distance between them nonetheless.

Her confidence faltered. Was she wrong about his feelings? Was she reading something into his behavior that only existed because she wished it to? Her heart twisted at the thought.

"We have already received several subscriptions, merely on Sir Ephraim's recommendation to"—he paused—"*collectors* of unusual books."

"Collectors?"

"Gentlemen who have nothing better in their lives than the accumulation of objects." His voice was light, but his eyes were oddly somber. "Acquisition is a substitute, I should think, for something more important."

"For what?" She held her breath.

He stared at her for a moment, then shrugged. "I have no idea, nor does it matter. Suffice it to say, such gentlemen usually have money to squander and I suspect they will make up the bulk of our orders."

"We shall have to hope there are a great many of them, then," she said slowly. "And hope as well that they place those orders as quickly as possible."

"I daresay we shall have some funds in hand by next week." He cast her a pleasant, if impersonal, smile.

She studied him with a rising sense of panic. When she'd last seen him he'd been confused and unsure. Now he was cool and remote, not at all the Jonathon she'd come to know and to love. It was as if he had indeed reached some sort of conclusion about his life and about her place in it. And not the conclusion she'd wanted.

This was not at all as she had planned. By this point he was supposed to be taking her into his arms. Begging her forgiveness for his hesitation up to now. Vowing his undying love. Urging to her marry him. They hadn't been with one another for six days. Six full days! Time that she'd hoped would help him see what was right in front of him. Help him sort out his feelings, feelings that she'd been certain were of a lasting and permanent nature. Feelings of love!

Could he possibly have spent all this time staring at her drawings and writing about the erotic quests of Summer and Winter without coming to acknowledge his feelings for her? Or at the very least his obvious desire? Why, the man wasn't even flirting. And there was no suggestion of desire in his eye.

Something was dreadfully, dreadfully amiss. Had he decided he didn't care for her at all? Surely she would not have been wrong about what she'd seen in his eyes? Felt in his arms? The fire that had leapt between them when they'd kissed?

Of course, if she was wrong she certainly had nothing to lose.

She stepped back, squared her shoulders and drew a deep breath. "Jonathon—Lord Helmsley—might I ask you a question?"

"In the interest of furthering our friendship." The slightest hint of a smile played on his lips.

"No," she said coolly, "in the interest of clarification."

"Very well," he said cautiously.

She clasped her hands behind her back and paced the room. "Do you truly believe I will be able to raise the money I need from this book for my sister's dowries?"

"Yes," he said firmly.

"And you believe I shall have something by next week?"

"I do."

She glanced at him. "How much?"

"A considerable amount, I should think."

"How considerable?"

"I can't say for certain, but I am confident—"

"Enough to provide for all three of my sisters as well as provide independence for myself?" Her voice was as hard and businesslike as his had been, but then this was no time for subtleties.

"I am confident about the ultimate success of this venture, but I daresay—"

She stopped, folded her arms over her chest and pinned his gaze with hers. "Do you think I am of strong character, my lord?"

He snorted. "Absolutely."

"Resolute, determined?" She narrowed her eyes. "Stubborn?"

He nodded slowly. "Why do you ask?"

"Because I fear I have deceived you."

He started. "What?"

"My strength of character, determination, stubbornness and all those other qualities that are of questionable virtue in terms of how society views proper young ladies—"

"Nonsense. Why, every woman in my family has very much the same—"

"Which is all very well and good if one is an Effington with wealth and power and societal connections and not virtually alone in the world with no fortune and the fate of one's sisters in one's hands!" she snapped.

His eyes widened. "I did not mean to imply—"

"Probably not." She waved away his words in a dismissive manner. "Regardless, I do not have the resources the women in your family do. In addition, I fear my strength of character is"—she searched for the right word—"limited."

"What do you mean, limited?" Caution sounded in his voice.

"I mean, my lord, at a certain point my strength fails. In truth, while I do try not to be, I am a very weak person. I do not relish the idea of poverty for myself and I will not condemn my sisters to it."

"But the book will eventually provide—"

"Eventually is no longer a possibility!" She drew a calming breath. "I received a letter yesterday. Whatshisname—Mr. Sinclair—will arrive within the week."

"And you shall have funds from the orders of the book within the week," he said firmly.

She shook her head. "It will not be enough."

"It will be enough to give you the time to find a husband of your own choosing."

"I *found* a husband of my own choosing." Her gaze caught his and they stared at one another for a long moment.

"I will not allow you to marry a man you do not wish to wed," he said quietly.

"Why not?" She held her breath. "What possible difference could it make to you?"

"I have long been friends with your cousin and I was under the impression you and I had forged a friendship of sorts as well. I would not want to see any friend of mine marry where she did not wish to do so."

"How do you propose to prevent it?"

"I . . ." He stepped toward her and her heart leapt. Then he blew a long breath. "I shall give you the money you would receive if you married. All of it. In advance, if you will, of sales of the book."

She stared in disbelief. "You would do that?"

He nodded. "I owe you that much. I did agree to marry you, even if I thought it was . . . well . . . no need to go into that."

"No need indeed. I am quite tired of hearing about it." Anger swelled within her. "You are that eager to get me out of your life that you would pay a fortune to do so?"

"No, not at all." He shook his head. "I am not the least bit eager. I have quite enjoyed the time we have spent together. More than I can say. It's simply that I feel a certain responsibility, an obligation, as it were—"

"An obligation?" Her voice rose. "And you would pay dearly to alleviate yourself of it? To assuage your conscience? Your guilt?"

"No, no, that's not at all what I mean." He ran his hand through his hair. "I do feel a responsibility, but I don't feel at all guilty. Well, perhaps a bit, but—"

"I don't want your money, and furthermore, I don't want

you." She pointed to the door with a hand that was kept from trembling only by sheer will. "Get out!"

"Fiona—"

"At the moment, my lord, this is my home, my sanctuary, as it were, and I do not want you here." Her voice was cold and hard and it was all she could do to keep it steady. She wanted to scream or cry or both. "It would be best if you took your leave."

"Fiona." Her own anguish sounded in his voice. He stepped toward her. "I don't want this to—"

"I don't care what you want, I want you to go!" She whirled around, grabbed the book off of the table and thrust it at him. "And take this with you. I don't want to see it or you ever again!"

He took the book reluctantly, as if he weren't entirely sure what he was doing, and stared at her. "Surely you don't mean that."

"You're right. I don't." She snatched the book out of his hands and hugged it close to her. "It's my book and it shall serve as a . . . a . . ."

"A what?" His blue eyes burned with intensity. "What shall it serve as?"

"A warning." She raised her chin. "Against false hopes and raised expectations and men who make promises they do not intend to keep."

He sucked in a sharp breath as though he had just been slapped. Regret washed through her for him and for herself.

"Now, please, go."

"As you wish." He turned toward the door, then turned back as though he wished to say something more. He stared at her for a moment, then nodded and strode out the door.

No! The word screamed inside her head and she started after him. She was nearly to the door when the realization of what had just happened slammed into her and snatched her breath away.

What had she done? This wasn't supposed to end like this. It wasn't supposed to end at all. At this point they were supposed to be well on their way to living the rest of their days happily together. But she couldn't make him love her any more than she could force him to marry her. And she'd been so certain. . . .

No, she *was* certain. She couldn't be wrong about this, about him. And surely Jonathon would never let her marry the American or anyone else. Or let her walk out of his life forever.

She had no idea what to do now, but she had to do something. Perhaps she needed assistance from someone who had far more experience with men than she had. Someone who had more experience with this man in particular. It was not yet too late. Jonathon Effington was the love of her life and Fiona refused to give up on him.

And until she was Mrs. Whatshisname there was hope.

Jonathon stalked down the sidewalk, his carriage following at a discreet distance, and noted that once again he was walking through the streets after yet another tumultuous meeting with Fiona. If nothing else, the woman was certainly keeping him fit.

What on earth had just happened?

Jonathon had spent the last few days doing nothing but staring at drawings of naked people or the newly produced copies of drawings of naked people. *Her* drawings of naked people. Or writing about the desire of two randy gods to possess lovely, nubile nymphs. Or begging favors from Sir Ephraim and paying exorbitant prices to craftsmen to work endless hours to get this blasted book produced. And every moment she'd been there in the back of his mind. Even when he'd slept he'd dreamt of her.

How had it gone so horribly wrong? This was not at all what he'd planned when he'd arrived with the copy of *A Fair Surrender* under his arm. He had thought she would be delighted with the book, and indeed she had been. He had further thought she'd show her delight with an expression of affection which he would then return, which would lead in turn to all sorts of interesting developments that he had thought he was prepared and even eager for.

That it hadn't happened that way at all was entirely his fault. From the moment he'd walked into the room and she'd smiled at him and, worse, when she'd gazed up at him with those luminous green eyes of hers, claiming to trust him implicitly with his absurd plan to rescue her. And believing, truly believing, that he would do so. Never had a woman looked at him like that. As though he were indeed her knight, her savior, her love. Her fate.

Without warning, something inside of him had snapped. At once he was completely overwhelmed and did what any drowning man would do when sinking beneath the waves. Plain and simple, he panicked. He had gasped for breath. He had clutched at anything that might provide salvation and had found it in, well, there was no other word for it but retreat.

He'd become cool, remote, reserved. He'd expressed his affection for her in terms of friendship. He groaned aloud. *Friendship?* And not primarily for her but for Oliver. Worse, he'd called her an obligation, a responsibility. What a dolt he was. What an idiot. What had come over him? He never used to be so stupid. Indeed he didn't recall ever being stupid before meeting her.

It was love, that's what it was. Why, hadn't he seen behavior every bit as stupid as his in every one of his friends on occasion? Especially Cavendish. No wonder they'd questioned his passion. It took passion to behave like an idiot.

Well, he knew passion now, by God. He'd found love and it was a dreadful, unpleasant thing. It was also too late. He had at last discovered what his father had discovered before him: the one woman in the world he could not live without. Pity he hadn't realized it when they'd first met. It certainly would have saved a lot of trouble if he had agreed to marry her and then had actually done it.

Now he was going to have to convince her that he wished to marry her. That she was not an obligation. That he loved her.

It wouldn't be easy, given his behavior today. But it would be a challenge. And hadn't he told his friends challenge was one of the qualities he had wished for in a wife? Fiona was indeed the perfect woman for him. She was everything he'd ever said he'd wanted. Everything he'd ever wished for. God help him.

Or rather, God help them both.

Twelve

The next night, anyone who was anyone in London and a great number of those who aspired to be anyone but were, in truth, still not entirely of consequence, flocked to Lady Chester's Twelfth Night Ball in hopes of being seen or seeing or for the simple, yet satisfying, purpose of being able to say one was there and thus elevate one's position to that of anyone . . .

"She is not at all as I expected," Warton said under his breath, his gaze firmly fixed on Fiona on the dance floor in the arms of yet another disgustingly eager gentleman. "Norcroft, you said your cousin was fat. With freckles."

"I don't believe I said fat," Oliver murmured. "Plump, perhaps, but not fat."

"She is plump in all the right places." Cavendish too could not keep his gaze from Fiona. It was most annoying.

Jonathon gritted his teeth. Still, they were his friends, and loyal friends at that. No matter how irresistible they found Fiona, they would not act on the attraction. Unlike every other man in the room.

"Look at them. They are like wolves with the scent of

fresh meat in their nostrils." Disgust sounded in Jonathon's voice.

"Lamb," Warton said absently, then glanced at Jonathon and winced. "My apologies."

"Accepted," Jonathon muttered, and stared at Fiona and her current partner.

Not that he, or anyone else, could tear his gaze away. Fiona Fairchild was a vision tonight, even lovelier, if possible, than when he'd first seen her. She looked like the goddess he had thought she was when he'd first met her in the library at Effington House. The copper tone of her gown matched the hue of her hair and he knew, even from this distance, the color would enhance the green of her eyes. Not that he could get close enough to see her eyes. From the moment Fiona, Oliver and Lady Norcroft had stepped foot in Judith's ballroom, Fiona had been the center of attention for every male who could walk, run or stumble in her direction. One would think they had never seen a goddess before.

"So, have you thought of something? Some sort of plan?" Warton glanced at Jonathon. "Anything at all?"

"He has filled my house with roses," Oliver said wryly. "My mother was most impressed, as were the younger Miss Fairchilds. Personally, I thought a dozen would have been more than sufficient. How many did you send?"

"One dozen for every month of the year," Jonathon muttered. "It was symbolic."

"And my idea, if you recall." Cavendish grinned. "The roses, that is, not the symbolism. I don't think there's a woman alive who can resist roses. Especially not in a lavish, extravagant and obviously costly display. Women like knowing a great deal of money has been spent to please them."

"It seems somewhat desperate to me," Warton said mildly.

"I *am* desperate," Jonathon snapped, then looked at Oliver. "Did Fiona say anything to you? About the flowers or me, or anything at all?"

"With the exception of the ride here—and do keep in

mind my mother was in the carriage with us, which does tend to inhibit discussion of certain matters somewhat—I have not had the opportunity to speak with my cousin about you." Oliver tried and failed to hold back a grin. "Although my mother did think the roses were far more significant than Fiona's offhand explanation of friendship and a shared interest in literature."

"Is your mother on my side, then?" Jonathon brightened. Having the support of Fiona's aunt certainly would not hurt his efforts.

"My mother is on the side of anyone who might be a potential husband for Fiona."

Cavendish narrowed his eyes in confusion. "I thought last night you said your mother didn't know about the stipulations of her brother-in-law's will."

"She doesn't, but she is well aware that Fiona is five-and-twenty." Oliver shook his head. "That in and of itself is enough to send my mother hunting for prospective husbands. She has brought up the subject on almost a daily basis since my cousin's arrival."

"Which might serve me well," Jonathon said thoughtfully.

"I still think you need a plan," Warton said. "A course of action."

"I am open to any suggestions." Jonathon's gaze lingered on Fiona. She smiled up at her partner and his stomach clenched. He didn't like that radiant smile of hers being bestowed on anyone save him. And he didn't like this business of being in love one bit.

His friends, however, thought his distress more than a little amusing, or at least they had last night. Jonathon had told Warton and Cavendish everything, from his first meeting with Fiona at the Christmas Ball to their disastrous parting yesterday. It had been a very long night, fueled by a great deal of liquor and, as the hour had grown later, had produced all manner of suggestions and more than a few plans to win Miss Fairchild's heart. None of which seemed even remotely intelligent in the cold light of day. Although Warton had pointed out, either late last night or early this morning, that none of the far-fetched ideas the friends had come up with were even vaguely as absurd as Jonathon and Oliver's scheme to sell books of nude drawings and prose of questionable quality.

The men had agreed, however, that Fiona absolutely had to be wed and blissfully happy long before she ever learned that there were no orders for *A Fair Surrender* nor had Jonathon ever intended for there to be. Given her reaction to his offer to provide her complete inheritance, the friends were confident she would not take this deception well either. And as much as they had all sworn oaths on each and every dead ancestor that had come before them never to reveal the truth to her, each and every one present knew that it was inevitable that someday, in some manner, she would learn the truth. No matter how many precautions a man took, women always learned the truth. At least in their collective experience.

"I said it last night and I shall say it again. I think you need to do something dramatic," Cavendish said. "Proclaim your love and your wish to marry her publicly. From, I don't know, the stage of a theater, perhaps. The Adelphi would do nicely."

Jonathon grimaced. "I don't think so."

"Between acts, of course," Cavendish scoffed. "I don't mean that you should interrupt a performance. That would be absurd."

"No," Jonathon said firmly.

"Fiona might not appreciate drama of that nature," Oliver murmured as if he were actually giving Cavendish's suggestion due consideration. "Besides, you would have to get her to the theater in the first place and that would certainly depend on what the production is, if there is a current production, and we've never seen Helmsley on the stage. He might be dreadful and humiliate himself and the rest of us in the process."

"We wouldn't want that," Jonathon muttered.

"The time is not yet right for dramatics. Onstage or off." Warton shook his head. "Although it may well come to that at some point. At the moment, however"—he paused thoughtfully—"I too think a grand gesture is called for."

Cavendish raised a brow. "Grander than twelve dozen roses?"

Warton nodded. "Much."

"But none of you have any idea what this grand gesture should be." Jonathon blew a long breath. "I could just fling myself at her feet and beg her forgiveness."

Cavendish snorted. "That wouldn't be the least bit grand."

"Or you could try, oh, I don't know, what's the word I'm looking for?" Judith's voice sounded behind him, and he turned toward her. "Honesty?"

"Honesty is only of worth when it comes to telling the most ravishing women in the room"—Warton stepped forward and took her hand, raising it to his lips—"that she is the most ravishing woman in the room." Warton's gaze locked with Judith's.

The most intriguing smile curved the lady's lips.

Jonathon stared at his two old friends. He didn't think they knew one another as more than passing acquaintances. This, however, seemed rather more significant than a polite encounter. He traded glances with Oliver. Was there something in the air tonight?

"Other than that," Warton continued, releasing Judith's hand, "honesty should be used only as a last resort in regards to women."

Judith laughed. "You are not married, are you, my lord?"

"To my everlasting gratitude"—Warton chuckled—"no."

"Honesty with women?" Cavendish shuddered, effectively breaking the moment he was apparently oblivious of. "It has never proved worthwhile for me."

"It's always worked well for Helmsley, though." Oliver studied him curiously. "Until now, that is."

"Under current circumstances, honesty might not be the best course," Jonathon said under his breath.

Judith hooked her arm through his. "Might I steal you away from this amusing group for a few minutes?"

"Lady Chester, I'm stunned that you would suggest such

a thing." Jonathon gasped in feigned surprise, then grinned. "They are not the least bit amusing, although they do think they are."

"I'm sure they do," Judith said. Her gaze caught Warton's for a fleeting moment as if there was something between the two of them, at once unacknowledged and irresistible. She nodded at the others. "Gentlemen."

They each murmured something in return, then Judith and Jonathon took their leave to meander around the perimeter of the ballroom.

Jonathon leaned closer and spoke softly into her ear. "What was that all about?"

"What was what all about?" Judith's tone was light, but there was a distinct flush on her cheeks.

"You and Warton."

"I barely know the man," she said in a lofty manner that prohibited any further discussion. Still, Judith and Warton? What an interesting idea.

Jonathon chuckled and she slanted him a sharp glance. "The more compelling subject of the evening, my dear man, is not me but you. Well?"

"Well, what?"

"Well, what are you going to do about Miss Fairchild?"

Jonathon sighed. "Does everyone in this town know everything about everyone?"

"Not everyone, but I certainly do." She grinned. "Not at all surprising, when you consider that I have become the confidante of a certain red-haired young lady. She paid a call on me just this afternoon."

"She did? Why? How?" Jonathon stared, then shook his head. "No, I don't want to know and I don't care." He paused. "What has she said to you?"

"I couldn't possibly reveal a confidence. It would not serve either of us well in the future." Judith signaled a waiter, who immediately made his way to them with a tray of champagne-filled glasses. They each took a glass and the servant vanished as quickly as he had appeared. "However, I will say that she told me more than enough to make me realize that you have lost your mind."

He snorted. "I already knew that."

"It would be most amusing, if I weren't so fond of you myself." She studied him curiously. "Did you know you look positively miserable? You've always been annoyingly happy. I don't believe I've never seen you look miserable before."

"I've never been miserable before."

"Because you have never been in love." It was a statement more than a question.

He met Judith's gaze reluctantly. It was somewhat rude to admit to a woman whose bed you had shared, no matter how long ago, that you had never before been in love. He blew a long breath. "No, never."

"Dear Lord, Jonathon, as remarkable as it seems, you appear even more distressed now than you did a moment ago." She smiled, leaned closer and rested her free hand on his arm. "I was never in love with you either, so you needn't look so stricken. As if you fear you have broken my heart by your admission."

Relief swept through him. Still . . . "Not even a bit?"

She laughed. "A bit, perhaps. And you?"

"More than a bit." He raised her hand to his lips. "How could I fail to have fallen under your spell?"

"How indeed?" she said wryly. "Even so, we both know you are a liar, the proof being the miserable state you now find yourself in. That, my dear, is truly love."

He grimaced. "Then I certainly have not missed anything up to now."

"Jonathon." She stared at him in disbelief. "You have missed . . . everything. Every emotion, every feeling, every sensation is heightened when one is in love. There is indeed much misery and doubt and indecision and, yes, the potential to behave like a complete and utter fool. But the glories of love are just as pronounced and extreme. For one thing, there is the rather remarkable way you feel inside." Her hand fluttered to her throat and she absently toyed with a pendant hanging from a chain around her neck. "As if part of you was always missing although you had no idea, and now, for the first time, you are whole." She stared unseeing at something very far away, something only she could see, and Jonathon wondered if she was still talking to him, or to herself. "It's the closest thing to pure joy one can know in this world." Her gaze met his. "That's what you have missed."

He stared at her, not entirely sure what to say in response.

"And furthermore, should I ever be so lucky as to feel as miserable again as you do right now, I shall thank God for that wretched state." She drew a deep breath, her composure at once restored, and smiled pleasantly. "Does that describe what you're feeling at all?"

"Better than I can say." He shook his head. "I could not put it into words as well myself."

"Perhaps you could put it better on paper? You are a writer, after all."

"I did, somewhat, in the story I wrote to match Fiona's drawings. I didn't intend it, but I can see my feelings in the words nonetheless. It may well be the best thing I have ever written. I was . . . inspired." He cast her a helpless glance. "What do I do now, Judith?"

"You are asking for advice?" She raised a brow. "Again?"

"You were not a great deal of help the last time."

"No?" Judith glanced at Fiona still dancing in the arms of another man and considered her thoughtfully. "I believe I told you to become friends, did I not? To ascertain your feelings toward her?"

Jonathon's gaze followed Judith's. "As I said. Your advice was not a great deal of help."

"Or you failed to follow it correctly."

"Admittedly a possibility," he said slowly, "although I do think we have forged a friendship of sorts."

"Friendship is an excellent beginning."

"Judith—"

"How can I resist you? You are as pathetic as a lost puppy." She heaved a resigned sigh. "And you obviously need assistance. I daresay you won't receive it from that group of friends of yours, none of which, from what I have heard, have ever been overly successful with the fairer sex.

"It's painfully apparent that you love this woman. If you

do not wish to see her marry someone else and disappear from your life forever, you shall tell her how you feel."

"It seems simple enough," he murmured.

She rolled her gaze toward the ceiling. "I doubt it shall be the least bit simple. You have acted deplorably, you know. I recommend a certain amount of groveling as well as begging her forgiveness."

He scoffed. "I shall apologize, but I shall certainly not grovel, nor shall I beg. I have never done either in my life."

"You have never needed to before now."

"That's true enough."

Fiona laughed at something her partner said and his heart twisted. Groveling, begging or whatever else was necessary was not too high a price to pay. "Well, there is no time like the present, I suppose." He handed Judith his glass and stepped toward the dance floor.

"Don't be insane. What are you thinking? Not here, and definitely not now." Judith scoffed and thrust his glass back at him. "At the moment, there are no more than a handful of us who know of Fiona's dilemma regarding her need to marry and the imminent arrival of the man her father chose for her. If you do anything to draw attention to the two of you here—and public groveling would indeed draw attention—it would spur no end of speculation as well as gossip. The truth is bound to come out, as it so often does."

"There is nothing especially scandalous about the truth. She cannot help the terms of her father's will."

"Not that truth, but what about your scheme to provide her sisters' dowries with a book of drawings of a questionable nature? Drawings produced by the young lady herself? Not to mention all the time the two of you have spent together without a respectable chaperone in sight?"

"Her drawings are art and quite respectable." Even as he said the words he knew there were a great many people who would not see them as art at all but simply, and scandalously, as drawings of naked people. "And when we worked together, the door was always open. There was never the least bit . . . that is to say . . ."

Judith raised a disbelieving brow.

"Yes, well, you may have a point," he muttered.

"Furthermore, I'm not sure you should declare yourself as of yet."

"Why not?"

Judith cast him a pitying glance. "She might not believe you."

"Surely she would...." He narrowed his gaze. "Why wouldn't she?"

"Did you or did you not use words like *responsibility* and *obligation* and even, I believe, *guilt*?"

"I might have." He did hate to admit to that particular bit of stupidity aloud.

"You cannot simply go up to her now and say: *I was wrong, Fiona, but I have come to my senses. I should have accepted your proposal at once because you are indeed the perfect woman for me.*"

"No, of course not," he murmured, although the thought had occurred to him somewhere between the discussion of grand gestures and discarding the idea of honesty. "Why not?"

"Because she might think your abrupt change of heart had nothing to do with affection and everything to do with an overly developed sense of honor. And she could decide she'd rather marry a man she's never met than one who is prompted by obligation and responsibility." She shook her head. "No, you have to start anew. You need to do now what you haven't yet done."

"And that is?" he asked cautiously.

"Court her, Jonathon, pursue her. I realize you have never done so with an eye toward marriage before, but I know full well that you do know how to charm a woman. The roses were an excellent start, by the way, if perhaps a shade excessive."

"I don't have time." He waved impatiently. "This American who expects to marry her could arrive at any minute. And then—"

"And then?"

"And then, you said it yourself, I could lose her." He

turned his gaze back to Fiona. Determination sounded in his voice. "And I will not allow that."

"So you need to claim her before he does? As if she were a new land to conquer? Plant your flag and all that?"

"Rather crudely put, Judith, but yes."

She studied him for a moment, then sighed. "You don't need a great deal of time to win her heart."

The music drew to a close and he watched Fiona's partner escort her off the floor. "Are you telling me she cares for me as well?"

"I would never reveal a confidence." Judith huffed. "However, I see no harm in telling you she too asked for my advice."

"And?"

"And I told her she should do what any woman in her position should do. She should be delightful and flirtatious and do her best to charm every man in sight. With one exception." Judith cast him a dazzling smile. "You."

Fiona absolutely refused to look in Jonathon's direction, at least when he might be looking back, or rather scowling back, although she was certainly aware of where he was and where he had been from the moment she'd arrived. No, to meet his gaze was to acknowledge his presence, and she had no intention of doing so. Beyond that, she was afraid he would see her feelings in her eyes, and that would not do. She was still more than a little furious with him. Besides, Judith had told her the best things for Jonathon were for him not to know exactly how Fiona felt about him and as well for him to see how desirable other men found her. Indeed, although the word *jealous* was not actually used, Judith's implication had been clear.

And Fiona was taking her advice to heart. She had never found flirtation the least bit difficult—indeed, she was something of an expert at it. It was as natural to her as her next breath. Besides, she was having a great deal of fun. She hadn't been to a ball like this one since before her father's death. Oh, certainly she had gone to the Effington Christmas ball, but only for the purpose of meeting Jonathon, and she had scarcely stayed any time at all.

Now she found herself whirling about the dance floor in the arms of one attentive gentleman after another. And even those who were not especially skilled at dancing were still more than adequate. She'd missed dancing more than she'd realized. Missed the joyous sense of freedom to be found in the music swirling about her and a sensation she suspected was very much like flying. She cast her current partner a dazzling smile and he grinned back at her with what could only be called hope.

She liked that as well.

Aunt Edwina was doing her best to introduce her niece to every eligible man present. In those moments when Fiona was between dances, there was no lack of gentlemen eager to fetch her refreshment or engage her in conversation of a frivolous nature. It had been far too long for that too. Conversation that had no other purpose than to tease and charm and provoke laughter. That was not the least bit significant and did not dwell on stipulations of wills or the prospect of poverty or responsibilities of any kind whatsoever.

Best of all, Jonathon Effington was aware of every dance, every glance, every smile, every laugh. It was apparent from the glower on his face that he didn't like it every bit as much as she did. Why, the man looked more than a little miserable. Good.

The music ended and her partner, a dashing fair-haired gentleman, offered his arm and escorted her off the floor. Out of the corner of her eye she noted Jonathon speaking with Judith.

"Miss Fairchild," her escort said, "before we reach your aunt and your throng of admirers, might I ask you a somewhat forward question?"

Fiona gazed up at him, fluttered her lashes and wished she could remember his name. Lord . . . Something? "I daresay it depends on the question."

He laughed. "I would very much like to ask your aunt for permission to call on you."

"Would you?" Delight bubbled through her. Lord Something's request was the sixth she'd received thus far, and the evening was not yet over. "I suspect my aunt would very much like that."

"But would you?"

"Oh, I couldn't possibly tell you." She shook her head in a chiding manner. "It would go straight to your head and I would hate to be responsible for such a thing."

Lord Something grinned down at her. "You, Miss Fairchild, are a delight."

"And you, my lord, should know such compliments will go straight to *my* head."

He laughed again. He really was charming and very nice, and under other circumstances Fiona would look forward to furthering their acquaintance. If she were still hunting for a husband he might well be toward the top of her list.

But she'd done a great deal of thinking since she'd told Jonathon she never wanted to see him again. He was the man she intended to marry and if he didn't want her, well, she saw no reason not to comply with her father's will and marry the American. If she were to be trapped in a loveless marriage, she might as well be a dutiful daughter in the process.

Fiona and Lord Something joined Aunt Edwina, who looked as if she were about to burst with the excitement of Fiona's successes. His lordship kissed Fiona's hand, gazed into her eyes, then took his leave. A momentary twinge of regret stabbed her that she might have misled him into believing she was available. Although she was, in truth, very much available. If one discounted the American, of course, and the fact that her heart was otherwise engaged.

Aunt Edwina leaned close and spoke low into her ear. "You are quite the belle of the ball, my dear. Why, nearly every eligible man of consequence here this evening has his eye on you." Her gaze slipped past Fiona and her smile took on a vaguely speculative quality. "No, I was wrong. There is no *nearly* about it."

She straightened and her smile widened. "Good evening, Lord Helmsley. What a pleasure to see you again."

Fiona braced herself and turned toward him.

"Good evening, Lady Norcroft." Jonathon took Aunt Edwina's hand and raised it to his lips. "You are looking exceptionally lovely this evening."

"Indeed I am, aren't I?" Aunt Edwina laughed.

"There is no one lovelier." Jonathon returned her grin.

A teasing light showed in Aunt Edwina's eye. "Except, perhaps, my niece."

"As she obviously favors you, of course." He turned toward Fiona. "How pleasant to see you again, Miss Fairchild." He took Fiona's hand and brushed his lips across it.

Fiona adopted a noncommittal smile, as if his very touch weren't enough to make her heart flutter or her knees weak.

"I must confess, my lord, I am pleased to see you here this evening." Aunt Edwina lowered her voice in a confidential manner. "I wish to speak to you about my niece."

"You do?" Jonathon said cautiously, his gaze flicked briefly to Fiona, then back to her aunt.

Surely Aunt Edwina could not possibly know anything about Jonathon and Fiona or, good Lord, the book? Fiona's smile tightened. "You do?"

"Indeed I do." Aunt Edwina met Jonathon's gaze firmly. "My dear Lord Helmsley, I wish to thank you for the friendship you have offered my niece since her arrival."

"I'd scarcely call it a friendship," Fiona said quickly.

Her aunt ignored her. "I know the two of you have found a mutual interest in literature."

Fiona released a breath she didn't know she'd held.

"Ah, yes, literature." His expression cleared. "We have indeed discovered that we have quite a bit in common when it comes to discussion of literature, particularly in regards to the classical writings of the ancient Greeks. Those works written by Homer, Sophocles, Euripides and others. She is extremely well versed."

"Really." Aunt Edwina's eyes widened. "Euripides? Fiona, I had no idea."

"I had excellent tutors," Fiona murmured.

"She is especially fond of Greek myths, legends and the

like. Specifically those that explain the workings of nature."
Jonathon smiled pleasantly. "In that respect I have found
we have a great deal in common."

"I must confess I have always been rather fond of myths
myself," Aunt Edwina said thoughtfully. "All those powerful gods chasing after young, nubile—"

"Aunt Edwina!" Fiona stared at the older woman.

Jonathon choked back a laugh.

"Come, now, Fiona, there's no need for embarrassment.
We're speaking of stories told hundreds of years ago, and
therefore they have the respectable veneer of age." Aunt
Edwina scoffed. "After all, it's not as if they were written
yesterday."

"Absolutely," Jonathon said smoothly. "Why, that would
place them in the category of—"

"Highly improper and not at all the topic of appropriate
discussion." A firm note sounded in her aunt's voice.

Fiona winced to herself.

"Quite." Jonathon's tone was somber, but a nasty glint of
amusement shone in his eye. He turned to Fiona. "Might I
have the honor of the next dance, Miss Fairchild?"

"Oh, I am sorry, but I believe my next dance is already
promised." Fiona forced a pleasant note to her voice.

"And yet"—Jonathon glanced around, disregarding a circle of admirers no more than a few feet away—"I see no one
here."

"Dance with the young man, Fiona," Aunt Edwina said
in a no-nonsense manner. "I shall be more than happy to
occupy the rest of these charming gentlemen until you return."

"You have my undying gratitude, Lady Norcroft." Jonathon flashed her aunt a smile complete with disarming
dimple and Aunt Edwina flushed in a most becoming manner. "Miss Fairchild." Jonathon offered his arm and there
was nothing she could do but allow him to escort her on to
the floor.

She plastered a smile onto her face and lowered her voice.
"You are incredibly high-handed tonight, Lord . . ." She

narrowed her eyes as if trying to place him. "Helmsley is it?"

He chuckled, took her right hand in his left, and placed his right hand gently but firmly just above the small of her back. There was nothing even remotely untoward about where his hands were or the distance between them. Even so, a delightful sense of warmth and anticipation washed through her simply being in his arms. "But you may call me Whatshisname."

"*Whatshisname* is already taken," she said loftily. "As am I."

"Not yet you aren't," he murmured, and swept her into the dance.

At once the world around her was nothing more than a kaleidoscope of bright colors twirling around the floor in perfect step with the three-quarter time of the music, as if they one and all were part of a magnificent ballet of beauty and passion and light. The four corners of the dance floor itself were bounded by groupings of large palms, creating a sense of exotic places and promises far from the here and now. And for a moment it was easy to forget how angry she was with him and revel in the warmth of his body close to hers and the solid, steady feel of her hand in his and believe that he did indeed care for her as much as she cared for him.

She lost herself in the music and the magic of being in his arms and made the mistake of meeting his gaze and knew she was lost there as well.

Before she realized it, he'd danced her behind one of the clusters of potted palms. This one served as a screen, concealing an open doorway. He drew to a stop and briskly escorted her out of the ballroom.

"What are you doing?" She glared at him.

"I must speak with you." His tone brooked no protest. "Alone."

"People will notice if we go off together." She glanced over her shoulder, but the palms obscured the ballroom and everyone in it. "There will be talk. I shall be completely ruined."

"In that immense crowd no one will note your absence.

And I shall have you back before the next set." He had a firm grip on her arm and it was obviously futile to resist. He directed her down a short corridor.

She huffed. "You're no doubt taking me to Lady Chester's library. You obviously have a penchant for libraries. Or rather, for clandestine meetings in libraries."

He ignored her.

"Do you have a rendezvous with a lady in Lady Chester's library every Twelfth Night ball?"

"Don't be absurd." He pushed open a French door. "Judith has never had a Twelfth Night ball before."

"Oh, so it's just the Effington House library on Christmas Eve that's the site of an annual assignation?"

"What?" He pulled up short and stared at her. "How do you . . . Did Oliver say something to you?"

"Oliver, Lady Chester." She shrugged. "Your holiday traditions are not a well-kept secret. Besides, I took Lady Chester's place this year, remember?"

"That I will never forget," he muttered, and released her arm. "If you would prefer the library, Judith's is small but serviceable. However, I thought you would like this."

For the first time she noticed her surroundings. It was as if she had stepped into a garden, and a distinctly tropical one at that. The outer walls, from what she could see that wasn't completely obscured by greenery, were made of glass, as was the ceiling. The air was moist and there was the faint sound of water coming from somewhere. The room was softly lit with gas sconces, flagstones were laid underfoot and the stars twinkled overhead.

"Oh, my." She gazed around in amazement. "This is . . ."

"Magic." He grinned as if he were responsible. "Welcome to Judith's conservatory." He nodded at a pathway. "You should see the rest. There is a banana tree in here somewhere. I must admit I know scarcely anything about plants, but Judith does go on and on about them, so I daresay I've picked up a fact or two. Come on."

He held out his hand. She hesitated for a moment, then placed her hand in his.

He led her down the path lined with palms and ferns and

plants she didn't recognize, most blooming in a profuse manner that defied the season. "Judith had this built shortly after her husband died, long before I knew her. It's been ten years since his death and she's never talked about him. At least not to me. I've always thought she poured the affection she had for him into all this."

She glanced at him in surprise. "What a romantic notion."

"I have any number of romantic notions," he said in a dry manner. "I am a most romantic chap."

They reached an open area dominated by a tall fountain, made of white marble and simple in style yet elegant nonetheless. The water splashed from one level to the next with a joyous abandon, the drops sparkling like fine diamonds or stars freed from the night sky.

"It's lovely," she said softly. "Truly lovely." From here one could well believe one had left the bonds of earth entirely and stepped into a grotto straight from Paradise itself. "It must be enormous."

"Not really. I don't think it's much larger than a fair-sized parlor, but it does give the illusion of size. Perhaps because it's so"—he glanced around wryly—"full."

"It is indeed," she murmured. Everywhere she looked, there was something new and unique to see: huge hibiscuses in bloom, numerous varieties of orchids and she caught the distinct scent of jasmine in the air.

"Miss Fairchild. Fiona."

She pulled her attention from what appeared to be a gardenia although much larger than others she'd seen, and turned toward him. "Yes?"

He squared his shoulders. "I owe you an apology."

"For?"

"For . . ." He shrugged helplessly. "Everything."

She studied him for a long moment. Her immediate inclination was to forgive him—for everything—and throw herself into his arms. That, however, did not seem like an especially good idea. She drew a deep breath.

"Not at all, my lord, it is I who owe you an apology."

His brow furrowed. "What? Why?"

"I put you in the untenable position of taking on a . . . a responsibility you had no desire for when I asked you to marry."

"But it was entirely my fault. I should never have jumped to the conclusions that I did, and even though I thought your proposal was . . ."

She smiled encouragingly.

"Well, something that it wasn't, I should never have accepted. Even as part of a hoax"—he shook his head—"it was unforgivable of me and I am not certain my behavior since then has been substantially better."

"I see." She wandered around the fountain, unsure as to what to say or do next. Better, perhaps, at the moment, not to say anything at all. She pulled off a glove and reached forward to catch a few drops of water on her fingertips. "What do you mean by your behavior since then?"

"I mean all that I've done, everything I've said." He ran his hand through his hair in obvious frustration. "It's difficult to explain."

"Try."

"You scare me, Fiona." He blew a long breath. "I have never been scared by a woman before, and I must say it's damnably—"

"Frightening?" She bit back a smile.

"Yes," he snapped, then sighed. "I have been thinking a lot about you and I and this situation . . . indeed, I have thought of little else since yesterday, little else since the moment we met really, and—"

"As have I." She shook the water from her fingers and straightened. "Would you care to know my thoughts?"

"I'm not sure," he said slowly.

She raised a brow.

"Go on."

"Very well. To begin with, I see now I should have shared my dilemma with my aunt immediately upon my arrival rather than taking Oliver into my confidence. By this time she would have found me an acceptable match, and one as well with whom I could be happy, at least given the enthusiasm with which she has herded every eligible man in my direction tonight."

"So I've noticed," he muttered, a distinct touch of annoyance in his voice.

"It's great fun to be sought after, you know." She grinned. "I have had a wonderful time this evening."

"I've noticed that as well." No, more than a touch of annoyance. Even jealousy.

She resisted the urge to smirk with satisfaction. "However, it is too late to rectify that mistake."

"It is?" His expression brightened.

She nodded and meandered around the fountain to examine a lovely deep red blossom she could not identify. "I have no intention of asking another gentleman to marry me."

"You don't?"

She cast him a wry look. "In that, I have learned my lesson."

He circled the fountain toward her. "Then . . ."

"Furthermore, I have decided, as much of the work is already done, that we should continue with our plans regarding *A Fair Surrender*. Regardless of whatever else might happen, it's something of a pity not to finish what we've started. Beyond that, I cannot imagine you would put your money into something that would not prove profitable eventually. It would be foolish to abandon a project that might be my financial salvation, as far-fetched as we both know that is, until such time as there is no other choice."

"That would be foolish." He nodded eagerly.

"However, you do understand I do not expect that salvation to come from you." She pinned him with a firm glance. "I will not take your money."

"Of course not," he murmured, then paused. "Even if it means you shall have to marry Whatshisname?"

"Mr. Sinclair." She nodded. "Yes."

"I see." He considered her for a long moment and she held her breath. "Now may I tell you what conclusions I've reached since yesterday?"

"Please do."

He stepped closer and took her ungloved hand. A shiver ran through her at his touch. "Fiona." His gaze met hers. He raised her hand to his lips. "I should like permission to call on you."

She stared at him. "Call on me?"

"Yes. In a formal manner." He turned her hand over and kissed her palm. "As men do in my position."

"In your position?"

Something wonderful simmered in his blue eyes. "Men who are interested in more than friendship."

"Oh?" She gazed up at him. Her heart thudded in her chest.

"I wish to do this properly." He released her hand and drew her into his arms.

"This is not especially proper," she murmured, but did not pull away.

His gaze never left hers. "I want to do all those things men are supposed to do."

"You have already sent me flowers," she said weakly.

"And you have not yet thanked me." His lips met hers.

"Thank you," she whispered against his lips.

For a long moment his lips on hers were little more than a gentle caress. Then he pulled her closer and she slipped her arms around his neck. He pressed his lips harder against hers and desire far too long suppressed erupted between them.

Her mouth opened to his and his tongue met hers in a demanding, greedy manner that she met and matched with greed and demand of her own. Sheer desire surged though her and she clung to him, unable, unwilling to let him go.

He pulled her tighter against him and she reveled in the hard feel of his chest crushing hers and the thud of her heart beating against his and resented the endless layers of clothing that kept her flesh from his. And wanted nothing more than to tear the clothes from his body and hers, right here beneath the stars with only the plants and the flowers to bear witness and the scent of jasmine in the air.

It was completely scandalous and quite irresistible.

Dimly in a distance muffled by rustling plants and the

sound of trickling water, she heard the murmur of voices. A part of her mind not fogged with desire realized they would be discovered, which could lead to Jonathon being forced to marry her. And a forced marriage would not serve either of them well.

Abruptly Jonathon released her and stepped away. At once she turned toward the nearest flower and slipped her glove back on over her damp fingers, all the while studying the blossom as if she had never seen anything like it before, which, in truth, she hadn't.

"And this is a *Zygopetalon*, an orchid found in the Southern Americas," Jonathon intoned in a dull manner as if he were a scholar and learned in such matters. It was most impressive, even if she suspected he had no idea what he was talking about. "In colder regions, I believe."

"Actually," Judith's voice sounded behind them, and Fiona breathed a sigh of relief, "it grows specifically at higher altitudes in Peru, Bolivia and Brazil. This particular specimen is from Brazil." Judith moved next to Fiona and studied the flower with the obvious affection of a true collector. "It's beautiful, isn't it?" She leaned closer and whispered in Fiona's ear, "I am not alone, my dear, and I would not have come if I had known the two of you were here. But never fear, we shall weather this storm and benefit from it." Judith met her gaze and there was a distinct hint of mischief there. She turned away from the orchid and Fiona followed suit.

"Miss Fairchild," Judith said in a light manner, "I believe you know the Contessa Orsetti?"

"Signorina Fairchild!" The bosomy Italian matron beamed and held out her arms as if to engulf Fiona.

"Contessa." Fiona forced a matching smile, dutifully stepped to the older woman and took her hands. "What a delightful surprise."

"My dear, dear Fiona." The contessa jerked her close and kissed the air by one side of Fiona's face, then the other. "How grand it is to see you again. I should have called on you, but . . ." She heaved an overly dramatic sigh, her bosom rising and falling in emphasis. "One has so many responsibilities and obligations."

"One does indeed," Fiona murmured, and carefully extricated herself from the older woman's grasp.

"You look"—the contessa studied her critically—"well enough, I suppose, given this ghastly climate." She glanced at Judith. "How do you survive your dreary English weather?"

"One wonders." Judith smiled politely.

The contessa turned to Jonathon and narrowed her gaze in suspicion. "And you are?"

"Allow me to present the Marquess of Helmsley, Contessa," Judith said. "Lord Helmsley is a very old friend of mine."

"Is he?" The contessa held out her hand to Jonathon in an imperious manner.

Jonathon politely took her hand and raised it to his lips. "A pleasure to meet you, Contessa."

"Lord Helmsley was kind enough to show Miss Fairchild my orchids until I was able to escape my other guests and join her," Judith said blithely, as if her request to have an unmarried woman shown anything by a gentleman without a chaperone present were the most natural thing in the world. "Miss Fairchild is interested in my orchids and Lord Helmsley is something of an amateur botanist."

"A botanist?" The contessa studied him as if she didn't believe Judith for a second. "You do not look like a botanist."

"Looks can be deceiving," he said smoothly.

"Hmph." The contessa snorted and the faint mustache above her lip quivered. "Do tell me, then, Lord Helmsley, which is your favorite?"

"My favorite . . . orchid?" he said slowly. It was painfully apparent, at least to Fiona, that aside from *Zygopetalon*, Jonathon didn't know one orchid from another.

"Yes, yes, which do you like best?" The contessa waved impatiently. "Let us say, of those that are here."

"It's difficult to select just one," he murmured.

"Do your best." The contessa snapped her fan. "Quick, quick, which is it to be?"

"If I am forced to choose . . ." he paused as if giving it considerable thought. "I should have to say the *Columnea schiedeana*, there behind you. A native of Mexico."

Fiona stared. How on earth did he do that?

"And one of my own personal favorites." Judith flashed Jonathon a congratulatory smile, and the faintest touch of jealously stabbed Fiona. It was ridiculous, of course, Judith was lending her assistance to Fiona. Still, Jonathon and Judith were such very good friends.

"The contessa wished to see the conservatory," Judith said to Fiona. "And, as I was to meet you here, I brought her with me."

"And better yet"—the contessa reached out and squeezed one of Fiona's hands in a conspiratorial manner—"I am not alone. You will be so pleased." She turned and called to someone behind her. "Bernardo!"

Fiona groaned to herself. Not Bernardo, Count Orsetti. The last thing she wanted at this particular moment, when she and Jonathon were finally coming to an understanding of sorts, was this particular unexpected encounter. For a moment she considered the possibility of escape, but as the only exit she was aware of would take her past the contessa and her son, she rejected that. Nor did she think there was really anywhere to hide in the conservatory.

"Signorina Fairchild! Bella, bellissimo Fiona!"

Count Orsetti practically shoved his mother aside in his haste to get to Fiona, although the contessa didn't seem to mind. He strode to Fiona, grabbed her hands and lifted them to his lips, all the while murmuring in a steady stream of Italian how he had missed her and how beautiful her eyes were and how her hair looked like molten sunlight. Fiona was fairly certain Jonathon did not speak Italian, but then again she would have wagered he couldn't tell an orchid from a daisy either.

She shot him a quick glance. Jonathon might not speak the language, but it was clear from the look on his face that he understood full well what the count was saying. Judith smiled in an innocent manner, but there was a wicked gleam in her eye. At once Fiona realized that somehow Judith knew exactly what the count's reaction would be when he saw Fiona again. And knew as well exactly how Jonathon would respond.

"English, if you please, Count." Fiona favored him with a pleasant but not overly affectionate smile and firmly pulled her hands from his. "As we are in England now."

"As you wish." He smiled in a tolerant manner as if her refusal to share in the intimacy of a language they alone might speak were not a rejection but a bond between them. It was a reminder of the man's overwhelming arrogance and as irritating now as the last time she'd seen him. "I am most delighted to find you here. I had not looked forward at all to my stay in London, but when I arrived and my mother informed me she had accompanied you here"—his grin broadened with a confidence that came from truly believing that every woman in the world was waiting to swoon at his feet or fall into his bed—"I felt God Himself was smiling down upon me once again."

"And yet you made no effort to call on her," Judith murmured.

"An oversight." Orsetti shrugged. "And one that is so easily corrected."

"Indeed." The contessa nodded in eager encouragement of her son. "Bernardo should make arrangements at once to call on—"

"Forgive me, Contessa, but"—Jonathon's gaze met Fiona's— "I did promise Miss Fairchild's aunt that we would be gone only a few minutes." He held out his arm to her. "Shall we, Miss Fairchild?"

"Yes, of course," Fiona said with relief, and took his arm. She had no desire to be trapped with the count and his mother, both of whom had long ago decided she would make Bernardo an excellent wife. The mother because of Fiona's societal connections, the son because Fiona would look good on his arm. As much as she now needed a husband, she had no desire for this one.

"I would be happy to escort Signorina Fairchild back to

her aunt." Orsetti bowed in a grand manner. "It would be my great pleasure."

"Nonetheless, at the moment Miss Fairchild is my responsibility," Jonathon said pleasantly.

"How very odd you English are." Orsetti studied Jonathon curiously. "I would never consider a beautiful woman as a responsibility."

Jonathon shrugged casually. "That explains a great deal."

It was all most polite and civilized, but underneath the veneer of proper behavior there was the definite feel of something primal. Not unlike jungle beasts ready to fight over a mate. Fiona had always rather liked having men fight over her and under other circumstances it would have been most amusing, but she would prefer to keep Jonathon far away from Orsetti. He was a man who had never been able to take no for an answer regardless of how many times she had said just that and how often she had made her disinterest in him clear.

"Lord Helmsley, please do escort Miss Fairchild back to the ballroom," Judith said smoothly. "Count Orsetti has obviously forgotten that he wished for me to show him my orchids. I should be quite disappointed if he did not allow me that pleasure." Judith gazed up at Orsetti in a most provocative manner that had nothing whatsoever to do with orchids.

"As would I, Lady Chester." Orsetti grinned down at Judith, immediately distracted from the pursuit of one woman to the intrigue offered by another.

"Yes, yes." The contessa huffed. "Show us the flowers."

Fiona nudged Jonathon and lowered her voice. "Perhaps we should . . ."

"Excellent idea." Jonathon nodded and quickly walked her back the way they'd come.

They didn't say a word until they were safely in the corridor with the door to the greenhouse firmly closed behind them.

"You have an admirer in the count," Jonathon said slowly. "He is quite a handsome man."

"Indeed he is, and he well knows it." She stared at him thoughtfully. "Are you jealous, then?"

"Don't be absurd. I have never been jealous." Jonathon's brows drew together in surprise. "Good God, I believe I am jealous."

"How perfectly wonderful of you." Fiona glanced up and down the corridor and then, before he could protest, leaned close and kissed him quickly. "I can't recall the last time I've been so flattered." She took his arm and they started back to the ballroom.

He chuckled. "Surely men have had cause to be jealous before?"

"Perhaps." She met his gaze. "But it was never of any real significance, as I never particularly cared before." They reached the ballroom entry and the screen of palms and paused.

His gaze caught hers, and what he might see in her eyes scarcely mattered, given what she saw in his. "And do you care now?"

"Yes," she said simply, and knew that at that instant a promise, unspoken yet there all the same, had been made.

A slow smile spread across his face and a sense of absolute happiness blossomed within her. Like a flower never before seen. He pulled his gaze from hers, cautiously looked around the palms, then held out his arms. "Might I have the remainder of this dance, Miss Fairchild?"

"I should be delighted, my lord." She beamed at him and stepped into his arms.

"Do remind me to thank Judith for her forethought in the placement of these trees so close to the perimeter of the dance floor. It was exceptionally clever of her."

"And most convenient as well."

"I fully intend to call on you tomorrow, you know." His gaze bored into hers. "Will I have to compete with other gentlemen for your attention?"

"Perhaps." She grinned. "It will do you a world of good to have to do so."

"I doubt it. I don't like this business of jealousy one bit, although I suspect I can bear it. For now." His hand tightened on hers. "I should prefer not to encounter Orsetti, however. I don't like the man."

She widened her eyes in an innocent manner. "And is there a reason for that?"

"I can think of one very good reason."

She laughed.

"But it is the oddest thing, Fiona," he said, preparing to step back onto the dance floor. "I know I have never met the man, yet I have the distinct feeling I have seen him somewhere before."

"Probably no more than a passing resemblance to someone else," she said lightly.

"Probably."

A moment later they had rejoined the dancers as smoothly as if they had never been away. Once again, in his arms, with the music filling her senses, it was impossible to think of anything but the memory of his lips on hers and the promise of tomorrow to come.

Thirteen

Later that night, or rather early the next morning, in the hour shortly before dawn when any civilized person of a respectable nature would be long abed and fast asleep, and any person whose level of civilization, as well as respectability, would not meet the high standards set by those who prefer slumber to something of a more strenuous nature in their beds would just be arriving home. Still others might well be in their beds in an attempt to be of a virtuous nature in anticipation of not being the least bit virtuous at a future date . . .

"Bloody hell." Jonathon threw off the covers, leapt out of bed and promptly smashed his knee on something unseen. He felt blindly around for his robe, stubbed his toe and bashed his elbow on yet another invisible object.

Damn it all, this room was awkward enough to navigate when fully lit. Now, in the dark of night, it was a death trap. Edwards would no doubt find him here in the morning felled by some curiosity or objet d'art or unidentified over-sized *something*, ornately carved by native artisans living in the upper regions of the Himalayas! He could see Edwards now, staring down at Jonathon's prone body, twisted and mangled on the floor, and hear the butler murmuring how this could have been avoided had his lordship simply listened to Edwards in the first place.

The butler had encouraged him to take the bedchamber vacated by Sir Nicholas. That particular room, per Nicholas's wishes, was scarcely furnished at all, at least when compared to every other room in the house. Jonathon, however, liked living in the chaotic jungle that best described his new home. Except—he banged his hip on something sharp—at this particular moment when the appeal of an overstuffed house diminished substantially. He stumbled his way in the general direction of a dresser aided by the faint starlight that drifted in between the crack of the window drapes, and suspected he had reached his goal when he smacked into something large and solid with surprisingly painful protruding knobs.

"Damnation." He sucked in a hard breath and groped for the matches and lamp he knew were here somewhere. Something crashed to the floor beside him and he ignored it. His fingers found the matches, he struck one, located the lamp and at last had light.

Good. He was covered in bruises just from crossing this one room. He'd probably kill himself if he attempted to make his way down the stairs without light. He shrugged on the robe he hadn't been able to find a moment ago, grabbed the lamp and headed for the library.

It wasn't that he couldn't sleep. Indeed, he'd been home for several hours and had had no trouble sleeping and sleeping quite well until now. His rest was no doubt the result of finally having come to grips with his feelings for Fiona and, beyond that, finally doing something about it.

He started down the stairs and ignored the fact that he really hadn't done anything of substance. Oh, certainly he had apologized, told her he wished to call on her formally and he had definitely indicated his intentions were of a permanent nature, although he had never actually mentioned marriage. Or love. For that matter, he really hadn't said much of anything, although he had planned on doing so. Hadn't he?

Circumstances had simply interfered, that was all. After he and Fiona had returned to the ballroom, they'd had no further opportunity for private discussion. They had managed only one more dance together and, given Fiona's popularity, even that was difficult to arrange. It wasn't simply that she was in demand, but the contessa had her beady little eyes fixed firmly on Jonathon's every move. Even Lady Norcroft appeared to watch Jonathon's activities closely. It had been most annoying. Did no one trust him at all? Or did they simply not trust him with Fiona? In which case, their caution was, admittedly, somewhat justified.

Still, while he hadn't had the chance to take her in his arms again or kiss her with the thoroughness she deserved, every time their gazes met across the room something intense and special and exciting passed between them. It was a palpable sense of anticipation, of promise, and Jonathon was amazed that everyone who looked at them did not note it. Or perhaps that was precisely why Fiona's aunt and the contessa had kept a close eye on him. Certainly Oliver, Warton and Cavendish had each commented, following Jonathon's return from the conservatory, on how he no longer appeared as miserable as he had previously. Indeed, he'd seemed positively jovial.

Jonathon reached the bottom of the curved stairway and turned in the direction of the library, moving a bit more cautiously given the tendency of the clutter in the house to reach out and attack him without provocation. Perhaps he should do something about the place before he brought a wife here.

A wife? Fiona?

Odd, the idea of a wife—no—the idea of Fiona as his wife no longer filled him with fear. Well, not as much fear. Obviously there was still some apprehension otherwise he wouldn't have hesitated to pour out his feelings, declare his love, ask for her hand and all that. Of course, he was well on his way to doing just that, or something close to that, when they had been so abruptly interrupted by the contessa and her son. *Bernardo.* Jonathon snorted in disdain and pushed open the door to the library. He could see why Fiona had no interest in him.

He opened the door to the library, held the lamp high to give him as much light as possible to avoid any further collisions and made his way to the desk.

Although, upon further reflection, Fiona hadn't actually *said* she had no interest in the count. In fact, she hadn't really said much about him at all. Oh, she'd commented on his arrogance and she had seemed relieved to leave his presence, but that could well be the natural reluctance of any woman to have a new lover come face to face with an old. Not that there was any evidence that the count had ever meant anything to her, although Orsetti was certainly overly affectionate toward her. And Jonathon was not her lover. Yet. Although she had offered him the opportunity and she was five-and-twenty and well versed in the art of flirtation and incredibly desirable and not the least bit shy or hesitant about what she wanted. . . .

Blast and damnation, did she share a past with *Bernardo*?

That was the question that had yanked him from a sound sleep. That and the continuing sense that he had seen the count somewhere before. And he had a horrible suspicion that he might well know where.

Her portfolio lay on the desk. He sat down and flipped it open. Quickly he paged through the drawings, looking for those depicting naked men. He found the drawing he was seeking and stared. Shock washed through him. He got up from the desk and quickly lit every lamp in the room until the library was ablaze with light. He returned to his seat and studied the drawing for a long moment.

He was right. He'd seen that face before. As for the body, had he seen that as well? Clothed, of course, but still, given the figure's height and build . . . He cursed under his breath. Companion indeed.

And more to the point, whose companion?

Fiona straightened her shoulders, lifted the knocker on Jonathon's front door and let it fall. This was the most improper thing she had ever done. She'd never gone to a man's

house before, uninvited and unaccompanied. But Jonathon
had been about to make all sorts of lovely promises and declarations. Who knew what might have happened had they
not been so abruptly interrupted last night? And she was far
too impatient to wait until he formally called on her for that
conversation to continue. Besides, she had a legitimate purpose above and beyond simply wanting to see Jonathon here
this morning.

She shifted the brown-paper-wrapped copy of *A Fair Surrender* under her arm and tapped her foot impatiently. Legitimate or not, most people would not view her visit as anything other than scandalous, precisely why she was here at
such an early hour of the day.

It had been a late evening for all of them. Her sisters had
not yet gone to bed when she and Oliver and Aunt Edwina
had returned home, and Fiona was confident everyone in
the household was now still asleep, with the exception of
the servants. With any luck at all, her absence would not be
noticed for hours. That she had managed to slip out the
door undetected and then find a hired carriage was something of a miracle in and of itself. But waiting now for the
door to open might be the most hazardous part of this entire endeavor.

She raised her hand to knock again and the door abruptly
opened. An older gentleman with a carefully nondescript
expression, obviously a butler, stared at her coolly.

She favored him with a pleasant smile. "Good day. I wish
to see Lord Helmsley, if you please."

"Who might I say is calling, miss?" the butler said without a moment of hesitation, as if it were not uncommon for
young women to appear unannounced at Jonathon's door
in the early hours of the morning.

To appear or to depart?

She brushed the thought aside. "Miss Fairchild."

"Of course, miss." A flicker of curiosity flashed in his
eyes, but he was too well trained to show more than that.
He ushered her into the foyer and took her cloak and hat. "I
will inform his lordship of your arrival." He nodded and

vanished into the shadows on the far side of a curved staircase.

She drew a deep breath. At least it appeared Jonathon was already up and about and the butler would not have to dislodge him from a sound sleep. From his bed. The image of rousing him from his sleep, or his bed, struck her, and it seemed a pity she could not do so personally. Yet.

"If you will follow me, miss." The butler reappeared out of nowhere and she started. Heat flashed up her face, although the man couldn't possibly know what she had been thinking.

"His lordship is in the library."

"Where else?" she murmured, and trailed after the servant to a door a scant few feet from the foyer.

The butler opened the door and stood aside to let her pass. She stepped into the library and wondered if she had been brought to the right room. If perhaps the older gentleman had been confused. This didn't look the least bit like a library.

"Come in," Jonathon's voice sounded from somewhere deeper in the labyrinth of assorted statuary and towering furnishings and ornately carved items of every sort and description.

"Good Lord, Jonathon, what on earth is this place?" The door closed behind her and she jumped. Not that she had anything to fear. Still, who knew what was lurking in the unseen depths of the room?

"It's my library." Indignation sounded in Jonathon's voice.

"Don't be absurd." Fiona stepped forward cautiously. Directly over her head were crossed spears held by enormous Nubian statues. It was the sort of thing one might see at an ancient palace. "Really, what is it?"

"It's my library," he said again.

"It doesn't look like a library."

His head appeared from behind a post or column or something of that nature with any number of other carved heads upon it. Depending on the light, a human head would probably blend right into the carvings. "There are books."

She snorted in disbelief. "Where?"

"On the shelves."

"And the shelves are?"

He sighed with annoyance. "Along the wall."

"Yes, of course. There must be walls . . . somewhere," she said under her breath, and moved carefully along what would be a pathway in a garden. Here it was simply a space between clutter, scarcely wide enough to walk through without her skirts catching on either side.

The place was fascinating, though, even if it was too overwhelming to take in all at once. Fiona suspected if she tried, her head might well burst. It would take years just to see everything in this one room alone. She hadn't really paid any attention in the foyer but wondered now if the rest of the house was like this.

"It looks like a museum," she murmured, catching sight of an odd-looking stuffed beast she could not identify. "Without the labels or placards, that sort of thing. Although you could certainly use labels or placards or . . ." Jonathon came fully into view and Fiona stared. "You're not dressed!"

"On the contrary, my dear, I am dressed. I have on silk trousers, a shirt and a dressing gown. I am simply not properly attired for callers, as I was not expecting company." He raised a brow. "It is exceptionally early for a call, isn't it?"

"Yes, but I thought it was better to come at this time of day when my visit was less likely to be noted and commented upon." She studied him for a long moment. "In truth, I'm surprised to find you awake so early. It's scarcely past dawn."

"I couldn't sleep." He glared at her as if she were to blame.

Something was definitely amiss here. She handed him the book. "I thought, as we are going ahead with the book, you would need this."

"Ah yes, *A Fair Surrender.*" He practically snatched the volume from her hands and tossed it on the desk, the only relatively empty space in the room. "Is there anything else?"

"Yes." Of course there was something else. There were any number of something elses, but right now the most important one was, what had happened since last night?

Annoyance rose within her. She had done nothing whatsoever to warrant this treatment, with the possible exception of paying an improper call at an early hour. And she had thought he would rather like her unexpected arrival. "I wish to discuss . . ." Her gaze fell on the paper-wrapped book lying on top of her portfolio. "The lithographs."

"What about them?" he snapped.

"I had a concern about their quality." Her tone matched his. "Given the speed with which they were produced."

He waved away her comment. "Their quality is excellent. You can scarcely tell the originals from the prints."

"Don't be ridiculous." She scoffed. "There's a huge difference between my drawings and your copies."

"Do you really think so?" He stared at her. "Perhaps we should compare them directly?"

"Excellent idea," she said sharply.

She stepped around the desk, brushing past him in the process. What a shame it was that here they were together, alone, with one of them scarcely dressed and the other trying to resist the temptation said lack of clothing presented, and all they could do was snipe at one another. It certainly wasn't her fault, she hadn't come here to argue with him. She had no idea what had possessed the man, but she was not about to allow him to run roughshod over her just because he was in a foul mood for some inexplicable reason.

She unwrapped the book, flipped it open, then drew her drawings out of the portfolio. She turned to the first lithograph, found the corresponding drawing and laid them side by side. "There. Now do you see what I'm talking about?"

"No." He shrugged. "I see no discernible difference."

In point of fact, the differences were mere quibbles, more

attributable to the quality of the different paper than anything else. The lithographers had done a very good job,
particularly if one considered the speed with which they
had worked. Fiona had thought so from the moment she'd
seen the sample copy. Still, she'd had to say something
when he'd asked if there was anything else.

"Perhaps you should look at these, then." She selected
another lithograph and the appropriate drawing. Again
there was no real difference, but she didn't want him asking, or demanding, that she leave before she discovered
what had upset him. "Well?"

"Again, I see no problem whatsoever." He considered
her for a moment. "However, we should examine the rest
of the lithographs and compare them to the originals." He
flipped through the book to one of her drawings of male
nudes, then found the original and laid them in front of
her. "Do you see a problem?"

She looked at them for a moment, then sighed. "Not
really."

"Look again," he said through clenched teeth.

She drew her brows together and stared at him. His gaze
was intense and more than a little angry. What on earth did
he have to be angry about?

"Very well." She huffed and returned her attention to the
pictures before her.

She really didn't see any significant differences. The lines
of the bodies were comparable, the variations in intensity of
shading and hues were similar, the facial expressions were
almost exact . . .

She froze and stared at the drawings before her. How
could she possibly have forgotten about this?

"Well?" His voice was curt.

She forced a casual note to her voice. "I see no difference
at all."

"Neither do I." His jaw clenched. "What I do see is a distinct similarity to someone I have recently met."

"Really?" She widened her eyes innocently. Under most
circumstances, Fiona truly believed honesty was the best

course. This, however, was not one of those circumstances. "I don't."

"Not at all?"

She shook her head. "No."

"Not even a little?"

"Not the tiniest bit."

"Come, now, Fiona." Jonathon's eyes narrowed. "This gentleman doesn't remind you of someone you know?"

"Not that I recall," she said blithely.

"He doesn't bear a resemblance to . . . Count Orsetti?"

"Oh, in passing I suppose there's a vague resemblance." She glanced at the drawings. "Only in that they are both Italian. Dark in coloring. Rather handsome—"

"This looks exactly like Orsetti." He smacked his hand on top of the drawing. "This is Orsetti! You drew Orsetti! Naked!"

"Don't be absurd." She huffed. "I most certainly did not."

"Is that or is that not Orsetti?"

"No." It wasn't a complete lie.

He stared in disbelief. "That is not Orsetti's naked body on that page?"

"It absolutely is not," she said in a lofty manner.

"It certainly looks like him."

"You've seen Orsetti without clothing, then?" she asked in an overly pleasant manner."

"Of course I haven't seen him without clothing!" He tapped his finger on the drawings. "But I'd know that face anywhere."

"Oh, the *face*. You're talking about the face." She raised a shoulder in a nonchalant shrug. "Well, that's another matter altogether."

His brow furrowed in confusion. "What do you mean, another matter?"

"The face is an entirely separate issue from the body."

"Fiona!"

"Very well, then, I admit it." She rolled her gaze toward the ceiling. "It is Orsetti's face—"

"Aha!"

"But it is not his body."

"What?"

"On occasion"—she chose her words carefully—"it became rather dull to be drawing the same model over and over again. Some of us then amused ourselves by . . ." She paused. It didn't sound at all good. "Using a different head rather than the one provided."

Jonathon sucked in a shocked breath. "You put one man's face on another man's body?"

"It was a . . ." She thought for a moment. "A joke. An amusing prank."

"A prank?" Jonathon's eyes widened. "You indiscriminately put one man's head on another man's body and call it a prank?"

She stared at him. His reaction was both unexpected and far too extreme for the circumstances. Besides, surely he of all people would understand a joke? "Yes, a prank, and as the true"—she searched for the right word— "*owner* of the head never knew of its use, nor, I might add, did the models ever see the finished work, it was a harmless prank, at that."

"I don't think it's the least bit harmless." Indignation rang in his voice. One would think it was his head that had been substituted for another.

She drew her brows together. "Why?"

"Because . . ."

"Because?" she prompted.

"Because if one didn't know it was a joke, one might be tempted to think—"

"To think . . . what?" Her voice hardened.

"That you"—he waved at the drawing—"and he . . ."

She narrowed her eyes. "That I and he what?"

"Well." Jonathon's voice faltered, and for the first time since her arrival he looked unsure of himself.

"That I had seen Orsetti naked?" she said slowly. "That perhaps Orsetti had seen me naked? Is that what you thought?"

He hesitated. He had the look of a man who has just

stepped in something unpleasant on the street and has no idea how to get it off his shoes. "No."

She gasped. "You did! You thought I and, worse, Orsetti? *Orsetti?*"

"You can certainly see how I would make such an assumption," he said weakly.

"I most certainly cannot! Orsetti is a pompous ass. How could you have failed to notice that? Did you honestly think that Orsetti is the kind of man that would appeal to me? The kind of man that I would draw"—she fairly spit the words—"*naked?*"

"Perhaps not, but—"

"Or do anything else with naked?"

"No, no, of course not," he said quickly, but it was obvious that he had indeed.

Anger flooded her. "It appears, my lord, that you have jumped to yet another ill-considered conclusion. Is this a habit of yours?"

"Only with you," he muttered.

"Do you honestly think I am the type of woman who would squander my virtue—"

Jonathon winced at the word.

"On an idiot like Orsetti?" She shoved at his shoulder. "Have I no sense? No intelligence? No taste?"

He stepped back. "Women have been known to lose their hearts to idiots—"

"I can certainly understand that!" *As I am staring at an idiot even as we speak!* "However, it's not the loss of my heart that was in question, was it?" She shoved him again.

Again he stepped back. "You can surely see how I might think—"

"I most certainly cannot." She pushed him once more.

"Ouch." He rubbed his shoulder. "That hurts a bit, you know."

"Good!" She emphasized the word with another push of her hand.

"Stop it."

She pushed again. "No."

"See here, Fiona." He grabbed her hand. "You have every

right to be angry. However, you cannot fault me entirely for this."

"I most certainly can." She tried to pull her hand away, but he held it fast.

"I may well have added two plus two together and come up with five, but your actions as well as your words, when construed incorrectly, as I freely admit I have done"—he met her gaze firmly—"might well lead one to believe you could have been freer with your favors than you have been."

She gasped. "I never—"

He jerked her closer. "Did you or did you not once say to me that you wanted to kiss me back when I kissed you?"

"I may have said something of the sort, but that scarcely means—"

"And did you or did you not tell me you no longer cared about virtue?" He stared at her, the look in his eyes daring her to deny his charge. "And that you wished to have me in the fullest sense of the phrase?"

She scoffed. "I never said the fullest sense of the phrase."

He snorted. "It was implied." He gazed directly into her eyes, his face a bare few inches from her own, the slightest hint of a smug smile tugging at the corners of his mouth. "And did you or did you not ask me to marry you when we had scarcely met?"

She glared up at him. "I was desperate."

"Are you desperate now?"

"No," she snapped. "Yes. I don't know. Nothing has changed. I—"

"Everything has changed." His voice was low and abruptly serious.

At once she was aware of her body pressed to his. Of her hand held against his chest. Of a tangible sense of inevitability in the air.

She held her breath. "Has it?"

"It has for me." He lowered his lips to hers. "And for you?"

"No."

He stilled.

"I still want to kiss you." She swallowed hard. "I still want . . . you."

He released her hand and wrapped his arms around her, pulling her tighter against him. "Good."

"You do realize there will be no turning back?" her lips murmured against his.

"I do." He pulled his lips from hers and kissed the line of her jaw.

Delight shivered through her and her head dropped back. His lips trailed over her neck and down the column of her throat.

She gasped. "You understand as well that I have never . . ."

"I do." His words murmured against her throat. "I surrender, Miss Fairchild."

Her hands flattened on his chest and the warmth of his body radiated through the silk of his dressing gown and his shirt. And into her soul.

His hands caressed her back and she turned her face toward his. His lips met hers in a manner firm and certain. Without hesitation. Without doubt. Without question. Fated. An overwhelming sense of certainty and irresistible need shivered through her. And surrender.

She pulled away and met his gaze. "I have always wanted to be the lady who joined you for a clandestine meeting in the library."

He smiled. "It scarcely deserves the name library."

"And yet, there are books." She threw her arms around him and pressed her lips to his with an eagerness that caught him unawares and knocked him off balance.

He staggered back a step. She struggled to maintain her footing. He caught his foot in something unseen, she grabbed for him and they both tumbled backward. And would have fallen to the floor had there been floor space to do so. As it was, Jonathon landed on his buttocks on something Fiona didn't see and she ended in a tangle of skirts and petticoats more or less on top of him.

He stared up at her in a wry manner. "I fear, Fiona, this library is not conducive to anything of a romantic nature."

He shifted and winced. "At least not without a great deal of pain."

"I don't care." She leaned forward, framed his face with her hands and kissed him, slowly, in a deliberate and sensual manner. She wanted this, wanted him, more than she had ever thought possible, and she was not about to let a museum of a house stand between them. "Although I should hate for you to be in pain."

He drew his head back and stared at her as if surprised by the seductive nature of her kiss or his own response to it.

"As would I," he murmured, pushed her to her feet, then stood. "I have had quite enough of this, Fiona Fairchild. We have been on this course from the moment we met." He pulled her to him and kissed her hard, then set her back. "I have wanted you since I first saw you in the Effington House library and I shall not let anything keep us apart now."

He grabbed her hand and started to make his way to the door.

"Jonathon!" She gasped with feigned shock. "Where are you taking me?"

"To my bed." He sidestepped a suit of armor. "It's past time."

"Indeed it is," she murmured, her skirts catching on a tall carving that looked tribal in nature and not at all friendly. "If the servants see us, they will talk."

He stopped and tried to untangle her. "If they talk, I shall fire them."

"What if I decide I don't wish to wish to join you in your bed?" she said, and impatiently pulled at the caught skirt.

"You won't." He furrowed his brow and tugged at the fabric. Abruptly it came free with a nasty ripping sound. He looked at her. "Will you?"

Her breath caught. "Absolutely not."

"It appears your cousin was right." He smiled wickedly and again headed for the door, pulling her behind him. "You are perfect for me."

She laughed and wondered that she wasn't the least bit hesitant to follow him to his bed or anywhere else. Of course, given what he'd said last night and more importantly what he hadn't, she was fairly confident he planned to marry her. But it simply didn't matter. She wondered at that too. Did all women who had reached a certain age without marrying decide to throw caution to winds and leap into the bed of the man they loved? Regardless of what happened after this, no matter whom she married, this, now, was what she wanted. And if she never got another thing she wanted for the rest of her life, at least she would have had this. She would have had him. She would have had love.

Jonathon reached the door, cautiously peeked out, then turned to her. "We shall make a dash for the stairs. Are you ready?"

The question hung in the air between them fraught with more meaning than he had intended. She nodded firmly. "I am."

He squeezed her hand and together they slipped out the door. She followed him down the short stretch to the stairway, then up the stairs and along a short corridor. He moved in a stealthy manner as if he were a thief and not the owner of the house. Still, it made her feel delightfully wicked and not simply apprehensive, although with each step closer to his bed she did note certain twinges of anxiety.

Jonathon threw open a door, stepped in, yanked her in after him and in one quick movement shut the door behind her, pressed her back to the door and kissed her. Long and hard, until the door was the only thing holding her up. Until her bones melted from heat and desire. Until she wanted nothing more than . . . more.

Skillfully, he turned her around and quickly undid the hooks at the back of her bodice, then pushed her dress down over her shoulders to her waist. His lips caressed the nape of her neck and she moaned softly. He untied the lone petticoat she'd worn and pushed it, together with her dress, over her hips until it fell at her feet. She'd dressed hurriedly, without a maid, and her corset was not as snug as it would have been otherwise and she realized, as the cool morning air mixed with the heat of his lips on her shoulders and the warmth of his hands at her waist, that she had fully expected them to come to this point. Had, in truth, wanted it. Planned for it.

She twisted around to face him and wrapped her arms around his neck. His lips claimed hers and his fingers ran over the front of her corset until they played over her confined breasts. She gasped at his touch, with anticipation and need. She pushed his hands away and quickly undid the hooks at the front of her corset and it too fell to the floor. He tugged at the ribbon of her chemise until he had it open to her waist and his hands cupped her bare breasts.

She rested her head against the door and arched her back upward to meet his touch. He pulled his lips from hers and bent to take one breast into his mouth. She laid her hands on his shoulders and let the feel of his mouth on her flesh wash over her. Through her. And tried to breathe. He shifted his attention to her other breast and she dug her fingers into his flesh. And again wanted . . . more.

Without warning he pulled away and, before she could protest, scooped her into his arms, kicked her dress out of the way, turned and took a step. And promptly bashed into something.

"Damnation!"

"What?" Her senses were muddled and she shook her head.

"This blasted room is as bad as that library," he muttered, and tried to make his way through the room with her in his arms.

"Dear Lord, it is, isn't it?" she murmured, looking around a bedchamber every bit as full as the library, with just as many odd curiosities and furnishings of an exotic nature. Although here the word *erotic* was probably more appropriate. "Fascinating."

"Oh, no. You are not going to be distracted by this . . . this . . . collection." Determination sounded in his voice. "Although"—he grinned down at her in a wicked manner—"there is something to be said for properly setting the stage, as it were."

He set her on her feet in front of what was probably the most unique bed she'd ever seen.

It was enormous, Chinese in style and looked more like a small room than a mere bed. It was canopied and had carved open-work panels around three sides depicting dragons and all manner of oriental creatures. An air of hedonistic mysticism encircled it as if this were a place where virgins were deflowered as sacrifices to an insatiable god and went eagerly with a smile upon their faces and an ache of need in their loins.

"Dear Lord," she breathed.

"It's impressive, isn't it?"

It was lacquered and light glinted off the finish as if it were alive. And it was . . . red.

"It's terrifying," she said under her breath. "And decadent. And . . ."

He raised a brow. "And?"

"And it fairly screams that its primary purpose is not sleep."

"Yes, well, I suppose. . . ." Jonathon looked distinctly uncomfortable. "I did not purchase it, you know, it came with the house, and I—"

"Jonathon." She turned to him and tugged at the knotted sash of his dressing gown. "You may not yet have realized it, but, as I am standing here clad in nothing more than my chemise, my stockings and my shoes, my primary purpose is not sleep either." She untied the sash and he shrugged the robe off. "At the moment I am concerned with nothing more than making certain you are as scantily attired as I."

"You have no idea how pleased I am to hear that." He yanked his shirt off over his head, tossed it aside, then pulled her back into his arms to kiss her thoroughly. Her breasts pressed against his naked chest, his arousal beneath the silk of his trousers was hard against her.

"I have some idea," she murmured.

He laughed, picked her up and laid her across the width of the bed, but even when she reached her hands over her head she still couldn't touch the panel that bounded the other side. The sheer size alone bespoke of frolicking of a carnal nature. She watched him take off her shoes, then slowly peel off her stockings until she was wearing only her thin chemise. He started to untie his trousers and she propped herself up on her elbows and watched him.

He hesitated, caught her gaze and grimaced. "Now I know how your models felt."

"Well, I have never seen . . ." Heat flashed up her face.

"It's somewhat intimidating, you know."

"I am sorry, I don't mean it to be."

"You have seen naked men before. Quite thoroughly, I might add, given the detail of your drawings."

"Yes, but men have never seen me naked before. Besides, that was an entirely different thing and completely impersonal. This"—she waved at the bulge in his trousers—"is most personal."

"Indeed it is," Jonathon murmured, drew a deep breath and slipped off his trousers.

Fiona stared. She had seen men fully exposed before in the name of art, but after the first few times it had become no more significant than when one was presented with an orange or a . . . a banana to draw. She had certainly never seen a gentleman's unmentionables at attention, as it were, prepared, erect and incredibly significant. It was at once daunting and exciting.

She scrambled to her knees, pulled her chemise up over her head and let it fall. Jonathon moved to the edge of the bed, tilted her chin up with two fingers and brushed his lips over hers until her mouth opened beneath his. His tongue met hers, he tasted of her, drank of her until she ached for his touch, and still he did not move closer. She could feel the heat of his naked body a few bare inches from her own and wanted to press her skin against his and knew he wanted it too. And with every moment she did not touch him, every second he did not touch her, desire swirled within her and grew.

At last, she placed her hands flat on his chest, on the rough hair that scattered over his skin and trailed down his abdomen. His muscles tensed beneath her touch. She trailed her fingers over the hills and valleys of his chest, exploring with a personal touch what she had drawn in an impersonal manner. Her hands drifted lower across the flat planes of his abdomen and she felt him hold his breath as if waiting. For her. She ran her hand over his member and it jerked beneath her hand. It was far harder than she'd expected and as soft as silk to the touch. She curled her fingers around him and he groaned and wrapped his arms around her, and together they tumbled backward onto the bed.

At once, passion exploded between them. Their arms entwined, their legs tangled together, their mouths were everywhere at once. She wanted, no, needed to touch him, to taste him, to feel the heat of his flesh pressed against hers. And needed him to touch her in return. To taste her. To make her his own.

He ran his hand up her leg, along her inner thigh to the juncture of her legs and beyond. She felt his fingers against her, felt her own slick moisture and a pleasure unlike anything she'd known before coursed through her. He caressed her slowly, easily, all the while his lips were on her shoulders, her throat, her breasts. His body moved against hers and her own body arched to meet him. She lost herself in the delicious sensations washing through her body, sweeping through her soul. And wanted more.

His fingers moved in an increasing rhythm until her mind, her life narrowed to include nothing beyond the extraordinary pleasure of his touch. Tension coiled inside her until she thought she would shatter into a thousand pieces. And wanted the shattering. Ached for it. Reached for it.

Abruptly he stopped and she clutched at him and groaned in a desperate manner that sounded completely foreign to her ear. As if it had come from someone else or somewhere else.

He shifted to kneel between her legs and she held her breath. He eased himself into her slowly. It was not quite as delightful as his caress, but still not unpleasant. A rather nice feeling of fullness, really. He paused, then thrust hard. She felt the tiniest stab of pain and gasped.

"Fiona?" he murmured against her neck. "Are you—"

"Yes, yes, I'm fine," she said brightly, although in truth it stung a bit. "Do go on."

"Do go on." He chuckled, and it reverberated through her.

She smiled. It did sound absurd, as if she were encouraging him to take a stroll in the park. Even so, she shifted a bit, and he settled deeper within her. Her body throbbed around his. He stayed still for a long moment, then slowly withdrew, and slid forward. It was intriguing and rather nice. He continued to thrust and pull back in an easy manner and the feeling became much more than nice. She wrapped her legs around his. The tempo of his movements grew faster, harder. She arched to meet him. Sensation, delicious and exquisite and unlike anything she'd ever imagined, flowed through her. Conquered her. Claimed her. Blood pounded in her veins in time with the beat of his thrusts.

The tension she'd felt earlier returned. The spring within her tightened.

Dimly she heard him groan. He shuddered against her and thrust again and again. Without warning her body exploded against his. She arched upward and waves of pleasure, basic and primordial and like nothing she'd ever imagined, surged through her and shook her body. And touched her soul.

He shifted and pulled her with him to lay side by side, still wrapped in each other's arms, their bodies still joined. She could feel the thud of his heart against hers, somehow more intimate, more personal even than their coupling, his heart beating as one with hers.

Her gaze met his and he kissed her. "Would you care to know what I am thinking, Miss Fairchild?"

"I believe I can feel what you're thinking, Lord Helmsley."

He grinned wickedly "Yes, well, there is that." He kissed her again slowly and she wondered if he realized she shared his thoughts.

He raised his head and gazed into her eyes. His voice was

light, but his eyes were dark with passion and desire. "I shall have to marry you now, you know. Now that you have ruined me."

"I thought as a man you were subject to different standards and could not be ruined." She could still feel him inside her and she adjusted her position slightly to keep him precisely where he was.

"I was wrong," he said in a lofty manner. "I am definitely ruined."

She moved to lie on top of him and ground her hips against his, delighting at the look of pained pleasure that crossed his face. "Odd, you don't feel the least bit ruined."

"I'm confident I can still function." Without warning, he rolled her over and settled deeper within her. "Apparently I was wrong." He grinned. "I am not ruined after all."

"No," she sighed, and moved her hips to encourage him. "You do not appear to be ruined, but we should make certain."

"Indeed we should." He chuckled, then raised his head to stare down at her. "I was wrong, you know."

"About being ruined?" She ran her fingers up and down his back. "Or about Orsetti? Or about—"

"Never mind." He fairly growled the words. "Suffice it to say, I have been wrong about any number of things."

She laughed and reveled in the way the sound echoed through her and him.

"And furthermore, I intend to let you remind me of how very wrong I have been every day for the rest of my life."

"Do you?" She smiled. "Then I gather you still intend to formally call on me?"

"I do indeed." He nuzzled the side of her neck. "Now, if there are no further questions . . ."

"Just one." She shivered, the way he did that was most delightful. "How did you know the name of the orchids in the conservatory?"

She felt him smile against her neck. "I know a little about a great number of things but not a great deal about any one thing."

"I see," she murmured, and surrendered herself to the pleasure of his touch.

A moment later Fiona realized he was wrong about that too.

There was at least one thing about which he knew a great deal.

Fourteen

Later that day, at a much more respectable hour for paying calls, if paying calls was what one had in mind and not something of a more scandalous nature . . .

"Oh, it was definitely the hand of fate." Judith accepted a cup of tea from Fiona. "What else could explain it?"

"A miracle, I should think." Fiona grinned. "Or simple luck."

"Nonsense. While I do subscribe to the notion that luck is always more important than skill in any endeavor, in this instance I believe there are greater powers at play. The very fact that you were able to pay a call on Jonathon and return home without anyone in your family having so much as an inkling of your absence definitely speaks of destiny."

"Still, it was very early," Fiona murmured. "Scarcely past dawn."

"And yet there were those who did not leave my ball until very early." Judith took a sip of her tea. "Scarcely past dawn. Given your activities and those of others I could name, the streets of London were a crush of comings and goings in the early morning hours. You are exceedingly fortunate you were not seen. Although," she said thoughtfully, "since the comings and goings were mainly of a clandestine nature, it's entirely possible anyone whose path you might have crossed was too busy concealing their own purposes to give yours a moment's notice." Judith smiled in a wicked manner. "It was a most successful ball."

Fiona laughed. Whether you wished to call it a miracle or luck or fate, it was indeed fortunate that Fiona's early morning assignation with Jonathon had gone undetected by anyone save his butler, who was hopefully as discreet as he was efficient. In spite of the hour, the man had actually found her a hired carriage to take her home.

"Of course, if Jonathon had escorted you home . . ." Judith said idly, "and you had been discovered . . ."

"There would be the devil to pay, and I should much prefer to avoid that particular price, if you please."

If Fiona had been caught returning home alone, she could probably have thought of some rational-sounding explanation about why she'd been out at that hour of the morning. But to be caught accompanied by Jonathon . . . She shuddered at the thought. "I have no desire for a husband who has been forced into marriage. Even if said husband is the only one I want."

"And the one who wants you," Judith said firmly.

"We shall see," Fiona said in an offhand manner as if she, and Judith as well, were not completely confident that Jonathon would declare both his affection and his intention to marry when he called on Fiona later today. Hadn't he said as much a mere few hours ago?

"I knew it would all work out, you know," Judith said in a smug manner. "I knew from the moment Jonathon first asked me for advice. And after last night, I had no doubts whatsoever."

"Really?" Fiona raised a brow. "Then your call today was simply to confirm your—"

"I am confident, my dear, not infallible." Judith smiled and sipped her tea. "Admittedly, I was dying to know what else might have transpired between you and he after that oh, so interesting encounter in the conservatory."

"I wouldn't call it the least bit interesting." Fiona grimaced. "I'd call it awkward and most annoying."

"I do wish I could have seen Jonathon's expression when he realized where he had seen the count's face before."

"It was . . ." Fiona laughed. "Memorable."

"I can well imagine." Judith shook her head. "Jonathon has never had to compete for anything, particularly women, I think because he's never met one before that he's truly wanted. And I have never known him to be jealous. Furthermore, he is not used to being wrong, nor is he the type of man to leap to unwarranted conclusions. All of which is no doubt extremely confusing for him. If he wasn't such a dear friend, I would find it most amusing."

Fiona sipped her tea. "But you do find it amusing."

"Apparently I am not as good a friend as I thought." Judith shrugged and set her cup down. "Nonetheless, you will soon be the Marchioness of Helmsley and the future Duchess of Roxborough, and I have had a hand in it, however slight."

"More importantly, my sisters will have the means needed to find a good match," Fiona said quickly.

"Yes, yes." Judith waved away the comment. "That is more important than marrying the wealthy, titled man that you love and living happily for the rest of your days."

"Perhaps not *more* important." Fiona laughed and Judith joined her.

"Well, as Shakespeare is continually saying in the guise of one actor or another, all's well that ends well, and I suspect this particular comedy will end in a most satisfying manner the moment his lordship calls on you. As much as I do hate to miss that"—Judith rose to her feet—"I still have a few other calls to make. Yours was not the only interesting thread left dangling at the end of the ball. Twelfth Night is obviously more fraught with possibilities than I had imagined." A satisfied twinkle lurked in Judith's eye. "It may well have to become an annual event."

"Judith." Fiona stood and took the other woman's hands. "I do thank you for coming here today. I had no one I could truly talk to about . . . everything. I couldn't take my sisters into my confidence. I certainly don't wish to set an"—she cringed at the word—"*immoral* example for them, and as for Aunt Edwina, well, in truth, Aunt Edwina is a continual surprise. I have no idea what she would say and I prefer not to find out. But I knew you would understand."

"An understanding nature is the curse of an interesting reputation." Judith heaved a dramatic sigh, then cast her a genuine smile. "I did mean it, Fiona, when I told you I wished to be friends. And as your friend I am curious." She studied the younger woman thoughtfully. "I know you're sublimely happy at the moment and certain you and Jonathon will spend the rest of your days together. Indeed I share that certainty, but what if, oh, I do hate to bring it up, but . . ." Judith's gaze met Fiona's. "What if we're wrong? About his feelings and fate and all of it? Men are odd creatures, by and large, and it's best not to count on any sort of rational behavior from them. It's been my experience they scarcely ever know their own minds when it comes to important matters regarding life and love and the rest of it. Have you considered that at all?"

"If I am wrong," Fiona said slowly, "if Jonathon doesn't care for me, doesn't love me, if he is not intent upon marriage, I shall have to face that." She drew a deep breath. "But I have no regrets about joining him in his bed. I should have, I suppose, it's quite wicked of me not to and probably stupid as well, but there you have it."

"Good." Judith nodded firmly. "Regrets are a dreadful thing. One cannot change the past, be it a decade ago or simply this morning. It is a waste of time to try to do so."

Fiona shrugged. "I'm not a child, I know my own mind and I know as well the consequences of my actions. I wasn't simply swept away by blind passion. I love him, and regardless of what happens I shall have the memory of being with him for the rest of my days."

"There are worse things to have in one's past than a good memory or two. Particularly if it involves love." Judith gave her a quick hug, then turned to go. "Oh, and by the way, I still want a copy of your book."

Fiona hadn't considered the book at all since this morning. If she was going to marry Jonathon, it was no longer necessary to proceed with it. Still, Jonathon had said it was in the hands of the printers and orders had been taken. Who knew how many copies had been produced at this point?

Judith leaned closer in a confidential manner. "I've always wanted to know someone named Anonymous. It makes me feel as though I am the protector of great secrets. Besides, it will serve as something of a keepsake for us all. Probably not something you will want to show your children. Or grandchildren. Although, perhaps my children . . ."

Fiona laughed. "I shall see to it that you receive a copy."

"I told Jonathon at the very start that I wanted one. And as he was only going to have a handful printed altogether, I did want to make sure I did not miss the opportunity to acquire one of my own."

"A handful altogether?" Fiona shook her head. "You mean initially, don't you? Not altogether. Just a few copies printed initially to use to solicit subscriptions and orders, that sort of thing?"

"No, I—" Judith's eyes widened and she nodded a shade too quickly. "Yes, of course, that's exactly what I mean. Why, I certainly couldn't have meant anything else. Imagine getting *initially* confused with *altogether*?" She laughed an odd sort of high-pitched laugh. "Obviously, too little sleep and entirely too much fun last night has left me somewhat confused today."

Fiona stared at her. Judith didn't seem the least bit confused, but she had a distinctly guilty air about her. And Fiona doubted Judith ever felt guilty about anything. "Is there something you're not telling me?"

"I really must take my leave." Judith started toward the door.

Unease gripped Fiona. "Judith? Is there something I should know? About the book?"

Judith paused in midstep and turned back to Fiona. "One of the hallmarks of friendship, of true friendship, is the ability to keep one another's confidences. I would no more reveal to Jonathon something you had confided to me than

I would tell you a secret he had told. At least not deliberately. Please do not ask me to do so."

"But—"

"Isn't it enough that you have found one another?"

"Well, certainly, but—"

"Do a few insignificant, oh, I don't know, *deceptions*, I suppose, really matter in the grander scheme of things?"

"I daresay it depends on the deception," Fiona said slowly.

"Nothing of any great significance, I can assure you that." Fiona's voice was firm. "It's the kind of silly thing that you will laugh about in your dotage."

"Tell the story to our children and grandchildren?"

"Something like that." Judith nodded and a few minutes later took her leave.

How very odd that was. There was obviously something about *A Fair Surrender* that Judith was not telling her, although Fiona couldn't imagine what it might be.

Jonathon and Oliver's original scheme was to have only a few copies printed initially and print additional copies as orders came in. It made perfect sense, although she'd never truly believed the book would ever make the kind of money she needed. Indeed, her purpose for working on it at all had simply been to spend as much time as possible with Jonathon. But Jonathon had been confident. Why, he'd guaranteed a profit for her. It was very sweet of him and quite gallant and . . .

And there was definitely something wrong. Something that had to do with the printing of the books, be it *initially* or *altogether*. She could wait and question Jonathon, of course, but it might well be better if Fiona had the answers she sought long before his arrival.

She had used the book as an excuse to pay one improper call today. Perhaps it was time to use it to pay yet another call.

Fiona stared unseeing out the carriage window. It was extraordinarily cold outside and not considerably warmer inside the carriage. In the back of her mind, she noted the cold and was grateful for it and the way it numbed her senses. Numb was preferable to anything else at the moment. She had no idea what to think and, worse, what to feel.

It had been a most informative outing. Sir Ephraim Cadwallender, publisher of *Cadwallender's Weekly World Messenger* and the proprietor of an impressively vast printing company, had been most charming if a bit taken aback to meet her, although he did recall having briefly seen her at the Effington Christmas Ball. Fiona was most charming herself. And completely dishonest.

She'd made up a ridiculous story about Lord Helmsley having mentioned a book he'd been writing involving artworks of an explicit nature. Well, surely the older gentleman could understand how her curiosity would compel her to seek out the book? Not for the art, of course, although she had spent many years living in Italy and considered herself well versed in art, but for Lord Helmsley's story. And, as his lordship was far too modest to ever show it to her himself, she thought perhaps she could purchase the book for herself.

Sir Ephraim had chuckled and said he would be more than happy to sell her a copy if of course they existed. He'd explained that even though Lord Helmsley had had the lithographs produced and the book printed with an unseemly haste and at an exorbitant cost, the entire endeavor was nothing more than an elaborate hoax. But then he'd said even as a boy Lord Helmsley had enjoyed a good joke regardless of the price. Sir Ephraim didn't know all the details, but there were a mere half dozen copies of the book printed and delivered to Lord Helmsley. His lordship had assured him there would be no more. It was something of a pity, Sir Ephraim had added, such a volume might eventually prove to turn a tidy profit.

Fiona had laughed with him, thanked him for his time and promptly taken her leave. Before the impact of his revelation could hit her and tear out her heart.

Was this the deception Judith had mentioned? That Jonathon had never planned on printing more than a handful of *A Fair Surrender* in the first place? And if that was indeed true, how on earth could it provide the money she'd needed? Money that would come through Jonathon allegedly to preserve her anonymity.

I shall give you the money you would receive if you married. All of it. In advance, if you will, of sales of the book.

Or perhaps come from him?

I feel a certain obligation to help you avoid the fate you so very much wish to avoid.

A heavy weight settled in her stomach.

You asked for rescue and I did not provide it. I have long thought of myself as an honorable man and I am not proud of my refusal.

The back of her throat stung with realization. How far would an honorable man go to assuage his guilt? To redeem himself in his own eyes?

I shall have to marry you now.

Fiona had long said she'd never force any man into marriage. Not out of honor or obligation or responsibility. She'd said it and she'd meant it.

Now it was time to live up to her word.

"Where on earth can she be, Oliver?" Jonathon paced across Oliver's parlor with one eye on the mantel clock. "I've been here nearly half an hour and no one seems to know where she has gone."

Oliver shrugged. "I wish I could tell you, old man, but I have no idea. If you haven't noticed thus far, my cousin has a mind of her own." He studied the other man carefully. "I'm not at all surprised she managed to slip out of the house without anyone noting her departure."

"Yes, yes, she's quite skilled at doing precisely what she wants," Jonathon said under his breath, ignoring the fact that it was that exact quality that had enabled Fiona to leave in the early morning hours to come to him. And, as Oliver had not met him at the door with a pistol in one hand and a minister by his side, Jonathon had assumed Fiona had managed to return home as surreptitiously as she had left.

Not that it really mattered now. Jonathon paused and looked at his friend. "I wish to marry her, you know."

"I assumed that, given the way you've not been able to stand still for more than a moment since your arrival. You have the look of a man about to jump off a cliff." Oliver grinned. "It's about time. I wondered what was taking you so long."

Jonathon raised a brow. "You couldn't have known it would come to this?"

"Oh, but I did. In truth, I never doubted it. After all, you had always said when you found the perfect woman—"

Jonathon snorted. "She is far from perfect. She is stubborn and determined and irritating. In many ways, she has no sense of propriety. Nude drawings of men, indeed. She's extremely flirtatious and outspoken and . . ." He blew a long breath. "And she is indeed perfect for me. Exactly what I have always wanted in a wife."

"It won't be easy, you know. Having Fiona as a wife."

"I don't expect easy. I expect"—Jonathon smiled wryly—"passion. Hers and, yes, mine. Grand and glorious and forever."

Oliver stared for a long moment.

"What now?" Jonathon rolled his gaze toward the ceiling.

"I'm simply thinking what a lot of money I could have made had I had the foresight to make one simple wager." Oliver shook his head mournfully. "One should always follow one's first instincts."

"You could have taken Cavendish and Warton for a great deal," Jonathon said in a dry manner. "My condolences that you did not do so."

"Don't be absurd. Neither of them would have wagered with me on this." Oliver grinned. "The wager would have been with you."

"So much for the loyalty of friends," Jonathon muttered.

Oliver laughed and Jonathon smiled reluctantly. It was good to have friends, those he could count on no matter what might befall him.

A low murmur of voices sounded in the foyer.

"I believe that's your intended now. Well, this is it."

Oliver slapped Jonathon on the back. "Best wishes, old man, and welcome to the family."

Jonathon huffed. "You find this all most amusing, don't you?"

"Only because it is." Oliver chuckled and strode to the door. "I shall be in the foyer, awaiting the happy announcement of your betrothal."

Jonathon patted his coat pocket as he had done a dozen times since he'd left his house to make certain his grandmother's ring was still securely in its jeweler's box. His heart thudded in his chest. Should he get down on one knee? Certainly a romantic gesture of some sort was called for. Damnation, why hadn't he thought to bring flowers? Or chocolates? Or something? He groaned to himself. He simply hadn't thought of anything beyond his express purpose. He was well used to charming a woman, but never with the intention of marriage. Bloody hell, he was an idiot. Again.

The voices in the hall sounded louder. Surely Oliver wasn't chastising Fiona for her absence? Jonathon chuckled. She would not take that at all well.

Fiona swept into the room, then stopped and slammed the door behind her. Jonathon winced. He certainly wouldn't wish to be in Oliver's shoes at the moment.

He adopted his most charming smile. "Good day, Fiona."

"Lord Helmsley." Her voice was cool. Blast Oliver anyway for putting her in such a foul mood. Well, Jonathon knew one sure way to improve her disposition.

He drew a deep breath. "Fiona, I wish to ask you a question."

"What a startling coincidence, my lord, as I wish to ask a question as well." Her green eyes glittered. "Several questions, in fact."

"They can wait. Fiona . . ." His nerve faltered. He waved at the sofa. "Perhaps you would like to sit down?"

"I prefer to stand," she said sharply.

"Very well." He laughed weakly. "But it's going to make things a bit awkward when I am down on bended knee."

She raised a brow. "And you will be on bended knee to beg my forgiveness?"

"No," he said slowly. Perhaps Oliver wasn't the target of her anger after all. "My intention was to ask if you will do me the honor of becoming my wife."

She narrowed her eyes. "Why?"

"Why?" He stared at her. No, Oliver definitely wasn't the target of her anger. "After this morning—"

"This morning?"

"Yes, well, after you and I . . ." He shook his head in confusion. "Damn it all, Fiona, you know what I am trying to say."

"Do I? I'm not the least bit sure of that." She studied him coldly. "Allow me to ask you a question."

"Of course." He racked his brains trying to think of what he might have done to invoke her wrath. Certainly when she'd left him this morning there had been nothing amiss. In fact, everything was quite wonderful between them. Or at least he'd thought it was.

"Tell me, my lord, do you take your responsibilities, obligations, honor, the giving of your word seriously?"

"Of course," he said staunchly.

She crossed her arms over her chest. "And would you take whatever steps necessary, do whatever was required, to meet those obligations and responsibilities and so forth?"

"Absolutely." What was she getting at?

"No matter how difficult it proved? How much, oh, I don't know, *deception* was involved? How much sacrifice was needed?" Her voice hardened. "How much it cost?"

"Yes, I suppose." None of this made any sense whatsoever. Judging from the look in her eye, it had something to do with whatever had upset her. And it was not going to be good. He searched his conscience. It was relatively blameless.

"Did you ever intend to sell copies of *A Fair Surrender,* or was it all simply a ploy?"

His stomach plummeted. "A ploy?"

"To allow you to surreptitiously provide me funding so that I was not forced into marriage? And were you planning to continue the deception until such time as I married and received my inheritance?" Her voice rose. "And was all this because you agreed to marry me, then felt responsible for my fate when you reneged?"

He braced himself. "Fiona—"

"Answer the question, if you please," she snapped.

He paused. "Which question?"

"Pick one!"

"Very well." It really wasn't that bad, at least not from his perspective. And he had fully intended to confess all to her at some point. Not now, of course, and possibly not for years. Still, it might be better to get it over with. Deception was not the best way to start their lives together. Besides, what difference did it make now?

He blew a resigned breath. "I never planned to sell copies of *A Fair Surrender,* although I must admit, I am quite pleased with the end result."

She glared.

"Scarcely matters now, I suppose," he said under his breath. "Aside from the scandal if the identity of Anonymous was discovered, you were right all along about the amount of money such an enterprise would generate. It would take years to make even a fraction of what you needed. I did indeed intend to provide you with funds to keep you from an unwanted marriage and to continue to do so for as long as was necessary. And yes, I concocted this scheme because I felt a certain responsibility toward you."

"And now?"

"Now . . . what?" he said cautiously.

"What is your plan now?"

"Now?" Relief washed through him. If she was asking about now, it surely wasn't too late. "Now I wish to marry you."

"Because of what happened between us this morning?"

"No. Yes." There was no good way to answer this. "In part, I suppose."

"Because you feel obligated?"

"No." He shook his head. "Because I *want* to marry you."

"And I am to believe you because you have always been so honest with me about your motives?"

"No." He clenched his jaw. "You're supposed to believe me because it's the truth."

"Ha! I'm not sure you would recognize the truth if it slapped you across the face!"

"I would," he said indignantly, then realized how stupid that sounded. Nonetheless, he was a bit angry now himself. "I did what I thought best at the time, Fiona. I couldn't simply abandon you to your fate. Yes, I felt a certain responsibility and an obligation to you. It was not your fault that I was not sincere when I agreed to marry you. But once the error was recognized, what would you have had me do?"

"You could have agreed to marry me and meant it!"

"But I want to marry you now! Doesn't that mean anything?"

"No! Not now. It's too late. You're too late." She ticked the points off on her finger. "You lied to me. You deceived me—"

"I did it for you!"

"Hardly! You tried to shape my life, my future, exactly as my father did. However, he truly believed his actions were in my best interests. Your actions were to alleviate your own sense of guilt for not being my salvation!" She drew a deep breath and met his gaze. Her voice was abruptly calm. It did not bode well. "I told you I would never force a man to marry me. I see little difference between forcing a man into marriage because of an indiscretion and marrying a man because I am a responsibility or an obligation."

His breath caught. "What are you saying?"

"What I am saying is that as much as I do appreciate your assistance, our association is at an end." Her voice was polite, formal, and struck fear into his heart. "I too have responsibilities and obligations, and I cannot meet them with lies and deception."

"Fiona—"

She clasped her hands in front of her in a prim, nononsense manner. As if the topic was no longer a subject of debate. "I shall adhere to my father's wishes and marry the man he chose for me."

He stared in disbelief. "You can't."

"Oh, but I can. And I shall."

"I will not allow it," he said staunchly, although he had no idea how to stop it.

She snorted in disdain. "You have nothing to say about it. Furthermore, you may consider any obligation you have to me discharged. However, I should offer my congratulations."

He was afraid to ask. "Why?"

"As I will not force you into marriage, you have won our wager."

His brows drew together. "What wager?"

"My virtue against your freedom."

"My freedom . . ." At once he remembered the wager discussed in a frivolous moment and shook his head. "I certainly never meant . . . why, it was not at all serious, nothing more than a joke—"

"I am weary of jokes!" Her voice rang with frustration. "Pranks, hoaxes, all of it! I am no longer amused!"

"I—"

"Whether it was a joke or not, you have won your freedom and I have lost what I wagered. If this were . . ."—she searched for the right word—"a *myth* there would be some great lesson here as to the origins of the universe or the beginning of the world. There would be a parallel between you and I and nature, but there isn't. I thought, when Oliver first suggested your name, that it was fate. It had to be. Surely it was more than coincidence that Oliver would name the one man in the world who once claimed my affection—"

"What?" His brows drew together.

She waved away his question. "I saw you years ago at an Effington Christmas Ball. I was scarcely more than a child and I thought you were the most wonderful man I'd ever seen. I even noted your rendezvous in the library with a lady."

He blew a long breath. "I see."

"I have long wondered what it would be like to be the lady in the library on Christmas Eve with you. I've wondered as well what it would be like to be the lady in question the day after the evening in the library." She smiled a humorless smile. "Now I know."

"It sounds like fate to me," he said quietly.

"Unless one is writing a myth or some other work of fiction, there is no such thing as fate or destiny. There is only life and what we make of it." She heaved a weary sigh, as if she were suddenly too tired to go on. "I think it would be best if you go now."

He didn't know what to say, what to do. He'd never felt so helpless in his entire life. A sense of panic rose within him and he pushed it away. "May I ask you a question first?"

She hesitated then nodded. "One."

"You said I once claimed your affection—"

"It was a long time ago and I was—"

"It's my question, Miss Fairchild, allow me to ask it," he said firmly. His gaze trapped hers. "Once, you felt some affection for me. Do you love me now?"

She stared at him for a long moment. "That is entirely too personal, my lord."

"Perhaps it is." He nodded thoughtfully. "Good day, Miss Fairchild." He turned and strode out of the room.

Out of the corner of his eye, he noted Oliver waiting in the foyer.

"Jonathon," Oliver called after him.

Jonathon ignored him and stalked to the front door. It opened for him at once thanks to a well-trained footman, otherwise he would have been compelled to kick the door down. He felt like kicking something at the moment. Once more he found himself walking the streets.

Fiona had every right to be angry with him. He deserved her anger and probably more. And perhaps claiming he did it for her was not the wisest thing to say. And yes, there had been some deception and, technically, a lie or two. But damn it all, he loved her. He wanted to marry her. He had felt a certain sense of responsibility and obligation in the beginning, but everything had changed since then.

He just had to convince her of that and he had to do it before she married Whatshisname and he lost her forever. It would not be easy. But now that he had found Fiona and love and passion and God knows what else that lay in the pit of his stomach and muddled his mind and made him behave like a total idiot, he was not about to give her up. He'd never especially believed in fate, but he did now, and if there was ever one woman meant for him it was Fiona Fairchild.

He had retreated, but only for the moment. Of course, he had no idea what to do now. Still, he had no intention of giving up, not as long as there was hope. And there was indeed hope.

Fiona hadn't said the words aloud when he'd asked if she loved him.

But surely the answer was in her eyes.

Fifteen

Two days later, an eternity if one is in the throes of having lost the one true love of one's life, yet not any significant time at all if one is attempting to come up with a brilliant plan to reclaim the heart of the aforementioned true love . . .

𝒷elle shut the door of the girls' parlor, flattened her back against it and announced in an overly dramatic tone, "He's here."

Fiona's breath caught. *At last.* She pushed the traitorous thought aside. It had been two endless days since she'd told Jonathon she was going to comply with her father's wishes. Two days in which to think long and hard about his actions and her life.

As much as she longed to do so, there was no getting around the fact that Jonathon had deceived her. He had done so in a grand manner and at no little cost, but he had deceived her nonetheless. And he had not done so out of affection or true concern for her future, but because he thought he had owed it to her. She was an obligation to him, no more important than a bill due to a merchant.

He had made no effort up to this point to change her

mind. There had been no outrageous display of roses, no notes of apologies, no anything. Yet he had said he wished to marry her. And surely, upon reflection, that could not entirely be due to any sense of obligation. Still, he had never mentioned love. And there had been no word from him.

Deception was no way to begin a life together. But he was here now and that had to be significant. Perhaps he too had spent these last days deep in thought. Perhaps he had come to the conclusion that he should not give her up without a fight. And perhaps . . .

She set her pencil down on the drawing she'd been working on absently, simply to get her mind off the more dreadful aspects of her life, and noted the face on the body of an ancient Greek god bore a strong resemblance to Jonathon's. She rose to her feet and drew a deep breath. "Very well, then, I shall see his lordship."

Belle looked confused. "Who?"

"Lord Helmsley."

Belle scoffed. "Lord Helmsley isn't here, it's Mr. Sinclair."

Whatshisname?

"And he doesn't look the least bit like his father."

Fiona's heart sank. This was it, then. "That's something, at any rate."

"In fact, he's quite, quite handsome, with a funny little scar just above his right eyebrow that makes him look dashing and adventurous. Like a pirate, I think, but a very good pirate. He's nice as well and most amusing." Belle studied her sister. "I would be happy to take him if you don't want him."

Fiona sighed. "I don't want him, but you can't have him."

Belle sniffed. "I didn't think you'd give him up."

"I would gladly give him up, but I can't if we are to comply with the terms of Father's will. And at this point I see no other choice."

"Pity you have to be the one to marry," Belle said. "Sophie and Gen and Aunt Edwina are with Mr. Sinclair right now, and I daresay any one of them would be happy to marry him. Aunt Edwina seems especially taken with him." Belle grinned. "Did I mention he was dashing?"

"Yes." Fiona smiled weakly. It scarcely mattered if he were the most dashing and handsomest man in the world. He was not the one she wanted. Nevertheless, regardless of how she had tried to avoid it, it now seemed inevitable. Whatshisname—Mr. Sinclair—was apparently her fate. And Jonathon Effington was not.

A few minutes later, Fiona squared her shoulders, adopted a pleasant smile and entered the parlor a step before Belle.

Gen, Sophie and Aunt Edwina sat on the sofa with looks approximating adoration on their collective faces. Even Gen, who was entirely too practical to be taken in by a handsome face, looked wide-eyed and just a bit stunned. And why not?

Whatshisname—Daniel Sinclair—stood leaning on the fireplace with a disarming grin on a face that was undeniably handsome. He was tall, with dark hair and darker eyes and yes, he was definitely dashing. He straightened when she entered the room and his eyes lit with appreciation.

Aunt Edwina rose. "Fiona, I should like to introduce Mr. Daniel Sinclair. Mr. Sinclair, this is my eldest niece, Miss Fiona Fairchild."

He strode to her, took her hand and raised it to his lips. His gaze met hers. "Miss Fairchild, I cannot tell you what a pleasure it is to meet you at last."

"A pleasure?" she said lightly. "Or a relief?"

He looked startled for a moment, then laughed. "Both."

"We shall leave the two of you to get acquainted. I daresay you have quite a lot to discuss." Aunt Edwina nodded at the girls. Gen and Sophie reluctantly stood and murmured polite goodbyes, herding Belle out of the parlor in front of them.

"But I just came in," Belle said under her breath.

"If you will excuse us for a moment?" Aunt Edwina cast Mr. Sinclair a brilliant smile.

"Of course," he murmured.

Aunt Edwina hooked her arm through Fiona's and

steered her out the parlor door, closed the door behind them and turned to her niece. "Your sisters told me about your father's will and his arrangement with Mr. Sinclair's father, but you should have told me, Fiona. I cannot tell you how angry I am about this."

Fiona winced. "I am sorry, Aunt Edwina. You're right, I should have told you, but it was humiliating to say it all aloud. Please forgive me."

"Oh, my dear child, I'm not mad at you." Aunt Edwina huffed. "Imagine in this day and age putting such stipulations on your daughters' futures. Why, if your father wasn't already dead I should be compelled to strangle him with my bare hands."

"The thought is most appreciated," Fiona murmured.

"Still"—the older woman eyed her niece—"he was right about your need to marry before you reach too advanced an age. And I must say, the gentleman he selected for you, even if he is an American, is most acceptable." A wicked grin curved Aunt Edwina's lips. "Indeed, he is quite charming and very dashing."

Fiona smiled in spite of herself. "So I've been told."

"However, the simple fact that Mr. Sinclair has turned out to be more than suitable does not mean you need marry him against your will." Aunt Edwina raised her chin. "I have a great deal of money and I am more than willing to provide you and your sisters acceptable dowries. Indeed, I should do it gladly in the knowledge that I am thwarting your father's wishes. Men can be delightful creatures, but they have no sense when it comes to matters involving life or love."

"I've been told that too. Thank you." She hugged her aunt. "I appreciate it more than I can say, but"—she drew a deep breath—"it is my responsibility to provide for my sisters."

"It is your life, my dear," Aunt Edwina said firmly. "And your decision."

"Indeed it is." Fiona nodded and returned to the parlor.

Mr. Sinclair smiled with obvious relief. "I was afraid you weren't coming back."

"Were you?" She studied him for a moment. "Why?"

"Given the circumstances, I was afraid that perhaps you . . ." He shrugged in an appealingly boyish manner. "I don't know, I just was."

He did seem nice enough, though.

"It is a bit awkward, isn't it?"

He snorted. "A bit?"

"Perhaps more than a bit, then."

"This is possibly the most uncomfortable moment of my entire life," he said wryly. "And that includes several moments that I was not entirely sure I would survive."

Her gaze flicked to the scar above his eyebrow. It did indeed make him look a little like a pirate. A good pirate. "Is this one of them, Mr. Sinclair?"

"Daniel, please. Given the situation, I think we can dispense with certain formalities." He ran his hand through his hair and the memory of Jonathon doing precisely the same thing under very similar circumstances flashed through her mind. She firmly ignored the image. "But yes, Fiona—" He glanced at her questioningly.

She nodded.

"This is indeed one of those moments. I believe my life is flashing before my eyes even as we speak." He shook his head in a mournful manner. "It's been a wicked, wicked life." He shot her a grin. "But fun."

Good Lord, the man was a pirate. She could well see Belle's attraction. She laughed in spite of herself.

"Fiona." He sobered. "Might I be completely honest with you?"

"Honesty would be a refreshing change, Mr.—Daniel." She settled on the sofa and gazed at him expectantly. "Do go on."

"Very well, then." He clasped his hands behind his back and thought for a moment, then grimaced. "I'm not sure where to begin."

"Perhaps if you begin with"—she braced herself— "exactly why you're here."

"That would make sense. All right, then." He drew a deep breath. "As I'm sure you're aware, my father and yours before his death arranged for a marriage between the two of us. I knew nothing about it until I recently arrived in Florence."

"You didn't?" She stared at him.

"No." He raised a brow. "Did you?"

"Not until after my father's death, when I learned of the terms of his will."

"So you did not agree to this marriage?"

She shook her head. "As apparently neither did you."

"That certainly puts things in a different light." He blew a relieved breath. "I don't mind telling you, I was not at all eager to come here. I wouldn't be here now if it wasn't for my father's insistence and the fact that you are heir to a great deal of money. Right now I could use a great deal of money. I have the opportunity for an excellent investment that could make my fortune and, well, that's neither here nor there, I suppose." He sat down beside her on the sofa. "But I have no desire to marry a woman who doesn't want to marry me." His brows drew together. "You don't, do you?"

"I can't say, I've just met you."

"Of course." He paused. "I do hope you're not disappointed."

"Not at all." She bit back a grin. "Are you?"

"Good God, no. I wasn't expecting"—he cast her an appreciative gaze—"*you*. But when your father tells you he has arranged for you to marry a woman of five-and-twenty because her father was afraid she'd never marry, you don't expect her to look like you."

"You expected old, ugly and desperate?"

"Indeed I did." He leaned closer in a confidential manner. "Frankly, I was just hoping for a good nature."

Fiona laughed.

"That's settled, then." He got to his feet. "Fiona, it has been a rare pleasure to meet you."

"That's it?" She stared up at him. "That's all you have to say?"

"I think so." He thought for a moment. "You don't want

to marry me, I don't want to marry you or, to be honest, anyone at the moment. So, yes, that's it."

"You don't know everything about my father's will, do you?" she said slowly.

"Aside from the part about us marrying, no."

"Do sit down, Daniel," she said with a sigh. "Let me tell it all to you."

Daniel took his seat and Fiona explained about her inheritances and her sisters' dowries.

He blew a long, low whistle. "That is a predicament."

"Indeed it is." She paused to find the right words. "Now allow me to be honest with you. My aunt has offered to provide my sisters with dowries if necessary to prevent me from marrying where I do not wish to do so. However"— she folded her hands in her lap and stared at them—"I have done a great deal of thinking in recent days. I am dreadfully tired of living with the uncertainty that I have lived with since my father's death. Of knowing my sisters' futures were my responsibility and not knowing what would happen. I want my life settled. I want to resolve this." She met his gaze firmly. "Daniel, I have a proposition that may be of interest to you."

He raised a brow. "A proposition?"

She nodded. "A business proposition. Or rather, I suppose, one could call it"—she drew a steadying breath— "a proposal."

"Bloody hell." Jonathon sank deeper in the chair, which had never especially been his favorite in the lounge of their favorite club but had become so in the last two days due to continued occupancy and inertia fed by regret, helplessness and a great deal of liquor. At least he'd been surrounded by his friends, although, upon reflection, they'd been of absolutely no help thus far. None had been able to come up with a brilliant, or even acceptable, idea on how to reclaim Fiona's heart. And Jonathon's mind had been entirely too muddled to be of any use whatsoever.

"That is a problem," Warton murmured. "Although you did realize it would come to this sooner or later."

Cavendish leaned toward Oliver and lowered his voice. "Refresh my memory. Who is Whatshisname?"

"The American, that's who he is," Jonathon snapped. "The one who is supposed to marry my . . . my . . ." What was she anyway? "My fiancée."

"Can he call her that?" Cavendish shook his head. "I don't think he can call her that."

"He did propose in a manner of speaking, but no." Warton shook his head. "I'm fairly certain if she doesn't accept, then she can't be considered his fiancée. She told you she never wanted to see you again, didn't she?"

"Not this time," Jonathon said through clenched teeth.

"That's right. That was when you offered to pay . . ." Cavendish winced. "We needn't go into that, I suppose."

"It scarcely matters." Oliver signaled to an attentive waiter for a drink. He had a great deal of catching up to do.

Oliver had just arrived bearing the news of Whatshisname's presence in London. It was good to have an informant in the house even if this was not what Jonathon wanted to hear. He much preferred Oliver's observations in the last two days of Fiona's state of mind, although admittedly the man had seen his cousin very little and strongly suspected she was avoiding him. Oliver's role in deceiving her had not endeared him to her.

"So, tell us about this Whatshisname," Warton drawled.

"Actually his name is Daniel Sinclair and, I'm surprised to admit, he seems a good sort," Oliver said. "I've had a long chat with him and I think he can be of some use to us. Or rather to Helmsley here."

"He can't unless he refuses to marry her." A tiny ray of hoped speared Jonathon's misery. "Has he refused to marry her?"

"Isn't that how all this started?" Cavendish said under his breath to Warton. "Someone's refusal to marry?"

"Only an idiot would refuse to marry Fiona Fairchild," Warton said wryly, then glanced at Jonathon. "My apologies."

"Accepted," Jonathon muttered.

"Sinclair hasn't refused to marry her, however he doesn't *want* to marry her," Oliver said.

"Then he's an idiot." Cavendish shrugged.

Oliver ignored him. "He doesn't especially want to marry anyone at the moment."

"Well, that makes all the difference." Warton sipped at his drink. "That makes him one of us."

"I thought you'd see it that way." Oliver accepted his drink from the waiter.

Jonathon pulled his brows together. "Regardless of what he wants, is he going to marry her?"

"That's where this becomes extremely interesting." Oliver leaned forward and lowered his voice. "Fiona proposed—"

"Again?" Cavendish raised a brow. "Does she do that a lot?"

"She's never proposed to me." Warton sniffed. "I might well have said yes. She has a face Botticelli might have painted and a fortune to match."

The other men stared.

"*I* am not an idiot," Warton said in a lofty manner, then nodded at Jonathon. "Sorry."

"Yes, yes." Jonathon waved off the apology and nodded to Oliver. "Go on."

"What she proposed was marriage," Oliver continued, "but one in name only and only for as long as was necessary to meet the terms of her father's will. In return, she'll give Sinclair a portion of her inheritance, a mutually agreed-upon amount that has not yet been determined."

"And he is willing to do this?" Jonathon studied Oliver closely.

"Indeed he is. Sinclair had no knowledge of the terms of Uncle Alfred's will until today. He came to see Fiona because he knew of her father's arrangement with his father and he felt obligated to do so."

Jonathon snorted. "He'd best not let her know that."

"He probably would have married her if she had expected him to do so, his family's honor and all that, but once he understood that she had no desire to marry him, he was more than willing to abandon the idea of marriage altogether." Oliver paused.

"Yes?" Jonathon said.

"It was Fiona who suggested they go ahead and marry," Oliver said reluctantly. "Sinclair needs money for an investment in America, something to do with railroads. Fiona will provide him with the funding he requires and at some point the marriage will be dissolved."

"I see," Jonathon said thoughtfully. Fiona had once suggested the possibility of a temporary marriage. And had said that it would very much depend on the type of man Whatshisname was.

"There's more." Reluctance sounded in Oliver's voice. "Fiona wants to marry as soon as possible. My mother is already planning a wedding."

Jonathon's stomach twisted. "When?"

Oliver grimaced. "Friday."

"Friday?" Jonathon stared. "That's three days from now."

"Should we send a gift?" Cavendish murmured to Warton.

"Not yet." Warton pinned Jonathon with a firm look. "What we need, what you need, is a plan. Not some ill-advised, poorly conceived stunt, but a serious, must-succeed, only-a-fool-would-fail plan to thwart this wedding and win Fiona for yourself."

"A plan?" Jonathon glared at his friend. "Why didn't I think of that?"

"Because you've been too busy wallowing in self-pity and misery?" Cavendish said helpfully.

Jonathon blew a resigned breath. He could deny it, of course, but it was true. He had indeed been wallowing and feeling entirely too sorry for himself to think in a rational manner. He'd never had to win a woman's heart before, no woman had ever meant this much to him before. And now he was out of time.

Either he took action now or he would lose her forever.

"You're right," Jonathon said slowly. "All of you. I have to do something and I have to do something now. I am open to any and all suggestions." He cast Cavendish a threatening glance. "Except for proclaiming my affection on a theater stage between acts."

Indignation sounded in Cavendish's voice. "I wasn't going to suggest that." He paused. "Although a grand gesture—"

"I have an idea," Oliver said. "But it will require the cooperation of Sinclair."

"Then I shall have to meet with Sinclair." Jonathon's voice was firm.

"No sooner said than done." Oliver stood and signaled to someone near the entrance.

"You brought him here?" Cavendish frowned. "Was that wise?"

"At this point, I'm not sure wisdom is as important as action," Warton said. "Even if it's wrong." He cast a pitying look at Jonathon. "The poor wretch has done nothing but mope since Fiona turned him away."

"He's in love." Cavendish's gaze met Warton's.

"And he's miserable," Warton said, and both men grinned.

"If you say it serves me right I shall have to shoot you both," Jonathon muttered.

A tall, dark-haired man strode toward them and Jonathon groaned to himself. This was Whatshisname? He'd been hoping the American would turn out to be short, fat and balding. There did not appear to be an inch of fat on him, he was disgustingly tall and had far too much hair. He looked like he could have posed for one of Fiona's drawings.

Jonathon and his friends rose to their feet.

"Lord Helmsley, allow me to introduce Mr. Sinclair," Oliver said in a formal manner. "Mr. Sinclair, this is the Marquess of Helmsley."

Jonathon stared at him for a long moment. Sinclair stared back without so much as a flicker of hesitation. An excellent quality in a friend, something to be wary of in a competitor. Sinclair offered his hand and Jonathon shook it. He had a firm, steady grip and Jonathon realized this was a man to be reckoned with. And realized as well having this man as an ally would be a very good thing.

Oliver introduced the other men and they all resumed their seats. Sinclair accepted a drink and an awkward silence fell on the group.

Jonathon drew a deep breath. "Mr. Sinclair—"

"Lord Helmsley—" Sinclair said at the same time.

Again silence fell.

Oliver cleared his throat. "Perhaps it would be best if I explained my idea."

"Perhaps it would be best if someone said something," Warton said under his breath.

Oliver continued. "Sinclair does not particularly want to marry Fiona."

"Not that she's not a beautiful, charming woman," Sinclair said quickly. "And not at all what I expected. You can well imagine what I thought when my father told me he and Miss Fairchild's father had arranged a marriage."

"She used to be fat," Cavendish offered helpfully.

Sinclair cast him a confused look, then continued. "It's not that under other circumstances, perhaps, I wouldn't be pleased to be matched with someone like her, although I would much prefer to select my own bride when the time is right. But at the moment, I have no desire to marry anyone."

"Nor do any of us." Warton paused, then grinned. "Except for Helmsley. He has always said when he found the perfect woman—"

"That's quite enough," Jonathon said firmly.

Warton chuckled and even Oliver stifled a smile.

Jonathon raised a brow. "But you have agreed to marry her?"

Sinclair glanced at Oliver. "Did you tell them everything?"

Oliver nodded.

Sinclair breathed a sigh of relief. "Then you know she is not interested in a real marriage. It's more in the nature of a business arrangement than anything else. She gets her inheritance, her sisters get their dowries and I get a substantial sum to allow me to pursue my own interests. After a time, the marriage is dissolved. Annulment or divorce. Here or in America." He shrugged. "We have not worked out that particular detail yet."

"So your only interest is in the financial aspects of this?" Jonathon considered him thoughtfully.

Sinclair winced. "It sounds so mercenary when you put it that way, but yes. Although I would like to point out Miss Fairchild's only interest in this marriage is financial as well."

"Helmsley here is always interested in a good investment," Oliver said casually. "One would think if you received funding from another source, there would be no need to wed Fiona."

Four pairs of shocked eyes turned toward Oliver.

"That's brilliant, old man." Admiration sounded in Warton's voice.

Oliver grinned.

"You would give her up?" Jonathon studied Sinclair closely. "Just like that?"

"She's not mine to give up. In fact, in the time I spent with her today I had the distinct impression"—his gaze met Jonathon's directly—"her affections have already been engaged."

Jonathon leaned forward. "Did you?"

Sinclair chuckled. "She didn't actually say it, but she did mention—in a most vehement manner, I might add—that she thought love was nothing more than a myth best relegated to fiction and how all men, with the possible exception of myself—"

"And me," Oliver interrupted.

Sinclair snorted. "Not you or her father either, for that matter. She said all men were cads with nothing more to their credit than a misplaced sense of obligation and responsibility and she preferred a marriage in name only to any other relationship with a man. Ever."

"Ouch." Warton cringed.

"It's been my experience," Sinclair said slowly, "that whenever a woman is that furious about men in general and that passionate about rejecting love altogether, she does so because she is, in truth, in love."

Jonathon thought for a long moment. Of course she loved him. How could he have doubted even for a moment? She loved him. He loved her, and damnation they were meant to be together. This was fate and he was not going to let her escape it.

"Then shall we call the wedding off?" Oliver asked.

Jonathon shook his head. "Not yet."

Resolve washed through him, and with it his spirits lifted. What on earth had been wrong with him? He'd never really had to fight for anything in his life, but it didn't mean he could not do so now. And there wasn't a doubt in his mind he would be victorious. Besides, love was involved, and that alone would conquer all.

Why, as his friends delighted in pointing out, he had indeed always said when he found the perfect woman he would marry her. And he was not about to let Fiona Fairchild make a liar out of him.

Jonathon smiled slowly. "You're right, Cavendish, this does call for a grand gesture. Grand and foolishly romantic and enough to make even the most hardened among us swoon with the sheer audacity of it."

Cavendish grinned. "I love grand gestures."

"As do we all." The tiniest beginning of a plan, grand and even outrageous, teased the back of Jonathon's mind. It would need development, but he knew, with the same instinct that led him to make sound investments, that it was good, even brilliant. His smile broadened and he turned toward Sinclair. "But first, Mr. Sinclair, let us talk railroads."

Sixteen

Three days later, the sun shone brightly and seemed, to any-one of a particularly romantic nature, to surely be a sign of good luck for those about to marry, as the sun did not rou-tinely shine, brightly or otherwise, in January in London. For those about to wed, nothing whatsoever seemed a good sign and the possibility of a miraculous event of some sort, even an intervention of the gods, to thwart the proceedings seemed more and more remote . . .

"Who are these people?" Fiona stared in horror at the gathering milling about Aunt Edwina's house. The doors between the main parlor and a secondary parlor had been thrown open to create a larger area, yet it did not seem large enough.

"Oh, friends for the most part," Aunt Edwina said brightly. "And really, my dear, there aren't that many."

"There are if one preferred to have no one at all," Fiona said under her breath. So much for allowing her aunt free rein regarding the plans for her wedding, but the older woman had been so excited at the mere thought of a wed-ding, Fiona didn't have the heart to tell her it was nothing more than a formality.

Her wedding. Fiona's stomach clenched at the thought. Of course she'd allowed Aunt Edwina to do as she'd wished because Fiona herself hadn't especially cared. She simply wanted it done with and it would be over soon. Within the hour she would be Mrs. Whats—Daniel Sinclair.

Daniel had been remarkably civilized about it all. She'd discovered he was quite nice and amusing as well. The kind of man a woman could fall in love with if she wasn't already in love. Since their agreement to marry, they had had several meetings with Oliver's solicitors, who had drawn up papers to be signed before the ceremony detailing their agreement. Fiona had been assured their marriage would meet the terms of her father's will and that they need not remain married for more than a year.

A year. It was a dreadfully long time but far better than forever. If Daniel hadn't been so decent, if he'd been greedy for her money or, worse, for her, she might well be trapped in an unwanted marriage for the rest of her life. In that, if in nothing else about this, she was fortunate.

"I cannot tell you what a help Oliver was in arranging all this. He thinks of you as a sister, you know." Aunt Edwina studied her niece. "I don't know what he's done to make you so upset with him, but hasn't he earned your forgiveness yet?"

"I have forgiven him." Fiona smiled weakly. "I simply haven't told him."

Oliver stood across the room speaking with two gentlemen, obviously friends of his, and her sisters, who were just as obviously flirting outrageously, if the expressions on the faces of the gentlemen with them were any indication. At least their future happiness was now assured, even if her own was questionable. Nonetheless, she would do what she had to do to fulfill her responsibilities.

Jonathon wasn't here, but then she hadn't expected him to be. Since that dreadful scene in this very parlor, she hadn't seen him or received a note from him or had any indication whatsoever that he still had feelings for her. If he ever did. It was entirely possible she would never see him again. At least not in the flesh. But he lingered in her mind every waking moment and in her dreams through the long, restless nights. And with every passing day, hope faded.

She had resisted the urge to page through her copy of *A Fair Surrender* and read the words he had written about passion and desire and seduction. She simply couldn't bear it. She'd wrapped the book once again in brown paper and stashed it in her trunk under some odds and ends, keepsakes of her childhood and her past, to eventually be forgotten. And packed all thoughts of Jonathon away as well, with hopes that he too would eventually be forgotten. So much for love.

Oliver's gaze caught hers and he smiled, said something to his friends, then started across the room toward her. He really had been wonderful in recent days and had accepted Daniel as a new member of the family, regardless of how tenuous that bond would be. He had assisted Daniel in handling all the legal aspects of arranging a quick wedding regarding licenses and whatever else was necessary. In truth, he and Daniel had become as thick as thieves. Who would have suspected a British lord and an American adventurer would form such a quick friendship?

"Fiona, you look especially beautiful today." Oliver cast her a genuine smile.

"Of course she does." Aunt Edwina huffed. "Although I do wish she hadn't been in such a hurry and we could have had a proper dress made for her."

"This is a proper dress," Fiona said with a long-suffering smile.

In truth, it was a lovely dress, pale yellow in color and more than appropriate for a wedding put together in a mere three days that neither the bride nor the groom was particularly eager for. Still, regardless of the circumstances, if Aunt Edwina had had her way, this wedding would be a spectacular affair never to be forgotten. The kind of wedding Fiona had always thought she'd have. But then that would be a celebration and not simply a ceremony.

"A proper *wedding* dress," Aunt Edwina said firmly. "Fiona, are you certain that you wish—"

"I do." Fiona nodded. Her aunt knew about the will but

did not know all the details of her agreement with Daniel.
And Fiona had no intention of telling her. "Daniel Sinclair
will make an excellent husband, he's a very nice man and I
intend to be happy with him." She glanced at Oliver. "Have
you seen him yet?"

"He's waiting for you in the library with the solicitor,"
Oliver said. "To sign the papers."

"Papers?" Aunt Edwina asked.

"Nothing of importance." Fiona raised her chin. "We
should do this."

"May I?" Oliver offered her his arm. She took it gratefully
and he escorted her out of the room. "I am sorry, Fiona,
about everything. I should never have agreed to Jonathon's
plan."

"No, you shouldn't have." They reached the library door
and she looked up at him. "But you were only doing what
you thought was best for me."

He cringed. "It sounds so bad when you say it."

"It was an absurd idea."

He grinned in a sheepish manner. "And yet, not my first
absurd idea and probably not my last."

She reached up and kissed him lightly on the cheek. "I do
forgive you, though. You were trying to be a good"—she
smiled—"brother."

"Remember that, Fiona." The look in his eye was
abruptly serious. "I just want your happiness. And I will do
whatever necessary, no matter how absurd, to assure that."

"There is nothing left to do." She drew a deep breath and
nodded.

Oliver opened the door and gestured for her to go in.
"There is something I must check on. I shall be no more
than a minute."

She stepped into the library and Oliver closed the door
behind her. At once she noted the large table she and
Jonathon had used for the work on *A Fair Surrender* had
been removed. An awful sense of finality rushed through
her. As if the removal of the table truly signified the end of
their work and everything else.

Daniel leaned against the desk and straightened at her approach.

She looked around. "Where is the solicitor?"

"I needed to speak with you alone." Daniel looked distinctly uncomfortable. "About the wedding."

She held her breath. "Have you had a change of heart?"

"Heart is precisely where the problem lies." Sympathy shone in his dark eyes. "Yours is not in this."

"It doesn't have to be. This is not a love match. This is an arrangement of business." Even to her own ears her words sounded hollow.

"No, Fiona," he said gently. "It's marriage. It's not to be taken lightly."

"I am not taking it at all lightly." The emotion she'd kept well in check up to now threatened to overwhelm her. She struggled to stay calm. "You agreed to this marriage."

"I did, and I am still willing to go through with it if you can tell me this is what you really want."

"It doesn't matter what I want." Desperation sounded in her voice. "This is what I have to do."

Daniel's gaze locked with hers. "Do you want to marry me?"

"Yes. Of course I do. Absolutely."

"Then say it."

"Very well. I want to marry . . ." She paused, then drew a calming breath. "I want to marry . . ." Her voice faltered. She couldn't make herself say the words. "You're right," she said quietly. "I know this is what I have to do, and you're such a nice man and charming and amusing and all any woman would really ever want, and God knows I could have done much worse, but . . ." She shook her head and tried not to weep. "No. I don't want to marry you."

"Then marry me." Jonathon's calm voice sounded behind her.

She froze.

Daniel shrugged. "Among the good qualities of mine that you failed to mention is that I have a romantic nature and a firm belief that a woman should always marry the man she loves." He took her hand and raised it to his lips.

"Don't think of him as a cad with a misplaced sense of obligation, Fiona." His eyes twinkled. "Think of him as your cad."

Daniel glanced behind her, nodded at Jonathon, then flashed her a grin and briskly strode out of the room.

For a long moment no one said a word.

"Fiona?" Jonathon's voice was tentative. She'd never heard him unsure before.

She summoned her courage and turned. Her heart thudded in her chest at the sight of him. She fought to keep her voice calm. "What are you doing here?"

"Before you say anything, hear me out," he said quickly. "I know you're probably still angry with me and I can certainly understand that. And in spite of my best intentions—"

She narrowed her eyes.

"—everything I've done since we first met has been a complete mistake in judgment. I can only attribute it to the fact that I have loved you from the moment you first appeared in the library, even if I didn't realize it."

Her breath caught.

"I know one cannot rectify a lie by making it the truth, but I have arranged to go forward with the plan, as it was explained to you, for *A Fair Surrender*."

"And if there's a scandal? If the true authors are discovered?"

He shrugged. "We shall weather it."

"We?"

"We." He stepped toward her. "I cannot promise that in the future I will not continue to do things that I think are in your best interest, but I will promise to be honest with you always from this moment forward.

"And in the interest of honesty, you should know that I agreed to provide Sinclair with the money he needs so that it was no longer necessary to marry you today. However," he added, "from a business standpoint, it is an excellent proposition, an exciting investment and I am confident we shall all make money together."

At once Oliver's newfound friendship with Daniel made perfect sense.

"I see," she said slowly. "So Daniel never intended to marry me today?"

Jonathon nodded.

"And once again you have spent a great deal of money to deceive me?" Although it didn't seem as important as it once had.

He thought for a moment, then grimaced. "Yes."

"For my own good?" And weren't there worse things?

"No, damnation, Fiona, for mine." He grabbed her shoulders and stared into her eyes. "I cannot live without you. These last few days have been an eternity and I have spent them in hell."

"Then why haven't you done anything about it!" Pain rang in her voice and she didn't care. "You stalked out of my life without a second thought!"

"I didn't know what to do! What to say! I had no idea how to make things right between us. I have been in a fog from the moment I left you. I've never been in love before." His gaze locked with hers. "I've been told that I needed a grand gesture, something absurdly romantic and completely outrageous to sweep you off your feet. But the more I thought about it, the more I realized that there is nothing grander than offering you my heart. Although, in truth it's already yours."

Her own heart lodged in her throat. "Jonathon—"

"Marry me, Fiona. Now. This minute. It's all arranged. The licenses, everything." His gaze searched hers. "It wasn't a complete deception, there was a wedding planned. Yours and mine. Will you marry me?"

She stared at him for a long time and finally drew a deep breath. "No."

His face fell. "But I love you and I know you love me and—"

"And if I am to marry the man I love"—she squared her shoulders—"I want a proper wedding. In a church. With your family and friends as witnesses and my sisters as attendants. I want Aunt Edwina planning it exactly as she thinks it should be. And I should like Daniel to be there as well—"

Jonathon stared in disbelief.

"—and I want Countess Orsetti and her son invited because I think it would be great fun just to see their faces and I want that nice Sir Ephraim in attendance and Judith and—"

A slow smile curved the corners of his lips.

"—and I want a terribly extravagant dress in the latest fashion and maybe doves and lots and lots of flowers—"

"Roses?"

"Twelve dozen at least. And most of all"—her voice cracked—"I want you."

And then she was in his arms. His lips pressed to hers and she clung to him. Something crumbled within her and she sobbed against him and he held her tight.

"I feared I'd lost you," he murmured against her hair.

She sniffed. "I thought I'd never see you again."

"So . . ." He drew back and looked at her. "To make certain I understand, you are agreeing to become Lady Helmsley instead of Mrs. Whatshisname?"

"I am," she said firmly, and hiccupped.

"But not today?"

"Not today."

"Good." He breathed a sigh of relief.

She raised a brow.

"Don't look at me like that. I am fully prepared to marry you today, but I too have a family that will not be happy if they are not made a part of this. Besides"—his blue eyes gazed into hers with love and a promise of forever—"I want to do this properly as well."

"You know, we shall have to tell Aunt Edwina and everyone here that the wedding they expect will not take place."

"Oliver is telling them now."

"You were that confident?"

"Not at all." He grinned. "Maybe a bit. Or perhaps I just hoped. Now . . ." He studied her curiously. "I have a question for you."

"Just one?"

"You were willing to enter into a temporary marriage, a business arrangement, with Sinclair." His gaze narrowed. "Why did you never suggest such an arrangement with me? I might well have been interested in such a proposition."

"You didn't want to marry at all, remember? Besides, with you, I didn't want it to be temporary."

"Why?" The soft timbre of his voice belied the intensity in his eyes.

"Because with you there was every possibility I would lose my heart. And when the marriage was at an end I would not be able to bear it."

"Why?"

"Because I love you." She smiled up at him. "I believe I have from the first night I saw you all those years ago."

"When you spied on me in the library?"

"You do realize your Christmas Eve trysts with ladies in the library during the Christmas Ball are at an end, don't you?"

"Absolutely not." He pulled her closer, a wicked light shining in his eyes. "I shall simply limit myself to one lady."

She laughed with a joy she could not contain.

"After all, you did say you had always wanted to be the lady in the library on Christmas Eve." He nuzzled the side of her neck and she shivered with delight and anticipation.

"And better yet, the lady in your arms the day after," she murmured, and her lips met his.

And knew she would indeed be the lady in his arms on Christmas Eve and the day after and every day to come.

Epilogue

Four weeks later . . .

"Nice wedding," Warton said, sipping his usual drink in his usual chair in their favorite club. "If you like that sort of thing."

"I don't." Cavendish shuddered. "Entirely too sentimental for my taste. Although Miss Fairchild, or rather Lady Helmsley now, was beautiful as always."

Oliver smiled. "Indeed she was."

"And she could have been mine," Sinclair said with a dramatic sigh. The American had yet to return to his own country, partially because of Fiona and Jonathon's desire to have him present at their wedding, but primarily because his initial arrangement with Jonathon had developed into an investment partnership including them all.

Cavendish snorted. "In name only."

"*Only* in the beginning." Sinclair grinned.

"Still"—Oliver swirled the brandy in his glass—"it seems to me it isn't the sentiment of a wedding that's distasteful as much as it is the permanence."

"I should think permanence is part of the appeal," Sinclair said thoughtfully.

Warton raised a brow. "Permanence appeals to you?"

Sinclair grimaced. "Not yet."

Oliver eyed him curiously. "You're under no pressure to marry, then?"

"None whatsoever. Unless, of course, you consider that little matter of my father having arranged a marriage for me without my consent." He took a sip of his brandy and shook his head. "Unlike you gentlemen, I have no title to pass on, no castle in the country to inherit and therefore, you would think, no pressing need for an heir. But my father believes he is building an empire and an empire needs a prince. I, on the other hand, am trying to build one of my own."

"How very American of you," Warton murmured, but there was a reluctant glint of admiration in his eye.

"I do think, however, that marriage, even for me, is inevitable." Sinclair shrugged. "And preferable to living your life alone."

"That's a nasty word *inevitable*," Warton said wryly. "As is *permanent*."

Cavendish leaned toward Sinclair and grinned. "I do actually have a castle in the country, you know."

Sinclair laughed.

"Still, Helmsley did look extraordinarily happy," Warton said, more to himself than to the others.

A low murmur of assent circled the group and faded to a considering silence. Each man sipped his brandy, thought his own thoughts.

It occurred to Oliver that these days were drawing to a close. Jonathon was the first to go. They would always be friends, of course, and he and Jonathon were now related as well, but no matter how close Jonathon remained with Oliver and the others, Fiona was now his closest friend. As it should be. They all had to wed eventually, and one day, probably soon, marriage and the responsibilities of family and position would separate them. Slowly and imperceptibly, perhaps, like the change of the seasons, but to be expected nonetheless.

"Rather a pity things have to change," Cavendish said,

and Oliver wondered if they were all thinking the same thing.

"I wonder who it will be," Warton murmured.

"Who will be what?" Oliver asked.

Warton started as if surprised he had spoken aloud. "The last one of us to marry."

Cavendish heaved a resigned sigh. "The last man left alive, you mean."

"We're talking about marriage." Oliver chuckled. "It's certainly been compared to imprisonment, but I daresay comparing it to death goes a bit far."

"Have you ever heard of a tontine?" Warton said abruptly.

Sinclair drew his brows together. "It's an investment program, isn't it?"

"Some kind of lottery?" Oliver said. "Or wager?"

"A little of all that, really." Warton thought for a moment. "If I recall correctly, subscribers contribute a certain amount to the tontine. The money can be invested or simply held. However, whenever a subscriber dies, his contribution is divided among those remaining. Eventually only one subscriber is left and the tontine is his. And I think," Warton said slowly, "we should form one."

"And the last man to marry wins?" Oliver's gaze met Warton's and he grinned. "We've wagered on nearly everything else through the years."

"Now whose equating death with marriage?" Cavendish muttered.

"Are you sure you want to include me in this?" Sinclair shook his head. "You scarcely know me."

"And yet we have invested a great deal in your railroad venture," Warton said. "This will be considerably less of a risk than that, although"—he cast a look of suspicion over the group—"people have been known to kill over a tontine."

"I'll do it." Cavendish nodded. "How much?"

Oliver shrugged. "It scarcely matters how much. The symbolism is the important thing."

"Then I propose"—Warton thought for a moment—"one shilling each."

"Then the winner receives a mere four shillings?" Cavendish shook his head. "Scarcely worth the effort."

"Then you can marry first and forfeit your shilling." Sinclair's voice was sincere but amusement shone in his eyes.

"Yes, I see your point." Cavendish grimaced. "Symbolism and all that. Very well, then, a shilling it is."

"Gentlemen, we should make this official." Oliver got to his feet and raised his glass. The other men followed suit. "Here's to the last one among us to remain."

"And for each of us who does not make it to that point, here's to the respective woman of our dreams," Sinclair said.

"Wherever she may be, whenever we may find her." Cavendish's voice rang with sincerity. "She awaits us as inescapably as the night awaits the day."

"Nicely said," Warton murmured to Cavendish. "Very poetic."

"There's more." Cavendish cleared his throat. "And in regards to that unknown lady in question . . ." He thought for a moment. "Let her be lovely."

Sinclair grinned. "Let her be rich."

"Let her be"—Warton paused—"forthright. As for the union itself"—he chuckled—"let it be painless."

Cavendish sighed. "Let it be passionate."

"Let it be blissful." Sinclair smiled.

"And gentlemen, above all . . ." Oliver raised his glass higher. "Let it be love."